VOYAGER
OF THE
CROWN

MELISSA MCSHANE

Night Harbor Publishing
Salt Lake City, UT

Cover design by Clarissa Yeo http://yocladesigns.com/

Map of Tremontane by Kay
Map of Dineh-Karit by Oscar Paludi

Dedicated to all the fans who wanted more about Zara

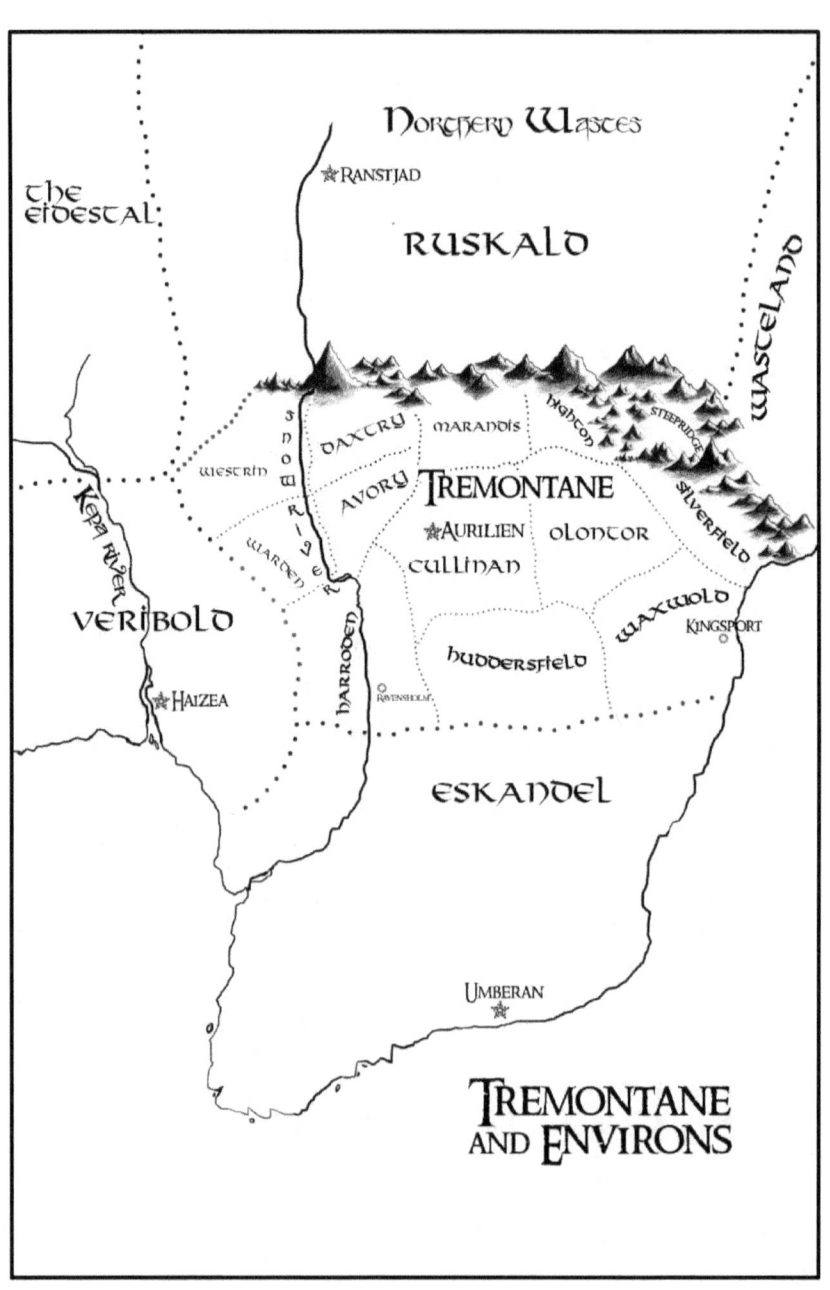

NORTHERN WASTES

RANSTJAD

THE EIDESTAL

RUSKALD

WASTELAND

SNOWRISE

WESTRIN

DAXTRY

MARANDIS

HIGHCOP

STEEPRIDGE

AVORY

TREMONTANE

WARDEN

AURILIEN

OLONTOR

SILVERFIELD

KEPA RIVER

CULLINAN

WAXWOLD

VERIBOLD

HARRODEN

KINGSPORT

HAIZEA

RAVENSHOLM

HUDDERSFIELD

ESKANDEL

UMBERAN

TREMONTANE
AND ENVIRONS

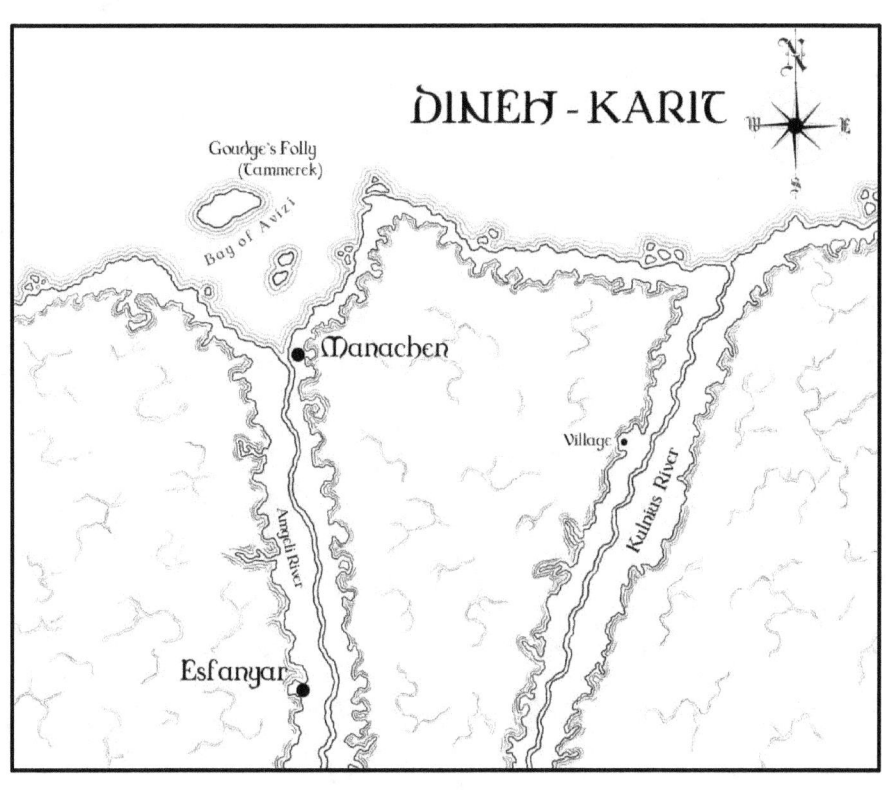

CHAPTER ONE

The chill autumn wind picked up again, tumbling red and gold leaves down Longbourne's main street, past the shuttered façades of houses and shops shut up tight against the coming storm. It was well after dawn, but the overcast turned the sun into a dim white disk that gave off little light and even less heat, and lanterns and Device lamps burned behind windows in every building but the one Zara North stood next to. That house, and its attached shop, sat dark and silent, waiting for their new owner. Zara cast her eye over the foundation, over the missing stones near the little-used front door—real business in Longbourne was conducted via the back door—and felt a pang at realizing they were no longer her problem.

A gust of wind carried more leaves that flew merrily past the loaded wagon, some of them fetching up against the horses' legs, and disappeared into the distance. Zara looked off down the street after them, toward distant Thorsten Pass. Verity's shop was just north of hers—she corrected herself again, it was north of where she'd used to call her own—and the lantern over the door swung and creaked with the wind. She could follow the leaves past the post office, the forge, Eleanor Richardson's laundry, the tavern, all the way through Longbourne and up the valley to where the mountains made a stark gray wall against the sky. It was so overcast she couldn't see Mount Ehuren, and the illusion of its absence made her shudder, as if Barony Steepridge was erasing itself.

She tossed one final bag, this one packed with clothing, into the back of the wagon. Its weathered, gray slats snagged the rough canvas like burrs, stopping it from rolling further. She was leaving, yes, she could never return, but it was ridiculous to let herself imagine her beloved home only existed so long as she was part of it. She glanced at her grandniece, who stood nearby, bundled into her coat and bouncing slightly on her heels against the cold. "You don't need to freeze your

1

nose off just to see me off," she said.

Telaine Garrett clutched her coat close around her and shrugged. "You picked quite a day to leave," she said.

"Happen I'd control the weather if I could," Zara said. The wind, carrying the smell of wood smoke from the nearest chimneys, whipped at her heavy cloak; she'd never gotten the hang of those newfangled fashions. Strands of black hair blew into her face, but she didn't push them away. It felt like weakness, acknowledging that the weather could discommode her. Her reaction to the wind was one of the few things she had control over. "Can't put it off any longer."

"I know," Telaine said. "You probably should have gone last year." Her nose was red, probably from the chill in the air, and likely the moisture in her eyes was because the wind carried dust as well as leaves. Telaine was sensible and level-headed, not given to sentimentality. She understood why Zara had to go. That didn't mean she liked it any more than her great-aunt did.

"Past time," Zara agreed. They both fell silent. Zara wished Telaine would go. She wished she'd stay. She *wished* her life wasn't so damned complicated.

"I'm sorry," Telaine said, and reached out to hug her. Zara, startled, put her arms around Telaine reflexively and hugged her back. The last person she'd hugged had been her sister Alison, the day before she died. It still hurt, though Alison had been eighty-three and was past ready to join her husband Anthony in heaven. Zara was now the last of her generation. And now she was leaving her family behind. Again.

"I won't write," she warned. "No contact. It's easier that way."

"It is," Telaine said. "But Uncle will know where you are, in case…"

They both knew there was no good ending to that sentence. Thanks to her inherent magic, Zara was likely to outlive not only her nephew, the King, but her great-grandnieces and nephews as well. Zara clenched her jaw against her own tears. No point crying over something she'd had almost sixty years to grow accustomed to.

She released Telaine and stepped back. "Have a good, long life," she said, and climbed up on the wagon's seat.

"Goodbye, aunt," Telaine said. Zara cracked the reins and the horse plodded forward. She kept her eyes focused on the road ahead, though she'd seen Telaine wave. She'd said her goodbyes to Ben and the children earlier; she didn't think she could bear any more pleading from her little namesake, who refused to accept that her great-aunt was leaving and wouldn't come back. That her house had already been sold, that the giant loom had gone down the mountain into storage the week before, that Zara had told everyone she was moving to Kingsport to have a larger market for her skilled weaving. That last was a lie, but she couldn't exactly tell her friends she was a deathless former Queen who needed to protect her secret. She prayed, as she always did, that the "deathless" part was untrue.

The wagon left Longbourne and made its slow way down the valley toward the pass. A sprinkling of rain, little more than heavy mist, struck her face. She pulled the cloak lower and tried not to hunch her shoulders. The tall grass was yellow, here at the beginning of autumn, but the golden coins of the aspens outshone its dry dullness. Dusty green pines to the left kept their dark color year round, unchanging unless something acted on them, fire or lightning or someone chopping them down. That was something she understood very well.

The ride down the mountain was unnaturally silent, without even the birds' cries to keep her company. All she heard was the rushing of the unseen river that flowed from the distant peaks and rippled over stones. It sounded like a distant party, conversation heard but not understood. She caught herself straining to understand it, and shook her head as if that would silence the murmur.

She wished she'd let Telaine come with her as far as Ellismere. She felt unexpectedly lonely, something she hadn't felt in seventeen years, ever since she'd come to Longbourne. The feeling made her angry, because Zara North wasn't weak, had never been weak. *You're starting a new life*, she told herself, *you ought to be filled with anticipation*, but after so many new lives, starting another one just made her tired.

Hank's face came to mind, as it sometimes did even thirty-nine years after his death. He'd been a good man, and she'd loved him dearly. She regretted never telling him the truth about who she was. She'd justified it by telling herself Zara North was dead, she was never going back to that life, and it wasn't her secret to tell, but the truth was she'd been afraid of how he'd treat her if he'd known she was the former Queen of Tremontane. So much better to be an ordinary woman with ordinary dreams.

Then he'd died, and to her shame she'd felt the tiniest twinge of relief that she wouldn't have to face the reality that he was aging and she wasn't. She should never have let herself try to make a life with him, but she'd been intoxicated with the joy of being free of all her responsibilities, and he'd looked at her the way he always did— She cut off that line of memory. Hank was dead. She'd moved on.

She came out of the pass and trundled along to Ellismere. She needed to decide where she was going next. Kingsport wasn't a bad idea, now that enough time had passed that no one in the great city would recognize Queen Zara North, but making a place for herself there now that weaving Devices were becoming more common would be difficult. She might be good at weaving—she'd had fifty-plus years to become good at weaving—but she didn't love it enough to fight for it. Ravensholm was another possibility, but that was a long way to ship the loom. And she found she was tired of little towns. She wanted the anonymity of a city, which made her laugh, a short, dry chuckle. She was already anonymous, just another ordinary woman among millions, but it was the wrong kind of anonymity.

The Hitching Station looked dull under the dark clouds that still threatened snow without delivering it. As she pulled into the yard, Josiah Stakely came out of the inn and strolled over to meet her. "Hey there, Agatha," he said. "Fine day for a journey."

She smiled at his witticism. "Fine day for a hot dinner, I think. Happen I can get one here?"

"Of course. Stew's about on, and Joanna made cornbread today."

4

"I'll be back in a bit, then. Got something to do."

Zara didn't really have anything to do; she just didn't feel like conversation, though she liked Josiah well enough and considered his wife a friend. She wrapped her cloak more closely around herself as she walked away from the Hitching Station toward the center of Ellismere.

The wind carried with it the biting sharp scent of snow, the promise of the season's first storm. Probably not more than a few flurries, but the children in Longbourne would shriek with delight and scrabble the fine drifts together to make marble-sized snowballs. Here in the lowlands, not even that much snow would stick, and the storm wouldn't be more than an inconvenience, certainly nothing that would delay her journey. Wherever she ended up going.

She stopped outside the city hall and bought a newspaper, but the wind rattled the pages so violently she went inside the telecoder office to read it. One of the operators looked as if he wanted to object to her using the place for shelter when she wasn't there on business. She fixed him with the blue-eyed North stare, and he subsided.

She'd tried, early on, to be demure and polite, modest and submissive, but it never lasted. Finally Hank had called her on it — *You weren't made to hide who you are* — and once she'd done laughing at that in private, she'd had to admit he was right. It wasn't as if Queen Zara North was the only forceful, quick-thinking woman in Tremontane.

She flipped idly past stories about politics and business, past the society pages, to the advertisements at the back. Those interested her more than politics these days. You saw so much of people's natures in the kind of things they asked for, whether it was employment or goods or even romance. More and more cottage industries were fading as Devices became more prevalent; there must have been two dozen advertisements for skilled Devisers and another score asking for men and women trained in the use of Device-powered looms, sawmills, or the tailor's trade.

She turned another page. Men and women seeking each other out. People offering things for sale. People looking for lost things. There might be an inherent magic for that last one, though if there were, prejudice against inherent magic was still strong enough that anyone possessing it wouldn't dare offer her services.

She turned to the back page, which was half-filled by a line drawing of a tropical beach lined with remarkably chipper palm trees, above which was the word ADVENTURE!!! in letters the length of her pinky finger. Below, in slightly smaller letters, she read:

THE CHANCE OF A LIFETIME!

EXPERIENCE FOREIGN TRAVEL!

MEET STRANGE AND EXOTIC PEOPLE!

ONLY A FEW SPACES LEFT!

She read on, then scowled. It was just an expedition into the jungles of southeastern Eskandel. They were thoroughly mapped and explored, but remained overgrown enough they looked like wild, uncharted territory. She'd gone once and had nothing more exciting happen to her than contracting a jungle fever her inherent magic had cured in a matter of hours when it should have taken days. *That* had required some clever talking.

And yet...the word ADVENTURE had caught her imagination. For a few seconds, before she had read the entire advertisement, her heart had beat faster at the idea of doing something...she wasn't sure what, but something different. Something Agatha Weaver would never do because it was bold and dramatic and attention-grabbing. But Zara North had been dead for sixty years now, and maybe she couldn't use her own name, but there was no need to hide anymore. The more she thought about it, the more she realized how much she wanted to do something outrageous. Not a week's journey into Eskandel's tame wilderness, but something truly different.

She threw the paper away and walked back to the Hitching Station. The snow had finally started falling, tiny specks that pricked her cheeks and hands, and everyone she passed had their heads down against the wind. As she entered the yard, she breathed in the rich, dark smell of beef stew and the higher, sweeter smell of cornbread, and her stomach rumbled.

She pushed the door open and was surrounded by the muggy warmth of the taproom and the quiet mutters of people conversing over their meals. "Josiah," she called out.

"I'll get you a bowl," the man said from beyond the door to the kitchen. She sat at the bar and pushed back her hood.

"Where's the farthest place from here you can imagine?" she asked when Josiah emerged. He blinked at her in surprise.

"That's an odd question. You planning to travel far?"

"Happen I might. Well?"

Josiah leaned against the bar and stretched out his long, thin arms. "I suppose north of the Eidestal," he said. "Not sure how hospitable that is."

"This time of year, happen it's unreachable," Zara agreed.

"Who's going to the Eidestal?" Joanna Stakely said. She set an armful of shot glasses on the counter and began putting them away out of sight. "Not you, Agatha?"

"What's the farthest away you can imagine?" Zara said.

"That isn't the Eidestal? Maybe Eskandel." Joanna polished a smudge off a glass with a corner of her apron. "Or—I suppose Dineh-Karit is further than that."

"It is," Zara said. "Though they don't let northerners into their cities." Dineh-Karit. The mysterious country on the southern continent, even more reclusive than Veribold. So reclusive they had no political relations with Tremontane or any of its neighbors. They'd rejected a Tremontanan embassy in her father King Sylvester's time, and she hadn't bothered to make overtures during her reign. She had no idea what Anthony and Jeffrey had done, whether they'd even made overtures, but in any case the Karitians weren't enemies and they weren't friends. Tremontane hardly even traded with them; Karitian merchants only went to Umberan in Eskandel, and northern merchants who wanted to trade with the Karitians in their homeland were confined to a large island called Goudge's Folly in the bay of Dineh-Karit's largest port city, Manachen.

"So you *are* thinking about it," Josiah said. "You're out of your mind."

"Why? Because I want a change? You know I'm going to be put out of business in a few years by these Devices."

"Yes, but...by heaven, Agatha, you're forty-five. Isn't that past time to settle down?"

Zara glared at him. "I've been settled down for nigh on twenty years. I think it's past time for a change, is what I think."

Josiah put up his hands palm-out in self-defense. "You know I didn't mean anything by it."

"Josiah lives with his foot in his mouth," Joanna said. "I think it sounds exciting."

Zara shrugged. "Can't say I've made up my mind," she said. "Happen I'll go to Kingsport and look about, see what kind of life I can make for myself there." She took a bite of stew and regretted it instantly, because it scorched her tongue and the roof of her mouth. She breathed in around the stew to cool it. "And who knows what might happen?" she said when she could finally swallow.

In her heart, she'd already sold the loom.

Five whirlwind days later, Zara stood in front of the small mirror in her rented room and examined her reflection. Yes, she could pass for thirty-two; she certainly didn't look the forty-five everyone in Longbourne and Ellismere believed her to be. Time to leave Agatha Weaver's life behind.

"I'm Rowena Farrell," she told the mirror, letting the name settle over her like a blanket. Almost her mother's name. "Rowena Farrell from Overton. It's nice to meet you." Ben Garrett was from Overton, and from what little he'd said, she'd gathered it was a small town near Aurilien whose citizens she wasn't likely to run into on the east coast.

Shedding her northeastern accent was harder than losing the name. She'd trained herself so well to say "happen" and "certain sure" it felt strange to say "maybe" and "of course" instead. "Miss Farrell," she said. "Mistress Farrell. Miss Farrell." No, on the whole it was better to be a Miss. No dodging inconvenient questions about her nonexistent husband. "Miss Rowena Farrell. Pleased to meet you."

She scrutinized the corners of her eyes and mouth, the lines extending from the sides of her nose. There were the beginnings of crow's-feet, which cheered her. Eighty-six years old and *finally* showing some wrinkles. She laughed, not too loudly because the walls of this inn were thin. If she looked to be in her early thirties when she was actually in her mid-eighties…no, she didn't want to do that math and work out how many more years she might live. She was starting an adventure and she refused to entertain depressing thoughts.

Finding a job had proved to be easy, and she hadn't even had to resort to the forged letters of reference "Rowena Farrell" came with. Sarah Falken, the daughter in Falken & Daughter, had sounded desperate for someone, anyone, who had a strong personality, was well organized and quick with numbers, and was also willing to travel to the farthest ends of the earth. Now Zara was their newest employee, setting out for Goudge's Folly to oversee the importer's inventory and receiving. It was nothing she'd ever done before, but that made it even more interesting. New job, new name, new country, new life.

She folded her spare shirt and tucked it into her bag, which lay on the elderly bed's sagging mattress. No doubt its lumpiness, and how scratchy the gray wool blanket was, had contributed to her sleeplessness the night before, but mostly she was eager to be off. She cinched the buckles and slung the bag over her shoulder. How freeing, to have all her worldly possessions in a single bag. The coach had arrived in time yesterday for her to go to the Bank of Kingsport and deposit most of her money. Her savings was a significant amount, and Rowena Farrell would want it when she came back from her adventure.

Zara had left the loom in its rented shed and sent a message up the mountain to Telaine: *don't need it anymore, turn it into a Device and sell it, give the money to my grandnieces and –nephew.* Heaven only knew what Telaine would make of that, but she'd do as Zara asked. Now Zara had a sizeable amount of coin in her bag, enough for her fare, she hoped, and as she settled the tab with the innkeeper, she breathed in the smell of warm ale that permeated the walls and tables and gave the woman a cheery farewell.

It was a beautiful autumn day, sunny, with a crispness to the air that spoke of apples and smoke and the promise of winter, which in this port city was milder than in Longbourne but still snowy. Kingsport was an old city, older than Aurilien, and it looked its age, but in a well-kept way. Centuries-old buildings, their half-timbered frames a study in dark and pale contrasts, stood like pieces of history against which men and women in modern dress looked like children playing at dress-up.

She caught a whiff of refuse that the Devices used to clean the streets would take care of later that night. Kingsport's citizens might be proud of their city's heritage and determined to preserve its historical character, but they weren't stupid enough to reject useful new Devisery. There were light Devices on lampposts lining the streets of even the slightly impoverished district she was passing through, though they were shaped to look like lanterns and would no doubt flicker like flames when they came on at night.

She stepped out of the way of a wagon drawing a load of crates that made the wagon bed sag alarmingly in the middle. Wouldn't it be interesting if that cargo ended up on the same ship she did?

She heard the harbor before she saw it, the *kraaaw*ing of sea birds and the shouts of wagoners mingling with the creak of wood and the snap of ropes. She came over the rise of the cobblestone street and saw the sea, blue-gray in the morning light and smelling of brine and mist. It was so vast she stopped at the top of the hill and watched it for a while. She'd never been to sea and had no idea what to expect, though she worried that seasickness wasn't something her inherent magic could prevent.

Another laden wagon rumbled past, forcing her to step off the street onto the sidewalk and bringing her back to the present. She followed the wagon down the hill, which wasn't terribly steep but would surely be slick and dangerous in winter. Not that she'd be there to find out.

Kingsport's harbor was a nearly perfect circle, easily defensible, though no one had ever attacked it in all the hundreds of years of its existence. Tall stone buildings with narrow slits for windows lining the curve completed the illusion of a city prepared for war. She came to the end of the street, where a rail prevented anyone from accidentally stepping over the edge of the sea-wall. The ancient black stones, set there in a time when Tremontane was a new country, reflected the sunlight dully, as if soaking it up against the coming winter.

Long splintery docks extended into the harbor, and dozens of tiny boats lay tied up to them—or were they ships? Some of them had one or two masts with sails furled tightly to them. Farther out in the harbor, the big ships rode the gentle waves that broke against the mouth of the bay, their masts and rigging like bare trees strung with spider's silk, though it was hard to imagine a spider capable of spinning webs strong enough to hold the men who clambered over the rigging like monkeys.

Steep, narrow steps set into the sea-wall took her down to the docks, where she walked, counting, until she came to the seventh pier. A rowboat was tethered there, overseen by a woman in a pea jacket and knit hat. She looked so perfectly the part of a sailor Zara said, "Miss Lyton?"

The woman turned. "Yes?"

"Rowena Farrell. Mistress Falken arranged passage for me on your ship?"

"Not my ship, but I take your meaning. This your baggage?" She pointed at Zara's bag. "Come aboard, and we'll take you to the *Emma Covington*. She's not ready to sail yet, but you might as well stow your gear now."

Zara clambered into the rowboat and settled herself at the front—no, the bow, she didn't know much about boats, but she knew bow and stern, starboard and port—with her bag on her lap. She watched Lyton and another sailor move about, neatly coiling rope and adjusting the oars. They weren't dressed in any special uniform, but then this wasn't a military ship, it was a cargo vessel that also carried passengers. She twisted around to look behind her, out into the harbor. One of those was the *Emma Covington,* soon to be her home for the next month or more. They all looked the same to her, but she didn't much care about their differences; she was eager to begin her journey.

The boat rocked, and she turned to see a young man, barely an adult, stepping over the side, one hand gripping a seaman's bag like hers and the other clutching his oversized belt. He was followed by a tall, handsome man who smiled at her appreciatively. She smiled back in a practiced way that said *Don't waste both our time.*

Lyton stepped into the boat and said, "Cast off," and the sailors pushed off from the pier, dipped their oars, and began pulling in long, smooth strokes out into the harbor.

Zara trailed her hand in the water and smiled at the young man, whose dark face had the wooden expression of someone utterly terrified. Out of the corner of her eye she caught the other man examining her closely, but she pretended not to notice. They'd all be cooped up together for more than a month, and there was no sense shutting him down hard without trying the polite way first. Zara turned around again to look at the ships. She wasn't even aboard yet, but she felt her adventure had already begun.

CHAPTER TWO

Zara stood at the rail and closed her eyes against the sun that turned the waves into glittering shards of glass. It was beautifully warm, the air smelled of salt, and an occasional breeze brushed her cheeks like a butterfly's kiss. It was hard to imagine snow and cold on a day like this, but if she were still in Longbourne, she'd probably be shoveling out the path between her house and Verity's shop next door, and Abel Roberts' grandnephew Enos would be preparing to drive the earth mover down the mountain to clear the pass. Today was her eighty-seventh birthday, and for the first time in as long as she could remember she didn't resent it.

It was hard to feel resentment, or any negative emotion, for that matter, in these balmy southern seas. They'd encountered only two storms on the whole trip; the food was plain but good and plentiful; her fellow passengers were, if not all friendly, not objectionable. And they were about two days out from Goudge's Folly. It was an excellent day for a birthday, even if she was celebrating it in private.

"Looking for land again, Rowena?" Gaston Digby came to stand beside her. His voice was teasing as usual. "Or for whales?"

"Not looking for anything this time," Zara said. "What about you?"

"You're the only thing worth looking at on this blasted ship," he said with a smile. Zara smiled back. Gaston was tall, fair-haired, extremely handsome, and fully aware of how attractive his physical attributes were. He had flirted with her relentlessly but without serious intent since they'd boarded the ship's longboat; she'd deflected his courtesies gracefully and chuckled over them in private. He was in his thirties, but they all seemed so *young* to her, with their enthusiasms and certainty that the world was theirs to conquer. And yet she had so little in common with those her own age, who were quietly — or not so quietly, given how vocal some of them were about their ailments and

13

ungrateful children—wrapping up their affairs on earth in preparation for heaven. If she'd been interested in developing a romantic relationship, which she was not, it was hard for her to imagine the kind of man she might fall in love with, except that Gaston wasn't it.

"What, you don't want to watch the sailors in the rigging?" she said.

Gaston shuddered. "Men were not meant to fly, and they certainly weren't meant to hang by their ankles from the topmast yardarm or whatever it's called. It chills my bones every time I look at them."

"Look at what?" Belinda Stouffer said, taking a position on Zara's other side. Her short brown hair fell forward over her eyes and she pushed it out of the way. "There's nothing out there but waves and more waves. By heaven, I can't wait for landfall."

"We were discussing Gaston's future career as a sail monkey," Zara said. Belinda, an independent merchant, had very quickly gone from being an acquaintance to a friend, and she and Zara and Gaston and Alfred Richfield, a shipping magnate's factor, spent most evenings together, playing cards or swapping stories.

"I'd pay money to see Gaston climb the rigging," Belinda said. "Wouldn't you, Rowena?"

"No amount of money could convince me to do that," Gaston said.

"I could forgive your gambling debts," Zara said.

"No need. I'm going to win everything back tonight."

"Not against Rowena. I've never seen anyone so good at poker."

"I'm lucky, I guess," Zara said, though the truth was she found poker simple after a long lifetime of observing people's faces, and sometimes played a bad hand to keep from looking too lucky. She leaned out over the rail again. "I think I see something. Is that a whale?"

The other two shaded their eyes. "It looks like a ship," Gaston said.

"That would be interesting," Belinda said. "Someone new to talk to." She was short and plump, half Zara's age and twice as outgoing.

"In the first place," said Gaston, "it's unlikely they're coming along our path, so we won't encounter them. And secondly, what's wrong with talking to *us*? Is novelty so important to you?"

"I'm *bored*. Novelty would help me stay sane."

Zara gazed out over the waves and focused on the distant ship. "Maybe it's a Karitian ship. *That* would be interesting. Do you suppose they'd even be willing to talk to us?"

"They're probably as bored as we are. That has to make a difference." Belinda stretched and yawned. "I'm going below to take a nap before dinner. I wish I'd brought more books." She turned to make her way down the stairs, but had to step aside for a tall, dusky-skinned woman who came up the companionway, followed by an equally tall and dark-skinned man. Neither of them behaved as if they'd noticed Belinda at all.

Zakhari Cantara and her brother Zakhari Arjan had come aboard at Umberan and stayed aloof from the other passengers since then. They'd said, in broken Tremontanese, they were working-class Eskandelics traveling to find work on Goudge's Folly, but Zara understood the Eskandelic language and was fairly certain they spoke Tremontanese better than they let on. That indicated they were upper class, possibly even children of a harem. They were circumspect even privately in their own language, but Zara also suspected they weren't siblings, but married, or at least betrothed, which raised a number of other questions Zara couldn't leave alone. It really wasn't any of her business, but she'd found over the years that if you were keeping a secret, other people's secrets could be a danger to you.

Cantara took Arjan's arm and they proceeded to stroll around the perimeter of the deck. Zara looked back out at the distant ship. It was probably only her imagination that it was closer. The thought filled her with inexplicable unease. "I think I'll go check on Eglantine," she said, and followed Belinda down the companionway. Eglantine Tucker had a nervous stomach and an equally nervous disposition, and she annoyed Zara because of her diffident manner that suggested she was waiting for the world to take care of her, but Zara wasn't cruel and didn't mind helping her in her illness. Much.

She descended into the muggy dimness of the passenger deck and knocked on Eglantine's door. At a muffled "come in," she entered, saying, "I thought you might be feeling poorly again."

"I really am sorry to trouble you," Eglantine said, "it's just that I feel so unwell." Her thin, high voice grated on Zara's nerves. She reminded herself to be kind and went to help the young woman sit up.

"I'll bring you something to drink that should settle your stomach, but you have to remember not to eat heavy food," she said. "It makes things worse."

"But that's almost all they serve," Eglantine said. "I can't not eat."

"Just…try, all right?" Zara said, feeling her impatience come creeping back. "Think about…how wonderful it will be to see your husband. Only a few more days now. Captain Proctor says we should see land tonight. Not *see* it, because it'll be dark, but be within sight."

Eglantine smiled wanly at her. "All right. You're too good to me."

You wouldn't say that if you could hear some of my thoughts. "It's no trouble. I'll be back in a bit."

The "special drink" was bicarbonate of soda mixed with boiled water, and Eglantine drank it without making a face for once. Zara helped her lie down and left her to rest. On the way out of the door, she nearly bumped into Theodore Jenkins. "Excuse me," she said.

"Sorry," he muttered, and brushed past, one hand on his belt as always. Theodore was about sixteen, though he acted younger, and although the belt didn't look like anything special, made of woven fabric instead of leather, it was obvious to Zara he was concealing something precious inside it. She watched him go, reflecting how Telaine's son Owen would probably look like him in a few years, though pale instead of dark. Theodore never said much, but he'd told them he was going to Goudge's Folly to finish his apprenticeship in Devisery with his aunt. Possibly his nervousness and shyness would disappear once he was safely on land again. Zara certainly never saw him go near the deck rails.

It was almost suppertime, but she went back up on deck anyway. The unknown ship was definitely closer. She didn't know any more

16

about ships than she'd learned in passing from the crew of the *Emma Covington*, but it seemed to be carrying more sail than theirs. She glanced around at the crew; none of them acted worried at all. It was probably nothing.

"Miss Farrell. It's a lovely evening, isn't it?"

Zara nodded, but didn't turn to face Mister Watson, the ship's first mate. "Very lovely."

"It's almost suppertime. You should go below."

His paternalistic tone of voice irritated her. "I'll go when I'm ready, thank you."

"You wouldn't want to delay the meal, would you? That's not very polite."

Zara ground her teeth. Watson always sounded polite, but he'd gotten on Zara's nerves the first day when he'd treated her like a child because she knew nothing of shipboard customs. And now he continued to treat her like a child and went out of his way to remind her of things she'd learned quickly to spite him. Men like him never failed to rile her, no matter how old she was. "They still ring the supper bell, don't they? I'll go then and not before."

"I really think—"

"Mister Watson," Zara said, turning on him, "I question whether your duties include monitoring my every action. Perhaps we should ask the captain to mediate? I'm sure he will love adding that to his undoubtedly busy schedule."

Watson's mouth went pinched with anger. "Miss Farrell, you are a passenger here, and you aren't allowed to decide what your rights are. It's my job to make sure you're safe."

"Again, Mister Watson, I'm more than willing to take it up with the captain. I believe, having paid my fare, I'm entitled to make a few requests, one of which is freedom from being hovered over by you like a particularly inept buzzard." She strode off toward the companionway—*end an argument on your terms*—and down the steps before he could do more than open his mouth for a retort.

Safely in her cabin, she sat on the bed and took a calming breath.

Now she was out of his presence, she was angrier with herself than with him. That had been the Queen talking, down to the syntax, and maybe nobody was looking for Zara North, but she'd spent so many years hiding that breaking those habits felt wrong and almost frightening, as if she weren't in control of herself. And self-control was something she'd always held dear.

Distantly, she heard the bell ring for supper, and stood and dusted off her trousers, though there wasn't anything to dust. She'd have to avoid Watson more diligently in the future. Better for both of them if he didn't have another opportunity to criticize her. Two more days, and it wouldn't matter.

Supper was, as usual, a cheery affair for Zara and most of the passengers, though the Zakharis kept to themselves and Theodore only spoke when spoken to. Afterward, while the steward cleared the table for the card game, Zara went up on deck again. The strange ship was definitely closer, and now she could see the sailors casting glances at it as they went about their duties. Captain Proctor stood near the wheel, having a low-voiced conversation with Lyton and the steersman.

On a whim, Zara approached them. The conversation cut off well before she could overhear it, but that wasn't what she was there for.

"Captain, what ship is that?" she said.

"Nothing to worry about," Lyton said. "Just another merchant vessel like us."

"It's moving fast for a merchant vessel."

"There's a storm coming in," Proctor said. "We've laid on more sail ourselves—that is, we'll try to make as much progress as we can before the storm catches us. Probably the ship will come alongside of us and we'll trade news."

Laying on more sail before a storm was foolish. Even Zara knew that. "Then it's a Tremontanan ship."

Proctor hesitated slightly. "Of course. There's nothing to worry about."

Zara thought about pressing the issue, decided Proctor wouldn't be more forthcoming than that, and nodded at him politely before turning away. The sun was sinking below the horizon, far to starboard, and the fading light caught the mystery ship's sails, turning them pale peach. She covertly observed the captain. He did not look like a man free of care.

So. That ship was almost certainly a danger to them. Was the captain hiding something about the nature of this voyage? Or was there something about the cargo someone wanted? Though they might simply be opportunists—but in any case, if that ship intended to board and pillage them, it wouldn't matter the reason.

She moved to the stern rail and looked northward, where masses of clouds blocked the starry sky. A fork of lightning shot through the air, the merest flash of light, then another, larger one streaked across the charcoal background. Even she knew it was time for the *Emma Covington* to furl her sails, but the vast swaths of canvas, dim gray in the fading light, billowed in the rising wind as if welcoming it.

The ship rocked, throwing Zara into the rail, and she clung to it momentarily before making her way back across the deck to the companionway. There was nothing left to do but wait, and pray, though she wasn't sure what to pray for—escape from their pursuers, or a safe journey through the storm? Either way, this would be a dangerous night.

She had trouble focusing on her cards and smiled weakly at Gaston and Belinda's teasing when she lost hand after hand, listening mainly to the sound of the wind from above. As the storm picked up, and the ship's movement became more noticeable, the game petered out, and eventually the four sat, not speaking, as the storm raged. The lantern above the table swayed with the ship, casting bleak shadows across their faces.

"This is a bad one," Alfred Richfield said. He hooked his thumbs through his suspenders and slid them up and down, the way he did when he was uncertain of something. "The captain would've said if there was any real danger, wouldn't he?"

Gaston shrugged. "Not much any of us could do about it if he did, right?"

"I'm going to check on Eglantine," Zara said.

She had to keep one hand on the bulkhead to avoid falling over as she went down the corridor. Distantly, thunder boomed, once, twice, and she listened for the sound of rain striking the deck, but heard only the bellowing of the wind. She knocked on Eglantine's door, then entered without an invitation. "Is your stomach still bothering you?" she said.

"Not much—isn't that strange?" Eglantine sat up on her bed. "I actually feel much better even though the storm is bad."

Another crack of thunder, low-pitched, then a nearer rumbling, and Zara stepped out of Eglantine's room in time to see a man falling down the companionway stairs to land heavily in an unmoving heap at the bottom. "What happened?" she began, taking a few swift steps in his direction, but before she could reach him, she heard shouting, and more sharp thunder, and she realized the noise was actually the sound of cannon fire and rifles.

She dropped to the floor beside the fallen sailor and tried to help him up, but saw dark blood spreading across his back and released his body. Behind her, Eglantine screamed. "Shut up!" Zara said, leaping at the woman and clapping a hand over her mouth.

"What's going on?" Gaston said, emerging from the mess room. "Sweet holy heaven, is that man dead?"

"Get back inside," Zara ordered. "Eglantine, don't scream or I'll have Gaston knock you unconscious, do you hear?"

Eglantine nodded, her eyes wide and terrified. Gaston gave her a confused look. "I can't—" he began.

"Just get inside." Zara did some pushing until she'd gotten all five of them into the dubious safety of the mess room. "The ship's under attack," she said. "Help me barricade the door."

"Under attack by who?" Alfred said.

"I don't know. Pirates, maybe. That ship, probably." She was aware what they were doing was pointless, that the pirates had all the time in the world to flush them out, that being safe from rifle balls didn't protect them from drowning if the pirates decided to sink the

20

ship, but it was all she could think of. Cannons roared again, and the ship lurched. "Maybe—"

Someone pounded on the door. *"You in there! What do you think you're doing? Come out now!"* The man's Eskandelic was rough, guttural and difficult for Zara to understand.

No one spoke. The same person pounded again and shouted, *"We aren't going to hurt anyone so long as we get what we come for!"*

"We don't understand! What do you want?" Eglantine cried out, ignoring the others' attempts to shush her.

There was a pause, then a new voice said in Tremontanese, "Something this ship is carrying. Nothing you need to worry about, darlin'. But if you *don't* come out, we're going to start shooting your friends. You don't want that, do you?"

Eglantine was crying. "Rowena, we have to go out there," she pleaded.

Some distance away came the fainter sound of a pistol being discharged, and a scream. "That was just an injury," the man said. "It could be worse."

"Rowena," Belinda said.

"We don't have a choice," Zara said. They shoved the table out of the way, and Zara opened the door. Immediately, rough hands grabbed her and passed her from one pirate to another, pushing her up the stairs to stumble onto the deck. A few bodies, including that of Captain Proctor, lay limp where they'd been shot, but most of the crew and passengers stood silently under guard by men and women dressed in ordinary clothing, not uniforms but not tattered or ragged either. They were of many nationalities, mostly Eskandelic, and all bore the grim look of people for whom violence was just another part of life.

The *Emma Covington* shuddered as the pirate ship, knocked about by the waves, grazed it; the two were dangerously close. Zara staggered as another blow nearly sent her to her knees. Only the grip of her pirate captor kept her from falling.

A pair of women climbed out of the cargo hold. *"It isn't there,"* one of them shouted in Eskandelic, and a third woman looked up from where she stood near the wheel. She was tall, with reddish-brown skin and ruddy hair to match it, and wore an ornate coat and several expensive-looking rings and bracelets. In her left hand she held a boxy Device of brass and shining dark wood about the size of her palm and extended fingers. She'd tied her hair loosely back from her face, but a few tendrils floated free, and as Zara watched, the woman drew an enormous knife, tucked the Device under her arm, and hacked one of the strands off at the roots. She thrust the knife roughly into her belt and crossed the deck to where the two women waited, brandishing the Device like a weapon.

"*It's somewhere on this ship,*" she said, tapping the Device on its glass top. "*You're not looking in the right place.*"

"*We looked everywhere,*" the pirate replied.

"*If that was true, you'd have found it,*" the woman said, and whipped her knife out of her belt and slashed the pirate's face so quickly the knife was back in her belt before the pirate could even scream. She clapped her hands to her face and took a step backward. "*Get out of my sight.*"

"Captain Ghazarian, ma'am," the woman said, weeping, and scuttled away to crouch near the rail. No one moved to help her.

Ghazarian turned her glare on the second pirate. "Well?" she said, this time speaking Tremontanese.

"It's not obvious, ma'am," the woman said, to her credit standing erect and fearless in front of the pirate captain. "We might have to unpack all the crates."

"Or we can try something else," Ghazarian said. She gestured, and two of her men dragged Lyton toward her. Lyton was holding her arm gingerly, as if it were broken, and she looked at the pirate captain dully. "You," Ghazarian said, "tell us where the Device is."

"Go to hell," Lyton said.

Ghazarian shrugged. "I will see you there," she said, drew a pistol from her belt, and shot Lyton in the face.

Eglantine screamed and fainted. Someone behind Zara vomited. Zara had trouble keeping the contents of her stomach down herself.

The pirates dropped Lyton's body to lie at Ghazarian's feet. "Does anyone else want me to defy?" she shouted. "You have the Device. I want it. I will spare you when I have what I want."

Zara didn't need Telaine's ability to hear lies to know that was a whopper. Either they could refuse to talk—not that they knew anything about whatever Device this woman wanted—and be killed one at a time, or they could help her find the Device and be killed all together. Zara cast her eye on the ship's boat. There were two of them, but this one was in a position to be lowered. Someone had clearly suspected trouble from the enemy ship. If they could start enough of a melee, possibly the passengers could be saved. It amused her briefly that she didn't think herself in need of saving. But where was Watson? Had he, too, been killed? The sailors would respond better to one of their own giving orders than a mere passenger.

"If you tell us what you want, we might be better able to help," Gaston said, and Zara's heart sank. He was going to try charm on Ghazarian, and he was going to get himself killed, probably get other people killed as well. "There's a lot of cargo on board. Or you could just take it all, let us go."

"I could, maybe," Ghazarian said. "It a Tremontanan Device is. Which cargo comes from there?"

Zara kept a neutral expression, though her heart beat faster. Mistress Falken had seen her cargo aboard the *Emma Covington* at Kingsport, and there were Devices in it—but household items, surely nothing a pirate would want? Then she heard Belinda, who stood just behind her, draw in a sharp, incautious breath. Instantly, Ghazarian's attention was on her. "You know something," she said.

"I...I don't," Belinda said, sounding so guilty no one could have believed her ignorant.

"Her cargo is Tremontanan!" Eglantine shrieked. "Take it and let us go!"

Zara groaned inwardly. First Gaston, then Belinda, then Eglantine—could none of them simply keep their mouths shut?

Ghazarian grabbed Belinda by the neck of her jacket and twisted,

23

choking her. "Where?" she said in a low voice. "Where is?"

Belinda scrabbled at her throat, her mouth opening and closing desperately in search of air. "Let her go! She can't tell you anything like that!" Alfred shouted.

Gaston took two steps and rammed hard into the pirate captain's side, snatching her pistol as he did so. Ghazarian stumbled, taking Belinda with her. Then the loud retorts of pistol and rifle fire rang out over the wind, sailors were turning on their captors, and Zara grabbed Eglantine and shoved her ahead and toward the ship's longboat.

Ghazarian turned on Gaston, drawing her knife and slashing at him so he couldn't bring her pistol to bear. Zara took advantage of the confusion to pull Belinda to her feet and help her stagger toward the longboat, coughing hard the whole way. "Help Eglantine!" she shouted in Belinda's ear, and stepped back out of the confusion, hoping to see someone else she might save.

It was chaos. More bodies, some of them not quite dead, cluttered the deck; sailors and pirates battled each other closely for possession of guns or knives. Zara saw Theodore Jenkins go down under the weight of a sailor twice his size, pushed into him by a pirate who'd thrust her knife deep into the sailor's stomach. The Zakharis were nowhere to be seen, and neither was Alfred.

She turned toward the pirate captain in time to see Gaston slump lifeless to the deck, blood covering his shattered chest, as Ghazarian thrust her recovered pistol into her belt. The pirate captain shouted orders that were lost in the noise of battle and the roar of the oncoming storm.

Zara raced for the longboat and shouted at the sailors nearby. All of them ignored her. Furious at the stupidity of it all, she climbed into the boat and worked at the ropes that would lower it into the dubious safety of the ocean. At the other end, Belinda did the same. It was awkward, and she was sure she was doing it wrong, but she had no other choice left.

Suddenly Eglantine stood up in the boat and screamed, "They're going to kill us! We have to go back or they'll kill us!" The boat rocked wildly, Zara lost her grip on the ropes, and one end of the boat lurched violently, throwing Eglantine over the side and into the steely gray waters below.

"Eglantine!" Zara shouted, craning to see over her shoulder where the woman had gone, fumbling desperately at the ropes to right the longboat. Slowly, too slowly, she and Belinda managed to lower it into the water. Eglantine had vanished. Zara clung to the side of the boat, searching the waves desperately for a sight of her, but there were nothing but foaming, choppy waves in all directions and the sound of rain hissing across the surface of the ocean toward them.

A shot cracked high above. "Rowena, we have to move," Belinda said, taking up one of the oars. Zara reached for the other, then shied away as something large and dark plummeted from the deck above to land half-in, half-out of the boat. It was Alfred Richfield. Zara grabbed hold of his suspenders and hauled him fully into the boat. Dark blood spread across the front of his shirt, but he moved when Zara felt his throat for a pulse.

"Not dead yet," he whispered. "Not dead yet."

Zara didn't think he'd be able to say that much longer, but she tore a swath of fabric from his ruined shirt, balled it up and helped him press it against his chest. "Hang on, and we'll get help," she lied, and she and Belinda began rowing away from the *Emma Covington.*

CHAPTER THREE

After only a few minutes, the full fury of the storm was on them. Zara and Belinda had to ship oars and lie down, protecting Alfred as best they could, while the rain and the waves and the wind tossed them in every direction. Zara curled up against her friend's body and prayed she wasn't about to find out if she could die by drowning. Would she just lie at the bottom for decades, or centuries, until someone pulled her out? She thought of Eglantine, who would never see her husband again, of Gaston dead on the deck of the *Emma Covington*, and found herself incapable of worrying about her own fate.

She had no idea how long it was they lay there, but eventually the waves calmed, and the rain turned from a pounding torrent into a quiet pattering. Zara and Belinda lapped at the water that had accumulated in the bottom of the boat, which tasted salty but was mostly rainwater. They tried to get Alfred to drink some of it, but he was barely conscious. It was a miracle he was even still alive — or could you call it a miracle when it really only prolonged his suffering?

When the sun came up, Zara pointed the bow of the boat southward. They had no idea where the storm had driven them, but Dineh-Karit was to the south no matter where they were now, and Zara knew from talking to Captain Proctor that the currents ran roughly southwest, so it was likely they weren't very far from the mainland. Zara told herself those were reasonable thoughts and not unjustified optimism in the face of certain death.

They rowed until they were tired, then rested as best they could. Zara tried not to think of the men and women they'd left behind. She should have made more of an effort to force some of them into the boat — but they'd had the look of sailors determined to retake their ship. Maybe she was the foolish one, running away before the battle was decided. She leaned back and closed her eyes against the tropical sun. No. The sailors of the *Emma Covington* were outnumbered and

26

poorly armed, and she'd done the only thing she could.

"...Rowena..."

She sat up. Alfred had his eyes open and was looking, not at her, but at something far distant in the sky—or possibly at nothing at all. "Rowena," he repeated. His voice was barely louder than a whisper.

"I'm here, Alfred," she said, moving to take his hand. Farther astern, Belinda lay sleeping with her mouth open, her breath whistling in and out of her nostrils.

Alfred squeezed her hand, the faintest pressure. "...dying..." he said.

Zara didn't believe in the comforting lie. "Yes."

"...need your help..."

"What is it?"

"...pocket..."

Alfred wasn't wearing a coat, and his shirt had no pockets. Zara felt along the outside seams of his trousers until she found a pocket slit with something hard and round inside. She reached in and pulled out an oversized pocket watch cased in bright brass, incised with a pattern of leaves around the outside edge. "Is this what you wanted?"

Alfred nodded, then coughed deep in his chest. "...not watch...Device," he said. "Agent...of the Crown..."

"You're an agent?" Zara lowered her voice instinctively.

He nodded again. "...what they wanted...Device..." He coughed less painfully. "...need you...to take it...Calliope Blackwood...on Goudge's Folly."

"*This* is the Device that pirate was looking for?" She'd thought it was hidden in Belinda's crates, whatever it was. It didn't look like anything worth killing over.

"Yes. Urgent...Blackwood needs it...it *cannot* be taken by...anyone else...promise me..."

"I promise." Immediately she wondered if she'd made a mistake, making such a promise to a dying man. It seemed unlikely she and Belinda would survive much longer than Alfred. But he sounded so urgent she found she couldn't deny him. "Calliope Blackwood on

Goudge's Folly. I promise. Just lie still now."

Alfred smiled. "Can't lie...much stiller than this," he said, and let out one final breath. Zara held onto his lifeless hand for a few moments, then laid it gently across his chest.

She looked more closely at the pocket watch, or whatever the Device actually was. It didn't look like a watch, once she examined it; it had no visible seam around the edge where a real watch would open, and the crown that ought to move freely to change the time was a solid part of the case. She pressed down on it and felt something shift inside. So it wasn't just a hunk of brass.

She put it away in her own trouser pocket. She had no compunctions about investigating the thing, but now wasn't the time. Belinda might wake at any moment, and Zara was sure Alfred intended her to keep the Device secret from everyone, even their friend.

She was staring southward when Belinda began stirring. "How's Alfred?" she said, then saw how still he lay and said, "Oh. I...suppose there was never any hope for him, was there?"

"Not really," Zara said, then realized how callous that had sounded and added, "He went peacefully. I don't think he was in any pain at the end."

"Should we...bury him at sea?"

"Maybe. But—isn't that land, over there?"

Belinda shaded her eyes and squinted. "I think it is. We could bury him there."

Zara picked up her oar. "We have to get there first."

They rowed all day and into the evening, taking occasional rests that became more frequent, and longer, as the day wore on. Zara's hands were almost raw, her magical healing barely keeping pace with the fierce rubbing of the oar handles on her skin. Beside her, Belinda rowed in near silence. Her breath came more heavily each time they took up the oars, but Zara didn't have time or inclination to coddle her. They needed to reach the shore, and she refused to give up.

The green haze on the southern horizon turned darker, then more solid, and by the time the sun kissed the horizon, they could see individual trees and a lighter smudge of shore. Zara had to control her eagerness, to keep pace with Belinda, but it was so hard not to make the oars fly. Finally, the bottom of the boat scraped along the sand, and Zara jumped out and dragged the boat higher onto the sand. "Help me," she said, but Belinda slumped over the oars and lay still. "Belinda, get up."

"I need to rest," she said. "Just give me a minute."

There wasn't a reason to hurry anymore, so Zara sat down on the hard, wet surface of sand, folded her arms across her knees, and let the wavelets lap over her feet. Her boots were already soaked from wading to shore, her trousers were damp in the seams and crotch, and her shirt was stiff with salt water, but she was alive and she intended to remain so. She laughed into her arms. As if she had a choice. Again, she felt no bitterness at the thought.

"Do you have any idea where we are?" Belinda said.

Zara scanned the sky. It was going to be a cloudless, starry night, and if she'd learned survival skills at all, she might be able to make use of that. "Not a clue," she said. "What worries me is not knowing whether we landed west or east of Manachen and Goudge's Folly. If we guess wrong, we could end up lost in Dineh-Karit for…"

"I know Captain Proctor was going to approach the shore and then sail west with the current. We couldn't have been driven that far off course, could we?"

"I don't know." Zara stretched and stood up. "Can you stand?"

"I think so." Belinda had to lean heavily on the sides of the boat to get herself upright. "What do we do with Alfred?"

Zara looked over the shoreline. Soft, low-growing scrub led to trees with fat trunks and branches that drooped under the weight of shiny dark green leaves. It was impossible to see more than a few feet beyond the tree line, and if not for the heavy scent of wet greenery she would have believed it to be a painting the artist hadn't bothered completing. "I didn't think about how we'd bury him," she said. "We should leave him in the boat for now and get some rest. I'm exhausted."

"I'm starving. Maybe we should look for food."

"I'm not sure it's a good idea to go too far from the shore."

"We can keep within sight of it. There has to be food here somewhere."

The sand went from being wet and clumping to dry and clinging, sticking to their damp clothes and working its way inside the seams. Zara led the way beneath the drooping branches, holding them carefully aside so they wouldn't hit Belinda. The cool evening air was muggy but not terribly oppressive—*that's one thing to be grateful for*, Zara thought, *that and practically no insects*. Beneath the trees, it was much darker, the leaves blocking the last of the sunlight, and Zara stopped almost immediately. "What are we looking for?" Belinda said.

Zara glanced back over her shoulder at the ocean. The myriad noises of birds and other nocturnal animals had cut off as they entered the jungle, which unsettled her. She half expected the ocean to be swallowed up by it. "That," she said, pointing at a papaya tree growing nearby. The upper fruits were still green, but the lower ones were a nice ripe orange, and Zara's stomach growled just looking at them. "They're still a little too high to reach, so we'll need a rock or a stick or something."

Between the two of them, they managed to gather five fruits and carry them back to the boat. It was full dark now, but they used Zara's small pocketknife to hack the fruits open and dove into the soft flesh, spitting out the bitter seeds. Zara tried not to look at the dark shape huddled in the bottom of the boat. They'd have to do something about him soon; in this tropical climate, his body would begin to rot quickly. Finally, full if not totally satisfied—she couldn't stop imagining a roast chicken with new potatoes—she scooted back above the tide line and threw the last rind away. "I'm so tired I don't care where I sleep," she said.

Belinda joined her and lay back on the sand. "And tomorrow we can make a plan."

"Tomorrow," Zara said, lying down with her hands pillowing her head. She was asleep in seconds.

"Rowena!"

Zara came instantly awake and sat up, spitting sand out of her mouth. Belinda was shaking her. "The boat's gone," she said.

"What?" Zara tried to rub sand off her hands and succeeded only in spreading it around. The sun was almost entirely above the horizon, and the shore was empty. "We didn't pull it up far enough."

"I guess not. What are we going to do?"

Other than be grateful not to have to dispose of Alfred's body? Zara sighed. "We'll have to go on foot. That won't be too bad so long as we choose the right direction."

"Which is still our biggest problem."

Zara thought their biggest problem was keeping Belinda from starving to death, but said only, "I think we have to go west. The *Emma Covington* was a long way east of Goudge's Folly, and I can't imagine it was blown that far off course. The same goes for us."

"That's as good a choice as any. And when we get to Manachen—"

"I can send word to Falken & Daughter and someone will come for us." *Assuming I can find someone willing to take a message.* Nothing about this was going to be simple.

They gathered more papayas—not many, since they had no way of carrying them except in Belinda's increasingly ragged jacket—and set off along the tree line. Birds clamored unseen in the tree tops, fighting or courting or possibly just giving each other the news of a couple of two-legged interlopers. As the sun rose higher in the sky, Belinda lagged behind. Zara, still fresh and unwearied, slowed to match her steps. "We should take rests," she said.

"All right," said Belinda, and immediately sat down. Zara sat next to her. "I wish I knew how far we have to go."

They'd come around a curve in the shore into a semi-circular bay, its water clear and blue and inviting. Zara thought about taking off her boots and wading in the shallows, but the idea of sand clinging to her feet and then filling her boots was unpleasant. "I guess we'll know when we get there," she said.

"This is hopeless, isn't it."

"Maybe. But I'm not giving up. We have food, we have a direction—"

"I've got nothing, Rowena."

Belinda's voice sounded dull, lifeless. "What are you talking about?" Zara asked.

"That cargo represented everything I had," Belinda said. "I had that and a few guilders, and now I don't have either. I took a chance—" She laughed, a sound as raucous as the birds' cries. "And to think I was afraid no one would want what I had to offer. Pirates weren't even near the top of my list of worries."

"It was a good gamble. The Veriboldan silk, I mean."

"I should have stayed in Umberan, let the trade come to me, but I was in competition with all those Eskandelic traders and it just— maybe I was greedy, but it made sense to try for a different market." She laughed again. "It's a stupid thing to worry about, given that we could die out here. Though I wish I knew what those pirates were after. They could have taken everything and left us alone, and Gaston and Alfred and Eglantine and all the others would still be alive."

The Device in Zara's pocket weighed her down with its secrets. "I don't think that captain, that Ghazarian woman, is the kind of person who leaves survivors."

"Probably not." Belinda stood up and brushed herself off. Then she gasped. "*People!*" she exclaimed, pointing. At the far end of the bay, two human figures had come into sight. Belinda took a few running steps, and Zara lunged, caught her arm and made her stop.

"We don't know who they are," she said. "They're probably Karitians, and they won't be happy we're on their shore. They might not care that we aren't here voluntarily."

"We can't run, Rowena, they've already seen us."

"True. But we need to be prepared for the worst." No sense pointing out they might not survive the worst. "Let's approach them slowly so we don't look like a threat."

Slowly, they made their way around the bay, walking on the damp sand near the water so their gait would be more even than if they'd stumbled along the loose, dry sand higher up. The first strangers were joined by two more, all four strolling toward them as if they wanted to seem nonthreatening, too. Zara rubbed her palms on her trouser leg, brushing off the rest of the sand. She had no idea what Karitians did to foreigners and didn't want to find out.

Then the others were close enough to make out features, and Zara's mouth fell open in astonishment. "Mister Watson!" she said. "How did you come here?"

"The same way you did, no doubt, Miss Farrell," Watson said in that unctuous tone that even under these circumstances annoyed her. "Our boat struck a reef and we were the only ones who managed to swim to shore. You had no other survivors?"

Zara looked at Watson's companions. Theodore Jenkins and both the Zakharis. Cantara had a couple of boards strapped to her left forearm and moved as if she were in pain. Arjan had his arm around her in a decidedly non-fraternal manner. "No," she said. "We were on our way to Manachen."

Watson laughed. "I'm afraid you're going the wrong way, Miss Farrell," he said. "Manachen is to the east of us."

"You're sure of that?"

"I've been a sailor for fifteen years. Of course I'm sure. But you shouldn't feel embarrassed at being wrong. Anyone not trained in the science of astronomy would have done the same."

Zara said nothing. She was sure her guess was right—but he *did* have the experience… She flushed, angry at herself for letting him get to her, and wanted to punch him in the face when his smile broadened. How dare he condescend to her!

"We have food, if you're hungry," Watson continued. He sounded as if he was rescuing them from the brink of starvation. As if, being lost, they were no doubt incapable of feeding themselves as well.

"Thank you, but we've collected food," Zara said, and took pleasure in the look of irritation that flitted across his face. She saw

Theodore's eyes widen as he saw the papayas Belinda was carrying. "Would *you* like some?"

"We—" Watson began, but Theodore already had his hand outstretched for a fruit, and Arjan wasn't far behind him. Arjan broke it open and helped Cantara eat; she made a face and spat out a half-bitten seed.

"Well, since we're all going to travel together now—or did you want to strike out on your own in the wrong direction, Miss Farrell?" Watson said with a mocking smile. "We might as well share what we've gathered." He took his papaya nonchalantly, but ate it as eagerly as any of the others. What had they eaten yesterday, that they were so hungry now?

"It makes sense for us to travel together," Zara said. "Don't you agree, Belinda?"

"Of course." Belinda offered half a papaya to Zara, who reflected it might as well be a very early dinnertime since they were all eating anyway.

She took a bite and gazed idly into the jungle. How long would it take for them to grow sick of papaya? For that matter, could eating nothing but papaya make them genuinely ill? Poison, whether actual venom or the tiny organisms that lived in improperly prepared food, did make her sick for a while, but couldn't kill her—at least, none of the poisons she'd had access to when she was trying to fake her death had done more than inconvenience her. Even so, she didn't relish the idea of being ill even for a short time, and none of her companions had her advantages. Maybe, with more of them working together, they could range farther into the jungle and look for other kinds of food.

"Let's move on, then," Watson said, tossing away the rind of his papaya.

"I think Cantara needs more of a rest," Zara said. She'd mostly meant to nettle Watson, but Cantara was sweating and did look as if she were having trouble standing.

"Better for Miss Zakhari to reach civilization and receive proper medical care," Watson said.

"And there's no sense us reaching civilization with her more seriously injured," Zara snapped back. "We can wait a few more minutes."

Watson pinched his lips tight shut. "Very well," he said finally, making himself sound like the King of Tremontane granting a poor supplicant a boon. Not that Jeffrey North was ever so supercilious as this man. Zara went to Arjan's side, where he was helping Cantara sit. "I thank," he said.

"You're welcome," Zara said, at the last minute deciding to speak Tremontanese rather than Eskandelic. They'd probably reached the point where the Zakharis' secrets didn't matter anymore, but revealing them at the tactically strong moment, whatever that might be, appealed to Zara. She smiled at Cantara, who smiled weakly back. Yes, no sense embarrassing the young couple in front of Watson.

It was barely five minutes before Watson said, "That's long enough. We're moving on." He didn't wait for Arjan to help Cantara up, just strode away across the sand. Zara glared at his back. He might know where Manachen was, but he'd lied about feeding the others — or at least exaggerated how filling that food was — and he had no concern for the well-being of an injured woman. Zara was certain he would lead them into disaster. She fell to the rear of their group and examined them all as she walked. None of them were capable of challenging Watson, if that became necessary — none but she. *You're imagining things,* she told herself, *you dislike him and you're looking for reasons not to follow where he leads.* But she couldn't help thinking she was making a mistake.

Chapter Four

The heat of the sun and the muggy air slowed their pace, though Watson insisted on leading the way and walked too rapidly for anyone else to keep up. The humid air drained Zara of whatever energy her inherent magic might otherwise have provided, which meant the others, except for Zakhari Arjan, were barely able to keep up the pace, and Arjan's attention was devoted to Cantara. The young woman's dark complexion was gray, and her eyes were glassy with pain or fever — *please, dear heaven, not fever.*

Finally Zara, glaring at Watson's distant back, declared loudly, "I need a rest," and sat down on the crumbling, damp sand. Belinda immediately followed her, and Arjan helped Cantara down and sat so she could lean against him. Theodore hesitated, looking in Watson's direction, then at Zara, and finally chose to sit some distance from the rest of them as if trying to find a middle ground.

Watson went another ten or fifteen feet before turning around. "We don't have time to rest," he said. He'd clearly been overexerting himself to spite Zara; his face was red and he was sweating, not that sweating did any good in this climate. "We need to reach Manachen as soon as possible so we can return to civilization."

"Some of us will collapse if we keep up the pace you're setting," Zara said. "A fifteen-minute rest and a shorter stride is what we need."

"If I wanted your opinion, I'd ask for it, Miss Farrell." Watson came back to stand over Zara, looming like one of the trees. He reminded her of a bantam rooster her friend Sophie had owned, back when Zara lived in Sterris, and the image was so amusing she had trouble not smiling. Instead, she gave him her coldest gaze and remained where she was. It was easy to intimidate when you had the higher ground, but Zara had never been one to take the easy route.

"Mister Watson," she said in a low voice that forced him to lean over to hear her, "your physical capabilities are admirable, but not everyone shares them. You might consider Mister Zakhari's probable reaction if his sister is hurt further. It won't make you look good if it comes to a fight between the two of you."

Watson glanced over at Arjan, who wasn't paying them any attention. Arjan was well-muscled, not like a laborer, but like someone who'd been trained to fight—another evidence he wasn't who he claimed to be—and he was a few inches taller and much broader in the shoulders than Watson. The former first mate threw back his shoulders and puffed out his chest, almost certainly unconsciously, and braced himself as if Arjan had already begun to throw a punch. "Mister Zakhari isn't the one challenging my authority," he said, matching Zara's low tones.

"I have no interest in taking on your responsibilities," Zara lied, "but even someone as competent as you can benefit from good advice."

"I question whether your advice is good," Watson said, and walked away, leaving Zara fuming on the wet sand. Bastard. Just because she couldn't navigate by the stars…! She stood up, brushing off her trousers, and went to help Belinda stand. Belinda's rosy complexion was red, and she was breathing heavily.

"Are you going to be all right?" Zara asked.

"I guess I have to be," said Belinda. "Wish I'd exercised more this last year." She hefted the makeshift bag containing what was left of their papayas and stretched.

"I'll carry that." Theodore had come up behind them and now held out his hand for the bag.

"That's all right," Belinda said.

"No, it's not. You have enough troubles, and my mam always says it's a gentleman's duty to help wherever he can."

It was the most Zara had ever heard the young man say. Belinda handed him the bag. Theodore nodded at them both, then walked away after Watson, who'd already started to move. "That was unexpected," Belinda said.

"We'd better get moving," Zara said. Arjan and Cantara were a few paces ahead of them, Cantara still moving slowly, but Watson had either taken Zara's advice to heart (unlikely) or was starting to feel the effects of the heat himself. In either case, Zara was glad not to have to keep up that punishing pace. She felt as if she'd sweated out every drop of water in her body —

"We need water soon," she called out.

"I'm aware of that, Miss Farrell," Watson said. "I'm looking for water right now. Unless you think you can do better?"

Zara ground her teeth. "Not at all, Mister Watson, I'm sure you'll be successful," she replied. It was true, she had no idea where to look for water. And there was something else they needed, something simple but counterintuitive, that she'd read about once years ago and now couldn't remember. Hopefully, it wouldn't be anything crucial.

They walked on through the undergrowth, just far enough under the trees to take advantage of their shade. The distant sounds of alien birdsong mingled with other cries Zara couldn't put a name to. None of it was nearby, probably because they were all making so much noise they wouldn't be able to hear a Karitian coming upon their little group even if he shouted a war cry at them. Though Karitians might not have war cries.

She knew so little about them. Aside from their isolationism, she'd heard they never traded for Devices, though she didn't know if that was because they didn't use them or because they built their own and thought them superior. Someone had once told her they had a strict caste system, though not what its basis was, and a woman in a bar back in Umberan had told her Dineh-Karit was as rich in source as Tremontane, though Zara hadn't taken that rumor seriously because the woman had never actually been to the southern continent. Supposition and guesses — not a good basis for drawing conclusions about an entire people.

Watson suddenly turned and disappeared into the jungle. Zara hurried past the Zakharis to catch up. "What are you doing?" she demanded.

"Following the scent of water," Watson said. "Unless you'd like us to continue without it?"

"We're too spread out. Wait for the others to join us."

"I don't recall inviting you to give me orders."

Zara turned and stalked away, back toward the end of the line. "Fool," she muttered under her breath. How this man had ever risen to a position of authority stymied her.

By the time she'd made sure the Zakharis and Belinda were together, Watson had moved only a short distance from the spot where Zara had confronted him. *Just enough to look like he isn't listening to me.* "This way," Watson said, and moved on.

Beneath the trees, there was practically no undergrowth, and following Watson was easy. It was dark and cool beneath the high canopy, and the raucous birdsong was louder. Zara brought up the rear of the group, just in case. The jungle was strange and beautiful, with vines twining about the thick tree trunks and hanging low from the distant tree tops. She'd never seen so many shades of green in her life.

High above, she saw movement, and tensed, but whatever it was moved on without hesitation. She had no idea what things lived in the jungle aside from the birds and no inclination to find out. Water, then more travel, and eventually they would reach Manachen...though what they'd find there was also an unknown. Suppose the Karitians didn't believe their story? Watson was unconcerned about the possibility they'd find trouble there, but she already knew Watson was an idiot, so it was down to her to come up with a plan.

Alfred's mystery Device, nestled deep in her trouser pocket, rubbed the outside of her thigh, and she reached in to touch it. Its smooth surface was warm—well, that made sense, it was snug against her leg, but working Devices, ones with a strong motive force, were always warm to the touch. Zara didn't dare take it out to look at it, even here at the end of the line, though now that the immediate crisis had passed, she had time to be curious. A Device carried by an agent of the Crown to a traders' colony, but sought by pirates, if that's what that Ghazarian woman was. She'd attacked the *Emma Covington* specifically to get Alfred's Device, and that didn't sound like typical pirate behavior. Not that she knew how pirates typically behaved. Even so, it was strange.

Ahead, she heard Theodore swear, and it startled her so much she ran to catch up to the rest. Watson was standing at the edge of a shallow pool, little more than a puddle. The water was black and stank of rot. "We can't drink that," Theodore said.

"Of course not," Watson said, though he'd lost most of his certainty. "We'll follow the stream that feeds it—"

"No stream," Arjan said. "Is nothing."

"I thirsty am," Cantara said. Her voice was faint enough Zara almost couldn't make out her words.

"Then we'll have to set off across country until we find a stream," Watson said.

"We'll get lost if we do that," said Zara.

"I think we're already lost," said Belinda.

"We're not lost." Watson stood straighter and made a visible attempt to regain his authority. "I know where we are. We just have to keep heading east."

"I think we should return to the coast," Zara said.

Watson sneered at her. "You don't know how to navigate, Miss Farrell, I think we've already established that. If we follow you, we'll no doubt end up traveling in circles."

"I think I know how to retrace the blindingly obvious path we made." She forced herself to breathe slowly. Losing her temper would do no good.

"We're more likely to run across water if we continue east," Watson said. "But if anyone wants to follow Miss Farrell, you're welcome to."

Belinda looked at Zara and shrugged. Theodore looked as conflicted as he always did. Arjan helped Cantara stand and without a word began heading east. Watson smiled at Zara and hurried to get ahead of the two Eskandelics. Theodore, with another uncertain look at Zara, followed him a moment later.

"We don't have much choice, Rowena," Belinda said. "I'll go

40

where you want, but I think it's better we all stay together."

"It is," Zara said, glaring at Watson's retreating back, then setting off after him. "But he's going to get someone killed, and the way our luck is running, it won't be himself."

The overland route was at least cooler and easier terrain. Belinda wasn't struggling nearly as much as she had been, which was a relief, and Zara could keep an eye on Cantara, who leaned heavily on Arjan and kept her injured arm close to her chest. They'd fallen into a pattern of gradually slowing their steps until Zara caught up to them, then walking more rapidly for about a minute before slowing again. Zara cursed Watson mentally. Those two wouldn't be able to keep going much longer.

She wiped sweat out of her eyes and blinked to clear her vision, then realized it wasn't her eyes that were going dim, but the level of light reaching the jungle floor. "It's getting dark," she called out. She wouldn't be surprised if Watson hadn't even noticed.

"We have plenty of light, Miss Farrell," Watson said, but he slowed until all six of them were gathered close. "Finding shelter is now our main priority."

"And food," Theodore said.

"Do we need a fire?" Belinda said.

"It's not that cold, Miss Stouffer," Watson said, so patronizingly he might as well have patted her head like he might an obedient child.

"I was thinking of animals," Belinda said, annoyed. "I know we haven't seen any, but that doesn't mean they won't come out at night."

"Where are you going, Mister Zakhari?" Watson said. The young man had helped Cantara sit, then walked a few more steps in the direction they'd been going.

"Water," Arjan said. His chin was lifted as if he were straining to hear some distant sound. "Water—near." He continued to walk, first slowly, as if feeling his way, then more rapidly. Watson cursed and followed him.

Zara went to help Cantara stand, but Theodore was already there, helping her put her unbroken arm around his shoulders. Taking short steps to accommodate Cantara's weakness, they followed the men and Belinda, who soon disappeared into the growing dusk. Zara did some inner cursing of her own. Why didn't anyone realize how important it was they stay together? Even Arjan was being impatient now.

She began to hear a sighing sound, like wind over stone, that turned into rushing water. Lots of rushing water. Then she smelled it, beautifully fresh and clean and cool, cutting across the muggy green funk of the jungle. Eventually, she saw Arjan and Belinda and Watson, their bodies partly obscured by the vines draping the nearest trees, and with slightly guilty impatience she left Theodore and Cantara and hurried forward to see what they'd found.

The others stood at the top of a steep bank, below which flowed a river wider than any she'd seen before, wider than the Snow River at the peak of its icy floodwaters. A little island, barely more than a sliver of land with a few bushes growing on it, lay about two-thirds of the way to the other bank. The river was mostly in shade at this time of day, but it still reflected the clear, cloudless blue of the sky, with white foam where the river met the bank. It smelled so good Zara almost wanted to dive into it, but it was moving fast enough that would be fatal.

"What is this?" Arjan said to Watson.

"Ah," said Watson. "Well, obviously—"

Arjan grabbed him by the lapels of his coat and shook him, hard. "This the Amgeli is not," he roared. "This the *Kulnius* is!"

"Let go of me, you idiot," Watson said, grabbing Arjan's hands and trying to break his grip. "Of course it's not—"

"I know something of Dineh-Karit's geography," Arjan said in remarkably fluent Tremontanese. "The Amgeli much wider is. You have taken us the wrong way!"

"The wrong way?" Zara said.

Arjan shoved Watson, who staggered but managed to stay on his feet. "We landed east of Manachen as you said," he told Zara. "We should have walked west to reach the Amgeli River, where Manachen is. Instead we far from Manachen and far from civilization are. My

Cantara cannot endure more of this. You have killed us all!" He turned on Watson again, raising a fist. Watson brought up his fists to defend himself. Briefly Zara entertained a fantasy about Arjan beating Watson to bloody pulp, then dismissed it.

"That's enough," she said in a cold, cutting voice. "Fighting won't solve this problem. Arjan, step away now."

Arjan, his fist still raised, took a step back, then looked at Zara as if he wasn't sure why he'd done it.

"That's right," Watson said. "I'm still the leader and you'd better respect that. If not for me, you wouldn't have escaped the ship."

"Because you hid in the longboat," Arjan said. "You a coward are."

"What good would my dying have done anyone? There was no way to help."

"You could have directed the sailors to flee the ship," Zara said. "You could have saved more people. Wasn't that your responsibility?"

"Miss Farrell, I don't answer to you, and I expect you to keep your opinions to yourself!"

"Please let's not fight," Belinda said. She looked as if she were near collapse. "Where do we go now?"

Zara took a calming breath and flexed her fingers, which had begun to cramp from being closed so tightly into fists. "Well, Mister Watson? Where do we go?"

Watson's eyes widened. He'd probably expected her to taunt him. Well, that was still an option if he didn't respond to her manipulation, but she didn't have time to make a play for the leadership of their group right then. She went on, not giving him time to interrupt. "We found water as you said we would. Arjan says this is the Kulnius. This at least gives us some idea of where we are. Where should we go next?"

"We should not follow him," Arjan said. "He is a fool."

I completely agree. "Unfortunately, he's the only one of us who can keep us on the right path, navigating by the sun and stars. Where next, Mister Watson?"

"I—ah," Watson said. "We should...if we follow the Kulnius south, we will find where it diverges from the Amgeli. Then we go north, following the Amgeli, until we reach the city."

"Karitians don't like northerners," Belinda said. "What makes you think they'll be happy to see us?"

"We don't have much choice at this point, Belinda," Zara said. "We should at least follow the river far enough to find a place where we can get water."

"Of course," Watson said. Zara wished she'd let Arjan hit him. "Let's move on."

Arjan took the sagging Cantara from Theodore. "I following you am not," he said. "We go alongside." Zara didn't bother concealing a smile from Watson, who glared at her before moving off down the river bank.

The river bank grew more shallow as the river wound in and out of the trees. The mysterious sounds grew louder, and as Zara kept glancing at the sky, gauging how much daylight they had left, she saw long-limbed creatures, pale against the dark canopy, swinging between the tree tops. Monkeys. She'd seen a few of them in the Umberan Zoo, but seeing them in their natural habitat took her breath away. There were so many of them—a family, a clan? She had no words for how they moved so gracefully, as if gravity was only something they'd heard about that didn't apply to them.

She stumbled, caught herself, and moved to catch up with the others. The river was flowing less swiftly now, and debris and logs swirled in its currents. Ahead, she saw some of the monkeys coming down to drink. They might never have seen humans before, judging by how carelessly close they came to their little group. What would it be like to hold one? Probably uncomfortable, as it climbed all over you and pulled your hair and screeched in your ear. They weren't tame, after all.

They were approaching a place where the river lapped against the shore, smoothly curving against it in a way that would carve out a deeper bank over years, maybe centuries. Watson ran ahead of the group—*he probably wants to make a big show of discovering it*—and squatted at the edge. "It's perfectly safe to drink," he said, as if they'd all been afraid it was poisoned.

Theodore was near him, but hesitated, looking at Arjan, who was almost fully supporting Cantara and was moving slowly. Zara stopped and took a deep breath. She felt uneasy, and she took another deep breath and tried to figure out why. The birds were still arguing with each other in the canopy, but the monkeys' cries were distant, almost too far away to hear. Zara looked upriver to where a family of monkeys drank. It was a rockier shore, and the water was less accessible, so why there and not where Watson knelt? "Mister Watson," she began.

"Miss Farrell, do you have yet another complaint? Did you want your water served in a tall glass with a chunk of ice?" Watson sat back on his heels and half-turned to look in her direction. "Or maybe—"

The water erupted. Watson screamed as the biggest lizard Zara had ever seen, bigger even than the alligators at the Zoo, lunged at him and seized hold of his shoulder, dragging him into the river. The floating logs came alive and converged on the screaming Watson. Blood filled the water, almost black in the afternoon light. Zara drew in a great breath and shouted, *"Run!"*

CHAPTER FIVE

"Stay with the river!" Zara shouted, grabbing Belinda by one arm and Theodore by the other. Theodore tripped and fell. With strength born of terror Zara hauled him upright and forced him to keep running. The monkeys scattered, chittering at them angrily as they passed. Zara looked back to make sure Arjan was following. He had Cantara in his arms and was stumbling along, not looking back as the terrible screams cut off. Zara couldn't think of anything but *away, get away*, but at some point her body, exhausted by the demands she'd made of it, gave out. She let go of Belinda and Theodore and sank to the jungle floor, breathing heavily. Beside her, she could hear the others doing the same. She closed her eyes and tried not to picture Watson's torn body, his desperate face. *Nothing you could do. It was too late for him when he knelt by the river.*

"What was that?" Theodore said. His voice was weak and breathy.

"Caiman," Arjan said. He sounded a good deal more hale than Theodore despite his double burden. "Though I have never seen one so large."

"It killed him," Belinda said. She sounded as if she were in shock. Zara opened her eyes. Belinda had her hands clasped tightly in front of her and her rosy complexion was pale. "It killed him."

"Belinda, look at me. Look at me," Zara said sharply, and Belinda turned her face in Zara's direction. She wasn't exactly looking at Zara, her eyes distant and unfocused, but it was good enough. "We're safe now. Watson was stupid and it got him killed."

"How could he possibly have known? We're just as stupid as he was. More, because I don't know anything about surviving in the wild!"

"We know to be more careful. It's going to be all right, Belinda. Don't be afraid."

Belinda nodded, but there were tears running down her face Zara

46

was certain she wasn't aware of. "Watson's plan was sound, though," Zara said. "Follow the river upstream. It will provide us with plenty of water. Then follow the Amgeli to the ocean. We'll have to take the chance the Karitians won't—" She stopped before she said *kill us on sight*. That was not a thought this group needed to entertain.

"We must find shelter soon," Arjan said, cradling Cantara in his lap. "And food."

"Let's keep moving, then," Zara said. "I imagine the nocturnal animals, whatever they are, come to the river at night. We need to make camp away from it."

"I saw more papayas," Theodore said. "Just a few yards from here."

"That's excellent, Theodore," Zara said. "Let's get a drink, gather food, then make camp and eat something. And we should probably set watches."

No one argued with her, which relieved her mind. Belinda would follow her instructions, and Theodore just wanted a clear line of authority, but Arjan was smart and utterly committed to keeping Cantara safe. Zara was certain he'd only follow her lead so long as it coincided with what he wanted to do. She was certain their only chance was in staying together, and the Zakharis would ultimately be helpless on their own. She'd have to lead Arjan to see that following her was the safest course of action.

Going back to the river was harder than she'd guessed, not because it was difficult to find, but because the memory of the thrashing water, of Watson's gurgling screams, made everyone hesitant to return. Zara took her fears in hand, straightened her shoulders, and strode briskly to the shallow riverbank, scattering monkeys as she crouched to scoop up delicious water and drink it down. The others slowly followed her lead until they were all kneeling or crouching beside the rushing flow. After a few mouthfuls, Zara felt less exhausted and more optimistic. Even the gnawing ache in her belly was lessened, though not so much that she wasn't interested in food.

She accepted some papayas from Theodore, who'd found a long

47

branch to bat the fruits down. Was it arrogant, believing she was the best choice to lead these people? Or just good sense? In all her years, in everything she'd done, she'd never been interested in power for its own sake, or for the sake of self-aggrandizement. She just knew what had to be done, and did it. Yet she felt deep satisfaction in seeing her plans come to fruition, in seeing some selfish or dishonest person receive a good metaphorical thrashing at her hands, so was that arrogance, or something else?

She took another papaya and tucked it with the rest into the crook of her arm. This was the wrong time to have that inner debate. Later, when they were all safe on Goudge's Folly, she could contemplate her motives and her abilities. Until then, she had to focus on keeping everyone from panicking.

They walked further into the jungle, looking for a place to sleep, until Zara realized none of them had any idea what constituted a good campsite and picked a spot at random. "I can light a fire," Arjan said, "but I see few sticks to make one."

"I think we shouldn't range far," Zara said. "We'll just have to set watches, and be alert. But for now, I'm ready to eat something."

They ate in exhausted silence, the only noise the quiet *pffft* of seeds being spat and the occasional *tick* when one struck a tree. The trees grew closer together where they sat, and Zara picked idly at the bark of the one next to her and found it was thin and peeled off easily. She kept herself from picking a larger patch and ran her fingers over the vines that wrapped around the tree. They were green and pliant at about head-height, but down near the ground they were thick and grayish-brown, like saplings huddling up for warmth. At least there was no need for a fire to keep them warm. If this had happened in the Eidestal, they'd all be dead by now.

"I'll take the first watch," Theodore said abruptly.

"That should be me," Arjan said.

"Why?"

"Because," Arjan began, then glanced at Cantara, who was mostly asleep in his lap. "Very well."

"I'll go third, then," Zara said.

"You shouldn't have to watch," Theodore said. "It's a gentleman's job to make a lady's life easier."

"Thank you, Theodore, but if three of us watch—" Zara glanced at Belinda, who was also asleep. "We'll all get more rest, doesn't that make sense?"

"All right," Theodore said, and pushed himself up stiffly. "And...call me Theo."

Zara nodded. If mortal danger didn't entitle you to a nickname, what would?

"I will wake you at your turn," Arjan told Zara.

"Thanks." This wasn't the best time to challenge him on his sudden acquisition of Tremontanese. Zara lay down near Belinda and put her hands behind her head so she could look up at the darkening canopy. The sun probably hadn't set yet, but the thickness of the leaves blocked out so much of the light, it felt like full night. She could hear the monkeys even if she couldn't see them, and wondered if they made noise all night long. If so, falling asleep was going to be a problem. She yawned and closed her eyes. Might as well make the best of it. She fell asleep wondering how long this journey would take them.

Someone was shaking her shoulder. "Rowena," Theo whispered in her ear, "get up."

Zara opened her eyes. "Is something wrong?" Why hadn't Arjan woken her?

"Maybe. There's something you need to see." Theo tugged on her arm, trying to get her to rise. Zara propped herself on her elbows and looked around. Belinda was still deeply asleep, her breath whistling through her nose as usual. The Zakharis were curled together nearby. "It's over that way," Theo whispered. She could barely see the dark shape of his arm stretched out to point.

She sat up fully and looked in that direction. A pinpoint of yellow light, barely visible past the trees, glowed steadily in the darkness. "A campfire," she said. "Or a really big lantern."

"What should we do?"

Zara watched the light for a few moments. It had to be either big or close for them to be able to see it through the trees. "Wake everyone," she finally said.

They huddled together, which made Zara feel as if they were sheltering against some invisible storm. "That could be someone who can help us," she said.

"Or it could be someone who couldn't care less what happens to us," Belinda said. "Or tries to kill us."

"We don't have a fire, so that person, whoever it is, doesn't know we're here," Zara said. "We don't have to approach him. Or her."

"But this could mean saving us," Arjan said.

"It could."

"Rowena, what do we do?" Belinda said.

"You want *me* to decide?"

"You were right every time Watson was wrong. I trust your judgment."

Zara looked around. Everyone, including Arjan and a sleepy-eyed Cantara, nodded at her. *Well, it's what you wanted.* "I say we approach him," she said. "And by 'we' I mean me."

"I stronger am. I should go," Arjan said.

"If I'm wrong, someone's going to need to help everyone else escape," Zara said, "and Cantara might need to be carried. I'm the sensible choice."

Arjan looked skeptical, but nodded. It was so nice when people didn't argue. Zara stood and brushed off her trousers where she'd knelt in the dirt. "Let's all get closer, so if something happens, you'll know right away."

They went as quietly as possible, which wasn't very quiet. The only thing that saved them, Zara thought, from being mistaken for a family of monkeys was the lack of undergrowth for them to crash through. When they were close enough to the light to identify it as a campfire, Zara motioned all of them to sit still and went on alone.

Her heart was beating rapidly, whether from fear or from excitement, she couldn't tell. Being effectively impossible to kill didn't

50

mean she didn't feel pain; in fact, it meant pain could go on forever if the person inflicting the pain knew what he was doing. But this person—or maybe people—could mean the difference between her friends dying in the jungle and all of them returning safely home.

She moved from one broad tree trunk to another, trying to keep quiet and out of sight. She wanted to see this person before he saw her. There was a tent that looked too small for more than one person, that was good. A box, too large for someone to carry; that meant—

A large shape moved near her, something that snuffled, and irrationally she thought of the caiman and stifled a shriek. In the next moment, she realized it was some kind of pack animal, a donkey or mule or something. She'd never been good at identifying animals beyond the basics. She clapped a hand over her mouth to hold back the sound that had already escaped her and leaned against the nearest tree. The donkey approached her and lipped her hand, slobbering all over it. This time, she managed to keep quiet, edging away from the animal and wiping her hand on her trousers. It followed her. What did the creature want?

A deep voice, speaking in a language she didn't understand, startled her. She froze again, not caring that the donkey was intent on licking her hand for whatever flavor she was. The voice said something else, still in the same language. Did he know she was there, or was he talking to the donkey? She heard someone shift, the sound of a chair scraping across the ground, and soft footsteps grew louder as the speaker approached. There was no way she could stay hidden, and after all, she'd gone there to talk to whoever it was.

She stepped away from the tree and held her hands out so it was obvious she was unarmed. "I'm sorry to intrude," she said. "I wasn't trying to sneak up on you." He wouldn't understand her, but she couldn't do anything about that.

A man, backlit by the fire, stopped with his hand outstretched to pet the donkey's neck. "Sweet heaven," he said. "I thought you were Karitian."

"You're Tremontanan," Zara said, startled.

"I was," the man said. "No wonder you didn't respond when I told you to come out into the open and stop skulking around. Where did you come from?"

"That's a very long story. I'll be happy to tell you," Zara added, "but I'd feel more comfortable if I could see your face."

The man patted the donkey's neck once more, then backed away from her. Zara followed. The man retreated almost to the fire and took a seat on a folding camp stool. "Satisfied?" It was hard to tell his age in the flickering light, but he had a handsome face, with a square jaw and dark eyes whose color she couldn't see in the firelight. His short hair was a streaky blond that looked like he spent a lot of time outdoors, and he was looking at her steadily, examining her as closely as she was examining him.

"My friends and I—"

"Friends?" He made a show of looking around the tiny clearing. "Do you keep them in your pockets?"

"We didn't know whose fire this was," Zara said, irritated by his sarcastic tone of voice. "Better to be safe than dead."

"You don't know I'm not dangerous. Or did you assume because we were born in the same place, we'd automatically be friends?"

"I didn't know you were Tremontanan when I approached, but I assume I'd have a better chance convincing someone who speaks my language to help me than a Karitian who probably *would* kill me on sight."

"That's a typical Tremontanan attitude, that all Karitians are bloodthirsty bigots."

Zara took a calming breath. Arguing with this man was pointless. Trying to gain his support was probably pointless too, but she had to try, for all their sakes. "I admit I don't know anything about Karitians except merchants' tales, so I'm sorry if I sound prejudiced. Are you going to let that stand in the way of helping us?"

"There's that 'us' again. Who are you?" He leaned forward with one elbow on his knee and propped his chin on his hand, settling in for a story with the same sardonic air that annoyed her before. It annoyed

52

her further that he didn't offer her a seat, until she realized he probably only had the one. Thinking about sitting made her realize how tired she was, how much she wanted to sleep, but she took a stance that would keep her from falling over if this went too long and began the story with the pirates attacking the *Emma Covington*.

She left out the details of the shipboard battle, left out the details of her fights with Watson as they traveled, and left out everything about Alfred's mysterious Device. When she came to the end, the man said, "None of you have any more sense than babies. Do you have any idea how long it takes to get from here to the junction of the Amgeli and the Kulnius? Let alone down the river to Manachen?"

"Of course not," Zara said, stung by how dismissive he sounded. "It's not as if we had much choice. Were you listening at all, or did you miss the part where we were shipwrecked?"

"Even so, you ought to know traveling along the coast is safer."

"Well, we do now, and thank you so much for that 'help.'" Zara turned away, wishing she dared slap him across that handsome, smug, annoying face.

"Wait," he said, and despite herself, Zara paused, though she didn't turn around. "What's your name again?"

"Rowena Farrell."

"The name's Ransom," the man said. "You all might as well stay the night here. The jungle can be dangerous if you don't have a fire. Sometimes even if you do."

Zara nodded curtly and went back to where she'd left the others, not bothering to conceal her path from Ransom. Quickly she summed up their conversation. "He's not going to help," she told them, "but he'll let us sleep near his fire tonight."

"Why won't he help us?" Belinda said.

"I don't know. Because he thinks he knows better than every other living person in the world how things should run? I think we should take advantage of the fire, and head back north in the morning."

"This journey will take long," Arjan said.

"There's no helping that. We just have to make the best of it."

"*Arjan, it will be all right,*" Cantara said in Eskandelic. It was only the second time Zara had heard her speak since the shipwreck. Arjan looked grim, but helped Cantara stand. Even the little sleep she'd gotten had done her good, because although she still favored her broken arm, she was moving more easily and looked like she didn't need Arjan's help to keep from falling down.

They returned to Ransom's camp to find him still sitting on the stool. He stood when they arrived, and said, "You didn't say anyone was injured."

"I didn't think you'd care," Zara said.

He gave her another sardonic look and went to Cantara. "Let me look at that."

Arjan stepped between them. "You do not touch her."

"I'm not going to hurt her. I'm a doctor. Or do you want her to go on suffering?"

Arjan held the man's gaze a moment longer, then stepped aside. Ransom guided Cantara to sit on the stool and gently removed the makeshift splint. Cantara hissed as he ran his hands over her arm. "It's broken," he said.

"We knew that," Zara said.

Ransom ignored her. "You'll want to hold her for this," he told Arjan, who knelt behind Cantara and put his arms around her. "This will hurt, but it won't last long." He gripped her arm in two places and bowed his head. Cantara let out a shriek, then sagged, unconscious. Arjan shouted and began to let go of her.

"Don't be an idiot," Ransom said without raising his head. "I'm healing her arm. It accelerates the natural healing process and it hurts like hell, but in a few minutes it will be over. You're Eskandelic, you ought to be more sensible about this."

"You should to warn," Arjan growled.

"Sorry, I thought I did. Now hold still. This isn't as easy as it looks."

The clearing went silent except for the donkey chewing something that by the sound of it was made of leather. Zara kept realizing she was holding her breath and let it out slowly, irrationally afraid of distracting Ransom even though she remembered Dr. Trevellian had never had any problem working around distractions. Not that healing magic worked on her; her own magic resisted it.

She wasn't sure how long it took, but eventually Ransom raised his head and released Cantara's arm. "There you are," he said, and pressed the tip of his forefinger to the center of her forehead. Cantara stirred and sat up, as far as she could with Arjan holding her. She moved her arm wonderingly. "Thank you," she said.

"You're welcome," Ransom said. "Now, will you make introductions, Miss Farrell?"

"We won't be here long enough for that to matter," Zara said.

"Nevertheless, it's polite, don't you think? You can call me Ransom," he added, addressing the group at large.

Zara grimaced. "Belinda Stouffer," she said, indicating the woman. "Theodore Jenkins. Zakhari Cantara and her husband Arjan."

"Welcome to my camp," Ransom said with a bow. "Now, why don't you all find spots around the fire. Nettles will give warning if anything large comes calling, but there's no point not using every advantage." He folded the stool and set it next to the box, then ducked inside the tent. Zara and Belinda looked at each other, and Zara could see Belinda was thinking the same thing she was: what kind of man *was* this?

She settled as far from the donkey — Nettles, what an appropriate name for his prickly owner — as she could, lay on her back, and stared up at the canopy again. At least they had a safe place to sleep for the night, and she wasn't going to think about anything beyond that until she had to. Beside her, Belinda rolled over and squirmed as if looking for a more comfortable spot. She looked so exhausted, almost as much as Cantara had; she wasn't in any shape for this kind of, hah, adventure.

A figure loomed up over them, dark against the firelight, then crouched. "I think you should take my tent," Ransom said to Belinda in a low voice. "You're suffering from dehydration and the delayed effects of shock. It's not much of a bed, but better than sleeping on the ground."

Belinda sat up. "But shouldn't everyone —"

"Go on, Belinda," Zara said. "He's right. No one's going to begrudge you."

"All right. Thank you, Dr. Ransom."

"Just Ransom," he said, and helped Belinda stand. Zara watched them walk away toward the tent, then went back to staring at the invisible sky. That was unexpected. A doctor, with inherent healing magic. What had brought a man whose talent and training would have made him rich in Tremontane to the jungles of Dineh-Karit?

Someone settled down on the ground where Belinda had lain, not too far from her. "She'll be all right in the morning," Ransom said. "Just needs some salt. Lack of that can kill a person here in the jungle."

Salt. That was it. "Thank you," she said. He hadn't sounded at all sarcastic then, nor turned his words into a sardonic reminder of how ill-equipped they were to survive in the wild. And he'd been unexpectedly gentle with Belinda and Cantara. Not that it made her like him more.

Ransom laughed, a deep chuckle Zara almost found pleasant. "I've got some in my supplies you can have," he said. "I'm not completely heartless."

"Heartless enough to abandon us."

"It's hardly abandonment if we weren't traveling together in the first place."

"Whatever you want to call it. You pointed out we're not prepared to survive in the jungle, but you're not willing to help us even though you are?"

Ransom blew out his breath. "I'm not going to drop my responsibilities just to play nursemaid to a bunch of strays."

Zara rolled her eyes. "Yes, you certainly look like a responsible man, you and your donkey in the middle of nowhere."

"You're awfully quick to judge, aren't you?"

"As quick as you are to criticize."

Ransom rolled onto his side to face her. "It's hardly criticism to point out the blindingly obvious."

"Well, it's not as if we chose this, so you're not criticizing so much as taunting us. If you were—"

"If I were what?"

The words *If you were dropped into my court, you'd be the one taunted* nearly escaped her lips. Where had that come from? She hadn't had a court in sixty years. "Nothing. I'm sorry. There's no point us arguing. Thank you for giving us protection tonight."

Ransom went silent. Zara thought about turning her back on him, but that would look too much like she cared enough to deliberately snub him. After a few moments, he said, "If you keep an eye on the monkeys, you can avoid the caimans. They won't drink where the monsters are."

"Thank you. I'd noticed that." There, she could be polite. It hadn't sounded the least bit sarcastic.

"What have you been eating?"

"Papayas."

"I'll show you a few other trees with edible fruit in the morning."

"Thank you."

They both fell silent again. Zara had begun to drift off when Ransom said, "You'll want to avoid the low-hanging vines. Some of them are snakes."

"How can you tell?"

"It's hard. Sometimes you just have to watch for the movement. Try to avoid them altogether."

Zara rolled onto her side to face him. "Too bad we don't have someone to show us the difference."

"If you'd—"

Ransom rolled onto his back and flung one arm over his eyes. Then he started speaking rapidly in the same language he'd used when she first approached his camp. She didn't understand him, but she knew swearing when she heard it. "I'm doing this against my will," he said finally. "You're all nothing but a burden. I have work to do and I don't have time to be your nanny. You had all better do everything I say, without question, or I really will leave you behind."

"Don't do us any favors."

"Oh, I'm not. I'm just softheaded enough not to want your deaths on my conscience. Go to sleep, Miss Farrell, and no more insults or I might change my mind."

Zara rolled onto her other side so she didn't have to look at Ransom. What kind of man could treat saving five people's lives as some kind of penance? He was infuriating, and it made her angry to have to depend on him. Well, it shouldn't take more than a few days to reach Manachen, and that would be the end of it. If he could keep them all alive that long, she'd forgive him any number of offenses. Maybe.

CHAPTER SIX

A beam of light shining directly into her eyes woke Zara the next morning. Of course, it would fit the kind of luck she'd been having that the lone sunbeam striking the clearing would find her. She rolled to her feet and brushed herself off, then stretched out her stiff muscles. Rowing all night, walking all day, sleeping on the ground — this wasn't what she'd had in mind when she set off for adventure.

She smelled hot rice, and her stomach growled. Ransom sat near the fire, stirring a small pot. In the daylight, the blond in his hair was brighter, and he looked to be in his mid-twenties. "There's not much," he said. "I didn't plan on feeding a horde."

"We're hardly a horde." He'd sounded annoyed, and her irritation of the night before returned.

"Yes, but you're still a drain on my supplies, and I was running low to start with."

"I'm sorry to inconvenience you. We'll eat fruit instead."

"I said you were a drain, not that I'd let you starve. But we'll have to take turns because I only have one bowl." He scooped some of the white mess into a chipped wooden bowl and extended it to her along with a similarly battered spoon.

"I'd rather you ate first," Zara said.

"Don't tell me you'd deprive me of the chance to patronize you? Eat. I'll go gather fruit. No time to hunt for more than that. We can make this last long enough to reach our destination."

Behind her, one of the Zakharis rose. Zara glared at Ransom, but took the bowl and began eating. It was sticky and bland and she'd never tasted anything so wonderful in her life. Ransom gave her another of those sideways smiles, took a curved, notched blade from beside the box, and left the clearing. A tuneful whistle drifted back to her, which only made her more irritated with their unwilling host.

She finished eating and filled the bowl again, handed it to Cantara,

59

then sat on Ransom's stool and poked at the fire. They might actually survive this, even if she wasn't sure just how far Ransom was willing to take them. If they could only return to the shore, they'd be able to find their way to Manachen...and then they'd have to convince the Karitians to take them to Goudge's Folly, or even to send a message so Zara's new employers could come for them.

She hoped Falken & Daughter cared about her in the abstract, since Mistress Falken Senior had never met her personally, but surely they wouldn't leave fellow Tremontanans (and a couple of Eskandelics) to the mercy of the Karitians? Ransom seemed to think the Karitians weren't as quick to attack as Zara had been told, but his perspective was probably skewed. Did he really live in the jungle? He had to have some contact with humanity, because rice didn't grow on trees. Or were there rice paddies in the jungle?

"That smells so good," Belinda said. "Are we taking turns?"

Zara accepted the bowl from Cantara and refilled it, handing it to Belinda. "Ransom went looking for more food. But eat as much as you can. It's got to be more filling than papayas."

Arjan and Cantara came to sit near Zara. "We thank you," Arjan said. "You kept us safe. I in your debt am."

"Really," Zara said. "Then you can tell me who you really are. Not brother and sister, that's for sure."

Arjan and Cantara exchanged glances. "They will not tell," Cantara said. Arjan scowled. "He thinks it safe anywhere is not," Cantara continued.

"Because safe it is not," Arjan said, but he was shaking his head in resignation.

"You're married? Betrothed? Lovers?" Zara said.

Cantara shook her head. "He is my *zuareto*."

Zara sucked in a startled breath. No wonder they were so nervous of being found out. "You fled your harem?"

"What's *zuareto* mean?" Belinda asked.

"It means Cantara is a wife of a principality, a member of the harem, and Arjan is the son of one of the other wives. Sweet heaven. Is

60

Zakhari really your name?"

"No. Takjashi."

One of the most powerful principalities in the Eskandelic government. Their relationship was so illegal it could mean their deaths. "Dineh-Karit might not be far enough away to protect you."

"She married her *son*?" Zara hadn't realized Theo was listening. Arjan leaped to his feet and advanced on the young man, fists raised.

"He's not her son, he's her stepson, and Arjan, don't you dare start a fight just because Theo doesn't understand how your families work." Zara put herself between the two of them and glared at the tall man. *Never show fear, even if he is taller and stronger than you.* "Arjan, none of us are interested in turning you over to your government. What happened? You spent too much time at home, you and Cantara?"

Arjan went back to put his arm around Cantara. "We had much in common," he said, "many scholastic pursuits. We did not realize the danger until it was too late. But a woman may not divorce a harem, and I thought my home to leave so Cantara's honor would not compromised be."

"I did not know my husband a violent man was," Cantara said. "It concealed from me by my sisters was, who embarrassed and ashamed of him were. I could not bear his touch and I sent for Arjan. He helped me escape. We cannot marry, but I will not leave him."

"That's unfair," Theo said. "You shouldn't have to stay married to someone who beats you."

"It our law is, that he remains our husband unless the harem chooses him to divorce. And it will weaken Takjashi such a thing to do, so they choose not." Cantara smiled at Arjan. "But in my heart I Arjan's wife am."

"That's up to you," Zara said, "and as I said, it's none of our business. But I'm glad you told us the truth."

"Truth about what?" Ransom said. He had a net bag over his shoulder, bulging with mangoes, bananas, and a couple of fruits Zara had never seen before.

"That Cantara is still feeling poorly," Zara said. "She shouldn't exert herself."

"I see," Ransom said. Zara didn't think he believed her. "I'll see what I can do about that. Everyone, eat up, and then we'll move out."

Zara helped herself to a banana—she hadn't had one in years, they didn't travel up the mountain well—and watched Ransom take Cantara by the hand. It was true, she still didn't look well, but then the wives of principalities didn't necessarily go in for physical exertion, not like the men, for whom exercise and swordplay, as archaic as that was, were a standard part of their education. Though she'd always looked strong enough, back on the ship. She already looked better from whatever it was Ransom was doing.

Zara spat a couple of seeds into her hand and turned away, feeling like an intruder. She prayed to ungoverned heaven nothing would happen to her that would require healing, because Ransom would definitely find out her secret, and she didn't want him knowing anything more about her than he already did.

They ate in silence, the heat and humidity already oppressive even though it couldn't have been later than eight o'clock. Then Zara and the others stood around awkwardly while Ransom took down his tent and packed his gear onto the donkey. Arjan offered to help, but Ransom waved him away. "I'm used to doing this myself," he said, "and you're technically my guests."

"So generous of you," Zara said.

"It *is* generous of me," he said. "You've already delayed me by a day. But I couldn't exactly leave you to wander the jungle and probably get killed. Now, where we're going is a lot more overgrown than this, and you'll need to stay close to me so you don't get lost."

"Aren't we going back down the river?"

Ransom shook his head and slapped the donkey's flank; the animal stepped out without complaint. "I've got a delivery to make, and I'm not abandoning that. You'll just have to come along south— unless you want to strike out on your own."

"As if we'd give you the satisfaction," Zara retorted.

Ransom shrugged and turned away. "It will take two days, best I can figure. Then we can head downriver and get you all to safety, at least as much safety as anyone can expect here."

Zara glanced at Belinda, who was already pink from the heat. They shouldn't waste time going wherever Ransom thought he needed to go, but they didn't really have a choice. She set off after Ransom and the donkey, praying she could survive this trip without killing the man.

It didn't take long for the tall trees to thin out, then disappear entirely, supplanted by shorter ones lush with bright green foliage that smelled of wet, rotting mulch. It wasn't exactly an unpleasant smell, but it was everywhere, and Zara soon gave up trying to breathe through her mouth and decided to endure it. Ransom cut a narrow path with his notched blade that forced them to travel single file, Theo right behind the donkey, then Belinda, then Zara, with Arjan and Cantara bringing up the rear.

After about half an hour, Zara saw monkeys filling the trees around them. These were a different variety, no bigger than the length of her forearm and golden-furred. Belinda kept stopping to look at them. "They're adorable," she exclaimed. "I wish I could hold one."

"It would just defecate on you," Zara said, but she had a secret wish to see if the golden fur was as soft as it looked.

"I've held one before," Theo said, "at a traveling menagerie. The fur's actually sort of bristly. Though that could have been because it was captive. I don't think the menagerie owner took good care of them."

"The Zoo in Umberan cares very well for its animals," Cantara said. "I have visited many times."

"I went once, years ago," Zara said. "There were much larger monkeys—except they said they were apes, and there was a difference."

"If you keep talking, you'll never see them," Ransom called out. "You're making enough noise I'm surprised the tamarins haven't all fled."

He sounded so sarcastic Zara replied, "They clearly have better judgment than you do."

"Meaning I'm a fool for taking you on?"

"Meaning they realize we're no danger to them."

"Oh, I'm fully aware of that." Ransom slashed twice at a thick branch. "Look out for the spider."

Belinda shrieked. Zara turned quickly to see a brown, furry spider the size of her hand scurry into the branches of a nearby tree. "Calm down, Belinda," she said. "I suppose it's poisonous?"

"Venomous, and no, it isn't. It just doesn't deserve to be struck at by one of you because you're frightened."

"I *hate* spiders," Belinda said, her breath coming even more quickly than it had been. "Hate them. Too many legs and too many eyes. You just know the only thing keeping them from hunting us is their size."

"Ransom said it was harmless. It was probably—"

"Don't say it was more scared of me than I was of it. I can tell you right now that's impossible."

"Don't worry," Theo said, brandishing a stick. "If they come too close I can fend them off. But I think Ransom's right that we shouldn't attack them if they're not attacking us."

"Very sensible," Ransom said. "Now, if you can stay quiet, we might see something interesting."

Zara bit back another scathing retort. He was annoying, his replies were almost always tinged with sarcasm, but he was right. Though it might not be the best idea to allow some of these animals to approach; the caiman couldn't possibly be the only dangerous animal in the jungle. She started to ask Ransom about it, then looked at Belinda, who was drawn in on herself trying not to touch any of the trees or bushes or vines they passed, and decided it was better not to frighten the others too much. *But don't wild animals only flee from humans if they know they're a threat?* she thought. *If we're the only ones they've ever seen…*

She looked far ahead to where Ransom cut a path, beyond the donkey. His arrogance annoyed her, true, but he was also confident where Watson had been brash, and even though she wouldn't have walked as far as the corner with him in Aurilien, she found she trusted him to get them where they were going in the jungle.

They walked on through the damp heat for hours, not stopping for dinner. Ransom handed back fruit and strips of dried meat for them to eat as they went. The low-hanging branches with their broad, vividly green leaves kept off most of the sun, but trapped enough moisture that Zara felt she was walking through fine mist. Ahead of her, Belinda was breathing heavily, but didn't have any trouble keeping the pace. Out of shape she might be, but she was also strong-willed, and Zara no longer felt fear for her.

She ducked under a branch and saw another spider, this one bigger than the first, with a shiny black abdomen streaked with red and spindly legs that clung to a web beaded with water droplets. It was beautiful and unsettling at the same time. The entire jungle felt that way to her, alien and beautiful, dangerous and compelling. Far in the distance she heard the hooting of what was either a different kind of monkey or a flock of large birds. It was impossible to see past the branches and the vines hanging low above the path.

Belinda ducked under one of those vines and said, "I can't imagine being able to light a fire here. Everything's so wet."

"I'm sure Ransom will think of something," Zara said sourly. His attitude toward his "guests" still annoyed her, even though a small, rational part of her considered what kind of errands a doctor might perform in the jungle and whether his impatience might not be justified. Not that it made her like him any better.

Belinda ducked under another vine and put her hand up to push aside another one. "He—" she said.

Zara saw the movement, one of the vines slipping over a branch too easily. She shouted, "*Move!*" and grabbed Belinda before she could obey, yanking her back and throwing up her own arm instinctively.

Sharp, agonizing pain went through her wrist as the snake struck faster than she could see, then convulsed, pumping venom into her arm. She gasped and tried to shake it off, but it wouldn't release her and kept thrashing. *It's more afraid of you than you are of it*, she thought hysterically, and tried swatting it with her free hand, with no result.

"Out of the way," Ransom said, shoving Belinda to one side. He grabbed the snake at the base of its jaw and tore it off Zara's wrist, flinging it far away into the bushes. "Keep your arm low, and don't panic, you're going to be fine," he said. He prodded at the two deep gashes on the side of her wrist, crouching to look at them rather than lifting her arm. "You'll be fine."

"What kind of snake was it?" Zara said. Her heart was beating too fast. That would bring the venom racing through her veins to her heart and lungs. She needed to calm down, but what made her heart race wasn't fear of the venom, but fear of Ransom learning her secret. He was going to try to do something about the venom, it would fail, and that would be it. "What kind?"

"It wouldn't mean anything to you."

"How serious?"

Ransom looked up at her, and she recognized the look on his face. It was the look of someone who had bad news to deliver and wasn't sure where to start. "You'll be fine," he said.

"Don't lie to me."

"All right, I *hope* you'll be fine. Does that satisfy you? Now, stop talking, it makes the venom spread faster."

"Shouldn't you suck the venom out?" Theo said.

"Swallowing this venom by accident could kill me, and I'm no good to anyone dead." Ransom gripped Zara's hand in his. His palm was smooth but hard, the hand of a man who worked for a living. "Hold her. She can't lie down for this."

Arjan and Theo took Zara's shoulders. Theo held on too tightly, but Zara didn't care. Her limbs were growing heavy, and she felt cold. Could she pretend his healing was working? No, she didn't have any idea what the effects were, and he could probably tell the difference. She concentrated on breathing slowly. She'd been poisoned before, not that it was the same, but—

All her muscles convulsed at once, and against her will she screamed at the sudden pain, like having talons embedded in every

66

part of her body and pulling in different directions to rend her into a hundred pieces. "It will pass," Ransom said, but he didn't sound certain. *No. He knows.* Then the pain struck her again, and she no longer cared what Ransom thought, or what he might discover. She couldn't control the spasms, which tore her out of her helpers' hands and made her collapse, thrashing, on the jungle floor.

Cold sweat built up on her face, her scalp, and all she could feel was Ransom's hand anchoring her to reality. She couldn't keep her fingers wrapped around his, but he held on to her tightly. She could hear him talking a great distance away, words she couldn't understand. Someone was crying loudly nearby. It sounded like the monkeys chittering. Then, with a final erratic thump, her heart stopped. Her muscle spasms slowed, then ceased entirely, and in the blessed relief of painlessness she let herself fall into death.

When she came to, her heart was beating, and she felt as if she'd been wrung out by a giant hand, all her muscles aching from the convulsions. She raised her hand to wipe the sweat from her forehead, and a terrified scream shattered the peaceful background noise of the jungle. Then Belinda was kneeling beside her, reaching out to touch her, then jerking her hand away. "You're dead," she said, "you can't be alive, you're dead."

"Move back, please," Ransom said, and Zara realized she was lying on a bed of something soft and squishy. "Miss Farrell, can you hear me?" Zara nodded. "The venom's worked its way through your system."

"Thank you," Zara said. *Might as well try to brazen it out.* "Your healing must have been effective."

Ransom's expression was carefully blank. "I suppose it was," he said. "You'll feel some lingering nausea and weakness, but otherwise you're fine. You're unexpectedly...hardy."

"Meaning I'm tough and hard to kill?" Was he playing along, or genuinely ignorant?

He favored her with one of those sardonic smiles. "Maybe it's not so unexpected. I think you could coerce Nettles into rearing onto his hind legs and dancing a jig."

"Easily. He's more sensible than his master."

"That's true. You won't catch me dancing a jig no matter what you say." He offered her his hand and helped her rise. Zara brushed fallen vegetation from her back and her head. Why couldn't they have found her a less filthy place to lie? Her legs were rubbery and her head and stomach ached. She tried to take a step and found Ransom supporting her. "Steady," he said. "Take short steps and give yourself time to regain your strength."

The others were huddled together, staring at her. "You dead were," Cantara said. "How can that be, that you now alive are?"

"It's not that unusual," Ransom said. "Once the venom had spent itself, her heart could start beating again. I realize it looks like death, but it's only a death-like state."

"You could have warned us," Theo said.

"Sorry, I thought I did. Well, Miss Farrell? Are you ready for us to proceed?"

Zara nodded. She still felt like vomiting, and her bitten arm was sore and felt twice its usual size, though it looked normal. She took a couple of wobbly steps, becoming gradually more sure of her footing, and soon was able to keep up the pace Ransom set. He certainly wasn't going to coddle her, not at that rate.

She ignored the continuing stares of her friends—were they friends, now? Could shared danger really be enough to build friendships on?—and followed Ransom deeper into the jungle. It was easier not having to meet their eyes, with all those remaining questions, but she could feel them watching her, and it was unnerving. She was certain Ransom knew her secret, and he clearly hadn't told the others. She disliked him, but she didn't think he was the type to pretend his healing talent was better than it was for his own aggrandizement. So he'd kept her secret, but why?

CHAPTER SEVEN

By the time the sun began to set, things had returned to normal—at least, no one was looking at Zara sideways. All of them stepped wide of the vines, the bushes, the trees, even the rotting leaves thickly coating the ground, which they shuffled through, hoping to scare away anything that might be hiding there. Zara kept up a normal pace, but all her attention was reserved for Ransom, striding along in front of the donkey as if nothing unusual had happened that day. It unnerved her more than the thought of more snakes hidden in the trees.

They made camp in a place off to one side of the trail where there was something of a clearing, and Ransom went around with his blade to widen it further. While he was doing this, Arjan gathered sticks and built a lopsided but serviceable fire, which he lit by some mysterious process Zara couldn't see. The fire smoked a bit at first, making Ransom say, when he rejoined them, "If we were at all interested in drawing attention, you'd have succeeded magnificently."

"Protection," Arjan said.

"I didn't say it was a bad idea." Ransom hauled a few boxes off the donkey, then the bundle that was his tent. "You could all help me get Nettles unloaded, you know."

"I was under the impression you didn't want our help," Zara said.

"I don't. But it's better than having you stare at me. And you, Miss Farrell, might start sharing out food. Who knows what might happen if you don't keep busy?"

"Total anarchy, no doubt. Or you might relapse into self-centeredness."

Ransom sighed, an exaggerated sound of despair. "Food, Miss Farrell, and don't make me reflect on the moment of insanity that brought us all to this point."

Zara didn't see the need to respond to that. She removed the net bag still full of fruit, most of which had gone mushy during the day's heat, then began rooting around in the boxes. Suddenly Ransom was at her side, gently but firmly closing one of the boxes. "Medicines," he said before she could do more than open her mouth to protest. "Anyone eating some of those would get a nasty surprise."

"It's not as if I knew that."

"Which is why I'm not calling you a fool. I'm not as sour-tempered as you seem to think."

"You haven't gone out of your way to prove otherwise."

"I might say the same of you." Ransom prodded a different box with his foot. "Staples. You could start chopping some of the roots, and we'll boil up a soup as soon as I have time to go for water."

"I—all right." That had been an almost pleasant conversation. Zara took handfuls of slightly dry squash and yams and went looking for a knife larger than the one she carried.

"He's not as bad as I thought," Belinda said in a low voice. She took some of the food from Zara and handed her a knife. "Here, I'll help. Chop them small or they'll take forever to cook."

"I had to make him feel guilty to get him to agree to take us," Zara said. "If he were a decent man—"

"He saved your life, Rowena. You didn't see—" Belinda's hand paused in her chopping. "Your arm swelled up to three times its normal size, and the wound was green and dripping. You would have died if not for him. Doesn't that entitle him to some credit?"

She'd forgotten how her healing must have looked from the outside. "I just don't like him, that's all. But I'm grateful."

"I think the two of you might be a little too much alike for comfort. There's only room for one queen in a hive."

Zara fumbled her knife and had to snatch at it to keep it from landing in the dirt. "We're neither of us queens, and this isn't a hive."

"You know what I mean."

"I suppose I do." She looked over at Ransom, who'd picked up the cookpot and was heading off into the bushes. "And it wouldn't hurt me to be nicer. But not much nicer. I think, if we're not careful, we'll end up doing what's convenient for him and not what's best for us."

70

Belinda shrugged. "He'll get us where we need to be, and that's all I care about." She took another yam and began chopping small, regular pieces much nicer than the chunks Zara was managing. "You really aren't much of a cook, are you?"

By the time the soup was ready, it was full dark, and they sat close around the fire and passed the bowl between them. Fortunately, soup was something Zara had learned to cook over the years, and between that and the fruit she felt full when the last drop was drained from the pot.

She sat cross-legged, soaking up the fire's dry heat that smelled deliciously of smoke and some spice that came from the wood itself. Humidity aside, she was glad she'd gone south rather than north to the Eidestal. She didn't really care for the cold. Was there someplace that was dry and hot? Haizea, the capital of Veribold, perhaps? She'd only ever been there once, when she was a child; maybe she could go there next. She smiled at herself. Lost in the jungle, and already planning a new trip. She probably ought to wait until she was safe on Goudge's Folly before she thought that far ahead.

"Miss Stouffer," Ransom said, "you'll take my tent again tonight." He was sitting on the ground rather than the stool, a show of egalitarianism that made Zara feel guilty at her annoyance with him.

"Maybe Cantara should take a turn," Belinda said.

"It's a one-man tent. I think Mistress Zakhari would prefer not to be separated from her husband."

"You should take the tent," Theo said. "I wouldn't feel right about you sleeping on the ground."

"I'm forty-four, Theo, not eighty-seven," Belinda said irritably. Zara successfully kept from choking on her last bite of papaya.

"And not terribly strong," Ransom said. "You'll slow us down if you don't get proper rest. If it helps, this isn't chivalry, but a doctor's opinion."

Belinda looked at Zara, who shrugged and shook her head. "All right," Belinda said. "But don't think I can't keep up, because I can."

"You've done well so far," Ransom said. "And speaking of rest,

71

we should probably settle in for the night. I want to make an early start so we can reach our destination before nightfall tomorrow." He stood and began banking the fire. "Stay close to the fire, though. No sense making ourselves more of a target than we already are."

Zara once again settled herself far from Nettles—she didn't like the way the donkey looked at her, as if he liked the way she tasted and wanted seconds—and tried to calm her thoughts. She raised her arm and looked at her wrist in the fading light. Two light dots of scar tissue, slightly raised, lay parallel to each other on the curve of her arm. No healing was perfect, and serious wounds left scars. With her other hand, she reached behind her head to finger the round circle of scarring beneath her hair, where Alison's pistol ball had shattered the back of her skull. It seemed like so long ago—well, it had been almost sixty years, but from her perspective that was almost no time at all.

"Let me see that arm," Ransom said in a low voice, sitting down beside her and taking her hand without waiting for her permission. She snatched it away from him, then felt ashamed of her abruptness.

"Sorry. I'd rather you didn't," she said, matching his tone.

"Because you know what I'll find?"

His hazel eyes were once again dark in the dim firelight, but for once he didn't sound sardonic, just amused. "Then there's no point to it, is there?" she said.

"I thought at first my magic had failed," Ransom said. "Then I realized what was happening. You heal yourself, don't you? Probably not consciously, either. I've never heard of anything like it."

"No one has." She hesitated—but she'd already put herself in his power, hadn't she? "Thanks for keeping my secret."

"By the looks of your friends, none of them knew, so I guessed you wanted it kept. And you can think what you like of me, but I know what it's like to have inherent magic in Tremontane, and I'd never betray one of my fellows."

"You can heal others. It's hardly the same."

"I still used to get suspicious looks from people, as if they expected me to turn into an Ascendant in front of them. So no, it's not the same, but I still understand. Somewhat."

Zara sighed and sat up to face him. "It's usually not an issue. I don't live a very dangerous life."

"And yet you're here in the jungles of Dineh-Karit."

"It's not where I wanted to go."

"Right. You were headed for Tammerek. That's its actual name, Goudge's Folly, that is."

"Still am, as long as you're willing to help us."

"I said I would, didn't I?"

"Your lack of enthusiasm doesn't fill me with confidence."

"You expect me to be enthusiastic about being thrown off schedule? People's lives depend on me, Miss Farrell, a lot more people than you five, and they won't be so understanding about the delay as I am."

Annoyance warred with guilt over feeling annoyed and won. "Then maybe you should have left us —"

"Stop." Ransom put his hand up between them, a barrier against her words. "You're angry, and I'm…difficult to get along with, and there's really no point to us fighting. I said I'd take you, but I thought you'd prefer honesty to me pretending this isn't a sacrifice that, by the way, I'm making on others' behalf. Can we call a truce between us?"

He didn't sound sarcastic or amused anymore, and Zara said, "You're right. I'm sorry."

"So am I."

She waited for him to leave, but he just sat there, half turned away from her, looking at the embers. She lay down, hoping that would encourage him to move on. Instead, he said, in an even lower voice, "So…how old are you?"

Her heart began pounding as if the venom still poured through her blood. "Didn't your mother tell you never to ask a woman's age?"

"My mother is a gossip. If she'd ever given me any advice, it would be to never let polite behavior get in the way of a good story."

"That's no way to talk about your mother."

"There's no other way to talk about her. How old?"

His persistence sharpened her tongue. "Why should I tell you?"

"No reason. I just want to know."

"Then how old are *you?*" She threw the question at him like a dare.

"Twenty-six. There, now it's your turn."

"I'm thirty-two."

"That's what I thought. How old are you really?"

"What makes you think I'm not thirty-two?"

"I'm not stupid. I know what the implications of your magic are. Anyone with my magic would."

"That doesn't mean you know anything about me."

Ransom turned and lay down next to her with his head propped on his arm. "Then don't tell me. You don't owe me anything."

"You're right. I don't."

Ransom was silent, his eyes fixed on her. *He's going to wait all night, and what will it hurt? And maybe it will stop him looking at you like...*she didn't know how to finish that sentence, except that his regard made her uncomfortably exposed, as if he could see through her skin. "I'm eighty-seven," she said.

His eyes widened. "Good heaven," he said. "A *much* older woman."

"Older than what?" She felt irritated all over again.

"Older than I thought. Sorry. I didn't mean to sound so surprised. It makes sense, actually. You act like someone who's had a long lifetime to become who she is."

"Oh." That was better than she'd expected from him. Maybe he really did want a truce. "Well, now that you know I'm so much more mature than you are, maybe you'll take my objections more seriously."

"Not likely." Ransom grinned at her. "You're still an infant as far as this jungle is concerned. If anything, you should have the wisdom to listen to what I tell you."

"Sounds like we're just going to go on clashing, then."

"Keep each other humble, rather."

"That sounds more mature. I can live with that."

74

"So can I. Good night, Miss Farrell."

To her surprise, the fact that he intended to sleep nearby didn't irritate her at all. "My name is Rowena," she said. "You know everything about me, you might as well call me that."

Ransom chuckled. "Don't expect me to share my first name with you in return. I hate it."

"I wouldn't. Ransom suits you."

He laughed again. "Good night, Rowena."

"Good night, Ransom."

The next morning was the same as the first: hot, muggy, and loud with the sounds of the jungle. They left the monkeys behind around noon, when they stopped briefly for Ransom to hand out food, but insects buzzed and hummed around them, diving at the fruit and whirring around their heads. A *ha-ha-ha* sound like the cough of a dying man echoed above them, and eventually Zara traced the sound to a flock of birds, sapphire blue and ruby red. The entire place reminded her of an old book she'd seen once, its pictures as bright as if the inks were still liquid on the pages. The jungle was lush, and swarming with life, and Zara breathed in the richness of it and couldn't remember what winter smelled like.

Rain fell that afternoon, hard, stinging rain like sheets of water pouring from the sky. They huddled together under the shelter of a tree whose trunk was too thick for Zara and Belinda combined to wrap their arms around. Its broad leaves were shaped like giant spoons, collecting water and then overflowing onto whoever was unwary enough to stand too far from the trunk. Zara pushed her wet hair back from her face and wished she'd thought to have it cut before leaving Tremontane. It reached the middle of her back, thick and black, and even though she kept it tied out of her face, it was dirty and slightly greasy, and her scalp itched. It was tempting to run out into the rainstorm and let it wash her clean, but she'd only be uncomfortable later.

"These storms are common in the afternoons," Ransom said. He'd pulled out a hat from one of the boxes, something shapeless with a wide brim that kept the drops off his face. "They don't last long. No more than fifteen or twenty minutes. But there's more water in one of these cloudbursts than falls during two hours in a northern storm."

"And it's warm," Theo said. He stuck his hand out to let the rainwater wash over it. "I've never felt warm rain before."

"This place much different than Eskandel's forests is," Cantara said. "They rich and green are, but not so overgrown as this." She looked as if she'd never been unwell.

"This is the best source for medicines in the world." Ransom crouched and sniffed a plant growing near the base of the tree, then fingered its spiky leaves. "This one, for example, is good for a poultice that treats boils and open sores. It's not mature yet, but there's quite a few of the adult plants growing near here." He took out a long knife with a leaf-shaped blade and took a few steps into the rain to cut sprigs off the bushes.

"Is that why you're here? Medicines?" Zara asked.

He favored her with his sardonic grin. "Not to be rude, but that's none of your business."

"It's a simple question."

"With a not so simple answer. One which I'm not giving you."

Zara gave up. "My apologies. It's not like *you know anything about me*."

The grin went from sardonic to amused. He really only had the two expressions, didn't he? "It's still none of your business." He opened the medicine box on the donkey's back, making it take a few steps away before settling down. Zara peeked over his shoulder. There were sacks, and little boxes, and bundles of herbs tied with colored strings. Ransom took out a ball of red silk thread and whipped its end around the green sprigs, then tied a knot and bit it off. "Curious?" he said. "Never mind. Rowena Farrell is always curious."

"I hardly think what's in that box is a secret, Ransom." Irritated, Zara turned her back on him.

"It's not, but I'm not inclined to take the time to explain it to you."

Ransom closed the box and removed his hat, shaking water from it and spattering Zara's boots, probably not on purpose. "Rain's letting up. Let's move on."

The jungle after rain was a very different place. The insects were gone, hopefully drowned, and the air smelled cool and fresh, like morning dew. Even the birds were quiet, subdued by the downpour or still hiding in the shelter of the trees. No one spoke; Zara couldn't imagine breaking the peaceful quiet with words. *Now would be a good time for some large animal to attack,* she thought irrelevantly, but started looking around more carefully anyway. Nothing approached them.

After about an hour, the peace the rain had left behind was supplanted by the usual hot mugginess of the millions of trees and bushes surrounding them. Wisps of steam rose from the wet leaves and from the boxes and bags perched on the donkey's back. Zara couldn't tell anymore if she was wet from rain or from sweat. She focused on Belinda's back, which rose and fell with her harsh breathing. She was holding up better than Zara had imagined, but she stopped occasionally and leaned over with her hands on her knees, shaking her head at Zara when she attempted to help.

"How much farther?" she asked the fifth time Belinda did this.

"Hours," Ransom said over his shoulder, not slowing.

"What is that in distance?"

"Distance isn't so important here as terrain. So it's hours."

"This feels like it's gone on forever," Theo said. He didn't look at all fatigued.

"Most of the country is still wilderness, settled only by a few villages," Ransom said. He hacked at a thick branch, then kicked it aside when it dropped. "The big cities all lie along the Amgeli until you get about two hundred miles inland."

"We're going to one of the villages?" Zara didn't expect him to answer—heaven forbid he cooperate with her—but he said, "Yes," and if it was a short answer, at least it was an answer.

They walked. The hundreds of different plants blurred together in Zara's vision into one solid mass of greenery. She became so accustomed to the noises the animals and birds made that she soon stopped hearing them, noticing only the lack of chirruping and howling when it paused. Her back and legs ached, probably not as much as Belinda's did, but she kept on putting one foot after the other, too weary to care if she stepped on another snake.

Ransom held up a hand for them to stop and handed Theo the donkey's reins. "Wait here," he said, unstrapping a hunting rifle from the donkey's side and moving on down the trail. Belinda sat down and put her head between her bent knees. "Are you all right?" Zara said.

"Just tired. Ready to stop for the night. Where did Ransom say we were stopping?"

"He didn't. Unsurprisingly. Just that we had to 'reach our destination' before sunset." Zara held out her hand. "You shouldn't stop now. It will just be harder when you have to get up again."

Belinda groaned, but let Zara pull her to her feet. Behind them, Arjan had his arm around Cantara, supporting her. Their "destination" needed to be close.

Ransom emerged from the undergrowth, his face grim. "We have to move quickly now," he said, "and as quietly as we can."

"What's wrong?" Zara asked.

"Nothing—yet." Ransom put away the rifle, took the reins from Theo and slapped Nettles gently on the rump. "But *najabedhi* has been here recently, and I don't want to meet him even in daylight."

"What's *najabedhi*?" asked Theo, but Zara already knew. *Najabedhi*, jungle panther, the animal on the North sign and shield. There was no record of why Willow North had chosen it, though she'd probably intended to intimidate her Council by reminding them she was swift and ruthless like the cat. Zara didn't want to meet it either.

"Panther," Ransom said to Theo. "The Karitians call it *horreus*, which means 'night terror.' This one's big, probably male, which is less dangerous than the female. If he's marking his territory, we could be in trouble, but otherwise they tend to stay away from other predators— and they know humans are as close to the top of the heap as they are."

"Do the men who live here hunt them?" Arjan said. He and

Cantara had come close to Zara as Ransom spoke.

"Yes. But I'm not a very good shot, so I'd rather not be one of them."

"I am," Belinda said, "but the way I feel now, I'm not sure I could hold a rifle without dropping it."

"You hunt?" Theo said.

"Don't sound so shocked. I was the County Cullinan amateur sharpshooting champion for ten years. National champion four times. But I'm in no shape for it right now."

"That's a pity," Ransom said. "Now let's move on. And try to stay quiet, if that's possible."

Zara wanted to say something sarcastic in return, but he was already down the trail several yards ahead of her, and the thought of the panther creeping up on them held her tongue. She had no idea whether they'd hear it before they saw it, whether it would attack the way the caiman had, and hoped they wouldn't find out.

Darkness crept up on them the way it did in the jungle, the air becoming saturated with evening light that glowed gold over the green leaves. Weariness had seeped into Zara's bones, and it was an effort to put one foot in front of the other. Ahead of her, Belinda stumbled, and Zara caught her. "We have to stop soon," she called out.

"Quiet," Ransom said. "It's not much farther."

There wasn't much to see, there in the growing dark, except the glow of the moonlight that struck the treetops high above. Zara pushed aside a branch. Was it her imagination, or was the trail growing wider? Ransom had put away his blade and strode forward more rapidly. He moved as if he'd seen something and was trying to reach it as quickly as possible. Belinda stumbled again, and Zara put her shoulder under her friend's arm and helped her walk, trying to keep up with Ransom. How typical of him not to think of their needs. What exactly was he doing?

A dark shape loomed up before them, and Zara had to pull up quickly to keep from running into Theo. The young man's face and arms blended with the night; she could see his eyes and not much else.

"Ransom's gone," he whispered. "He just disappeared."

"He's here somewhere," Zara said. "He wouldn't waste his time taking us into the jungle and abandoning us when he could have left us back at his camp."

"Then where is he?" Theo sounded like he was on the verge of terror.

"I don't know. We have to stay put." She said that last to the Zakharis—she didn't dare even think their real name—who'd come up from behind. Cantara looked far less exhausted than she had the day before.

"We can't stand here all night," Theo insisted. "We have to move on."

"Ransom's coming back, and he won't be able to find us if we move." Zara squeezed Theo's shoulder. "Don't be afraid."

"That's very sensible advice," Ransom said, emerging from the bushes. "Come with me."

"Where did you go?" Zara said. Now that he'd returned, she could afford to be annoyed with him.

"Ahead. Just come along." He took Nettles by the reins and started walking without looking to see if they were following. Zara swore under her breath. Wherever they were going had better have beds.

The bushes were thinning out, and soon Zara could see the moonlight clearly, a warm glow that gave just enough light to keep them from tripping over roots and small plants. Then they were out of the bushes and back among the tall trees. Zara looked up at the distant canopy. Moonlight struck the leaves—but no, it was coming from beneath the leaves, and it was too orange for moonlight. Fire, like dozens of campfires or a hundred torches, made the leaves glow and cast their elongated shadows on the branches above. Dark shapes too regular to be natural clung to the thick trunks, and heavy strands like the biggest spider web in the world hung between them. It was all so strange to her exhausted brain she rubbed grit out of her eyes and looked again. Still there.

"Up," Ransom said. He was standing next to a ladder made of

short sticks bound together by long, fuzzy ropes. "And I hope none of you are afraid of heights, because sleeping on the ground isn't an option."

Belinda immediately took hold of the rungs and began climbing. Ransom steadied the ladder for her and said, "One at a time."

Theo, then Cantara, then Arjan climbed out of sight. "Afraid?" Ransom said.

"Hardly. Who'll hold the ladder for you?"

Ransom nodded, a quick jerk of his head over his shoulder, and Zara stifled a gasp as two men appeared next to him. They wore short skirts of leather and were bare-chested. Each man bore a club as big around as her thigh and neither of them looked happy to see her. "Go ahead, Rowena," Ransom said. "Who knows what trouble the rest of them have gotten into?"

Zara took hold of the rungs and, not looking down, began the long ascent.

CHAPTER EIGHT

The ladder led to a small, square platform of planed lumber, so unexpected Zara stood on it for a moment without moving, feeling she'd stepped out of the jungle into a different world. Another ladder stretched upward from it. She took hold of the rungs and climbed again. Two more platforms interrupted the ladder before she came to the top, where she clambered over the edge of a much larger platform, feeling a tug on her trousers as they caught on the rough lip. She knelt there, breathing heavily from the exertion, grateful to be done climbing. Then she stood, slowly, and looked around.

The others stood a short distance away, huddled together like a tiny flock of bedraggled sheep. Facing her was the biggest man she'd ever seen, nearly seven feet tall with broad shoulders and an enormous belly not restrained by the leather skirt he wore. If the men below had been unfriendly, this one looked as if he were mere seconds away from erupting into violence. His being unarmed wasn't a comfort; he could probably beat her to death with his fists alone. *Or just shove me off the platform*, she thought. She squared her shoulders and regarded him without fear.

"Rowena," Arjan said, "where is Ransom?"

"Coming," Zara said. The big man shifted his weight and crossed his arms over his chest. In the firelight, his dark skin glowed golden, and light sparked on the copper hoops he wore in his left ear, five of them running up the edge of it and into the cartilage. Zara didn't take her eyes off him. "There's nothing to worry about."

"That man has me very worried," Belinda said. "Maybe you should come over here."

Zara didn't move. "He's not going to hurt us."

"Again, so sensible," Ransom said, pulling himself over the edge. "This is Kossrek Tamun, the…I suppose you could call him the ruler of this village." He spoke in Karitian to Tamun, who regarded him dispassionately, then responded with a few curt words. Ransom glanced at Zara, then spoke again, longer this time. Tamun looked Zara up and down as if assessing her. He said a few more words. Ransom snapped back a response that made Tamun's eyes widen.

To Zara's astonishment, the giant laughed and slapped Ransom on the back. Ransom laughed with him, but it sounded forced. Tamun shouted, and dark-haired men and women came from nowhere, smiling and bowing with both hands placed palm-together in front of their navels. Theo gasped and ducked his head. None of the people were wearing shirts, male or female. Zara regarded him sympathetically, remembering her first, hah, exposure to an Eskandelic resort in which nudity was the norm. So many bare breasts...well, he could probably stand to have his horizons broadened.

"Go with them," Ransom said. "They'll feed you and give you a place to sleep. I have things to take care of."

"What were you and Tamun talking about?" Zara said.

"Just negotiations."

"Negotiations that required him to look at me like I was a side of beef?"

"Don't worry about it. I'll explain later."

Zara stepped in front of him. "That's not good enough."

Ransom took her by the shoulders and moved her to the side. His eyes were shadowed with tiredness. "I have to get my cargo stowed. It will have to be good enough. Please, Rowena, show a little common sense and patience?"

Zara scowled. "Meaning I don't usually?"

"Meaning I trust you to keep the rest of them from doing anything stupid. I'll be back later." He bent to take hold of the ladder and disappeared over the side. Zara glared at the place where he'd been. He was abrupt, but it had been a compliment, and that made it hard to stay angry with him.

She had to run to catch up with the others, her feet thudding across the platform of more planed lumber. Where could they get that in the middle of the jungle? Torches made a puddle of light ahead, illuminating wooden walls and a doorway hung with a blanket woven in an intricate pattern. She almost stopped to examine it, saw how far ahead the others were, and left it for later.

She passed several more of the wooden houses—were they houses?—before reaching the others, who were crossing a wooden bridge with woven ropes for handrails. The bridge, too, was made of short planed planks and moved unpleasantly as Zara stepped onto it, like a snake shifting underfoot. She waited, watching the others spaced out along it like beads on a string, before crossing. Thank heaven it was dark and she couldn't see the ground below. She'd never been in a position to learn whether she was afraid of heights and didn't want to find out on a rickety bridge heaven knew how far above the ground.

There were more torches on the far side of the bridge, and Zara could see clearly the building they were approaching. It encircled the trunk of an enormous tree, with wooden shingles the length of her forearm covering the roof and a hollowed-out curve of wrist-thick vine fastened just below the lowest shingles, positioned to catch the heavy rains that rolled off the roof and funnel them into…Zara traced the path with her eye. There was the rain barrel, off to the left. Large windows pierced the wooden walls, these made of woven branches rather than planed wood, and light streamed from within.

Zara caught up to the others as they hovered near the doorway. "Let's go in," she said, seeing one of the women who'd been their escort holding aside the blanket and gesturing for them to enter.

"Where did Ransom go?" Arjan said.

"He's unloading his cargo. Come, I can smell food."

"I can't look at her. It's unseemly." Theo had his head ducked so low his chin was trying to merge with his chest.

"It's their culture, Theo, it's not unseemly," Belinda said.

"I mean it's wrong for me to look. Mam says to respect all women."

"If this is how they dress all the time, it must not be disrespectful in their culture." Belinda patted him on the shoulder and went inside, ducking under the blanket. Zara prodded Theo, and one at a time they all entered.

The trunk of the tree filled the center of the room like a giant guest, its bark rosy and smooth. Walls to either side, both with blanket-covered doorways, made the huge room cozy. A brightly woven cloth was spread on the floor near the entrance, and the woman who'd held the blanket for them indicated they should sit around it. Zara sat cross-legged and rolled her shoulders to ease the tension. She could smell roasted meat somewhere nearby, and the sweeter scent of yams, and her stomach rumbled. If the villagers were going to feed them, they couldn't be that antagonistic to northerners, could they?

One of the blankets moved, and three people came through. Two of them bore steaming dishes; the third held a pile of large, fat leaves and a stack of wooden cups. He set a leaf and a cup in front of each of them, smiling and saying something in rapid Karitian. Zara picked her leaf up. It was mostly round, with a crease down the middle for the stem, and it was glossy dark green on the front, nearly black, and pale, almost white on the back.

The man returned and gently took the leaf from Zara, set it back down flat in front of her, and one of his companions scooped out mashed orange yams, cooked soft, onto the leaf. The other had tongs with which he picked up a large helping of shredded white meat and dropped it next to the yams. The first man leaned past Zara to pour a thin stream of water into the cup. It smelled like minerals, but not in a nasty way. Zara looked from the leaf "plate" to the server, who was a woman about thirty with a pleasant smile. "How do I eat this?" she said, miming chewing.

The woman's smile grew broader. She reached down and pretended to pick up the meat, brought the imaginary morsel to her lips and chewed. Then she made a scooping motion near the yams with two fingers and put both into her mouth.

Well. That was interesting. Zara nodded and said, "Thank you." She picked up some of the meat and ate it, examining the room as she did so. The walls were hung with smaller squares of woven fabric she itched to examine. The weave was lumpier than that of her great loom,

85

suggesting either that these were novice efforts or they were using unfamiliar techniques. Her eye passed over one of the Karitians, the older man who'd brought in the leaves, and her hand stilled before dipping into the mash. "Stop," she told the others.

"What is it? Is something wrong with the food?" Belinda asked. Theo was already sucking on his fingers.

"Something's wrong with them." Zara looked at their servers more closely, then at the dishes they held. "They're playing a game with us."

"I do not understand," said Arjan. "What game?"

"'Let's see what we can get the stupid foreigners to do,' that's the game." Zara pushed her leaf aside and stood. "Those are some very nice metal pots you have there," she said to the woman, pointing at the pan containing the mash. "And you've got ladles that are just as nice. I think you have utensils somewhere, and I wouldn't be surprised if you have plates, too."

The woman looked at her without comprehension. "You don't speak Tremontanese, do you?" Zara said. "Well, I don't speak your language either, so this will have to do." She lifted the ladle and pretended to use it as a spoon, pointed at the ladle, pointed at herself and then the others, then repeated herself. The woman glanced down at the cloth, then smiled and said something to the man with the leaves. He replied in a cranky tone, and she shook her head and left the room, followed by the other two. Zara sat down. Now was when she'd find out if she'd been right.

A minute later, the man reappeared. He held a fistful of cutlery, forks and spoons, which he distributed. "Plates?" Zara said, pointing at the leaf. He shook his head, looking confused.

"They really do use *rashedek* leaves as plates," Ransom said, taking a seat between Cantara and Theo. The man handed him a fork and spoon and disappeared into the back. "Saves a lot of effort. I take it you figured out their little game?"

"You could have warned us," Zara said. The yams were growing cold, but they were still delicious.

"They judge visitors by their behavior. It's not my place to interfere." The server woman reappeared with her companion and smiled at Ransom. He said something that ended in a question, and she responded at length while Ransom nodded. Finally, when she wound down, he said one last thing that made her smile even more broadly before she left the room. Ransom started eating as if he hadn't eaten for days. Zara spun her fork in her fingers; it was stainless steel, completely incongruous against the *rashedek* leaf.

"What did you say?" Theo asked. He was still using his fingers to mop up the last of the yams on his leaf and kept his eyes firmly on his food, not looking at the women.

"Doctor-patient issues. Not your business," Ransom said.

"I take it they're going to let us stay tonight?" Zara said.

"I told you Karitians aren't as bigoted as northerners think."

"But they wouldn't have been so friendly if you hadn't been along."

"You're welcome."

"I ready for sleep am," Cantara said. Zara leaned back, stretching her thighs. She could use some sleep herself.

"They have guest quarters," Ransom said, but he glanced at Zara as he did so, as if there were something he wasn't saying.

"And?" Zara said.

"And nothing. If you're done eating, they'll take you to where you can sleep." Ransom applied himself to his food and said nothing further. Zara regarded him narrowly. There probably wasn't any point to pushing him into speaking again.

There were two men waiting outside the eating house, both tall and thin, wearing woven belts dyed red over their leather skirts. They pointed off into the darkness, but didn't move, and after a moment Zara decided there was no point in waiting for more from them and led the way in that direction. The platform ended in another swaying bridge, where Zara kept tight hold of the ropes and pretended it was an ordinary sidewalk. It had to be perfectly safe, because the villagers used them all the time. She kept her eyes fixed on the far side.

At the other end of the bridge stood a man and a woman, both also wearing the red belts. Once everyone was off the bridge, they led the way across a platform to several small round huts with the unique drainpipes and rain barrels. The man pointed at Theo and Arjan and waved at one of the huts. Cantara made a noise of protest, and Arjan, who had his arm around her shoulders, drew her more closely to him. "No," he said, shaking his head for emphasis. The man and the woman had a short, low-voiced conversation that ended with the man pointing at Arjan and Cantara and then at the hut. As the Zakharis entered it, the man pointed at Theo and Belinda and waved at another hut.

"So it's all right for me to share a hut with a man so long as it's Theo?" Belinda exclaimed. "I don't understand these people at all."

"Let's just sleep," Zara said, "and tomorrow we can go north again." She moved to follow Belinda, but the man stopped her with a hand on her shoulder and shook his head. "Oh, for heaven's sake," she said. "Look. I realize you can't speak my language, but can you understand I just want to sleep?"

The man shook his head again and pointed in the opposite direction, at a hut much larger than the others. "No," Zara said. "With my friends." The man shook his head more vehemently and pointed again. He and the woman looked worried, the kind of worry that said they thought they were going to be in trouble. "Fine," Zara said. "I'll see you in the morning, Belinda." She stomped across the platform, enjoying how the thuds of her angry footsteps echoed. So long as the hut had a bed of some kind, she didn't care where she slept.

There was no light inside the hut but what came from torches outside through the window holes, so she stood for a moment to let her eyes adjust. There was a bed, though it was more of a mattress on the floor; it was a big square sack stuffed with something that rustled when she sat on it. She took off her boots and her socks, which were damp, and rubbed her toes. Her feet smelled of jungle, but then, so did the rest of her.

She freed her hair from its leather tie and tried to finger-comb the tangles, then gave up. Now that she was sitting, she realized she ached everywhere with exhaustion. *Think how tired you'd be without your inherent magic fighting off all those little muscle strains*, she thought, and lay down. There was no pillow, but she didn't care.

She was just drifting off when the blanket covering the door moved and a dark figure entered the room. Instantly she was on her feet, backing against the wall for whatever protection that might give. "Who are you?" she said. "Get out of here *now*."

"It's me," Ransom said. "Sorry. I thought you'd already be asleep."

That made no sense. "Can't we talk in the morning?"

"Yes. But this is my hut."

"Your—I'm sorry, they made a mistake. I'll go sleep with Belinda." She crossed the room to the door, and Ransom put a hand on her arm.

"It's not a mistake. It's...complicated."

"Then uncomplicate it. Why did they put me in your hut?"

Ransom sighed and released her. He sat on the edge of the mattress and began taking his boots off. "These villages have a precarious existence, living between the old tribal ways and the new civilization," he said. "They take advantage of new technology, but they haven't given up blood feuds and vendettas. This means there's always a shortage of young men and most of the villages are barely at replacement level of reproduction. So the role of young women is primarily seen as childbearing and -rearing."

"That's an interesting cultural lesson, but it doesn't explain anything."

"I'm getting to it. The ruler of a village—there's this custom that the chief has the right to, um, impregnate any unattached young woman, or at least try to—"

"Sweet heaven, Ransom, that's utterly barbaric!"

"And he decided he wanted you."

Words choked her. "I'm not Karitian," she managed, "I'm not part of his village, and I couldn't—"

"He knows that. I think he finds you attractive and was using custom to get what he wanted. So I had to tell him you belong to me.

I'm sorry."

"You—"

"I realize it's awkward."

"*Awkward?*"

"Look at it this way. There *used* to be a custom that a man and a woman had to consummate their love in front of witnesses to prove who the father of a child was."

"*Ransom!*"

"That was centuries ago. I thought it would give you perspective."

Zara closed her eyes. "You couldn't have told him to go to hell?"

"I was hoping to avoid bloodshed."

"Would they really kill us just for denying their ruler his...rights?"

"I was thinking more about his blood, when he told you what you had to submit to. He's not a bad man, just a selfish one."

"He's a rapist!"

"Any of the young women in this village would go to him willingly. He meant his interest in you as a compliment. Don't be too quick to judge." He set his boots and socks near the door and began to stretch out on the floor.

"What are you doing?" Zara said.

"Going to sleep. I'm exhausted and I've got a full day ahead of me tomorrow."

"You don't have to sleep on the floor."

"I'm certainly not going to let you do it."

He picked the strangest times to become chivalrous. "There's enough room for both of us," she said. "Unless you're afraid I'm going to attack you in your sleep."

Ransom sat up. "At least you're not a restless sleeper. I'd hate for your snoring to keep me up all night."

Zara lay on the bed. "You're hilarious. Sleep where you want, but I think it's stupid of you not to take advantage of this bed."

"You're right." Ransom lay down on his side of the mattress. "I imagine this isn't what you thought you'd be doing when you left Tremontane."

"Not even a little bit. I was going to Goudge's Folly for work."

"What do you do?"

"I'm going to oversee inventory for an importer based on the island."

"That can't be what you've done for...what is it, seventy-two years since you became an adult?"

"I was a weaver for a long time. This was meant to be the start of something new."

"I can see that. It's certainly a difference."

His tone of voice, carefully neutral, made her realize she'd told him far more than she'd intended to share. It irritated her that she'd been so easily drawn, and she said, "How long have you been a doctor?"

"Six years. I was in training for nine years before that." He didn't sound disturbed at the sudden change of subject.

"And what brought you here? Never mind, I forgot. A question with a complicated answer."

Ransom laughed quietly. "I was trying to get away from my family. They wanted things for me I didn't want for myself."

"That's not a complicated answer."

"It is if you know my family. They're...have you heard of the Resurgence?"

"No."

"It's a growing movement centered in Aurilien that wants to remove the stigma of inherent magic, make it something people don't have to be afraid of. My parents—my whole family, really—became involved about eight years ago. Heavily involved. Donations, fundraisers...it became their whole lives. I graduated, received my medical degree, and came home to a hero's welcome. Except it wasn't that they were proud of what I'd achieved, they were eager for what I could do for the Resurgence."

"Was that why they got involved? Because of your magic?"

"I think it was a sense of moral superiority. Helping the downtrodden, et cetera. Which I suppose makes them not quite so opportunistic, if they only thought of using me afterward. But they definitely wanted to use me. And I had other plans."

"And you couldn't have stayed in Tremontane without clashing with them constantly."

"You see the problem. It wasn't good enough for them that I was using my talent openly; they wanted me to be a devoted supporter of the cause. So I left."

"Why Dineh-Karit? Surely there are places closer to home where you could do what you do."

"Because I'm needed here." He shifted beside her. "There are a lot of healers in Dineh-Karit. It's got as much source as Tremontane, maybe more, and there's no hatred or fear of inherent magic. But people with *useful* inherent magic, like healers—the city dwellers look down on the people who live in the jungle, and mostly leave them to fend for themselves. The unspoken corollary being no one's going to weep great tears if they die. And if they do take it on themselves to help, they try to change their customs 'in their best interests.' The villagers need people who'll help them without trying to force change on them."

"I'm not sure that custom about impregnating single women is something that needs preserving."

"No. But it's down to them to make that choice. It's already disappearing as some of these villages learn to overcome the pride that makes them go to war over any slight. But telling them they need to build houses on the jungle floor? Or to put on more clothes in this climate? It's wrong."

"Well, why *don't* they build on the ground?"

"Predators. *Najabedhi*. And a lot of food is only available near the canopy. Plus, they have some amazing views." He yawned widely enough that she could hear it.

"I'm sorry, I'm keeping you up," she said.

"Well, you'd want me to answer these questions eventually. Might as well do it now as when we're going down river."

"So you're staying with us."

"I told you I would, didn't I? Besides, why would I deprive myself of the joys of your interrogations?"

"You don't have to answer."

"I'm hoping to build up debt so you'll have to answer mine."

"You have questions for me?"

"Don't sound so surprised. You've lived a long life. I can only imagine the things you've seen and done."

"That really is a conversation for another time. It's far too late for me to tell you any of that."

"That sounds like a promise."

"It's a maybe." It might just be the weariness, but suddenly the idea of telling someone was compelling. Not her identity, naturally, but other things, like the history she'd lived, or how it felt to leave people behind. "Go to sleep, Ransom."

"Yes, ma'am," he said, amused, and to her surprise the "ma'am" was unsettling, as if he were taunting her about her age. It made no sense, so she pushed the feeling to one side and let herself drift into sleep.

CHAPTER NINE

A heart-chilling scream propelled Zara out of bed and across the room—what room? She'd been dreaming of the palace, which had become a maze of endless passages, and it took her a moment to remember this was Ransom's hut. Another scream pressed her into the wall, which caught at her hair. She looked around wildly and saw in one of the windows a monkey, black-furred with its head thrust forward, that pursed its thick black lips at her. It screamed once more, then pulled itself up onto the roof; its footsteps pattered away and then were gone. Zara closed her eyes and waited for her heart rate and breathing to return to normal. That would not go at the top of her list of favorite ways to wake up.

Eventually, she pushed away from the wall, disentangling strands of hair from the woven sticks comprising it, and went to look out the window the monkey had been at. Thick leaves hung low, blocking the view, and the sun streaming through them cast a green light over her, as if she were looking at a stained glass window made of emerald and jade. A depression in the mattress was the only sign Ransom had been there. Why had he left her to sleep instead of rousing her?

Her bladder demanded her attention. Now, where would people who lived in trees relieve themselves? Chamber pots they dumped over the side? She poked around and found, not a chamber pot, but a small niche covered by a wall hanging, containing a waist-high box with a hole in it. She sniffed. The faint odor of human waste, not strong enough to be offensive, rose up from it. After a long moment's indecision, she used it. Probably she was doing it wrong, but she couldn't wait any longer.

She examined the rest of the room while she was sitting. Colorful woven hangings depicting animals she'd never seen before—or were they imaginary?—decorated the walls, their weave as fine as anything she could produce. They were very different from the blanket covering the doorway, which was probably waterproof based on the coarseness of the fibers and the thickness of the weave. It would be interesting to speak to the Karitian weavers, not that she was capable of that.

Something pressed against her thigh. She laid her hand on the lump and remembered the Device. Well, she wasn't likely to get a better chance than this. She finished her business, pulled the Device out, and sat on the mattress to examine it. Solid case, stem and crown that didn't move, leaf pattern around the round edge. She tugged at the crown, then tried pushing it, and again heard a tiny, faraway *thunk* like the smallest footstep imaginable. She twisted the crown while pressing down, and with a click, it rotated, the barest motion. That was progress.

She twisted it again, and again it clicked. She heard nothing else from inside the case, so she kept turning it until it was back to where she'd started. She hoped. She hadn't kept track. Well, she'd learned something. She put it away, pushing it deep into her pocket so it wouldn't fall out or move around. Whatever it was, she'd promised to deliver it, and losing it after bringing it all this way would be awful.

Zara pushed the blanket aside and stepped onto the platform. The air was clear and cool and smelled of growing things, and wasn't very damp, though the humidity would become intolerable later in the day. Nearby were dozens of huts, all clustered around thickly-growing tree trunks. Some of the huts were made of the same woven stick walls her—Ransom's—hut had, but most were made of planed lumber as the platform was. The blankets covering the doorways were vividly colored and elaborately patterned, and Zara saw no duplicates anywhere. Her desire to see the looms increased.

She smelled bread baking somewhere nearby, and the rich scent of meat, and her stomach complained. Maybe she should return to the place they'd eaten the night before. Her worn boots made a thudding sound against the boards, which creaked in harmony: *THUD-creak, THUD-creak*. No one would be in any doubt she was approaching, but she wasn't trying to hide.

She began to see people, mostly half-naked women carrying net bags or baskets and a few scrambling, naked children, their dark brown hair long and bound up on the top of their heads to make horses' tails. The women were all shorter than she was and wore their hair cropped so it curled over their ears, which bore multiple piercings with gold or silver or copper hoops that glinted in the indirect light.

Everyone stopped to look at her as she passed, though the women were polite about their scrutiny and the children gaped openly. One of them who looked to be about eight years old fell into step behind her, raising his bare feet and stomping them on the platform in imitation of her. She turned and smiled at him. He scampered away to hide behind a woman, peeking out from behind her leather skirt with wide, dark eyes. He reminded Zara so much of Telaine's son Owen she felt a moment's pang of homesickness. "He's bold," she said, and the woman regarded her with a lack of comprehension, so Zara smiled again and continued on her way.

It was growing warm under the canopy, not as warm as it had been on the ground, but sweat prickled under her arms and she longed more than ever for a bath. There was probably no point, if they were just going back into the jungle, and she'd have nothing to wear but her old filthy clothes, but the idea was so compelling she had a hard time shaking it.

She retraced their steps of the night before to Belinda and Theo's hut, peeked inside, and found it empty. Arjan and Cantara were gone as well. Why hadn't anyone bothered to wake her? She put her hand on her rumbling stomach. Someone, somewhere, had to know where she could find food.

Eventually she came to the edge of the platform, which had ropes strung around it, probably to keep people from stumbling off in the night. Or the day. Zara peered over the edge, standing as far back as she could. The platform had to be at least eighty feet off the ground. Eighty very long, terrifying feet. If she fell, it wouldn't kill her, it would just leave her with shattered bones and organs pierced by broken ribs and a skull fractured into pieces. How long would it take her to heal from that? And she'd be in agony the whole time. She took a few steps back from the edge and contemplated the bridge. It was two feet wide, too narrow for more than one person to walk abreast, with nothing but a pair of ropes for someone to hold onto. Crossing it in the daylight was out of the question. She'd just have to beg food from one of the women living on this platform.

"Rowena! Come eat with us!"

Belinda waved at Zara from the other side of the bridge. Zara swallowed, trying to moisten her suddenly dry throat. She had to cross. Zara North never let fear rule her. "Coming," she called out, proud of how her voice didn't waver. She put a tentative foot on the first plank and nearly jerked it back when the bridge quivered. Carefully, she took a step, then another, gripping the ropes so tightly she had to make a conscious effort to unclench her fingers every time she took a step. A bird flew beneath the bridge, and she stopped, heart pounding, feeling the bridge sway slightly with her movements. *No. No fear.*

She closed her eyes and took another step. That made it worse. Belinda was still standing there, watching her. What was she thinking? That Rowena was terrified for no reason? Except there was a reason, there were eighty good reasons for her to be afraid of this bridge. She tried walking faster, which made the bridge sway more, and that unnerved her enough that she made herself go even faster, hoping to reach the far side before the whole thing tipped her over and sent her plummeting to the ground below.

"It's fun, isn't it?" Belinda said when Zara took the last few running steps onto the relatively solid ground of the platform. "My father built us children a tree house when I was young, but this is so much better."

"You're cheerful this morning."

"I feel more rested than I have been in days. Well, obviously I am. And this place is delightful. The people are so nice, even if we can't understand each other." Belinda began to walk away. "Come, there's food, and then I think Mister Tamun wants to show us around. I don't know why he'd do it, there must be better things a ruler can do with his time, but Ransom said it was polite to accept."

"Where is Ransom?"

"I don't know. He ate breakfast with us, and then he was gone. Why did they put you in with him?"

"I don't know," Zara managed. "It saved room, probably. Why didn't he wake me?"

"You needed rest. You've been working harder than anyone." Belinda put her hand on Zara's arm. "Thanks for helping me. And saving my life. I don't know if I could have survived that snake bite, even with Ransom's healing."

"I don't mind," Zara said. Belinda's gratitude made her feel uncomfortable. Most people's gratitude did, come to think on it. She did what needed doing, usually what no one else could do, and it felt wrong to accept thanks when she was only being herself. Accepting thanks was one of the things she still hadn't mastered, even in eighty-seven years of life.

The hut where they'd eaten the night before was, in daylight, bigger than Zara realized and smelled deliciously of cooked, spiced chicken and fresh fruit. With the windows on either side of the door frame and the ragged wooden shingles of the roof, it looked like the face of a man with a giant blue and white mouth in need of a haircut. She inhaled the scent of food again and had to make herself walk slowly and not rush to the door. She'd never been this hungry in her life.

"Good morning," Cantara said. Theo nodded at Zara, his mouth full of food. Sitting cross-legged beside him was Kossrek Tamun, who looked less menacing in the warm light of day but still gave Zara the impression that violence was an option if they stepped wrong. She smiled pleasantly at him and let one of the villagers fill her leaf-plate before eating as daintily as her starving stomach would let her.

After eating her fill under Kossrek Tamun's glowering eye, she and her friends followed him across the platform. Everyone they met bowed to him, hands crossed on their chests and heads lowered; Tamun acknowledged them with a complicated ceremonial wave. A memory came to Zara from the distant past, of riding through the streets of Aurilien and waving at cheering citizens. If she hadn't had this…gift…would she still be alive, receiving those accolades? It all seemed so far away, but not like a dream — more like a story she'd read once that was so real it seemed she'd lived it. Which she had.

Tamun led them to the edge of the platform and another bridge. This one — Zara had to swallow against the dryness in her throat again — was longer and, sweet heaven, sloped downward. She could hear the noise of the river now, a rustling, airy sound beneath the constant cries of the brightly colored birds who swooped the length of the village and roosted in the canopy just above.

She hung back as the others crossed. None of them seemed at all bothered by the fact that they were high enough for birds to fly underneath them. If she'd been at all willing to look down, she was sure she'd see clouds below the bridge. When she made it across she surreptitiously fanned herself with her shirt to dry the sweat she'd broken into halfway across. This was ridiculous. She wasn't afraid of anything.

She fanned herself again, wishing the morning cool had lasted longer. She wasn't quite daring enough to take off her shirt and uncomfortable brassiere and go naked like the other women, though it would be so comfortable to be wearing a skirt. Tamun was speaking and gesturing, and Zara tried to pay attention to what he was showing them. The construction of the huts, probably, and the way they cooked their food over…could they even have fires up here? They had torches, so it couldn't be that dangerous. And maybe she'd see the loom, assuming the villagers were the ones who wove the fabric.

Tamun stood at the edge off the platform, so Zara made herself go as far as the ropes and look down. "It's a sawmill," Theo said, his dark face alight with interest. "It's where they get all the lumber."

Far below, perched at the edge of the fast-flowing river, was a sawmill that was the virtual duplicate of the one outside Longbourne. Tiny figures went in and out of it, some of them loading lumber onto carts, others guiding logs out of the water into the shallows. It looked so much like the mill back home Zara couldn't help feeling another pang of homesickness. That was unacceptable. She could never go back to Barony Steepridge, and it was ridiculous to entertain those feelings.

"I'm ashamed to say I thought these people were savages," Belinda murmured, though Tamun wasn't paying any attention to them and no doubt didn't speak their language. "Do you suppose that's why they showed this to us?"

"They must be proud of it," Zara said in the same low voice. "Ransom said they've adopted new technologies even as they've kept their old customs. I wonder if the rest of Dineh-Karit—the city dwellers, I mean—patronize them as much as we would have."

Tamun put a hand on Zara's arm, and she jerked away without thinking. To her surprise, Tamun looked puzzled rather than offended. Then he laughed and patted her shoulder, and said something in Karitian. He gestured, and said, "Come," in thickly accented Tremontanese.

"Oh, heaven, he speaks our language," Belinda said, her rosy face crimson with embarrassment.

"I'm sure he only knows a few words." Zara waved at the others to follow Tamun, and prayed he wasn't going to leave the platform.

To her astonishment, Tamun not only didn't leave the platform, but for the next hour took them from hut to hut, showing off dozens of Devices. Few of them were cased in metal the way Zara was accustomed to, but the wood and vines of their construction were very fine, and their functions were more sophisticated than Zara would have guessed. There were Devices for doing household tasks like cooking and sewing clothes, Devices that raised and lowered small platforms to the jungle floor, other Devices that did things Zara had never even thought of wanting a Device to do. Tamun demonstrated a box like the one she'd used to relieve herself that morning, filling her with relief that she'd guessed its use correctly. She pushed the button that whisked the waste away she didn't know where, and felt increasingly embarrassed at the assumptions she'd made about these people just because they ate off leaves and didn't wear as many clothes as she did.

She turned away and heard, distantly, the thumping, rattling sound of a loom. Without considering whether it was impolite or not, she walked away from their little group and followed her ears to one of the largest huts she'd seen so far. Its walls were only waist-height; poles held up the shingled roof, letting the sun fully illuminate the loom. The man operating it glanced up as she approached, but turned his attention immediately back to his work. Zara leaned against one of the poles and closed her eyes, enjoying the noise it made. It, too, felt like a memory, even though it had been no more than six weeks since she'd sat at her loom for the last time, finishing the last bolt of cloth. She breathed in the indefinable smell the loom gave off.

She nodded at the weaver, one craftsman to another, then turned away as Tamun passed by with the others. She trailed at the back of the group again, then had to step farther back as a couple of naked children ran past her. She turned to watch them go and saw Ransom seated on a stool with a child on his lap, gently feeling her throat and then holding her eyelids open to peer into her eyes. Zara watched the rest of the examination, fascinated, until he set the girl down and wiggled her nose gently, making her laugh and run away past Zara. Ransom took another child on his lap and said, "Interested in medicine?"

"Just surprised to see you have a soft side."

"Don't worry, I'll be my normal irascible self by the time we leave." He took his extremely modern stethoscope from around his neck and handed it to the child to play with while he examined the boy's feet.

"Is this something you do often?"

"Every time I come through this way. Give the children a physical examination, treat infections and larval infestations—it's a real problem out here. Do some healing if necessary. But mostly I bring medicines so they can take care of themselves without depending on me."

"That sounds generous."

"They pay me in supplies and a little coin. It's a business relationship."

Zara observed how gently he held the little boy. "I can see that."

Ransom retrieved the stethoscope. "Did you see the loom?"

"It's marvelous."

Someone wrapped their arms around her legs. A child, no more than two, looked up at Zara and smiled at her, saying something in Karitian. Little Julia was only a year older. Homesickness again swept over Zara, and she had to blink hard to dispel the tears that tried to form. No crying. Not ever. She'd long ago come to terms with her barrenness, and Telaine's children had been enough to satisfy her desire for her own. She squatted and picked up the little girl. Like the others, she almost looked Eskandelic, with her brown skin and hair, though all the Karitians Zara had seen had brown eyes, not the hazel or gray that were typical of Eskandelics. "Hello, little one," she said. "You remind me of my niece."

The little girl kissed Zara's cheek, then wiggled to get down. Stunned, Zara released her and watched her run away. She touched her cheek. They were so trusting at that age, so quick to give affection.

"I didn't know you have family," Ransom said, standing and waving the lingering children away.

"Since your inherent magic is healing and not mind reading, that doesn't surprise me," Zara snapped. What she didn't need was this man trying to dig more secrets out of her.

"Sorry," he said. "None of my business."

His carefully neutral tone of voice made her feel ashamed. "No, I'm sorry. I shouldn't have snapped at you."

"I'd have done the same if you'd pried into my family life. It's not something I like to think about."

He turned to leave, and Zara said, "One of my grandnieces knows my secret. I lived near her family for the last ten years. She has three children, and I had to leave them all behind because my young face was starting to cause talk. I don't like remembering them. Too painful."

Ransom bowed his head. "I see." He glanced back over his shoulder at Zara. "I have a sister I haven't seen in five years," he said. "We were close, growing up, but then she got involved with the

Resurgence, and I...well. She wrote to me for a year, before I left Tammerek for the jungle, and every word was recrimination. I'm glad your family memories are better than mine."

It was more honesty than she'd ever thought to hear from him. "Thank you," she said.

Ransom smiled at her, for once not sardonic or amused, just...friendly. "Let's go have some food, and then I have some more work to do, but we should be able to leave this afternoon."

Zara shuddered. "Is that ladder really safe to descend?"

"The villagers use it all the time." Ransom looked at her more closely, then said, with his usual sardonic air, "But they also have a lift to bring things to and from the jungle floor. I'm sure they'd let you ride it."

"Don't do me any favors." Embarrassment sharpened her tongue.

"As if I'd do anything to put you in my debt. It's not as if I care about your secrets." He grinned at her. "You can watch my supplies, keep them from flinging themselves over the side. That's a long way down."

Zara refused to let herself shudder a second time. "I'd be happy to do you a favor," she said. "And you can stop prying into my affairs."

"Gladly," Ransom said, as if she'd promised him a treat instead.

After dinner, which was a salad of unfamiliar greens and chopped vegetables with round flat bread and more water, Zara waved away her friends' invitation to explore and settled herself outside the dining hut, watching the villagers pass. All of them glanced at her as they walked by, though none of them stopped or said anything, even to each other. Their conversations picked up when they were several feet past her, hushed words that no doubt were about the strangers the doctor had brought with him.

Most of the passersby were women, which made sense given Ransom's comments about the role of women in this society. They carried baskets or bags and sometimes trailed children, just as the men and women of Longbourne did. Zara observed how they interacted with one another, made note of friendships and rivalries and dislikes, and enjoyed the feeling of not fighting through the jungle undergrowth, watching for snakes and *najabedhi* and poisonous plants.

"I'm surprised you aren't off poking your nose into every corner you can find," Ransom said. Zara looked up at him. He wore his usual sardonic expression, but there was no malice in his voice.

"How do you know I'm not?" she replied. "People are far more interesting than corners."

"And what have you learned?"

"That people are the same wherever you go. Though I'm surprised those two—" she pointed—"haven't come to blows yet."

"They have, in the past." Ransom extended his hand to help her up. "And will again. You're observant for an old woman."

"It's because I'm an old woman I'm observant. Are we going somewhere?"

"We're going down river. I thought I'd show you the lift. Let you keep an eye on my things. Wouldn't want them stolen on the way down."

Zara shrugged. "It's nothing to me whether I take the lift or the ladder," she lied.

"Well, I'd appreciate it." He grinned and winked at her before heading off across the bridge. Zara shuddered and followed him, slowly, pretending not to see him ostentatiously waiting for her at the far side.

The lift turned out to be a six-foot square pallet with ropes surrounding its perimeter like a smaller version of the platforms. Two of the villagers were piling boxes and sacks onto it, arranging them in a neat pattern that kept the lift balanced, though it looked sturdy enough even for Zara. Ransom strolled up to the two young men and said something that made them laugh and look at Zara. One of them said something in a low voice, punching Ransom lightly on the arm. Ransom pretended to be injured and replied in an even lower voice. The two men looked at Zara again, this time curiously, and one of them said something that had to be a question. Ransom nodded, and the two men broke out into uproarious laughter.

Zara folded her arms across her chest and glared at Ransom. "What did they say?"

"They congratulated me on my conquest and wished me joy of our union," Ransom said. "They think you're beautiful, for a northern savage."

"What a compliment," Zara said sourly. "Young men only think about one thing. It's tedious."

"I guess everyone's young to you," Ransom said. He wasn't smiling anymore. "Let me give you a hand."

"I—" Zara began, but he'd already taken hold of her waist and lifted her across the divide. Zara wobbled, sat down more quickly than she'd intended, and put out both hands to steady herself. From this position, she couldn't see the ground, and the muscles of her back and legs relaxed. "Thanks," she said.

"Stay where you are, and you'll be fine," Ransom said. "Though it's just as far to the ground on that thing as it is on the ladder. Don't worry, nobody's fallen off the lift in at least three years. And I'm sure the ropes aren't worn through at all."

"Ransom!" Zara began. It came out as a squeak, so she cleared her throat to try again, but he was already receding from view. It made her angry that he'd been so abrupt, so dismissive, when they'd been getting along so well…oh, heaven, what had she said about young men? She'd forgotten he was young, too. Guilt welled up inside her and she ruthlessly pushed it away. He hadn't been offended; he was just permanently cranky, that's all, and if he *had* been offended, it would pass. Drawing attention to it by apologizing was a bad idea. It wasn't as if they were friends.

Whatever Device lowered the lift did it smoothly, keeping it perfectly level, and Zara never felt a moment's fear—though she wasn't brave enough to move to the edge to look over. At the bottom, a couple of villagers waited to unload the boxes, though neither of them offered to help her, which pleased her. She stood on slightly wobbly feet and stretched.

"Oh, I wish I'd thought to ask to ride down!" Belinda said. "It must be just like floating."

"It was comfortable," Zara said. Arjan was stepping off the ladder, and Zara looked up to see Ransom descending. She turned away and said, "Aren't we walking?"

"They're loaning us a boat," Theo said. He took up one of the sacks and handed it over to a man standing in a boat with high, lacquered sides, who stowed it somewhere in the bottom. "Actually, they're loaning Ransom a boat, and it's big enough for all of us to ride."

Attached to the rear of the boat was a corroded, tarnished brass and silver Device hooked over the stern gunwale. Its long tail curved and flexed like a fat snake, splashing the water where it struck the surface. A wooden wheel bound with brass perched atop the body of the Device, and a tiller extended forward from it. Zara went to look at it more closely. Why didn't Tremontane have these? Suppose you could make a giant one and never have to depend on sail again? Or maybe that was impossible, and that's why Tremontane didn't have them.

The boat bounced against the dock to which it was tethered, but only lightly, and the man loading the cargo had no trouble staying balanced. The current of the river foamed against the boat's hull and the struts of the pier.

"Us, but not the donkey," Cantara said, making a face. "It would make much noise and smell, I think."

"Nettles is better behaved than that," Ransom said, coming up behind them. "But he won't fit, so he's staying behind. Possibly as a hostage. Getting this thing back upstream is going to be a misery."

"Then why don't we all walk?" Zara said.

"Because I want this over with as soon as possible, and river travel will cut our journey's time in half." Ransom glanced briefly at Zara. "You're not afraid of the river, are you, Miss Farrell?"

So he *was* offended. Stupid. "Of course not. I liked ocean travel, and I'm sure the river can't be much different. What happens when we reach the coast?"

"This boat is faster than a sailboat and more maneuverable, but it's still not much more than a rowboat, so it won't be safe for us to go out of sight of land. We'll follow the coast to Tammerek, drop you all off, and I'll wave you a merry goodbye as I sail away into the sunrise. Metaphorically speaking."

"Is Tammerek what they call Goudge's Folly, then?" Belinda said.

"Yes. Now, all of you, into the boat, and find seats. It's going to be tight quarters, and we'll have to pull in to shore at night, but we'll be rid of each other soon enough."

"Don't do us any favors," Zara said. Even for Ransom, that was harsh. "We wouldn't want to put you out."

"Too late for that," Ransom said. "Settle in, and I'll cast off." He spun the wheel a couple of times, and the tail of the Device began thrashing rhythmically, like an oar that could row in all directions at once. The boat strained harder against its tether, a fish ready to leap downstream to the sea. Zara took a place near the bow where she could watch the river. It was coincidental that it was far away from their unwilling guide. It was better not to give him an opportunity to clash with her.

The river flowed by like liquid glass, not as fast as the river near Longbourne where the sawmill was, but fast enough that Ransom was probably right and they'd make good time. And then she'd be at Goudge's Folly, ready to start her new life. After this, it would probably seem boring. She told herself boring was good.

Chapter Ten

The river carried them along at a fast clip, fast enough that Ransom used the Device mainly to keep the boat near the center of the river and away from rocks. At times, the river slowed enough that Zara could appreciate the land slipping away past them. It was cooler on the river, cooler and less humid, which she thought was strange given how close they were to the water. A million shades of green spread out in every direction, turning the water muddy with their reflections, and Zara would have been tempted to dabble her fingers in the current if she hadn't remembered the caimans. She sat at the prow and amused herself by pretending to be a figurehead, bringing luck to their voyage. A figurehead. Thank heaven those days were far behind her.

She heard quiet conversations going on behind her, Belinda talking to Cantara, Theo asking questions Ransom answered curtly but not unkindly. So he was going to take his bad mood out only on her, was he? More guilt surfaced. She never thought of him as young—never thought in terms of his age, when his experience in these surroundings made him far wiser than she was despite the sixty-year difference in their ages. *He overreacted, it's not your fault*, she told herself, but she was having trouble believing it.

They floated downstream until the sun was low and the trees cast long black shadows over the river, then Arjan, taking a turn at the helm, steered the boat to the western bank, where the ground sloped shallowly to the river and provided an easy berth. Zara scrambled out and took hold of the prow to help pull it onto shore. "We can do that," Arjan said.

"And it will be easier if we all help," Zara said.

"There's no point in arguing with her," Ransom said. "Even if her efforts would be better spent unloading the food."

Zara let go of the boat and stepped back, crossing her arms over her chest. "I'm sure you know best, captain," she said.

"I do, Miss Farrell." Ransom took her place and began pulling. "Water, fire, food, in that order — unless you have a better idea?"

"I'm surprised you'll let anyone do any of the work, given that you're such an expert on doing everything."

"I don't think getting water takes much skill. Maybe you could do that."

"I will." Zara snatched the pot out of its box and stormed away upstream. Safely behind a couple of bushes, she leaned over to fill the pot, as far from the shallows as she could so she wouldn't collect too much silt with the water. She'd forgotten he was a stubborn, selfish man who had to be prodded into doing the right thing. The sooner they were parted, the better.

"Rowena?" Belinda stood a short distance behind the bush. "Is something wrong?"

"Of course not," Zara lied. "It's just been a long day. I'm sorry I'm so short-tempered."

"I don't think that's it." Belinda came to crouch beside her on the bank. "I've never heard you be so rude before."

"I never had so much provocation." More guilt. Provocation was no excuse. She was eighty-seven years old, and she should have better self-control than that. "Everything will be all right in the morning."

"I hope so." Belinda picked up a pebble and flung it across the river. It skipped six times before sinking. "I think — never mind."

"What?"

"Nothing. Just what I thought before — that you and Ransom are too much alike to be comfortable companions. Come, let's go back and get this water boiling."

Ransom was gone when they returned. Arjan, building a fire, said, "He goes to hunt, but I do not know what."

Cantara said, "I wish we do not need him. He…I think the word 'resent' is. Resents us."

"He's a man of his word. He'll take us where we need to be even if he's resentful," Zara said.

"I thought he was starting to like us, though," Theo said. "He was rude to you, Rowena."

"Well, I was rude to him in return. Not that that makes it all right." Zara set the pot over the fire and went to help Belinda cut vegetables. *You need to apologize,* the tiny voice of her conscience said. It was far too morally correct for an imaginary thing.

Ransom pushed through the bushes, and Belinda screamed. Zara shot to her feet. A gigantic pink snake draped around his neck and hung down nearly to his knees. "Ransom!" she exclaimed, then realized the snake had no head and wasn't moving except when Ransom did. "Oh," she said, breathing out in relief.

"Worried about my safety?" Ransom said with his familiar sardonic grin. "Or the snake's?"

"Worried it was trying to eat you," Zara said, rallying. "We'd be trapped here without you."

"Ah, pragmatic to the end." He set down the rifle and heavy blade and unlooped the snake from around himself, revealing that it was pink because its skin was gone. It had been slit down the middle and its guts removed. "I thought fresh meat might be welcome."

"I cannot eat that," Cantara said, her brown skin gone pale.

"Don't worry, it's not venomous. This kind strangles its prey. And I skinned and gutted it far from camp, so it won't bring predators down on us." Ransom dropped the snake in a heap in front of Zara. "If you cut it into sections, I'll roast them."

"Of course," Zara said. The thing looked slimy, and had bits of dirt clinging to it from where it had landed on the ground, but she felt no distaste. And even if she had, she wouldn't give him the satisfaction. "Knife, Belinda?"

Ransom's grin became amused. "I should have known you wouldn't be overcome by anything this jungle threw at you."

"Nor anything you throw at me, apparently," she shot back, and began cutting thick...could you call them steaks? At any rate, thick pieces out of the dead snake. Ransom laughed and walked away.

Snake meat turned out to be delicious, if somewhat gamy, and Ransom was right: fresh meat revived them all. There was more than they could eat, so Ransom put the leftovers in a sack and hoisted it high above the trees, some distance from where they slept. "It probably won't be disturbed," he said, "but if it is, whoever gets it is welcome to it."

"Do you mean it might attract predators?" Theo said.

"Possibly." Ransom shrugged. "Not likely. But I think, with Nettles not here, we should set watches tonight. I'll go first, then Arjan, then Theo."

"Then me," Zara said.

"I think three is sufficient, Miss Farrell."

"Then four will be even better. Unless you think I'm not capable of screaming an alarm?"

"I think you're capable of waking a battalion if you choose. But it's not necessary."

"And I say it is."

"Do you ever let anyone be chivalrous on your behalf?"

Zara glared at him. "What exactly do you think you're protecting me from? A lack of sleep?"

Ransom shook his head. "Do what you like. Four watches is probably better. Now — go to sleep."

Zara settled some distance from the fire and watched Ransom pace its circumference. He managed to steer wide of her while behaving as if she didn't exist, which took some doing, and her conscience began prodding her again. She closed her eyes and tried to sleep. The ground was hard, with very little topsoil to cushion her, and after a moment she opened her eyes and rolled onto her side. Ransom had finished his circuit and was now sitting with the rifle across his lap and his back to the fire, on the side opposite her, and despite herself she had to smile. They were both behaving like babies, and as the older and far more mature, it was her job to do something about it.

She rose quietly, hoping not to wake Belinda or Theo, who slept nearby, and went around the fire to sit beside Ransom. "It's a quiet night," she said, and it was. The sound of the river drowned out all the nearer sounds, the insects humming or whistling and the night birds calling to one another.

"It was until you started talking," Ransom said.

Zara bit back an irritated retort. "I'm sorry," she said.

Ransom was silent for a moment. "Sorry for what?" he finally said, in a tone of voice that said he knew exactly what she was talking about.

"For being rude to you, even indirectly. For making crass generalizations. I never remember how young you are. I apologize."

More silence. "I'd think someone of your age would always be conscious of other people's."

"I'm usually more conscious of how people behave. Sometimes the youngest are the ones who are most mature. And you'd be surprised at how immature the elderly can be." She laughed. "I tend to forget I'm one of the elderly."

"And you don't think of me as young."

"I don't think of your age at all. Not when you have so many irritating habits to define you instead."

Ransom chuckled. "Like being rude to an old woman who makes snap judgments about the youth of today?"

"Like telling me I'm not fit to stand watch because I'm a woman."

He shrugged. "I occasionally break out in a rash of chivalry. Don't hold it against me."

"I won't. So long as you don't let it override your good sense."

"I'm flattered you think I have any."

Zara smiled. "I don't think you could survive out here without it. And…thank you. Again."

"For what?"

"For guiding us. I hope you know we appreciate it."

Ransom shrugged. "You're not that much of a burden. I'm just cranky and set in my ways."

"Well, so am I. But I think, between the two of us, we can get everyone to Goudge's Folly safely, and you can be back to your old ways."

Ransom looked off into the undergrowth. "Right," he said. "You should get some sleep if you're going to insist on taking a watch."

"All right," Zara said, mystified by his abruptness. She went back to her place, but continued to watch him as he sat by the fire, hunched over slightly and perfectly still. When the firelight started to burn her eyes, she closed them, and soon afterward dropped into sleep.

She slept peacefully until Theo shook her awake, then stretched and made the circuit of the camp. She left the rifle on the ground near the fire; she didn't know how to shoot and this didn't seem the time to learn. Arjan and Cantara were nestled together as usual, Arjan with his arm draped protectively around his *majdran*, though it was unlikely he thought of her as his stepmother no matter what word you used. She hoped again that Goudge's Folly was far enough away from Eskandel to protect them.

Belinda lay on her back, her breath whistling in and out of her nostrils in a sound too light to be called a snore. She'd borne up well, never complaining even though Zara knew she wasn't strong enough for a journey like this. Could she make a new life for herself, penniless as she now was? No doubt whatever job she took, she'd end up running the business in five years.

Theo was already asleep again, one hand clutching his belt. She wasn't sure anyone else had noticed how tightly he always held on to it—wasn't sure *he* realized how tightly he held it—and she was reluctant to simply come out and ask him. It was probably no mystery, just the money his father had given him for the journey, but she was curious and tempted to investigate it while he slept—no, that would be a betrayal of the trust that had grown between them, and that wasn't worth satisfying her curiosity.

And Ransom. She paused for a moment next to him. He looked his age when he slept, young and vulnerable in a way that made her embarrassed to look at him, as if she were trespassing on private ground. Why had she told him so many truths about herself? Come to think on it, why had she wanted to share those secrets in the first place, let alone with a total stranger? But then, he'd been candid with her, too, telling her about his family in that level tone without a hint of his usual good humor.

113

Being a thing, a figurehead — that was something Zara understood, even though she didn't resent having been Queen and hadn't had it forced on her by a family who didn't care anything about her personally. Did Telaine know about the Resurgence? Zara couldn't begin to guess how her grandniece would feel about an organization that wanted to make it possible for her to be open about her inherent magic, though she had a suspicion Telaine might not be keen on giving up the edge of being secretly able to hear lies that were spoken to her.

She watched, listening to the river, until the sky grew light and she could see the murky outlines of trees clearly, watch the leaves quiver in the faint morning breeze. It would disappear by noon, so she took pleasure in the moment. The jungle was beautiful, even when it was trying to kill you.

Something rustled in the undergrowth, away from the river, and Zara tensed, listening for more. Silence. Then more rustling. Zara glanced back at Ransom. If this turned out to be nothing, he'd mock her, but was that really a good reason not to be sensible? He would know better than she what kind of danger this was. She knelt at his side and gently shook him awake. A moment's confusion flickered across his face, then he focused on her. "Trouble?"

"I don't know. Something's moving in the bushes over there."

Ransom rolled to his feet and moved swiftly to the far side of their camp, picking up the rifle as he went. The thing, whatever it was, disturbed more bushes, but farther away. "Stay here," he said. "It's probably just a wild pig or some kind of monkey."

"If whatever it is attacks you, you'll need help," Zara pointed out.

"And if something comes on the camp while we're both gone, we're going to feel stupid."

"It's almost dawn. Nothing's going to attack the camp unless it's this thing. You need my help."

Ransom rolled his eyes. "Is there anything I can say that will convince you?"

"No."

"Then stay behind me, and stay quiet. We'll probably just have to scare it off."

Zara followed as closely as she dared. The sounds of the jungle at night were unfamiliar, as if the animals of the day were replaced by completely different ones, which might be true. Zara ducked vines and pushed aside trailing branches, praying the snakes were all still indoors and asleep. She had no desire to be bitten again. The smell of plants crushed underfoot mingled with the richer smell of rotting vegetation, a smell that was almost alive itself. Somewhere nearby, a monkey screeched and went instantly silent. Zara pictured a baby monkey being hushed by its mother as she put it to bed. Were the monkeys as bothered as she by the loud chirruping and whirring and humming of the millions, maybe billions of insects?

Ransom stopped and held out a hand behind him, waving her to silence. Zara froze mid-step. Then Ransom swiftly raised the rifle to his shoulder, and the underbrush exploded with the sounds of grunting and leaves rustling. Something rushed past Zara, making her wobble and begin to fall. A hand steadied her. "Wild pig, and a young one," Ransom said. "Wish I'd been quicker. They're much tastier than snakes."

"I never thought I'd regret not catching a pig," Zara said.

"Well, as long as we're out here, let's see if we can't find some food. And we'll take that bag of snake meat back to camp."

"It didn't taste so awful. It's not sausage and eggs, but it can't be that bad a breakfast."

"You must have slept well. That was almost optimistic." Ransom pushed aside some low-growing branches and held them for Zara to pass. "There, those are pineapples. They don't usually grow around here, but I'm not going to reject heaven's gift." He set down the rifle, drew his notched knife, and held the dusty green spikes growing from the plant's top steady while he slashed at the base.

"I've never had pineapple. Is it good?"

"Delicious. Juicy, sweet and tangy, very filling. We can drink—"

A scream rang out over the trees, cut off by the sound of a gunshot. Another shot, and then something flew into the sky and exploded with a fiery pinkish-red light. It burned itself out just as another flare exploded near it.

"That's our camp," Ransom said. He dropped the pineapple and grabbed the gun. "We have to get back."

"Wait," Zara said, grabbing his arm. "Those flares were either a warning or a summons. Either way, whoever's at our camp isn't friendly and has friends somewhere else. We need to be cautious."

"That gunshot might mean someone was killed."

"We won't do them any good if we get ourselves killed as well."

"Then follow me. Keep close behind. If we can sneak up on them…"

"Let's wait to make plans until we see what's there."

Ransom set off, more slowly this time, and Zara followed him, watching where he stepped and following as closely as she dared. She caught a branch he pushed aside and released it gingerly behind her. That wild pig had better not be in the area anymore, because if they stumbled on it, so much for stealth.

Nothing looked familiar; she hadn't been watching their trail closely, and now she cursed herself for having left the camp unguarded. She should have woken everyone, or at least stayed behind…and been attacked, or captured, or killed, whatever the fate of her companions was. At least Ransom hadn't criticized her for her mistake, though he might only be waiting to do that until they discovered what had happened. She hoped it wasn't the kind of mistake that had just gotten one of her friends killed.

CHAPTER ELEVEN

She heard voices in the distance that grew louder with every step until she could almost make out what they were saying: men's voices, a couple of women, arguing over something. She didn't hear anyone she recognized, which could mean Belinda and the others were...she refused to consider that possibility. Only one shot, so — *Stop borrowing trouble.*

She took a few more steps and nearly tripped over Ransom, who'd stopped and crouched behind an overgrown bush taller than either of them. "Through there," he whispered, and Zara crouched beside him. Ransom pushed aside the lowest branches, giving them an unobstructed view of their campsite.

The first thing Zara saw was Belinda, sprawled on the ground with her hands flung out. Zara swallowed a cry of horror. If Belinda was dead, there was nothing Zara could do about it. A stranger crossed in front of their hiding place, someone wearing tattered trousers and boots dark with water stains. Beyond that, beyond Belinda, another stranger held Arjan fast in his grip. Arjan had blood running down the side of his face and looked furious. Zara couldn't see Theo or Cantara. She heard the sound of bags being emptied and boxes being kicked open. *"Not here,"* someone said in Eskandelic. *"There aren't any Devices at all."*

Another stranger stepped in front of Arjan and punched him in the stomach, making him groan. *"Where is it?"* the woman said. Arjan said nothing. She punched him again. *"Talk, or I start hurting the woman."*

Cantara screamed, *"We don't know anything! Leave us alone!"*

Ransom nudged Zara. "Six," he whispered, holding up six fingers for emphasis. "See if you can pull some of them away, and I'll attack the ones who stay."

"I'll get lost if I try to draw them from the camp," Zara whispered

117

back. "You have to go."

"Not to be insulting, but there's no way you can overpower even one of those people."

"Then you circle back around to help. We don't have much choice."

Ransom scowled, but began backing away. "There are three to the right," he said. "Go that way and approach from the side closest the river, then get everyone onto the ship."

"I know what to do. Give me a minute to get into position."

Ransom was gone almost before she finished speaking. Zara, still crouching, moved as quietly as she could, keeping low and staying in the shade of the giant trees around which bushes and tall grass grew intermittently. She wished she could take advantage of the more open spaces, which were easier to travel through and didn't have all those noisy plants for her to disrupt, but she needed camouflage more than she needed speed.

Cantara shouted again, and Arjan cried out in pain, then his captor issued a long stream of commands in Eskandelic she didn't have time to listen to. These had to be the pirates who'd attacked the *Emma Covington*; it was too much of a coincidence that there were two groups looking for a Device. How they'd found them...but there was no time to worry about that.

Zara ducked under a low-growing plant with skinny jade-green leaves and realized the smell of water had grown stronger just as she came out on the riverbank. The boat was drawn up a dozen yards away, and there was the path they'd made that wound through the shelter of the trees across bare ground. That would take too long. They'd have to make a straight run for it.

"Hey! You there! What are you doing?" Ransom's voice rang out clearly through the morning air.

"*Who's that?*" the pirate woman said. "*Don't let him get away! You two, stay here!*" Then there was the sound of running feet, crashing through the undergrowth, and Arjan groaning, and then nothing. Zara cast about for inspiration. Ahead, under one of the trees, she saw a fallen branch, bent and shedding its thin bark. She ran and picked it up. It was heavy and awkward, but better than nothing. She moved off down the path they'd made, this time needing silence rather than concealment.

She stopped several feet back from the camp and ducked to one side, holding the branch at waist height to keep it from tangling in the vines hanging from the trees. As she neared their camp, she saw the head of one of the pirates, arms akimbo, and realized this was the man holding Arjan. She'd hoped to attack the other and let Arjan take advantage of the distraction to free himself, but he hadn't looked capable of fighting back.

She tried not to think about the possibility that he couldn't get himself to the ship. She might be able to carry Belinda — *she's alive, she's just unconscious* — but Arjan was far too heavy, possibly too heavy for her and Theo combined. She had no idea what condition Theo was in, but she guessed the other pirate had him in hand. Well, it was a good plan — no, it was a terrible plan, but it was the only one she could think of. If Theo was alert and in a position to fight, if there really were only two pirates, if Belinda wasn't dead…there was a lot of "if" involved, but she had to act quickly and pray it was enough.

She stood swiftly, took two steps, and brought the stick around in a great sweeping arc at the pirate's head. It connected with a satisfying *thunk*, causing the man to grunt in pain and then, to Zara's surprise, collapse, taking Arjan with him. The other pirate cried out in surprise, and as Zara burst into the clearing, stick raised, Theo broke free of the man's grip and smashed his nose with a two-fisted punch. Cantara leaped to her feet, pivoted, and kicked the man in the throat in one smooth motion that had Zara gaping. A trained *arakeli* dancer? The Takjashi would definitely never stop hunting them.

The man choked, gagged, and covered his face as Cantara followed her kick by scything his legs out from under him and punching him in the stomach as he went down. Theo leaped on him, struck him and kicked him until the pirate lay curled unconscious on the ground. Zara grabbed Theo's shoulders and said, "That's enough!

We have to get everyone out of here!"

"Where's Ransom?" Theo panted, his eyes wild and his hands shaking with fury.

"Making a distraction. Help me."

Cantara was already at Arjan's side, trying to get him to rise. "They say they will kill us if we do not give them the Device," she said. "I do not know what Device it is."

"Even if we had it, they'd kill us anyway once they got it," Zara said. She got her shoulder under Arjan's arm, and he stirred and groaned. "Theo—"

"I can stand," Arjan said, but he wobbled, and Theo had to support him. Zara ran to Belinda's side and felt for a pulse. Still alive, thank heaven. She rolled Belinda onto her back and wormed her arms under her shoulders and knees, then heaved, grunted, and managed to stand. She staggered after the others, who had realized—or at least Theo had—where they needed to go. Belinda stirred, muttered something incomprehensible, then fell unconscious again. She had a fist-sized lump on the side of her head, but otherwise seemed unharmed.

"Get him into the bow," she told Theo, who helped Arjan move to the front of the boat, then began unshipping the oars. Zara laid Belinda near Arjan; it made the bow sag, but not much. Zara got out of the boat and began shoving.

"We can't leave Ransom!" Theo said.

"We won't. We just have to be as close to pushing off as possible when he comes."

Arjan groaned again and sat up. "I can steer," he said, stepping over Belinda and nudging Cantara to take his place. "No, I a fool am not, I well am not, but I think if they catch us I will not care if I well am."

"All right. Cantara, watch Belinda." Zara left the boat and took a few steps back toward the clearing. She wished she hadn't had to leave the branch, which hadn't been a great weapon but had at least kept her from feeling totally helpless. She wished she had some way to tell

Ransom they were safe. Pity their magics weren't the power of shared thoughts, though aside from this one moment, that would be an extremely awkward inherent magic for two virtual strangers to share. She certainly didn't want Ransom knowing her secret thoughts and she didn't think, curiosity aside, she wanted to know his.

There. Footsteps, approaching rapidly. Zara took a few more steps toward the clearing and was about to whisper Ransom's name before a stranger came running out of the undergrowth and knocked Zara over.

The stranger's surprise gave Zara time to roll out from under the woman and grab her wrist before she could bring her pistol to bear. In the next second, Zara realized her assailant was the pirate captain Ghazarian. Zara slammed the pirate's wrist into the mucky ground, once, twice, and the third time the woman's fingers splayed open and the gun spun away from them both.

Ghazarian twisted, yanked away from Zara's grip, and punched her in the stomach, driving the air out of Zara's lungs and making her gasp for breath. Ghazarian tried to sit up, and Zara, dizzy and seeing light-rimmed black spots, slammed her forehead against the pirate's and heard the woman hiss with pain. Immediately, she rolled away, felt something hard dig into her shoulder, rolled again and came up with the gun. Ghazarian, who'd almost risen to her feet, froze.

Zara kept the pistol trained on the woman's chest and stood, slowly, not letting her aim waver. "Back away," she said.

"That yours is not," Ghazarian said.

"Doesn't matter, does it, if I'm the one holding it."

"We only want the Device," Ghazarian said. "Give it to me, and you may walk free from us."

"Forgive me for not believing you." Zara began edging in the direction of the boat. Far away, she heard more shots, and shouting. Ransom needed to come soon. "What Device? Not that it matters, because we don't have any."

"You do, I know." Ghazarian took a step in Zara's direction, then froze again when the wavering pistol settled more firmly on her. "I can tell."

121

"Well, you're wrong." Zara began backing toward the boat. Perfect silence from her friends, thank heaven, because what she didn't need was a distraction. "Something valuable, no doubt? What kind of Device do pirates find valuable? Something to make your piracy more effective?"

Ghazarian bared her teeth at Zara. "You know because it yours is."

The tree branches began shaking with someone's passage. Ghazarian's smile turned nasty. "You will die for denying me," she said.

"So much for the honor of a pirate. No, I forgot, pirates don't have honor."

The undergrowth parted, and Ransom emerged, coming up short when he saw the little tableau. His hands were empty. "Rowena," he said, breathing heavily, "we don't have time for this."

"Get in the boat, Ransom," Zara said, her gaze unflinching. Ransom went wide around Ghazarian, but instead of getting into the boat, he came to stand behind Zara. "I said get in the boat," she repeated. Sweat was sliding down her back and her temples, and her stomach muscles ached from being hit.

"I'll guide you," Ransom said in her ear. "Start walking. I won't let you fall."

"Where's the rifle?"

"I dropped it when I was running. Stupid of me. Now, walk."

Zara took a step backward. Ghazarian followed, and Zara cocked the pistol. The tiny click seemed unnaturally loud against the background noise of the river. Even the insects had stopped whirring, as if holding their breath against the outcome of this battle. Zara took another step back, and this time Ghazarian stayed put. Her cinnamon-dark skin was mottled red with fury. "I will find you," she said, "and I will kill you much. You will suffer."

"Big words from the woman who lost her gun," Zara said, continuing to walk backward with Ransom a steady, reassuring presence behind her. "I hope it doesn't have sentimental value."

By the look on Ghazarian's face, she didn't understand the word "sentimental." "You," she began, and the bushes behind her rustled again as another pirate emerged, then another. They brought up their pistols, and Zara said, "Drop them if you don't want to see your captain bloody on the ground."

The man and woman glanced at Ghazarian. "Do it," she said through gritted teeth, and the pirates dropped their pistols.

"Kick them out of the way," Zara said. "Harder." The pirates glared at her, but did as she said. "Please tell me we're close," she said in a low voice.

"We're almost there. You *do* know how to shoot, right?" Ransom said.

"Let's hope we don't have to find out," Zara replied. Her heel kicked the side of the boat, and she wobbled a bit, then raised her foot high to step over the side. Ransom had his hands around her waist, steadying her. She lifted her other foot, stumbled, and fell into the bottom of the boat. Ghazarian lunged.

"*Go!*" Zara shouted, and fired her pistol at the pirate captain. Ghazarian ducked, and Zara fired again, cursing when she missed once more. Why hadn't she ever learned to shoot a pistol? *What use did you ever have for weapons when words were just as deadly?* she thought, shooting again, missing again.

The boat was moving more rapidly now, Ransom at the Device, and Zara flung herself into the bottom of the boat as the pirates recovered their weapons and began shooting back. Zara fired again, not trying to hit anyone, just hoping to distract them. She could feel the current taking them, moving even faster. "More power," Ransom told Theo, then grunted in pain. Zara shot one final time and turned to see blood spreading across Ransom's back.

She cried out and looked for something to stop the bleeding. Ransom sagged over the Device, and Arjan and Zara pulled him out of the way so Arjan could take over. Another bullet carved a furrow across the port side, making Cantara scream and jerk away. Then the bullets stopped, and all Zara could hear was distant shouting over the roar of the river.

"We have to get to shore," Zara said. "Head for the other side."

"We should go as far as possible from them," Arjan said. His voice was weak, but he had no trouble controlling the Device, steering as she instructed.

"Ransom's hit. We have to stop the bleeding." Zara leaned harder on Ransom's back and heard him groan. "Quickly."

Ransom said something too quietly for her to understand. "What was that?" she said, leaning close to his mouth.

"Not that bad," he whispered. "Can heal...if the bullet is out."

"It's not."

"I can tell, Rowena," he said with a wry smile, and despite her fear she couldn't help smiling back. "Someone has to...take it out."

"You mean me."

"Put me...in your debt."

"Stop being ridiculous. As if that mattered."

Ransom took a shallow breath. "Tools in kit. I'll guide you."

"I can't promise I won't make it worse."

"Just...get it out...I'll do the rest." He closed his eyes. Zara sat up.

"We need solid ground for this," she said. "I—*Belinda!*"

Belinda was sitting up and had a hand pressed to her head. "Why are we on the boat?"

"Don't you remember? You attacked one of those pirates with nothing but your fists!" Theo said. "Left her clawed up, too, before she hit you."

Belinda looked at her fingertips, which were slightly bloody, and shuddered. "I don't know if I wish I remembered that moment of heroics or if I'm glad I've forgotten it," she said. She ran her fingers in the water and dried them on her shirt. "Oh, heaven, what happened to Ransom?"

"He'll be fine. We just have to get to safety." Zara realized she was still holding Ghazarian's pistol and tucked it into her waistband. It felt like a trophy. "Are we almost across?"

"The current's stronger now," Theo said. "But we're making progress."

Zara watched the opposite bank draw gradually nearer. "We'd better be," she said.

She lost track of time, watching the bank creep closer as she kept her hands pressed firmly on Ransom's back. She was sure he was conscious, though he said nothing; none of them spoke, Theo and Arjan intent on wrestling the boat across the river with the recalcitrant Device, Belinda with her hands on the starboard gunwale, leaning toward the bank as if she could propel the boat faster with the weight of her desires. Cantara sat curled at the prow, staring at the water. Red birds with green and yellow wings swooped overhead, indifferent to their troubles; they, too, were silent. The sound of the river filled Zara's ears, the roar of a thousand people all cheering them on, and she clung to that image as the torn rag she was using grew gradually redder.

She had drifted into a numb, mindless state when a bump, and then a grinding sensation, told her they'd reached the shore. She sat, indecisive as to whether to stand or stay where she was, while Arjan and Theo dragged the boat up onto the bank, probably farther than was strictly necessary. Ransom moved, pushing himself up with one arm, and Zara said, "Don't."

"Have to…on the ground," he whispered, then to her horror pushed himself into a sitting position and began to rise.

"Stop it! Arjan, help me," she said. Ransom leaned forward and caught himself on the gunwale.

"It's all right," he said in a surprisingly strong voice. "But we don't have much time."

"I don't understand," Zara said.

Ransom sat up again, and Arjan awkwardly dragged him out of the boat without prompting any cries of pain. "I can cut off the nerves surrounding the wound for a while," he said, "long enough to guide you in taking the bullet out."

"We had to leave everything behind, Ransom. What am I supposed to do?"

"Medical kit's in the boat below the stern seat," Ransom said. "We only unloaded what we were going to use. We still have the kit, the medicines, and some food. We can survive for weeks on that."

"He wrong is," Arjan said.

"I think he's joking. Let's find a soft place to put him."

Thick-bladed striped grass grew long about ten feet from the water's edge. Belinda and Cantara stomped down a ten-foot-square section that Arjan and Theo laid Ransom face down on. Zara lugged the stained leather bag containing Ransom's tools and set it down near him. Ransom propped himself on his elbows and dug around in it. "This," he said, handing Zara a long forceps of stainless steel, "and this."

Zara took the scalpel he handed her and examined the edge. "You want me to cut you *more?*"

"Possibly." His face was shiny with sweat, though the morning was still cool. "You'll need to cut my shirt open. Scissors in the bottom of the bag."

"Can't I just push it up?"

"Why does it not surprise me that you're arguing with me?" Ransom lay back down and raised his arms to put his hands beneath his head. "Just do it, Rowena."

Zara dug out the scissors—they were the biggest scissors she'd ever seen in her life—and cut his shirt up the back, folding it to each side. "Now what?"

"It's not that deep. See if you can use the forceps to—" he let out a gasp. "Yes. That."

"I thought you couldn't feel anything."

"Only the pain receptors are numb. You're touching the bullet."

"I can't see it."

"You'll need to widen the wound, then. Make a deep cut—don't be afraid."

Zara swallowed. "You're the one who should be afraid. Giving me a knife and telling me to stab you in the back. Are you sure that's a behavior you want to encourage?"

"Don't stab, cut. Yes, like that."

It felt like cutting pork for stew. Zara pushed away the grotesque thought and set the scalpel aside. "This can't be how bullet wounds are treated."

"It isn't. It's just—" He gasped again. "Just the only option. Now, can you see it?"

She prodded the wound with the forceps. "I think so."

"Very gently, get the forceps around the bottom of it and pull. Slowly. I'm getting to the end of how long I can safely keep those nerves shut off, and if you have to dig around to recover it—"

"Shut up. I know what to do." This was no harder than fishing a bit of eggshell out of a bowl of sticky, slippery egg whites. Nothing to it. She had a steady hand, he was lucky—

The forceps slipped. Zara cursed. "What?" Ransom said.

"Hold still." She carefully removed the forceps. She could see the bullet now, slick with blood in the middle of red, torn flesh. Cantara made a noise, then fainted, and Arjan caught her and lowered her to the ground. "I could use a smaller audience," Zara said through gritted teeth. Belinda and Theo moved back.

Ransom cried out in pain. The sound struck her to the heart. "Sorry," she whispered, "almost done," and she reached back in with the forceps. Ransom cried out again, then went limp. Zara cursed and groped for the bullet, no longer caring if it hurt—he wasn't in a position to feel anything. She felt the forceps close around something hard and pulled it out, steadily, then dropped the bullet on the bed of grass and sat back, breathing heavily. She tossed the forceps next to the bullet and cut the rest of Ransom's shirt off, then bound it over the wound. If she'd been the one hurt, her body would have already begun knitting itself back together. Would she have healed around the bullet, or would it have pushed itself out as the flesh healed? Heaven send she never had to find out.

"He'll be fine," she assured the others. "We just have to wait for him to wake up so he can heal himself. Then we can get back on the river."

"Those pirates will keep chasing us!" Arjan said. "They looking for a Device back on the *Emma Covington* were as well. Why do they think we have it?"

"It's a mistake," Theo said, but he clutched his belt tighter.

"I think it time for honesty is," Arjan said. He was still supporting Cantara, who was conscious but ashy. "The pirates found us twice. They have a way us to find. It must a thing we carry be. Who has such a thing?"

"You don't trust us?" Belinda said.

"We do not know each other before the shipwreck," Arjan said in a harsh, unfamiliar voice. "On ship it does not matter what secrets we have. Now a secret might kill us. We have said our secret, Cantara and I. It reasonable that you do the same is."

"I don't have any secrets," Belinda exclaimed. "I don't have anything but what I'm wearing."

"I'm not hiding anything," Theo said. Zara could hear the guilt in his voice.

"You're hiding whatever that belt is," she said. Both Theo's hands flew to his belt.

"It's just money," he said. "Well, not money. Gems. My father sold property in County Cullinan for my aunt and this is the proceeds."

"Prove it," Arjan said.

"I can't, not without picking it apart—but you can feel it." Theo unbuckled his belt and handed it to Arjan, who felt along its length, squeezing it between his fingers and thumb.

"It lumpy is," he said. "It may truth be."

"I believe him," said Belinda.

"Rowena hasn't said anything," Theo said, snatching his belt away from Arjan and threading it through the loops of his trousers. "What do you know?"

Well, this is dramatic, Zara thought. Casually, displaying no signs of guilt, she dug in her pocket and came out with Alfred's Device. "I think this is what they want."

All four of them burst out into shouts and accusations. "You could have gotten us killed!" Belinda said. "What were you thinking?"

"And you thought *I* was hiding secrets," Theo said with a trace of smugness.

"You could have given it to them, and Arjan would not have been beaten," Cantara shouted.

"How dare you treat us thus?" Arjan said. He advanced on Zara with his fist raised. Zara stuffed the Device into her pocket and stared him down with the steely North gaze.

"That's *enough*," she said, and everyone went silent. Arjan stopped a few feet from her, still tense as if he might strike her if she said the wrong thing. "This belonged to Alfred, and he entrusted it to me before he died. I didn't know the pirates had any way of tracking it and I certainly didn't mean to involve all of you. But it wasn't my secret to keep. And I intended to tell you all about it once we were safe." That last was a lie, but only a partial one. Keeping Alfred's secret was one thing, but endangering five other people superseded that need. "I'm sorry you all had to be involved in this, whatever it is."

"Well, that's interesting," Ransom said, rolling over and making the awkward bandage shift, "but I think that story should wait until we're all recovered enough to hear it. And I'm going to need a bath."

CHAPTER TWELVE

They waited, exhausted from terror, as the day wore on and Ransom lay still on the bloody bed of grass, healing. Zara leaned back against a tree and watched a trail of tiny ants circle around her boot and across the bare ground toward a cone of dirt, where they disappeared. Everything else in the jungle was built to such a large scale it was disconcerting to see anything normal-sized, even if it was just ants. She closed her eyes and drew in a breath of muggy air. She was so tired of being *damp* all the time. When this was over, she was definitely going to Veribold. At least there she spoke the language.

"So Alfred was an agent of the Crown," Belinda said. "I never suspected."

"The good agents aren't suspicious," Theo said. "Do you think he knew how dangerous the Device was? I mean, dangerous to him if the pirates found it."

"I think the attack surprised him," Zara said. "In the sense that he wasn't expecting pirates. Obviously he knew discovery was possible."

"What does it do?" Cantara said.

Zara pulled it out of her pocket again. She'd handed it around to everyone but Ransom, who was preoccupied, to examine. "I don't know. I haven't wanted to investigate it too closely. If I broke it, and it was something urgent… Theo, what do you think?"

"I have no idea," Theo said, holding out his hand for it. "If I could crack it open, I might have a better idea, but I can barely see the seam." He clicked the stem of the Device around in a complete cycle again. "Odd. I didn't notice before, but the leaf pattern shifts with every click."

The others gathered around. Cantara prodded one of the leaves. "It raises," she said. "I can feel the bumps. It is like *seltirian*. A…language for those who cannot see. It too uses bumps."

"I don't suppose you speak this language?" Zara said. She still

130

hadn't told them she spoke Eskandelic and tried not to feel guilty about that. She was keeping so many secrets it was a wonder she didn't erupt.

Cantara shook her head. "It might not enough for a complete language be, only…nine bumps. I do not know how many combinations that is."

"362,880," Theo said immediately. "I have a knack for numbers," he said defensively when everyone turned to look at him. "Anyway, it's enough for a language. More than enough. This could be some kind of communication Device." He handed it back to Zara.

"But why?" Zara fingered the outlines of the leaves before resetting the Device to what she hoped was its base setting, assuming it had one. At least, it was the setting that made the Device's surface smooth. "A telecoder uses far fewer symbols and lets you communicate instantly from any distance. This…well, suppose you could encode a message in it, send it to someone else who knows how to trigger the message? That seems needlessly complicated."

"What matters is that the pirates want it and they have some way to find it," Ransom said. He was still lying on his stomach with the bandage wrapped tightly to his lower back, but his voice was strong, if a bit muffled by the grass. "We need to get rid of it."

"I promised Alfred I'd deliver it," Zara said.

"You didn't promise Alfred you'd let yourself be killed over it," Ransom said. "It's dangerous."

"Then we'll have to deliver it quickly."

"Or we can bury it here, get as far away as possible, and let the pirates track it down."

"That's not going to happen."

"I don't recall putting you in charge of deciding our fates."

"I don't recall inviting you to make decisions for me."

"Maybe he's right," Theo said. "Alfred wouldn't want us to get killed. Much as I'd hate to leave it behind."

Zara stood and thrust the Device back into her pocket. "The pirates are on the wrong side of the river, and they're on foot, because there's no way they have the kind of Device this boat has to take them upstream," she said. "If they want this thing, they're going to have to go farther south to find a ford or go north to their ship. In either case, we have the advantage of them. And I'll be damned if I let that murdering pirate get her hands on this Device. So I say we get back on this boat and get to Goudge's Folly as fast as we can. If you're not interested, then set me down on the opposite shore and I'll walk north and west until I get where I'm going. But I *am* going to make this delivery."

The others were silent. Far above, the ha-ha bird let out its raucous cry and was echoed by two others. Then Ransom groaned and got slowly to his knees. "You should consider a career in piracy," he said, peeling away the bandage to reveal bloody, scarred, unwounded skin. "Or at least as a professional blackmailer."

"It's a fair offer."

"And one you know we won't take. All right. You make good points. Let me clean myself up and find a new shirt, and we can be on our way."

Zara sat down. "It wasn't blackmail," she muttered.

"No, just a really effective reminder," Belinda said. "Whatever that Device does, it can't be safe to let that Ghazarian woman have it. And we're the only ones who can do something about it." She sat down beside Zara. "I wish my head didn't hurt so much."

"You should have Ransom look at that."

"I don't like bothering him when he was hurt worse. Maybe later."

"Sooner rather than later," Ransom said. He'd taken his boots off and was rolling up his trouser legs. His back beneath the blood wasn't as pale as Zara would have guessed, though still not as suntanned as his face and forearms, and his chest was lean and muscular. He waded into the river and began scooping up water to splash over the streaks of blood, making the small pouch he wore around his neck bounce as if it were mostly empty. "Thank heaven my spare clothes are back behind the medicines. I don't relish being food for insects."

Zara realized she was staring and turned away, feeling

embarrassed in a way she hadn't back at the village. Those were strangers, and Ransom...*He's worth looking at*, she thought, and felt even more embarrassed. She was old enough to be his grandmother, which was an unsettling thought all by itself.

Soon he came back, dressed in a relatively clean shirt and tucking it into his trousers. "We'll eat first, then see how far we can travel this afternoon," he said, "if that's all right with you, captain."

"You're hilarious," Zara snapped, but without malice. "I think we should eat as we go."

"I agree," said Arjan. "Let us go quickly."

Ransom shrugged. "I've no objections. But you'll sit up front again. No handling the Device for you."

"Why not?" Zara exclaimed.

"Because your hands are shaking and you're at the edge of your reserves." Ransom took both her hands in his, still damp from the river. "Sit down, Rowena."

Zara settled herself in the bow and accepted a piece of fruit. Mango. She was sick of tropical food. What she wouldn't give for a nice steak, or a bowl of chicken soup with big chunks of meat, or even a fresh apple. She bit into the mango and pretended it was a pear. At the stern, Ransom had his hand on Belinda's forehead, and Belinda's lips were taut as if she were in pain. How odd that making someone better meant inflicting pain first, with healing.

Arjan pushed the boat off and clambered aboard, and they started back down the river. Zara fell into a fugue state, watching the water pass the prow of the boat. Maybe Ransom was right about her physical condition. She certainly felt exhausted, even though all she'd done was creep around the bushes...and knock a man unconscious with a branch nearly as long as she was...and hold off a pirate captain with a gun she didn't know how to use...and dig a bullet out of a man's body...if you lined all those things up together, she'd had a very busy morning. She curled up in the bow, put her head on the forward seat, and fell asleep.

The next she knew, the boat was bumping up onto the shore, it was nearly full dark, and she felt more rested than she had in days, even counting the night she'd slept in Ransom's hut. "We're stopping?" she said.

"We can no longer see to avoid dangers," Arjan said, extending a hand to help her out of the boat. "And the next stretch rocky is. We will need to go carefully."

"But for now, we're going to sleep," Ransom said. "Though I think, as I know you're going to insist on taking a watch, you should go first, since you've already done enough sleeping for three people."

"You could have woken me," Zara said, irritated by his amusement.

"We tried," Belinda said, and she sounded amused too. "You said something about coffee and 'not before six-thirty' and we decided not to risk you hitting one of us."

Zara's face was hot. How far back had her sleeping brain roamed? Thank heaven she hadn't said anything incriminating. Not that any of them suspected her deepest secret. "Sorry," she said. "I'll take the first watch."

They didn't build a fire, so Zara had only the light of the waxing moon to watch by. They'd made camp in a natural clearing under three trees whose branches were low enough to the ground to feel like they were inside a giant black tent, silver moonlight limning the leaves and making strange patterns on the ground. Zara saw a huge spider climbing into the branches and thanked heaven Belinda wasn't awake to see it. She made a wide circle around the camp, outside the sheltering branches, and listened to the night noises, the insects and the hooting of nocturnal birds. Something big passed nearby, but didn't stop to investigate, so Zara just stood straining to hear it until everything was silent again.

She fingered the Device in her pocket. How stupid was she, to have made that speech? If she was wrong, if the pirates could return to their ship before they reached the ocean, they were all dead, and it would be her fault. She went to sit in the center of the circle of sleeping bodies. She couldn't be wrong, that was all.

She woke Ransom with no more than a few words of warning

about the large shadow, then curled up in the warm spot he'd left and slept.

It took most of the next day for them to navigate past the rocky shoals and into calmer water. The current flowed more slowly the wider the river got, and the noise of the water diminished, sounding less like a gale-force wind rushing through trees and more like a quiet reception with fifty people all talking at once. Zara insisted on taking a turn at the boat's propulsion Device and sat next to Ransom, trying to keep the boat moving in a straight line. Neither of them spoke. All the questions Zara wanted to ask him seemed too personal to air in public, so to speak.

She remembered sitting next to him by the fire two nights before, how it had been such a relief not to be sniping at each other anymore. *Are we friends*, she wondered, *or is this just propinquity?* It had been a long time since she'd known anyone who'd matched her wit for wit. *And he's handsome*, a tiny voice whispered, and she steered too sharply to the right before calming herself and correcting her course. Handsome had nothing to do with it. They'd be friends no matter what he looked like.

She shifted position, and the butt of Ghazarian's pistol dug into her side. "I forgot I had it," she said aloud, startled.

"Had what?" Ransom said.

"Ghazarian's pistol. Too bad we have no bullets. I'd love some of that wild pig."

"You've been in the jungle too long if you can speak of wild pig with longing." Ransom glanced down at the pistol. "I don't know much about firearms, but it looks nice."

"May I?" Belinda said, taking the pistol and sighting along the barrel.

"I thought you used a rifle," Zara said.

"It's my preferred weapon, but I'm an expert with several kinds of gun Devices." She turned it over in her hands. "It's a fine weapon. She'll regret losing it."

"Well, I don't know what I'll do with it. Do you want it, Belinda?"

"You have it by right of conquest, I think." Belinda tucked it neatly back into Zara's waistband. "Though I think she'll want it back."

"She already wants the Device. She can hardly hunt us down twice over." Zara wiped sweat from her forehead and wished she had a way to tie her hair more securely.

In the bow, Cantara sat up, making the boat rock. "That is the ocean," she said. "We are here!"

"Don't get too excited," Ransom said. "We still have to reach Tammerek, and this boat isn't exactly stable. We'll be slower out in the ocean, even if we stay close to the shore. And if those pirates followed us..."

"We must have outrun them," Belinda said.

"I imagine we have about a day's lead on them. Once they get back to their ship..." His words trailed off again.

"If we stay in the shallows, they will not follow us well," Cantara said. "I have sailed all my life and I know where safe water is."

"I'm relieved to know someone knows what she's doing. I've never taken one of these things out into open water before." Ransom nudged Zara. "Let me take a turn. We'll go until sunset, then find a place to camp."

"We might want to consider traveling longer than that," Zara said. She leaned forward, pointing at an object that looked like a large fly with skeletal wings settled on the skin of the ocean. "That's Ghazarian's ship. A day's head start might not be enough."

Ransom handed the Device's tiller back to her. "Hold the boat steady," he said, and leaned over the side to make some adjustments. "I don't like the way the motive force is flickering. It's supposed to do that to show when the source is running low, but I know they put in a fully imbued one and those are supposed to last for weeks."

"You could have said something," Zara said.

"I just did. This is the first I noticed it." He took the tiller from her hand and adjusted the wheel that controlled the speed. The boat moved fractionally faster. "Let's see how far we can get before dark."

Even with the wheel turned to full, the boat slowed more as it approached the mouth of the Kulnius, where the river's current warred with the ocean waves. Zara glanced at Ransom occasionally; his mouth was grim, and he kept his eyes as often on the distant ship as on the water before them. Sunset was on them by the time they reached open water and turned left to follow the coast. "Do you see a longboat?" Ransom asked Zara.

"I don't." She scanned the shoreline. "That's bad."

"Why is it bad?" Theo asked.

"Because it could mean they've already returned and are on their way to their ship. And if Ghazarian can track the Device, she'll know to come after us." Zara recalled the brass and dark wood of the Device the pirate captain had had on the *Emma Covington*. It couldn't track Alfred's Device perfectly, or they'd have found it then, but it was good enough to get Ghazarian close, and then…cannon fire, rifles, and they'd all be trapped in this stupid boat and killed.

"I think we'll go a little farther," Ransom said. "Cantara, I think you should steer. How well can you find your way in the darkness?"

"Well enough, but we should not linger," Cantara said, changing places awkwardly with him. "Seeing better than feeling is, in these waters."

Zara moved forward to the bow and peered into the growing darkness, though it was unlikely she'd be able to see any reefs or rocks or other marine dangers. Beside her, Belinda stared across the sea toward the pirate ship, anchored several hundred yards off shore. "It's not coming nearer," she said.

"Do you really think those pirates made it back to their ship already?" Theo said.

"They might have hidden the longboat well." Belinda turned away from her watch to look at Theo. "I hope they've just hidden it well."

"We need to stop," Cantara said. "I will find a place."

"They have to have seen us. Why aren't they following?" said Theo.

"They probably have orders not to sail without their captain."

Ransom was a dim shape now amidships. "We can't afford to stop. Ghazarian might return soon."

"We will go beyond their sight and hide. If the pirates come, they come, and we will fight. But it safe to continue is not."

"Strong words," Ransom said, but he sounded approving. "No fire tonight. Just in case."

They pulled the boat up on the shore and handed out the last of the food. Zara nibbled her dried meat and settled in more comfortably on the mound of dried grass she'd made for herself. They'd have to hunt for food in the morning, which would slow them further, and Ransom was right, the boat was traveling more slowly now. She should have insisted the villagers give them an extra imbued motive force — but, then, she hadn't had any idea how the Device worked or what made it run, so how could she have known to do that? *You should have made it your business to learn*, she chastised herself, and bit off another mouthful with ferocity. No sense dwelling on what was past. Time to plan for the future.

The pirate ship was a blotch on the ocean in the moonlight. She wished she understood more about sailing, whether the ship's behavior meant something good for them. Maybe the currents nearer the shore were too strong. Maybe their ship was too large to come in close to the shallows. Zara swallowed the last of her food and lay back. There was no point dwelling on possibilities either. They had to move as quickly as possible, and pray heaven was on their side.

There was something digging into her back. She moved the grass aside and dug through the sand, found nothing. She smoothed it back over and tried to settle down again, but the moon was too bright, the ground too lumpy, and she couldn't stop seeing Ghazarian's furious face as she stared her down. She'd made an enemy, not that it mattered, but the idea propelled her off the ground to pace the edge of the jungle where it met the strip of land barely worth calling a beach. She wasn't afraid of the pirate captain, but she also wasn't stupid enough to think she wasn't dangerous. Zara wished she knew just how much the pirate's honor, if you could call it that, was bound up in finding and destroying her. Having to keep one eye constantly looking over her shoulder would be exhausting.

"Rowena," Ransom called in a low voice. She went to join him where he stood near the water's edge. "Stop pacing and go to sleep. Your watch will come soon enough."

"I'm too restless. I just need to walk around a bit."

"Well, you're making me nervous."

"I am not."

"True. But when I catch sight of you moving out of the corner of my eye, I twitch because I think you're a predator. Stay put."

Zara sighed and looked out over the ocean at the dark blotch, lit by a few specks of light. She could only tell what it was because she knew what to look for. "Sorry."

"You can stand here and talk to me, if you can't sleep."

"And *that's* not a distraction?"

He chuckled. "You hear that? The insects and the monkeys and the snuffling of pigs? When that noise stops, you'll know we're in danger. You talking isn't going to distract me from that."

"Oh." Zara glanced at him; he was watching the ship. "And I suppose you have more impertinences for me?"

"I want to know who you are. Who you were, all those years."

"I told you. I was a weaver."

"That can't have been everything."

A flash of a memory, of sitting on the marble throne of Tremontane facing down the Magistrix of the Scholia, came and went so swiftly it stunned her. "It wasn't," she said, "but you don't need to know the rest."

Ransom turned to face her. "No weaver moves like a predator," he said. "You're used to taking charge."

"I am. But, to use your favorite phrase, that's none of your business."

He shrugged. "You're right. It's not." He went back to looking out across the waves. "How old were you when you found out?"

"That I wasn't aging?" She turned that question over in her mind.

139

"I was thirty-one."

"That's a long time to look younger than you are."

"Nobody thought to question it." Who was going to challenge the Queen on not looking her age?

"So how did you end up living near your grandniece?"

"Why does this feel like a one-sided conversation?"

That made him laugh. "I'm not nearly as interesting as you are," he said.

It made her feel uncomfortable, though she didn't know why. "I've lived the last fifty-odd years quietly," she said. "That's not very interesting. Besides, you're not telling me anything about yourself, Dr. Ransom."

"It's just Ransom," he said. "My surname is De Witt."

"Oh." It sounded familiar. "Should I know the name?"

"Possibly. It's an old, well-to-do family in Aurilien. I don't trade on it."

"But you said you wouldn't tell me your given name."

"I have two given names. In addition to my detested first name, my parents named me after my maternal uncle Ransom—my mother was a Ransom before she adopted into my father's family. They hoped it would induce him to leave his fortune to me."

"Did it work?"

"Now who's prying?"

"I answered your questions."

"Some of them. Answer for answer, Rowena."

Zara sighed. "All right. What's your question?"

"How did you come to live with family? Did they all know your secret?"

"No. My grandniece…came to live in my home town and figured out the truth. Gave out that I was her father's half-sister so we didn't have to hide our relationship, at least as far as that was possible. Now, your turn."

"My Uncle Ransom is the only one of my relatives I can stand. He's not infected by that Resurgence nonsense, for one. I lived with him while I was in medical school. He's never held my name against me."

"I apologize if this is too personal for even our newfound understanding, but couldn't you adopt into his family?"

"If I wanted to start a war, sure. I still care enough about my family not to want to hurt them. I suppose I hope someday they'll come to their senses, or at least understand my point of view. Were you ever married?"

"What?"

"Sorry, I thought it was your turn to answer."

"Have you always been this persistent?"

"It's a doctor's most important quality. Well, no, the most important quality is the ability to cure your patients. But persistence is part of that."

Zara couldn't hold back a laugh. "Yes. I was married once."

Ransom was silent. "What, no more questions?" Zara asked.

"I just realized," he said, his voice somber, "how that story must have ended. I'm sorry."

His sudden seriousness left her wordless. "Thank you," she finally said. "It was a long time ago. He never knew the truth."

"What were you planning to do?"

"I didn't have a plan. I loved him, and I wanted a normal life. He died in an accident before it became an issue."

"I see."

"You think I was wrong."

"It's not my place to judge you." He turned to look at her again. "I'm serious about that. I can barely imagine what your life must be like."

"It's...not so bad." *Was* it so bad? She'd had so many moments of happiness, it seemed wrong to dwell on the negatives. "I've seen a lot. Two wars, the growth of three countries. Changes in Devisery. I was—" She could tell him this, it didn't give anything away. "I remember the first telecoders. They were huge, and it cost a fortune to send messages. Now they're the size of a shoebox and people use them as casually as breathing."

"See, that's exactly what I meant," Ransom said. "You've seen so much and you're going to see so much more."

"I suppose. I try not to think about it. It's hard leaving people behind."

"That, I can imagine." Ransom dug his toe in the soft sand. "You really should try to get some rest."

"I will. Good night, Ransom. And…thank you."

"For pestering you with impertinences?"

"For reminding me my life doesn't have to be tragedy."

His blond hair shone in the moonlight. "I suppose," he said without turning around, "it depends on what you do with it."

His voice, always deep, had taken on a somber tone again, and she wondered what he was thinking, but decided they'd had enough of a heartfelt conversation for one night. *Admit it*, she told herself, *you like talking to him, and telling him things is a release.* She fell asleep thinking of Longbourne without sorrow.

Chapter Thirteen

The moon had set by the time Arjan roused Zara for her watch. She stood at the edge of the water, straining to see the pirate ship, and listened to the raucous nighttime noises of the jungle. Ransom was right: if anything dangerous came near — anything large, probably — all those smaller animals would go still. Even so, after realizing there was no way she'd see the ship move until dawn, she paced the edge of the jungle, breathing in its moist warmth that smelled of humus and green and slapping away insects. Getting out on the ocean in the morning was going to be a huge relief, if only to get away from the bugs.

When the sky began glowing pale pink, she prodded everyone awake, then stood watching the eastern seas. The ship was still there, its sails catching the dawn light like pale white membranes against the lowering haze of morning. It took Zara a moment to realize what that meant, and then a chill shot through her. "The ship is on the move," she said. "We have to leave immediately."

"We have to gather food, Rowena," Belinda said. "It's still a day or two to Goudge's Folly."

"But they don't have to stop," Theo pointed out. "We can't afford to either."

"All the more reason to gather food enough to last," Ransom said. "But hurry."

There wasn't much to gather without spending too much time going inland. They piled up mangoes, papayas, and wild bananas with their enormous seeds, so unsatisfying, but better than nothing, and arranged things in the little boat as best they could. Then Arjan and Theo shoved the boat into deeper water, and Ransom at the tiller guided them westward. Zara sat beside him, now and then glancing back. She couldn't tell if the pirate ship was drawing nearer, but it felt as if it loomed over them, waiting its moment to blast them with cannon fire.

"We should stay in the shallows," she said, "where they can't follow us."

"It a bad idea is," Cantara said from her position in the bow. "We slow here are. We need the current us to Manachen to carry, and that far from shore is."

"The motive force is definitely weaker now," Ransom said. "But I think it will get us where we're going." But Zara was looking at him as he spoke, and his mouth was set in that grim line again.

"I suppose we can always row," Theo said, sounding hopeful. No one said anything.

They made their way slowly along the coast, carried along by the current and the Device. Zara stopped looking behind them at noon. There was no point, when it was clear the pirate ship was gaining on them. She ran her fingers in the rushing water and tried not to see how hard Ransom had to steer into the waves to keep from being thrown off course. He must be regretting the impulse that had led him to throw in his lot with theirs. Not that any of them had suspected pirates, when this all began.

"How close do they have to be before they begin firing their cannons?" Belinda asked.

"They won't use the cannons," Ransom said, "not if they want to retrieve that Device. They'll shoot us —" He closed his mouth abruptly and put his hand on the wheel of the Device as if he could turn it up past full, where it already was. Belinda hunched her shoulders.

Sunset came, and Zara risked one glance at the following ship. The pirates were no more than a mile behind them, their sails once again catching the light of the setting sun. "We can't afford to stop," she said to Ransom.

"I know. We'll have to take our chances with the current, and hope the moonlight is enough."

"The moonlight will help them, too."

"Why don't we focus on the positive?"

"What's that?"

"Well, there could be snakes in here with us."

Zara chuckled. "Let me take the tiller," she said to Ransom. "You sleep for a while."

"I can manage," Ransom said.

"I know, but Cantara will need to steer once it's full night, and she's sleeping now," Zara said, pointing to where Cantara and Arjan were curled up together. "I'll take a turn for an hour or so."

"I don't know how they can bear to sleep," Belinda said. She'd taken Cantara's seat in the bow and was clutching the gunwale as if to keep herself upright.

"We'd all better find ways to rest, because we can't stop." Ransom handed Zara the tiller and settled himself. "Wake me if the pirates come," he said with a smile.

More time passed. Zara handed the tiller to Cantara and napped fitfully amidships, her head on Belinda's leg. She dreamed of being rocked to sleep in her mother's arms, though she was an adult and her mother was a giant with blond hair like Alison's. Then she dreamed of Hank and woke herself with tears running down her face, though she couldn't remember the dream or if they were happy or grieving tears. Finally dawn came, and she woke to find Ransom back at the wheel and the pirate ship closer than ever. Close enough for rifle fire? It depended on what kind of Devices they had. She judged the distance. If they had black powder rifles, they might have begun shooting already; their range was still longer than the new rifle Devices, according to Telaine. So they were still safe — for now.

"Rowena, take over," Ransom said. He had the expression of a man who'd been chewing over some unpleasant truths and come to an unpleasant conclusion. "I have an idea."

"What is it?"

"I think I can get the Device to give us more speed, but it won't last long. Possibly enough to get us to Manachen, but maybe not."

"How far are we?" Theo asked.

"Half a day, at our current speed. Those pirates will catch us in an hour if they continue as they've been doing. I think I can give us maybe half an hour's boost in speed, which should be fast enough to take us most of the way to Manachen. Certainly enough to outpace the pirates. Then we can row the rest of the way. But, if I'm wrong, they'll catch us when we're dead in the water."

Zara looked at her friends and saw nods and gestures of assent. "Do it," she said.

She kept the boat as steady as she could while Ransom leaned over the back with his head dangerously close to the thrashing Device, which had been turned to low but still moved. "They're—" Belinda began, then shut her mouth. None of them needed a reminder.

Ransom sat up and took the tiller. "When I give the word, turn the wheel to full," he told Zara, who gripped it tightly. The Device was making strange clunking noises along with its usual throaty purr, and the boat shuddered, then shuddered again, like a bull trying to shake off a persistent fly. Everyone grabbed hold of something. Ransom twitched the tiller one way and then the other, holding out his free arm and sighting along it. "Now," he said. Zara spun the wheel to full.

The boat jerked, the Device roared, and then they were flying across the waves, bouncing as they crossed them. Everyone except Ransom and Zara screamed, Ransom because all his attention was focused on keeping a straight course, Zara because the wheel was trying to spin out of her hands. It was terrifying, and exhilarating, and Zara looked back once, briefly, to see the pirate ship receding at an incredible rate. Then she had to focus on the wheel again. "I can't hold this for long!" she shouted over the noise of the Device.

"Find something to tie it off with," Ransom shouted back, "a strap or something." His knuckles were white on the tiller, and she could see the tendons in his neck standing out.

"How long can *you* hold on?" she said, leaning closer.

"As long as you don't insist on conversation," he replied, but he gave her a tight smile that blunted the harshness of his words.

Zara looked around, didn't see anything that might work for a strap, and called out, "Belinda! Take off your belt!"

"What?"

"Your *belt*, give me your belt!"

146

Belinda crawled back to her and worked her belt free. "Why?"

"Need to hold the wheel steady." She directed Belinda in tying the wheel into the "full" position, then sat back and rubbed her sore wrists. "Let me take that!" she said to Ransom.

"You're not strong enough," he said. It looked as if his hands were shaking.

"Then Arjan!"

She changed places with the Eskandelic, and with some jerking of the boat from side to side, Arjan took Ransom's place. Ransom immediately collapsed into the bottom of the boat and began laughing. "Is there something funny about all this?" Zara asked.

"I can't believe that worked," he said, gasping for air. "There was a good chance it would explode and take all of us with it."

"You could have said that!" Theo exclaimed.

"It was a risk of death versus certain death if they caught us." Ransom sat up and ran his hands through his hair, scratching his scalp. "In a few minutes we'll slow enough that it won't be so hard to stay on course. Fifteen or so minutes after that, we'll be out of fuel and have to row."

Zara looked back at the pirate ship, which was once again a speck on the horizon. "Let's hope it's enough."

Half an hour later, the Device sputtered, and its purr dwindled to a hum and then went silent. They all sat for a moment, listening to the sound of the waves striking the boat and the sea birds calling to one another. Then Arjan reached into the bottom of the boat and unearthed an oar. "Time to row," he said, and he and Ransom fitted the oars into the oarlocks.

Compared to the speed with which they'd sailed across the waves, rowing seemed to get them nowhere. Zara sat in the bow once again and watched the coastline slip past, so slowly it was barely noticeable as progress. She didn't look back at the pirate ship more than once. It was closer than it had been, and she didn't need the knife-edged dread of seeing it get closer still. A tiny island slipped past them on the right, just one of many dotting the curve of the coast. None of them were large enough to give them shelter or be anything but a trap.

The water was dark and warm, and she dipped her hand in it and sniffed the salty brine. How long had it been since she'd stood on the deck of the *Emma Covington* and contemplated snowy Longbourne? She'd almost lost count of the days. So much had happened it felt like an eternity.

She turned around to look, not at the oncoming pirate ship, but her fellow fugitives. Ransom and Arjan had removed their shirts and were pulling smoothly in tandem. How would things have been different if they'd all gone west instead of east when they first landed? The pirates might not have been able to catch them before they reached Manachen and Goudge's Folly, and would have followed them into the city, and who knew how many people they might have killed in their attempt to retrieve the Device?

And they would never have met Ransom. Would never have drawn him into this mess, more to the point. Funny how he no longer seemed to mind, given his initial reluctance to help them. His shoulders were starting to redden, though no doubt he could heal sunburn easily enough. Not that she was looking. She turned her back on him and tilted her head to let the breeze cool her cheeks.

"They're closing in again," Belinda said.

"They have the wind," Cantara said, "and this current helps them as well as it does us."

"I could take a turn," Theo said.

"We're fine," Ransom said with a grunt. "Not much longer."

"How can you tell?" Zara said.

"I can't. I was being optimistic."

"We're coming to a promontory," Zara said. "I can't see beyond it."

"Then I'm not just being optimistic. The Bay of Avizi is around that promontory." Ransom wiped sweat from his forehead. "We might actually make it."

"The Bay of Avizi...that's where Goudge's Folly is?"

Ransom nodded. "If we're lucky, we'll be far enough ahead of our pursuers to make it to the island. If not, we'll have to land in Manachen and take our chances there."

"How dangerous is that?" Belinda said.

"Depends on who we talk to. Some of them are more…unfriendly than others. But they'll just harass us before sending us on. They don't like foreigners in their country."

"Isn't Goudge's Folly their country?" asked Theo.

"It a…I do not know the word," said Arjan. "Our countries pay to be there."

"You mean a lease," Belinda said.

"Yes. A lease. Part Veribold, part Eskandel, part Tremontane. A lease for fifty years, but Dineh-Karit can revoke it if they choose. They do not choose because it brings them wealth."

"It's strange, having a piece of Tremontane all the way out here," Theo said.

"Not stranger than if we had an embassy in Dineh-Karit. That would be a piece of Tremontane too." Belinda stretched. "I feel so much more optimistic. How about something to eat?"

Zara and Theo took the oars while Ransom and Arjan ate, then traded places. Eventually they came around the point of land into a bay big enough to hold a fleet of ships the size of the *Emma Covington*. A city lay like a scruff of rusty moss on the curve of the bay, bisected by a river larger even than the Kulnius, with peaked red roofs catching the noon sunlight. Nobody spoke, but Zara could feel the relief coming off everyone, including herself. Arjan and Ransom rowed faster. Zara took one last look back at the oncoming pirate ship before the promontory blocked it from view. Surely they were fast enough, even rowing, to make it to safety.

Fifteen minutes later, she said, "Why are we slowing?"

"We fighting the current are," Arjan said. His voice was tight and breathless.

"Oh, heaven, there they are," Belinda said, once again gripping the gunwales. Zara didn't turn around, feeling irrationally if she could only keep the distant city in her sights, they would make it. They'd come too far to lose at the last minute.

"Keep pulling," Ransom said to Arjan. His voice sounded tense, too.

Zara twisted her hair up and tied it in a knot that would probably fall down in a few minutes. She made herself breathe slowly, in and out. She listened to the slap of the oars against the water and the quieter sound of the waves striking the boat, the louder cries of sea birds flying in and out of the harbor, and, more distantly, the hum of a bustling, thriving seaport. The wind carried with it not only the briny smell of the ocean, but the more distant smells of wood and stone heated by the sun, the smell of civilization.

Goudge's Folly was visible to the right, a gently peaked rock covered in buildings that looked similar to those of Manachen. That was a surprise; she'd expected northern architecture. Maybe Dineh-Karit had evicted its citizens from Tammerek in order to give it to the northerners. That suggested they wanted northern trade and weren't as averse to dealing with foreign savages as she'd thought. She shook her head violently. They were facing death, and she was thinking about politics and trade? She had very skewed priorities.

She turned to face the oncoming pirate ship. It was so close she could see pirates clinging to the ropes and even standing at the rail, looking back at them. She needed to have a plan. If she gave them what they wanted…no, they'd just kill all of them. And she didn't want that Ghazarian woman to have the Device. She could throw it overboard — she'd be breaking her promise to Alfred, but better that than letting the wrong person have it, and he'd as much as said it was crucial that didn't happen. There was a way to get everyone free, but it depended on Ghazarian's greed outweighing her hatred of Zara…still, it was better than nothing.

"We're not going to make it," Theo muttered.

"Don't give up," Belinda said. "We're getting close. There are a lot of little boats nearby, so they won't be able to shoot us without someone noticing."

"We do not know if they care," Cantara said. "Steer right."

Their course shifted marginally to avoid a boat, smaller than theirs but also Device-propelled, crewed by a couple of young Karitians wearing nothing but loincloths. The Karitians stared at them. Zara smiled and waved, though her mind was shrieking at her to find a solution, fast. The Karitians seemed uninterested in the pirate ship, which was now only a few hundred yards behind. They just sped away, still staring back at the northerners as if they couldn't believe what they saw. So, no help from that quarter. "I have an idea," Zara said.

"Why does that sentence strike dread into my heart?" Ransom said.

"Just keep rowing. It might not matter."

"We're not going to make it," Theo repeated.

"There's another boat coming after us," Belinda said. "It's got a Device like ours and it's moving really fast."

"*Nakati*," Ransom said. "Sort of…harbor police. They may be after the pirates and not us."

"You don't sound certain," Zara said.

"That's because it might be in our best interests to be arrested. It would get us away from the pirates."

"…And?"

"They might convict us of something serious. Karitian prisons aren't kind to foreigners. And we're not entitled to due process."

"I am not happy with this," Cantara said.

"We have to keep rowing until one or the other catches us." Ransom wiped his forehead again. "Prayer might be in order."

Belinda closed her eyes. Theo clutched his belt more closely. Zara watched first the pirates, then the rapidly approaching *nakati*. The pirates at the rail of the ship were readying gun Devices, stubby-nosed pistols and not rifles, thank heaven, but another few yards and they'd be close enough to fire.

"Don't stop rowing," Zara said.

She stood up in the boat, flinging out her arms for balance, then shouted in Eskandelic, "*If you shoot, I'll drop it!*" She displayed the Device, holding it high over her head, then stretched out her arm so a single movement would send it plummeting into the ocean.

"*Rowena!*" Arjan shouted.

"What did she say?" Ransom said.

"Don't stop rowing," Zara said again, wobbling but maintaining her balance. The pirate ship continued toward them, more slowly now as men and women on its deck began heaving to and slowing its momentum.

The pirates at the ship's rail looked confused. One or two of them brought their pistols to bear on her. Zara, unflinching, shouted, "*This is what you want! Shoot me, and you'll lose it forever!*"

"*You're a liar,*" Ghazarian said, shoving a few men aside to stand at the rail. "*I knew you had the Device.*"

"*As if I'd tell the truth to you,*" Zara said. "*You want it, you let us go. We'll go to the shore and I'll leave it here in the boat.*"

"*I think I don't trust you, liar,*" Ghazarian said, and raised a pistol to point directly at Zara's head. Zara felt like laughing. *I've already been shot through the head once,* she thought. *You'll have to try harder than that to frighten me.*

"*I think you don't have a choice,*" she said. "*Shoot me, and it's gone. Take my offer, and everyone gets what they want.*"

Ghazarian didn't lower the pistol. "Rowena, this dangerous is. She will not allow us to go," said Arjan.

"For the love of holy heaven, will *someone* tell me what kind of insane deal she's brokering?" Ransom said.

From behind her, someone shouted at them in Karitian, short, terse syllables whose meaning Zara could guess. Ransom let out an exasperated noise and replied at length. "*Put it down and you will live,*" Ghazarian said.

"*I think not.*" Sweat was running down Zara's back. The Karitian was closer now, still shouting, but Zara had her back to him and didn't have time to worry about what he might be saying.

"Rowena, you need to sit down. That *nakat* is very nervous about

152

all the weapons," Ransom said. He sounded as if his patience was fraying. Zara carefully sat down, but kept her hand with the Device extended over the side of the boat. The Karitian spoke again, more loudly, and his words seemed aimed at Ghazarian's ship instead of theirs. *"I don't speak your stupid language,"* Ghazarian retorted.

"That is unfortunate, I speak yours," the Karitian said. *"Remove the weapons and putting down the guns. It illegal is to bring foreign Devices into Bay of Avizi."*

Ghazarian didn't move. Zara didn't take her eyes off her. Then, almost in her ear, someone fired a gun, and one of the pirates screamed and collapsed on the deck, making his neighbors recoil. *"That a warning is,"* said the *nakat*. *"We do not second ones give."*

There was another long moment in which Zara couldn't breathe. Then Ghazarian cursed and lowered her weapon. *"Personal Devices are allowed, yes?"*

"You must prove so," said the *nakat*. *"You will have an escort to your anchorage and an escort to the customs. Do not threaten again or we will not so friendly be."*

Zara withdrew her hand, glaring at Ghazarian. Her heart was slowing from its rapid pace. One obstacle down, but—

The *nakat* said something to Ransom, who replied at length. Zara wished she dared ask him what he was saying, but for all she knew, he was bargaining for their freedom.

The conversation went on for a while, during which the second *nakat*, the woman handling the tiller of their Device, listened in silence. Zara wondered if she'd been the one to fire the gun. Both the man and the woman wore loose tunic-like shirts of linen with no sleeves and skirts of the same fabric, dyed crimson and blue so they looked like the ha-ha birds. Their black hair was cut short in the same style, and their dark brown eyes were emotionless, as if holding six people's fates in their hands happened all the time and meant nothing to them. That might even be true.

Finally, Ransom turned to them and said, "I've explained we were all going to Tammerek and have no intention of landing in Manachen.

Except we have to, if we want to find passage to Tammerek. So it's complicated."

Zara caught a glimpse of the female *nakat* watching them curiously. She was convinced the woman spoke at least some Tremontanese. "Meaning we have to go on shore, but we're not staying, so the rules are different?"

"Exactly. I had to make some promises. We won't be allowed contact with anyone but an approved representative of the government. We'll probably have to pay a fine, and it might be heavy. And—" He drew a deep breath and looked Zara in the eye. "We have to surrender Ghazarian's pistol…and that Device."

Chapter Fourteen

"All right," Zara said. She pretended not to notice the female *nakat*, who was still watching their exchange.

"But—we can't!" Belinda exclaimed.

"Of course we can. It's *not important*," Zara said, flicking her gaze at the Karitian and willing Belinda and the others to take the hint. The last thing they needed was to suggest this Device was anything out of the ordinary.

Ransom was nodding, slowly. "They'll lock them up and return them to you when you're on the transport to Tammerek," he said. "The idea is to avoid cheap, inferior Devices polluting the market."

"Our Devices—" Theo began hotly.

"Are nothing like the ones the Karitians have," Zara said. Sweet heaven, could no one use simple reason anymore? "We *don't want to interfere*, do we?" She extended the Device, and then the pistol, to the female *nakat*, who put them into a metal box under the bow seat of the boat and locked the box with a tarnished key she put into a pouch at her waist.

Theo opened his mouth, then, puzzled, subsided. The male *nakat* brought out a grappling hook that looked like it might be a weapon itself, with heavy barbs on all three points and a spike at the place where they joined, and his companion steered their boat around until he could hook it to the bow of Ransom's boat. With a jerk, the crippled boat leveled out, and the *nakat* paid out line from a winch so they could be towed, gently but inexorably, into the harbor.

When the distance was great enough between the two boats that they couldn't be overheard, Ransom said, "Quick thinking."

"I don't want them to search for an excuse to look at it closely," Zara said in a low voice. "Am I right that the woman speaks Tremontanese?"

"I think so. The *nakati* have to be at least bilingual to handle

155

clashes between the northern savages and honest Karitian sailors."

"But what happens now?" Belinda exclaimed. "We don't have any way to pay for transportation, let alone a fine!"

"I think I can talk them down to a stern warning, especially if Ghazarian makes enough of a stink to be truly obnoxious," Ransom said. "They might have sympathy for anyone she was pursuing, northerner or not."

"And I can promise Falken & Daughter will pay our fare to Goudge's Folly," Zara said, but she felt less confident than she sounded. Whatever had happened to the *Emma Covington*, the Falken cargo was certainly lost, and Mistress Falken Senior might not be thrilled at the prospect of bailing out an employee she'd never even met.

"We don't have to," Theo said. "Where's the scalpel?"

"Theo — oh!" said Cantara as Theo scooted back so she sat between him and the *nakati* in their boat. He pulled off his belt and began feeling along its edges.

"That's not your money, Theo," Belinda said.

"My aunt won't begrudge me," he said, accepting the scalpel from Ransom and carefully cutting the threads at the inner seam. "Besides, even if she did, she doesn't know how much money is coming to her. How much do you think they'll ask for?"

"Let me see what you — holy heaven, Theo, that's at least two fortunes!" Ransom exclaimed, then glanced over his shoulder to see if the *nakati* had heard that. "These two stones should be more than enough. I'll try to get away with giving them just the one, keep the second in reserve." He tilted his palm so the diamonds caught the light, then tipped them into the pouch he wore around his neck.

"Will the others be safe, now you've cut it open?" Belinda asked.

"I think I can fold it so they won't come out."

"Or I can stitch it closed," Ransom said.

"I wouldn't think you'd have need of sutures," Zara said.

"I don't. But I have a sewing kit." He grinned at her embarrassment. "What, you think because I live in the jungle like a savage, I don't have at least a few of the trappings of civilization?"

"Do it quickly, because they're coming up to a dock," Theo said.

By the time the boat came to a bobbing halt, Ransom had stitched up the belt and returned it to Theo. Zara kept a close eye on the *nakati* during the procedure, but neither of them looked back at all. Presumably the northern savages, being unable to go anywhere, were no threat. She climbed up the short ladder out of the boat with no assistance and then stood on wobbly legs until the ground stopped moving quite so much. Belinda, surprisingly, was able to stand on her own. It seemed like an eternity since they'd been on solid ground. "This way," Ransom said, but Zara was already following the *nakati* down the wooden pier.

She felt small, here in this harbor that was so unlike those of Kingsport or even Umberan. Even the smells were foreign: the wet wood of the pier smelled of cedar, the briny tang of the air was tinged with cinnamon and cloves, and from somewhere in the distance came the sweet scent of oranges. It would have been beautiful if she hadn't been so tense. Karitians stared at them as they passed, though most of them seemed curious rather than antagonistic. Zara nodded politely at each one who caught her eye, but couldn't muster a smile. She looked across the bay at misty Goudge's Folly. Who was Goudge, and why had he or she thought a settlement in Dineh-Karit was a good idea?

The docks were all east of the river Amgeli, which was broader even than the Kulnius and flowed lazily into the bay, defiant of the waves trying to push it back. Manachen, straddling it, looked like two cities joined by white bridges that gleamed as brightly as the river. The coast continued on the west side of the river, but rose high above the ocean in a series of sheer cliffs, atop which houses stood as if preparing to leap into the water below. The red roofs made Manachen look as if someone had swiped a giant paintbrush across the city. It was beautiful, and alien, and Zara found herself straining to see anything that might break the uniformity and make Manachen seem less forbidding.

Between the harbor and the island, ships and tiny boats turned the bay into a vast sweep of colorful movement. The brightly painted little boats all had Devices to propel them along, and they zipped about the harbor like swarms of dragonflies. By contrast, the ships were all drab grays and browns except for the gaudy designs painted on their hulls, abstract lines and curves that almost resolved into pictures, or letters in some alien alphabet. Were they words in Karitian? Zara was beginning to regret not learning their language, though how was she to have known it might be useful someday?

They left the pier for stony ground and turned right toward rows of narrow, bright blue buildings with those same peaked red roofs she'd seen from a distance, set on the stone as precariously as birds perched on ice, with nothing to keep them from blowing over in a stiff gale. They were laid out as regularly as a division of soldiers with red caps, standing stiffly to attention, and didn't look as if they could hold more than a dozen people at once. Each had a single window that looked out on the harbor, and there Zara saw the only differences between them: some of the windows were open to catch the sea breezes.

Beyond those were weather-blasted warehouses, much larger and with roofs of black tile, their doors wide open to admit the bales and crates being loaded or unloaded from wagons. They too were spaced regularly, with barely enough distance between them for a wagon to pass through. Zara could see six wagons from where she was, all of them identical, all of them pulled by whirring, wheeled brass and wood Devices rather than horses or cattle. It was unnerving, as if Manachen had been designed by a sculptor who kept using the same molds, over and over again.

The only familiar things were the sounds: the *kraaaw* of the sea birds, the creak of wet and warped wood, the unintelligible distant shouts of men loading cargo onto boats or wagons. If she closed her eyes, she might be in Kingsport—except Kingsport was never this hot or muggy. Then again, if she closed her eyes she might trip and fall, so she wouldn't be doing that.

The male *nakat* went to one of the narrow buildings, one whose window was open, and climbed a few short steps to rap on a narrow door. The woman carried the metal box Alfred's Device was locked inside. Zara kept a close eye on it without looking like she cared. One slip, and she might never see it again.

The door opened, and an older woman in the same crimson and blue uniform poked her head out. The *nakat* spoke to her briefly. She glanced over Zara and the others with a total lack of interest. "Inside," she said in Tremontanese, and they all trooped up the steps, Ransom in front and Zara at the rear. She wasn't sure why she held back, except that she'd never regretted standing back long enough to assess a situation. Ransom could speak for all of them; she could observe, and be prepared for the worst.

She'd been right about the holding capacity of the narrow buildings. This one had a single room inside, and if there'd been half a dozen more in their group, it would have been very crowded. The air was drier and marginally cooler inside, probably because of the cylindrical brass Device chugging away on the back wall. Other than the Device, the room held nothing but a mahogany chair with eight spindly, round legs supporting a basin for a seat and an ebony table with six equally spindly legs and a trapezoidal top. Despite its alien appearance, Zara was certain it was not a matched set. Between that, and the weathered appearance of the unpainted walls, this struck her as a room of afterthoughts. Even the Device was corroded, though the rust made a lacework pattern that might almost have been intentional.

The older woman sat in the basin chair and drew her legs up to sit cross-legged. It looked comfortable. "You approach Manachen without papers," she said, "and with illegal Devices."

"We were going to Tammerek," Ransom said, "and were forced off course. And the Devices are personal property, not intended for trade or sale. We meant no disrespect of your laws."

"Meaning is not in the law," the woman said. "We cannot see your intentions. This is punishable in law."

"We understand, and beg leniency. We will not interact with the citizens of Dineh-Karit and will stay only long enough to find passage to Tammerek."

"Not enough. There is a fine. Twenty *meshet*. Each."

Zara saw Ransom's back go rigid. "That is a heavy fine," he said.

"Heavy fine for heavy wrong."

"We don't have that much."

Wonderful. They'd found one of the greedy hard-liners. Zara turned her attention to the *nakati*. The woman was impassive. The man looked uncertain. He glanced at their little group and saw Zara watching him, then lowered his eyes. Ashamed, was he? Too bad she couldn't think of a way to use that.

"We have some," Ransom continued, "and if you allow us to contact our people on Tammerek, we will have the rest."

"Not good enough." The woman gestured dismissively.

"Not good enough for whom?" Zara said. Everyone turned to look at her at once. Ransom looked as if he wanted to shout at her. Well, they were about to be thrown in prison, so she couldn't make things worse. She hoped.

"What say you?" the woman said. She looked as if she'd just heard a cat sit up and speak Karitian.

"I'm asking about your government. Who decides the fines?" Zara kept her posture relaxed. No sense antagonizing the woman with an aggressive stance.

"They are by law," the woman said. The male *nakat* shook his head, almost imperceptibly.

"But they vary according to the crime, yes?" Zara said. The woman nodded. "And the fine is to compensate the government for having to deal with lawbreakers."

The woman's eyes narrowed. "Who are you to know such things?"

"It's obvious. And I imagine some of the fine pays your salary, doesn't it?" *Or, more likely, your bribe.*

"Rowena," Ransom said in a low voice. She ignored him.

"I have one question," she went on, cutting across the woman's next words. "If you put us in prison for not paying the fine, and your government gets no money out of us—loses money, having to house

160

and feed us in prison—do you benefit from that personally, or not?" Her heart was beating too rapidly, but this was both exhilarating and terrifying, because if she'd judged this woman wrong, if she was more proud than venal, they would all be finding out whether Karitians fed their prisoners or not.

The woman leaned back in her chair, narrow-eyed as if she were thinking hard. "How much have you?" she finally said.

Ransom tipped the diamonds onto the desk. Zara kept her eyes on the woman and not on the stones, and saw her eyes gleam. She touched the stones, then said, "It is enough for all but one. Choose."

Belinda gasped. Zara said, "We can get the rest if you give us time." *And access to Theo's belt.*

"No time. Dineh-Karit does not treat with foreigners. Choose."

"I'll stay," Ransom said.

"Are you out of your mind?" Zara shouted.

Ransom moved swiftly to take Zara's arm. "Don't be a fool. The Zakharis can't be separated. Theo and Belinda wouldn't last two hours in a Karitian prison. And you have a mission." He smiled that crooked, sardonic smile. "Once you're on Tammerek, find a negotiator and give that person a *lot* of money. He or she will come back here and release me. It shouldn't take long."

"This isn't even your journey! You didn't want to be here!"

"Sometimes life takes you places you weren't expecting to go. Don't worry about me. I speak the language." He pulled the pouch over his head and pressed it into her hands. "Just in case."

"We can give them Theo's belt!"

"That would be fatal. She couldn't turn in that much in fines without being investigated. And it's too large for a bribe. She'd have to kill us, and possibly the *nakati*, to keep it a secret. Just do as I say for once?"

"Ransom—"

He stepped away from her. "You've spoken the law's verdict," he said to the woman, "and these two are witnesses." He nodded at the *nakati*. "If these five don't return to Tammerek along with their possessions, the law will punish you."

The male *nakat* nodded vigorously and said something in Karitian, then repeated in Eskandelic, *"We will find a boat for you."*

"But...you can't stay!" Belinda wailed. "This isn't right!"

"It's how things are in Dineh-Karit," Ransom said.

The woman unfolded herself and came around the desk to face Zara. "You go," she said, "and do not come back." She gestured at the *nakat*, who opened the door and motioned for them to leave.

"I want my Devices back, please," Zara said, pointing at the box. The woman glared at her, but snapped her fingers at the female *nakat*, who unlocked the box and handed Zara the Device and the pistol. Zara shoved the Device into her pocket and the gun into her waistband, staring down the *nakat*. She was so furious her hands were shaking. Ransom staying behind—oh, hell, that name was all too appropriate right now!—that stupid greedy bitch of a Karitian! She closed her fist on her shaking and turned to follow the others out the door.

"Wait," Ransom said. She turned in time for him to take three rapid strides across the tiny room and kiss her, hard, his lips firm on hers and one of his hands burying itself in her mass of filthy hair. "That's not a goodbye," he said when he released her, his eyes fierce. "I *will* see you again."

Stunned, Zara took a step backward, her eyes fixed on his, then stumbled as her heel caught the stairs. She had to turn around to catch herself, and by the time she reached the bottom of the steps, the door was closed and he was gone.

She hurried to catch up to Belinda, her heart pounding, the memory of his kiss still on her lips. What was he—how—he couldn't— She was having trouble thinking straight, didn't even know where they were going. Why—?

"If I weren't so upset, I'd gloat over being right," Belinda murmured. "I *thought* he was interested in you."

"You saw that?"

"I was only a foot away. Of course I saw that. Now we *really* have to get him back."

"*Belinda!*"

"I'm kidding. It's either that or run gibbering mad across these docks. Aren't you afraid they'll go back on their word?"

"Terrified. Though I think the *nakat,* the man, is honorable. He certainly wasn't happy about his superior. I think she's extorted far more people than just us. Bribery might be part of their system, but that didn't feel right." She laughed bitterly. "Not that I know anything about it."

They were back on the pier again—or, not again, because it was a different one. The *nakat* leaned over a pink and green boat moored to the pier to speak to a woman dressed in a loincloth and a sort of brassiere of twisted dark green fabric. He gestured out across the bay toward distant Goudge's Folly.

"Though I'm surprised you didn't realize, what with all the time you were spending together," Belinda continued. No one else seemed to be listening, but she spoke in a low voice regardless.

"I'm too old for him," Zara said.

"Not that old. If you were a man and he were a woman, nobody would think anything of it."

"No, I mean—it's not possible."

"I just saw some excellent evidence to the contrary. How long do you think it will take to find someone who can release him? We certainly have the funds."

"Belinda—"

"Why don't you save all of those objections for when you see him again?"

Zara gave up. It was impossible. She was far too old to be thinking of romance, and certainly not with someone young enough to be her grandson. And he knew who she really was, mostly, so what was he thinking? She must look awful, messy hair, beet red face—*I will see you again,* she heard him say in memory, and it started her heart beating faster again. She was a fool, and she needed to concentrate, because until they were all on Goudge's Folly, none of them were safe.

The *nakat* straightened and gestured to them. "*She will take you to*

Tammerek," he said in Eskandelic.

"What will happen to our friend?" Zara demanded, not moving.

"Prison is not dangerous," he said, his eyes darting everywhere but in her direction.

"Don't lie to us," Arjan said. *"What will happen?"*

The *nakat* backed away. *"You should send help soon,"* he said, and ran back the way they'd come. Arjan's face was grim. Zara was sure she looked the same. He gave her a hand down into the boat, then settled himself next to Cantara amidships. The boat pilot deftly maneuvered them away from the pier and out across the water toward Goudge's Folly.

"Will this take long?" Zara asked. The pilot looked at her with incomprehension. *"Will it take long?"* she repeated herself in Eskandelic, then, feeling desperate, in Veriboldan. The woman's face cleared, and she smiled.

"It is only half an hour," she said in the same language. *"This is a fast boat."*

"How do you speak Veriboldan?" Theo asked.

"I learned it a long time ago," Zara said, feeling every one of her eighty-seven years aching through her bones. Theo subsided, and then there was nothing but the sound of the Device purring like the largest cat Zara could think of. Did *najabedhi* purr? She closed her eyes and cursed herself for thinking of irrelevancies, but it was either that or trying not to imagine what Ransom was going through. How bad *were* those prisons? Would it matter that he had healing magic? Surely even the Karitians valued that over nationality.

None of that mattered. They would reach Goudge's Folly in half an hour, they'd find a negotiator, and they'd send that person back over immediately. Ransom might be back before nightfall. Possibly earlier. It was hard to believe it was barely after noon, so much had happened. He'd kissed her. He'd meant it, too. Not a goodbye. Zara closed her eyes against memories. She had to stay focused, because Ransom was counting on her.

The sun hammered down on her head like heated brass, tempered not much by the wind kicked up by the rapidly moving boat. The pilot steered deftly around other boats like a lunatic, making Belinda squeak every time they came close to colliding with one of the bright flying specks that veered close and then were gone. It was a dance, children spinning and leaping around the grown dancers that were the ships, gracefully curving into the harbor or settled at rest here and there throughout the bay, and if her muscles weren't knotted with hot tension, she'd be able to appreciate it better. Was there a pattern to it, or was it all just the kind of randomness that could leave an innocent man trapped in a foreign prison—she shook her head to fight off the visions her fiendish imagination insisted on showing her.

She wished the Device really was the pocket watch it seemed to be, because it felt like much longer than half an hour before Goudge's Folly went from being a shape misty with distance to a massive rock looming large and bright before them. It had to be an illusion that the little red roofs were so much more welcoming there.

The island rose to a gentle, flat-topped peak of verdant green, below which lay hundreds of roofs, mostly red, but some blue or tan and one or two stark black like spots of char on a multicolored tablecloth. It looked as though Goudge's Folly had been settled for generations, which made Zara wonder how long northerners had been here, and how much longer they had to go on the lease. What would happen to all of them if Dineh-Karit decided it didn't like foreigners polluting its waters anymore? Living on Goudge's Folly had lost its appeal.

Traffic at the Goudge's Folly docks was even heavier than it had been in Manachen, and it took the pilot some time to find a place where they could exit the boat. Zara got off last, afraid the pilot might demand money from them—had the *nakat* even paid her?—and unwilling to give away Theo's secret, but the woman just turned the boat around and zipped away toward the mainland. At least something had gone their way that day. Two things, if you counted not being captured or killed by pirates.

She joined the others at the end of the pier. "What now?" Theo said.

"I'll find Falken & Daughter and see if I can get an advance on my salary. You'll find a negotiator," Zara said.

"We've still got plenty of gems," Belinda said, but quietly.

"Those aren't ours."

"I told you, my aunt won't mind," Theo said. "And he saved our lives."

"We all his friends are," Cantara said. "This trouble our fault is."

"It's the fault of that pirate Ghazarian, and let's all not forget that," Zara said. "All right. Let's start asking around for a negotiator. That has to happen first, anyway."

The docks were a messy jumble of enormous warehouses and scattered customs houses so comforting to the eye, so *northern*, Zara almost relaxed. If there hadn't been that tiny voice in the back of her head screaming at her to *hurry hurry hurry*, she would have enjoyed being back where people spoke one of the three languages she did. As it was, she felt choked with impatience as they sped across the docks, looking for something that might be a harbormaster's house, preferably a Tremontanan one.

Finally, Belinda said, "There! That's the sign!" Zara looked where she pointed and saw a familiar green and brown sign and shield bearing the triple peaks of Tremontane. They ran faster, dodging sailors and burly men loading wagons, until they stumbled in the door of the harbormaster's house, nearly knocking over someone who was exiting at the same time.

"We need a negotiator," Zara demanded of the room at large.

"This isn't the place to go for that," a tall woman wearing a harbormaster's uniform said. "And you could stand to be a little more polite."

"We have a friend in a Karitian prison who needs help *now*," Zara snarled. "Excuse me if politeness isn't at the top of my priorities."

"Good heaven," said another woman standing nearby. She was about sixty years old and had a face like a cheerful, wrinkled apple, but her voice was aghast. "Dearie, nobody gets out of a Karitian prison."

"He told us to find a negotiator and send a lot of money," Theo said. "Just tell us where to go."

The room was silent. "You're wasting your time," said the harbormaster finally, "but if you go to the Tremontanan embassy, they'll have someone there who will tell you what I just did."

"Thanks," said Zara. "Where's the embassy?"

"Straight out the harbor gate, down that street," the harbormaster said. "Third street on the right, follow it as it rises—the slope's about a quarter mile—then turn left and it's the fifth house on the right. Looks like the Justiciary, if you've ever seen that."

"I have," said Zara. "Thanks."

"Good luck," said the wrinkly woman, but she didn't sound very encouraging. Zara ignored her and rushed back out the door, once again nearly knocking over someone trying to enter. Was everyone on Goudge's Folly trying to get in her way?

"Let's go," she said, and they ran.

CHAPTER FIFTEEN

Goudge's Folly was as hot and humid as Dineh-Karit, hotter because there were no great trees to hold off the sun, and running was like slogging through flower-scented soup. They ran anyway, down the street from the harbor, until Belinda, panting, said, "I can't do this, I'm sorry," and slowed to a walk. The rest of them returned to her side. "You should leave me. I'll catch up."

"If we separated are, we may not find each other again, and we have lost one person already today," Arjan said. "We should not exhaust ourselves."

Zara bit back an impatient reply. "Let's keep moving. It won't take long."

They walked down a long road lined with the same trees and plants they'd forged a path through only days before, but tamed into a semblance of cultivation. Shops and houses peeped out from the riot of plants thick with red and purple flowers shaped like trumpets; jewel-like birds the length of Zara's pinky finger darted in and out, dipping their needle-sharp beaks into the flowers and then zipping away again. Zara found herself watching the flight of two of those birds around and under an airy verandah that encircled one of the houses, caught herself, and picked up the pace. Beside her, Belinda was red-faced and breathing heavily, and Zara felt the smallest pang of guilt at pushing her friend so hard, but it couldn't be helped.

The buildings they passed were all Karitian, or at least Zara assumed the wide windows, the broad verandahs, and the gently-sloping roofs were designed for tropical weather. They were as identical to each other as the ones on the Manachen docks had been, at least in construction, but were painted in bright colors that clashed with one another. The bold individualism cheered Zara, made her feel as if they weren't completely alone in a foreign land. The faces were all Tremontanan as well, though no one paid any attention to the scruffy and probably odorous strangers, two of whom were Eskandelic. That cheered her further. Tremontanans as a whole were many things, but xenophobic wasn't one of them.

They turned right at the third street and found themselves in a neighborhood of more obviously Tremontanan-inspired buildings, thick-walled and with steeply sloping roofs, though still painted in garish colors. "Bet those houses are miserable in summer," Theo said.

"Bet they're miserable now," Belinda said. "Is it me, or is the street sloping up?"

"It you is not," Arjan said. "I feel it too."

The street sloped gently up for about a quarter mile, slowing them further, and Zara had begun to regret insisting they stay together when it came to an end, sharply turning left. They'd left behind the commercial district, if that's what it was, and everything at this end of the street was giant mansions built in the Karitian style, all of them white with red roofs, all of them set far back from the street along curving drives paved in small white stones that glittered in the afternoon sun. "Fifth on the right," Zara said, and they ran again, Zara breathing in a second wind that propelled her up the new street, which sloped even more steeply, to the fifth mansion on the right.

It did look like the Justiciary, which had been rebuilt the year she took the throne. Its front was one long colonnade of white pillars that bulged slightly in the middle, beyond which she could barely see the mansion's cool façade. It lay some distance from the street, past a white ironwork gate wide enough to admit one of those Device-propelled carts from the Manachen docks. Zara ran ahead of the others and fell on it, winded. It didn't open.

"Can I help you with something?" A young man in a forest green and walnut brown Tremontanan attaché's uniform appeared in front of her, on the other side of the gate.

"We need a negotiator," Zara panted. This climate would be the death of her, if that were possible. "They told us to come here."

"Are you Tremontanan citizens?"

His tone of voice was so skeptical Zara wanted to shout *Do we look like Karitians to you, idiot?* and rattle the bars again, but she said, "Three of us are. These are our companions from Eskandel. We're here on behalf of another Tremontanan citizen who's been unlawfully detained in Manachen. Please let us in."

The man frowned. "Wait a minute," he said, and walked up the sparkling drive so slowly Zara wished she could propel him along with a good swift kick to his green and brown backside.

"Why won't he open the gate?" Theo said. He leaned on it, breathing as heavily as Zara was.

"He afraid is," Cantara said. "We do not look like reputables."

"Well, he'd better hurry back," Belinda said, but she sounded uncertain.

They waited. Insects buzzed around Zara's head, undeterred by her shooing them away. Belinda sat on the ground with her back against the gate and her eyes closed. Theo had his hand on his belt again, though this time he was fingering the lumps inside, counting. Arjan paced while Cantara watched him.

Zara put her hand into her pocket and rubbed the surface of the Device. She had no idea how to find Calliope Blackwood and, at the moment, no interest in finding her. This Device had brought them nothing but trouble, and maybe that meant she ought to find Blackwood first, get rid of the thing, but Ransom—she had to stop thinking about him, what he might be enduring right then. He would be all right. They would get him out.

The crunch of boots on gravel heralded the return of the attaché. "You can come in," he said, pointing at Zara and Belinda and Theo. "The Eskandelics stay."

Arjan said, furiously, "We—"

"We've traveled a long way and we're all tired," Belinda said. "Please let them come in with us and rest for a while."

"They're Eskandelics. They can go to their own embassy."

The man's stubborn, smug face, his stance that said he enjoyed exercising power over people, filled Zara with white-hot rage. "What's your name?" she said, walking up so she was within inches of him.

"Reginald Dyer," the man said, as if his was the proudest name in Tremontane.

"Mister Dyer," Zara said, "we are here on behalf of a Tremontanan citizen whose family is extremely powerful. You will open this gate. You will let *all* of us in. You will precede us to the Embassy and you will take us to someone who has the power to free this man. And you will do all of this, Mister Dyer, because if you do not, someone else will, and when that happens I will make it my mission in life to break you so far down your family will need a special dispensation from the King himself to find you again. Do we have an understanding?"

The attaché took an involuntary step back. "I," he began, and Zara fixed him with the blue-eyed North glare that had reduced Counts and Barons to stammering fools. "Ma'am," he said, and unlocked the gate. Zara swept past him the instant it was open, forcing him to scramble to get ahead of her, and strode up the path, still burning with righteous fury.

"Sweet holy heaven," Belinda said. "You're terrifying."

"Yes," said Zara, "I am."

The door to the Tremontanan Embassy was made of some tropical hardwood Zara didn't recognize. Mister Dyer had it open well before they got there, but before they could enter, someone cursed, then shouted, "Shut the damn door, man! D'ye want all the insects in this heavenforsaken place to eat me alive?"

Zara crossed the threshold and was struck by a blast of cold air that was such a contrast to the muggy heat outside she immediately drenched in sweat. Belinda gasped in relief. The others crowded in past the attaché, who shut the door, and Zara turned her attention to the woman crossing the foyer toward them.

The foyer was at least fifteen feet tall and windowless, big enough to make Zara feel small, but the woman approaching her now was large enough to match her surroundings. She was taller than Zara, probably in her late forties, and hugely fat, and her hair was cropped close to her head in a style Zara envied, with her own hair falling down in back and her itchy scalp. The woman's white shirt and trousers looked so comfortable Zara was again aware of her grubby condition, of the place where the knee of her trousers was torn, and the desire for a bath became nearly overwhelming. "Who are you?" the woman demanded.

"We're looking for a negotiator," Zara said, skipping the niceties. "Our friend is imprisoned in Manachen and we need someone who can get him out."

"Don't be a fool. No foreigner leaves a Karitian prison," the woman said. "I hope you said your farewells."

"He told us enough money and a good negotiator would be enough. We have the money. We just need someone who speaks the language and understands their customs. Or laws. Or whatever it is they use to decide what passes for justice."

"Come with me." The woman turned on her heel and walked away, not waiting for them. Zara and the others hurried after her. "It's impossible," the woman said as they walked. "The Karitian government hates foreigners and only allows its citizens to do business with us because they levy a high tariff on foreign goods. They don't think we deserve justice the way their citizens do."

"But this is an embassy. Don't you treat with them?"

"Hah. This is an embassy in name only. We've got no power here, nothing but a veneer of respectability. And we throw excellent parties." The woman flung open a door that led to a room even chillier than the foyer. Zara had never seen anything so opulent outside the palace. The walls were draped with red silk a debutante wouldn't be ashamed to be seen in; the sofa and three armchairs were upholstered in gold-shot silk brocade; the desk and cabinetry smelled of varnish and money. The woman threw herself into the chair behind the desk and gestured at the room in general. "Have a seat."

The others sat. Zara remained standing. "Ma'am," she said, "this is urgent. There must be something you can do."

"Sit down," the woman said, and there was steel in her words. Zara sat. "Look, I'll be honest with you. We can send a negotiator, and we can send money. But even if they do release your friend, it could take weeks. And surviving inside a Karitian prison for weeks…what you get back might not resemble your friend anymore."

Zara clenched her fists in frustration and realized she was still holding Ransom's pouch in her left hand. She'd completely forgotten about it. "Wait," she said, and opened it, rummaged through the scant contents. A couple of letters, a signet ring—"His name is De Witt," she said. "Ransom De Witt. Does that matter to you?"

The woman's jaw went slack with astonishment. "*Daniel* De Witt?" she said. "The boy's been lost for five years, and—you can't possibly mean the same man. Or did you think to use a dead man's name to rescue your friend? Because I don't like being played."

"He didn't give his first name," Zara said, wondering in passing what was so wrong with the name Daniel. "But he gave me this before we parted." She held out the signet ring. It was incised on both sides with a tiny sign and shield bearing what looked like a fox and a wreath of laurel leaves, and the insignia on its face was an intertwined D and W.

The woman took it gingerly, as if she was afraid it might burn her. "By heaven, it's the De Witt sign and shield all right. You—"

"Don't say we stole it," Zara said. The fury began to fill her again, and she took it in both hands to bridle it. Intimidating that stupid sergeant was one thing; if she said the wrong words to this woman, Ransom might stay in that prison forever. "It's his ring. He's got letters from his family, though I think he'd prefer we not read them. I swear it's him. We have to get him out."

The woman set the ring on the desk and stared at it. Then she said, "Damn."

"Find us a negotiator," Zara said.

"It doesn't change anything," the woman said, "except now we have to try, or the De Witts will never stop battering at us for losing their only son." She pushed back heavily from the desk and pulled a bell rope dangling near it. "I almost wish he'd stayed lost."

"I'm sure he's very sorry for inconveniencing you," Zara shot back.

The woman raised an eyebrow at her. "Sharp words," she said as the door opened and a slender young man with a pencil-thin mustache entered. "Get on the telecoder," she said. "Send a message home that...dear heaven, I don't even know what to say...tell them we'll need another diplomatic letter to the Karitians."

"But—" the young man said.

"I know, James, but there's no other way. Tell them Blackwood is waiting for a reply."

"Wait," Zara said as the young man closed the door behind himself. "Are you Blackwood? Calliope Blackwood?"

The woman nodded. "Ambassador to Dineh-Karit, for my sins."

"Then I have something that belongs to you," Zara said, and pulled the Device out of her pocket and laid it on the desk.

Blackwood shot out of her seat, knocking the chair over. "Sweet heaven," she whispered. Then she grabbed the rope and pulled on it hard, several times. "Cancel that," she told James when he reappeared, looking startled. "Don't send any more telecodes until I give the word." She snatched up the Device and clicked through the settings a few times. "What happened to Alfred?"

"He died. We were attacked by pirates. He asked me to bring this to you."

"Oh, Alfred," Blackwood said quietly. "He was a good friend of mine. I thought his ship had simply been delayed, but..." She set the Device back on the desk. "Out," she said. "James will show you to a place where you can clean up. You all look exhausted. No, don't argue with me," she said when Zara and Belinda both began to protest. "This is going to take some time to sort out, and there's no sense you all sitting around in those filthy clothes. Go. I'll summon you when there's news."

Seething over "summon," Zara did as she was told. They filed out into the hallway.

"It's something," Theo said. "At least she's going to try."

"How did you know they would care about his name?" Cantara

said.

"Excuse me," James said, emerging from Blackwood's office behind them. "If you'll follow me, there is a washroom just up the stairs."

"He told me his family back in Aurilien was important," Zara said as they all trooped after James up a long, curving staircase with a bannister made of the same exotic-smelling hardwood as Blackwood's office furniture. "I just didn't know how important. I made a guess."

"A good guess," said Arjan. "I think it will take less time than they imagine."

The washroom had two basins, both with hot and cold running water supplied by Devices on the taps. They took turns, once James was gone, washing their faces and hands and splashing water on their necks, drying with the many fluffy towels in the cupboards, and looking out the washroom window over the hills of Goudge's Folly. The embassy was nearly at the top of the hill, and even though it wasn't a very tall hill, it looked out across the bay to where Manachen was a dim splotch of rust red. Zara stood there for a long time, trying not to think. There was nothing more she could do. *Hurry*, she thought in Blackwood's direction, *hurry*, and closed her hands on the smooth windowsill, warm despite the cool air. It had to be a Device that kept the embassy so chilly, which Zara had never heard of; Devices to warm a room, surely, but to take the heat out…that was quite an innovation. *Yes*, she told herself, *think about Devices, think about what else is possible, don't think about —*

Someone came running up the stairs. "You, ma'am," James said, panting. He pointed at Zara. "Miss Blackwood wants to see you."

Fear filled her. She ruthlessly stomped it down and followed James, but by the time they reached the bottom of the stairs, she was running. She dashed through Blackwood's door and found the woman sitting at the desk, staring at Alfred's Device. The leaf engravings were raised in one of their patterns, but to Zara's surprise they were also glowing a faint green, as if there were a motive force inside the thing leaking light from the cracks. "She's here, your Majesty," Blackwood said to the air.

"*Thank you,*" a man's voice replied. It came from the Device. Zara's mouth fell open. Sweet heaven. No wonder Alfred had been so insistent no one else get their hands on it. A Device that let you speak to someone at a distance—a far distance, if this was—

"*This is Jeffrey North, ma'am,*" the voice said. "*Calliope, would you leave us alone for a moment?*"

"Of course, your Majesty," Blackwood said, giving Zara a skeptical look, but shutting the door quietly behind her.

"*She's gone?*"

"Yes. Is that…is that really you?" His voice was tinny, as if he were speaking into a metal box, and she hadn't spoken to him in decades, but if she could believe in a Device that spoke, she could believe this was Jeffrey North.

"*Yes. I realize it's unexpected.*"

"That's not the word I would use, but…yes. Jeffrey, I don't even know where to start."

"*I imagine you're not going by Agatha Weaver anymore, so I couldn't call you by name, but I knew you were there. I've been following your progress—what under heaven have you been doing?*"

"We don't have time to chat, Jeffrey. How do we get Ransom De Witt free?"

"*Tell me your name, first. I have to be able to give Calliope instructions.*"

"Rowena Farrell."

"*All right. The first thing you need to know, Rowena, is that tensions between our government and the Karitians are high. They have Devisery that lets them intercept telecodes and they've used it on us. They already knew our embassy was spying on them, just as we know they spy on us, but now they're in a position to act self-righteous and deny us any requests we might make.*"

"Meaning you can't send a negotiator. They might kill Ransom if they knew he mattered."

"*Right. But we also can't let a Tremontanan citizen rot in a Karitian prison. So I can't not act.*"

"But what can you do?"

"*Send a private negotiator. Someone Tremontanan who isn't affiliated with the government.*" There was a pause. "*Someone with experience at getting people to do things her way.*"

She'd known where he was going with that before his final thin and echoing words had faded. "I don't speak Karitian."

"*They won't expect you to. Not all Karitians are selfish bigots, but it seems a majority of the ones in power are. I think their political structure encourages it.*"

"Let's save the political analysis for later, shall we? We're going to need a lot of money, Ransom said."

"*Calliope said you had funds.*"

"We do, but they're not exactly ours. I was hoping the government could pay for it."

"*We don't have much in the way of liquid assets there. It might be faster if we reimbursed you. Who is 'we'?*"

"I was shipwrecked with some of the passengers on the ship I was traveling on. It's a long story I'd be happy to tell you later."

"*I'd appreciate it. Anyone else who'd made the trip you did, I would have worried about.*"

"Thanks. I was perfectly safe." She didn't mention the snake. Or the pirates. Though… "We were pursued by people who wanted this Device. People who had a way to track it."

Jeffrey cursed. "*Are they still in a position to follow you?*"

"Possibly. They were apprehended by the Karitians as well."

"*Because there's something else I want you to do on the mainland. Something Alfred Richfield was meant to attempt.*"

"Jeffrey, I'm not an agent. I'm not saying I'm not willing, but I'm not qualified."

"*This won't take much. We have agents in Manachen—a couple of naturalized Eskandelics who can pass for Karitian. I need to communicate with them and, as I said, we can't use the telecoder. All you have to do is take this Device to a place Calliope will direct you to and let me have five minutes' conversation with them. Then, depending on what they tell me, you'll either bring the Device back to the embassy or leave it with them.*"

"That's impossible. I don't look Karitian."

"*There are Tremontanans in Manachen. Most of them are servants, people working off fines. Calliope will help you disguise yourself. You meet with the agents, release De Witt from prison, and come back to Goudge's Folly.*"

Zara shook her head, then remembered Jeffrey couldn't see her. "I'm not leaving Ransom there one second longer than I have to. I get him first."

"*This is far more important than one man's life.*"

"To you, maybe. Besides, if Ransom knows the city, he'll be able to guide me better than some hard-to-follow directions."

Jeffrey was silent for so long Zara began to wonder if he'd turned off the Device on his end. "*All right,*" he finally said. "*De Witt first. But don't linger in Manachen. I wouldn't ask this of you if there were any other way, you understand?*"

"What's family for, if not to ask outrageous favors?"

Jeffrey laughed. It sounded like the cough of a dying man. "*I'll be in your debt again.*"

"I'll have to think of something outrageous to ask of *you*."

"*You're well, though? I wondered why you'd gone so far afield.*"

"I just…wanted something different. I'm perfectly well. And now I should go, if I'm going to perform your outrageously dangerous task."

"*Thank you. Get Calliope back here, will you? She'll tell you the rest once I've instructed her.*"

Zara went to the door. Blackwood was hovering some distance down the hall. Zara didn't think she'd been listening in, but she gave the woman a cool stare as she passed and was relieved to see she didn't flinch the way a guilty person might have. Or she just had the same iron-clad nerves Zara did. Well, they hadn't said anything incriminating except the comment about family, and Zara would defy Blackwood to make something of it.

She went back upstairs and found the others in a lush sitting room, with velvet carpet that matched the purple velvet upholstery of the chairs. It looked like an upscale mausoleum. "Well? What was that about?" Belinda said.

"It's complicated," Zara said, "but the fundamentals are they can't send an official negotiator without causing an international incident. So they're sending me instead."

"You mean us," Theo said.

"No. Just me."

"You cannot," Arjan said. "That lunacy is."

"All five of us going in there at once will only make things worse," Zara said. "I'll go as a private Tremontanan citizen. Theo, I'll need as many of those gems as you can spare. The government will reimburse your aunt."

"If you go, they might keep you as well," Cantara said. She was holding tight to Arjan's hand and her whole body was rigid. "We cannot do this."

"They're not going to keep me. And the alternative is Ransom sits there in prison until he dies. This is the only way."

Belinda stood and paced from her chair to the one small window and back. "You're right," she said. "This isn't something we can do. But surely there's someone else? Someone who speaks Karitian, for heaven's sake!"

"If there were, they'd send him. And I'd let him go. Trust me, Belinda, I know how ridiculous this sounds, but I have to do this."

"You'll do it," Theo said. "We saw you talk down that man. If any of us have a chance, it's you." He took off his belt and began picking at the seams. "I wish I knew how much these were worth."

"Maybe someone here can tell us," Belinda said. "You'll need to know how much to ask for in reimbursement. Those, plus the two Ransom—" She stopped and turned away.

"Excuse me," James said from the doorway. "I'm to take you to your rooms now. Feel free to bathe and change your clothes before supper."

"I have to go now," Zara said.

"You have to wait until morning," said Blackwood, coming up behind James. "The Karitians won't see you at this hour of the afternoon, and I'll need to prepare you anyway. I'm sorry," she added, holding up her hands when they all began to protest, "but that's the way it is. De Witt should be safe until morning."

"You don't believe that," said Zara.

"No." Blackwood turned away. "But there's nothing more to be done, save pray the Karitians listen to you. For his sake, I hope you're persuasive."

"So do I," Zara said.

Chapter Sixteen

After the chill of the embassy, even the muggy coolness of a Karitian morning had Zara sweating before she reached the end of the drive and had the gate opened for her by a subdued Mister Dyer. A woman dressed in a loose tunic and wide-legged linen trousers, both of them a soft rose, waited there with a carriage built like a teacup, fancifully painted with silver flowers on a pale green background. There was nothing about the woman or the carriage to suggest they had anything to do with Tremontane's government. Zara herself was dressed in a white sleeveless tunic and trousers similar to the woman's, though hers held a number of secrets Zara suspected the woman would never guess. More to the point, she hoped the Karitians didn't guess them either.

She climbed into the carriage without assistance and brushed her hair back over her shoulders. It felt so good to be *clean*, even if she was sweating. She'd wanted to put her hair up, let the breezes cool her neck, but Blackwood had warned her that would make her appear to be putting on airs. *Only upper-class Karitians wear their hair up*, she'd said, *and you don't want to look like you're saying you're their equal.*

She'd had any number of other warnings. Let the Karitians speak first. Give direct answers. Don't let them see how much money you have—Zara hadn't needed to be told that. She crossed her legs and leaned back, feeling the little pouch—Ransom's pouch—settle between her breasts. She'd been coached in how much to offer and whom to offer it to, in what to say and what not to say (*You're bribing them, but that's crass, so you never suggest it's a bribe*, Blackwood had said) and now she was as prepared as she could be. She watched the flowering trees pass and tried not to think about the price of failure.

She saw other carriages like hers passing, more than they'd seen the day before. Apparently they'd arrived during the hottest part of the day, when most people were napping indoors, which was just another way in which this adventure had gone wrong. The woman flicked the reins at the horse, who stepped out more spryly. The heat didn't seem to bother it, but Zara still felt sorry for it. She plucked at the neck of her tunic and fanned herself with it. Definitely Veribold after this. She'd just have to make her apologies to Mistress Falken and make Jeffrey give her enough money to repay her fare and take a ship back north.

The horse's hooves went from clopping on the hard-packed earth to tapping on the wooden docks, and the wheels rattled more loudly. Then the carriage was pulling up to one of the piers, and Zara hopped down. "The third boat, ma'am," the driver said, pointing. "She'll be waiting for your return."

"Thank you," Zara said, and strode briskly toward the indicated boat. It was painted lemon yellow and its Device shone bright brass. The pilot was lounging with her feet on the gunwale and a bright red woven hat shielding her face, but sat up quickly when Zara cleared her throat.

"Sorry, ma'am, I was just resting my eyes," she said, and Zara realized she was barely more than a child, bright-eyed and enthusiastic. She might have been Theo's twin, down to the closely shorn head. Zara envied her her loincloth and skimpy brassiere. "Let me help you. You don't mind going fast, do you?"

"I *love* going fast," Zara said, and before she was finished speaking the young woman had spun the wheel to full, and the boat zipped away from the pier, knocking Zara back in her seat. She sat up and gripped the gunwale, thinking, *Faster*, and as if the girl could read her mind, the boat sped up until the pilot had to put her hat under her feet to keep it from flying away.

At this hour, the Amgeli had no tide to fight, and small boats zipped up and down stream, pulling in to shore to hand off parcels and then speed away again. Zara watched them, counting how many times each went between the larger ships and their…might as well call them docks, though mostly they were platforms on the shore of the river. The brightly colored boats were confetti on the waves, the propelling Devices made sparks of gold in the sunlight, and the whole thing was so cheery and indifferent to the injustice of the Karitian government it made her want to scream.

As they approached the Manachen piers, the pilot said, "I'll stay here as long as I can, but that's only an hour. Then I'll have to cast off and return later, and I might not be in the same place. That's what the hat's for, so you can see me at a distance. So if you take longer than an hour, you may have to wait for me a bit." She flapped the hat in Zara's direction. "Any questions?"

"Yes. What's your name?"

The young woman laughed. "Cerise. We're here. Good luck, ma'am."

They were approaching a pier where stood a couple of female *nakati*, watching them closely. Before Zara had even set foot on the pier, the taller one said, "Foreigners are not allowed in Manachen."

"I am here to negotiate a release," Zara said, speaking slowly enough to be perfectly intelligible, but not enough to be insulting. "I ask permission to be escorted to the *godozi* for this purpose alone, after which I will return to Tammerek. I will not speak to any Karitians unless I am spoken to. I swear to obey the laws of Dineh-Karit while I am on its ground."

The *nakati* looked at each other. Zara waited. Finally, the shorter one said something in Karitian to her companion, who nodded. "Come with us," the taller one said. So, they were going to pretend only one of them spoke Tremontanese. Zara couldn't see the point in that, but knowing more about your enemy than she knew of you was always valuable.

This early in the morning, the breeze carried only the faintest scents of brine and tar, and Zara inhaled shallowly and made herself relax. This would work. Bracketed by the *nakati*, she walked past the ranks of narrow houses, none of which had their windows open this morning, and the identical warehouses, which were already busy with wagons loading and unloading. Only a few of the drovers paid her any attention, and that was in the form of ostentatiously refusing to look at her. Other men and women in the gaudy *nakati* uniform were more obvious in watching her. They held themselves in readiness to attack her if she stepped wrong. Zara felt the Device in its special pocket brush her leg. She'd left the gun Device behind, obviously, but if anyone thought to search her, she might be joining Ransom in prison.

Beyond the warehouses, a street wider than any Zara had seen before stretched deep into Manachen. It was big enough a row of houses might be built down its middle, leaving enough room on either side for two ordinary streets. She tried not to gape, but it was hard not to want to explore, to learn more about this isolationist and antagonistic country. To the right, hidden by red-roofed buildings, was the river, whose rushing murmur was the only thing she could hear. Manachen was as silent as if it were midnight.

No one within the city wore the loincloths of the sailors; most of them wore narrow, sleeveless robes in bright colors that brushed the ground as they walked. They draped closely enough to reveal that brassieres were not an invention this country embraced. Filmy gauze coats or cloaks, if you could call anything so lightweight that, were layered over the robes and pulled over the head to obscure the face. These people, unlike the drovers, ignored Zara so completely she was sure they really didn't see her. It relieved her mind somewhat. That would make the second part of her job easier, if foreigners were invisible.

They walked down the center of the plaza-like street. Zara's armpits itched and her neck was sweaty and hot. The sandals Blackwood had given her were little better than leather soles with thongs strung through them, and her feet hurt every time she took a step on the hard concrete pavers of the street. Nicer shoes would have been more appropriate as well as more comfortable, but the second part of her job, again, required something different. She resisted the urge to scratch. *How much farther do we have to walk?* she thought, then felt ashamed of complaining, even internally. This was nothing. Ransom had to endure far worse.

The architecture of Manachen was identical to what she'd seen on Goudge's Folly. She saw no signs of individuality anywhere, though she didn't draw any conclusions from that. In large cities in Veribold, home owners were taxed according to the construction of their houses: so much for window boxes, so much more for a blue instead of a brown roof. So the homes were very plain, and you couldn't assume anything about the owners' personalities from looking at their houses. Even so, the uniformity unnerved her. It might not say anything about individual Karitians, but it certainly suggested things about their culture.

Something nagged at her, something strange about the city, and it wasn't until she passed a few doors that looked like shops that she realized she couldn't smell food. Any Tremontanan city—any *northern* city—this size would be thronged with vendors selling sausages or fruit or sweets, filling the air with delicious aromas. And the place was virtually silent. There were no carriages, just pedestrians, the shopkeepers didn't call out to passersby advertising their wares, and she couldn't see or hear a single person talking to his companions. She became eerily aware of the noise she made, the slapping sound of her leather soles on the pavers, the swish of her trouser legs against each other, and the distant rush of the river, and had to bite back the urge to sing just to break the silence.

The *nakat* in the lead veered sharply to the left, taking them down a narrow alley between two of the buildings. A woman on a verandah stood up to watch them pass. Zara looked up and met her eyes; the woman didn't look away. She looked…pensive? As if it mattered to her what happened to Zara. It must look as if she was being led to her doom. Zara nodded to the woman and smiled as they passed her, and got a tentative smile in return. Not all Karitians were bigoted, Ransom had said. Maybe he was right.

The alley terminated at a paved semicircle in front of—Zara stumbled in surprise. It looked exactly like the Tremontanan embassy, down to the bulgy pillars and the exotic hardwood of the door. It was getting harder for her not to be judgmental of the Karitian culture, if it couldn't produce a variety of architectural styles. "Do not speak," the tall *nakat* woman said, and held open the door so Zara could pass.

Even the foyer was the same—fifteen feet tall, many more than that across, big enough to make her feel small, except she refused to be intimidated by it. It was dry and comfortably cool, not as frigid as the embassy, and smelled of dust. Zara rolled her shoulders to shift her hair a bit without looking like she was uncomfortable. The *nakati* led her to the center of the room, the smaller one made a "stay put" gesture, and the two women went back out the front door. Zara took a relaxed stance that would let her stand comfortably for a long time. She anticipated she'd need it.

About five minutes later, one of the three doors that led elsewhere into this building opened, and a man entered. He wore a narrow, sleeveless robe and gauzy over-robe like the civilians she'd seen, but in *nakati* blue and crimson, and with his beaky face and too-widely-spaced eyes he looked even more like a ha-ha bird than the *nakati* did. He regarded Zara with an expression that said he didn't like the way she smelled, then said something in Karitian.

"I apologize for not speaking your language and beg your indulgence in speaking mine," Zara said. It was one of three phrases she'd had to memorize. The rest was up to her.

The ha-ha man gave her another long look. "You are a negotiator," he said. His Tremontanese was precise, though marred by a thick accent. Zara guessed it would be a matter of pride with these people not to speak the foreigners' languages as precisely as they were able to do.

"I am," Zara said.

Another pause. "The *godozi* is busy. Come back in an hour."

"I'll wait." Zara shifted her position to make it clear she was capable of standing there all day.

The ha-ha man regarded her for another moment. Possibly he was lining up sentences in his head that the foreign woman couldn't counter. Then he turned and left. Zara drew in a deep breath. *They'll try to make you leave and come back later,* Blackwood had said, *but if you do, they'll keep putting you off. If you stay, it will make them uncomfortable enough to deal with you just to get you out of there.*

186

What if they try to remove me by force? Zara had asked.

They won't lay hands on a foreigner, Blackwood had said, *it's beneath them,* but she didn't look certain. It didn't matter. If they made her leave, she wouldn't go quietly.

She waited, counting her heartbeats, examining the identical doors, wondering what kind of wood they were made of. It was a shame the Karitians didn't want open trade, though so far Zara had only seen ways that trade would benefit Tremontane. Who knew what kinds of things they could do for Dineh-Karit?

The door opened again. The ha-ha man sailed in, his gauzy robe fluttering like wings around him. "The *godozi* is very busy. He may not be able to see you today."

"I'll wait."

"Come back later. Or tomorrow."

"I'll wait."

The ha-ha man hesitated. This time, it looked as if he genuinely didn't know what to do. Then he turned around and left again. Zara went back to examining the doors and calculating what kind of profit a company might make in importing the wood. She had to do a lot of guessing, but it kept her from going mad.

A different door opened. This time, it was a ha-ha woman. She wore her dark brown hair piled high on her head and pinned with a pair of long sticks. Jewels dangled from the end of each. "You will come with me," she said.

The hallway beyond was narrow but tall, arched like a bethel back home, though no place of worship would be built from that exotic wood. Windows near the curved ceiling let in a diffuse light that made the hall seem even cooler than it was. Tremontane really should see about developing those room-chilling Devices. Summers in Aurilien could be brutal, though now that Zara had spent time in Dineh-Karit's jungles, her definition of "brutal" was somewhat different.

The walls were painted the same red as the *nakati* uniform and hung with small round paintings Zara didn't have time to examine. It reminded her of her grandfather's sitting room in the palace, somber and dark and cluttered with those round miniatures Grandpapa was so fond of, though that had always smelled of cedar and this hall didn't smell of anything in particular. She hadn't thought of those rooms in years.

At the far end of the hall, the ha-ha woman opened another door, and Zara stepped through into a brightly lit round chamber carpeted in white, with a row of circular windows near its domed ceiling. It was empty except for a table and chair identical in shape to those of the woman on the docks, the greedy bitch who'd stolen Ransom's freedom. These were definitely a matched set in glossy ebony with shining steel legs, like silvery insects making off with planed lumber. A man sat cross-legged in the chair, his narrow robe rucked up around his thighs and his over-robe billowing out around the chair, falling nearly to the floor. "You are the negotiator," he said. His Tremontanese was better than that of the other two Karitians.

"I am," Zara said.

"We do not know you."

"I'm a private citizen negotiating on behalf of the prisoner's family."

"You do not have a letter of authority."

This was the first hurdle. "Those are issued by the government, and we recognize Tremontane currently has no authority with regard to Karitian matters. So no, I don't have a letter of authority."

The *godozi* tapped his fingers on the smooth ebony surface. It was reflective enough to show the shadowy inverse of his fingers, like a pair of hands plotting something diabolical. "Which prisoner?" he said.

She'd sent the official request ahead, earlier that morning. He knew which prisoner. "The man taken at dock seventeen yesterday just after noon. He is accused of trespassing on Karitian territory and refusal to pay the fine."

"That is a serious crime."

"Which is why I'm here to make amends. I am willing to pay the fine, plus the administrative costs incurred by the Karitian government in holding him." Code for "bribe."

"And you think this will be sufficient."

"I think reasonable people are always capable of coming to civilized agreement."

Tap, tap, tap. "The fine is twenty *meshet.*"

Zara removed the pouch from around her neck and dug into it, coming up with a handful of stones she kept concealed from the *godozi.* He looked impassive, but Zara knew curiosity when she saw it, and she was even more familiar with greed. This might work out, after all. She thought back over the quick lesson she'd been given in Karitian currency and the relative value of Theo's gems and plucked one from her palm.

"It is a reasonable fine," she lied. It was the same amount the chief *nakat* had demanded, and Ransom had behaved as if it was extremely unreasonable, so she now knew three things: the *godozi* had spoken to the *nakat*, the *nakat* had been open about what they were willing to pay, and the *godozi* was a greedy man who'd want to squeeze every drop of blood from her stones. But the fines were not negotiable, unlike the "administrative costs" she'd have to pay next, so she handed over the gem with a straight face.

The *godozi* set it on the desk in front of him. It was a lovely square-cut emerald Zara wished she could wear as a ring. "It is acceptable," he said. "But there are costs. Processing the prisoner. Food. A cell to himself—we cannot expect Karitian prisoners to share a cell with a foreigner. Other expenses."

Zara waited. *Don't speak unless you're addressed,"* Blackwood had said. *They'll increase the amount of the bribe if you break with tradition in any way. Be patient. Remember, they want your money more than they want De Witt.*

"Many expenses," the *godozi* said. "One hundred *meshet.*"

Zara barely twitched. "Too much," she said. "That could house five prisoners."

"You question me?"

"I demonstrate my respect for your country by being familiar with your laws." Another memorized line. *The bribe has to be the right amount,*

Blackwood had said. *He'll test you by asking for too much. If you accept his first demand, he'll know you're desperate and will deny your request — possibly for days.* "I know you are civilized enough not to spend more on prisoners than you have to."

Tap, tap, tap. "Fifty *meshet*," the *godozi* said. "For our trouble."

"Naturally," Zara said, counting out a couple of diamonds and setting them down next to the emerald.

"It is enough." The *godozi* pushed one diamond to line up more precisely with the other gems. "Come back in two weeks and he will be released."

Zara's heart beat faster. "His family wants him returned now."

"That is not our problem. Two weeks is what it takes to process a prisoner's release."

"I see." Zara stirred the hidden contents of her palm with her index finger and watched the *godozi's* eyes follow the movement. "More administrative costs."

"Yes."

"We are willing to pay to expedite that process."

"It is expensive."

"How expensive?"

"Eighty *meshet*."

Now, was this fee negotiable, or not? "And how soon will he be released with the help of eighty *meshet*?"

The *godozi* smiled. "This afternoon."

"Agreed." Three more gems joined the line.

"He must be valuable, to spend so much." The smile broadened.

"His family cares about him. And, of course, he is in an important line of work."

The smile disappeared. "What work?"

Warning bells went off inside Zara's head. Karitians didn't have a problem with inherent magic, and healers were respected everywhere. Wouldn't he have at least tried to mitigate his imprisonment by telling them he was a healer and a doctor? Too late now. "He's a doctor," she said.

The *godozi* tapped his fingers more rapidly on the table top. The gems quivered with the vibrations. "A doctor. And a healer?"

Zara briefly considered lying to the man. "Yes."

"Of course," the *godozi* said. "Very important to Tremontanans."

"We just care about him as a person." That sounded incredibly stupid. Zara mentally kicked herself.

"Then let us see. Twenty *meshet* for the fine. Fifty for administrative costs. Eighty for expediting the release. Have I forgotten any?"

"No. You've been most generous."

"Yes." He unfolded his legs and stood, swept the gems into his palm, then hesitated with his hand still outstretched. "No. I have forgotten. One thousand *meshet*. For the removal of a valuable magical resource from Dineh-Karit. A healer is a valuable resource indeed."

Chapter Seventeen

"I don't see how he can be a healer in Dineh-Karit if he's in prison," Zara said.

"He will be permitted to work off his fine by the department of the *falrek*," the *godozi* said, and held out the emerald. "One year, and his term will be complete."

Zara took the emerald and held it concealed in her hand with the rest of the gems. "That's unacceptable. One year for a twenty *meshet* fine—"

"Do you disrespect our laws?" The *godozi* looked as if he very much hoped she did.

"No, of course not. But he is a Tremontanan citizen and has obligations that will not wait a year."

"He should have considered that before coming here." The *godozi* smiled pleasantly. His eyes glittered at her. "We must be compensated for our loss."

Zara breathed in slowly, deeply, then released it. This was just another part of the game. The question was, what part? "I understand," she said, and the man's smile broadened. "One thousand *meshet* instead of the fine and administrative costs."

"In addition to. It is a separate matter. And I have considered further. The price is two thousand *meshet*."

Big mistake, my friend. Zara had to hold back a smile of her own. The *godozi* thought he'd won because she couldn't walk away from this. He was a petty, greedy little person and she would crush him like a bug. And enjoy it. "Very well," she said, pouring the gems back into the pouch. "Let's go."

He blinked, his smile fading slightly. "Go to where?"

"To speak to whoever is responsible for prisoners working off their debts. The *falrek*, correct? You've convinced me of how reasonable your government is, and I'll be happy to work with your superiors.

192

Can we do this quickly?"

"I will take the money to them," the *godozi* said, holding out his hand.

"Oh, I don't think so. You said it was a separate matter, yes? So it must be a separate authority. It's too much money for me not to deliver it personally. But I'll be happy to tell the *falrek* how...eager...you were to help. Two thousand *meshet*, yes?"

"That is not necessary."

"Of course it is! I'm sure they'll want to know the name of the man who wanted to do their jobs for them. What was your name, again?"

"I—" The man put his hands down on the desk and seemed surprised when the gems fell out. He quickly gathered them up and put them away somewhere in his robes. "I must send word to the prison," he said, and fled.

Zara breathed in deeply again and closed her eyes. He'd given her all the power in that negotiation; now to see if she'd pushed him too far. She kicked herself again for being so stupid as to give valuable information away. Never tell them more than you have to. The question now was, would he give Ransom's secret away to the *falrek* and risk Zara coming into contact with them? If she had to go to that department, she'd tell them of the *godozi's* attempt to extort money from her in their name, and he'd suffer for it, but suppose they made a similar demand on their own behalf? She didn't think she had a thousand *meshet* in gems.

Minutes passed, slow as syrup. She stayed where she was, only shifting her weight to ease her legs. Light from the round windows made spots on the wall that traveled with the sun, sliding gradually down until they disappeared. Noon. She'd been there for more than three hours. She stood on one leg, lifted the other and stretched it, then repeated the movements for the other leg. She ought to feel hungry, but her stomach was too tense. What was the *godozi* doing, anyway? She hadn't misread him, she was certain of it, but she had no idea what the repercussions were of being caught in extortion, and if his fear of punishment was greater than his fear of her...

The door opened. Zara pretended she hadn't been fidgeting. The *godozi* entered, and said, "I have forgotten the fine. Twenty *meshet*."

"Oh, of course," Zara said, her heart pounding. He'd given the emerald back to her. She felt around in the pouch until she came up with it and handed it over.

The man put it away in his robe and said, "You will be taken to the prison now. Do not speak to anyone. The prisoner will be released to you and you will both go immediately to your boat to return to Tammerek."

"But what about—" She couldn't resist needling him.

"Karitians will not endure the touch of a foreign savage, no matter his gift." The *godozi* was looking at a spot on the wall behind her. "We need not involve the *falrek*."

"If you're sure…" Zara hung the pouch around her neck again and dropped it inside her shirt. "Thank you for your patience."

The *godozi* continued to ignore her. The door behind her opened, and the ha-ha man entered. "With me," he said, and Zara followed him.

They went out by a different door into the heat of the noonday sun, but Zara didn't care that sweat sprang up under her hair and her arms immediately. *You're not safe yet*, she reminded herself, her heart pounding more rapidly than the heat would account for.

The streets were practically empty, and Zara remembered what Blackwood had said about everyone staying indoors through the hottest part of the day. It certainly seemed reasonable right now, with the sun radiating off the pavers and filling the air with the acrid smell of hot concrete. It might also help her with Jeffrey's mission, assuming she could get Ransom out in time. *You're not safe yet*.

The ha-ha man kept up a smart pace, and Zara had trouble keeping up with him, but didn't dare ask him to slow. They went west, judging by the sun, and the river became gradually louder until they came to a bridge nearly as wide as the plaza-street arching over it.

It was cooler on the bridge, though not much so, and sweat was running down her back and had saturated the band of her brassiere by the time they reached the far side and entered a warren of narrow streets and tiny buildings, each surrounded by identical verandahs and capped by red roofs. Zara tried not to shrink in on herself, but some of the streets were narrow enough that she and the ha-ha man had to walk single file, and she couldn't help feeling like she might brush up against the houses if she weren't careful. Karitian uniformity might be catching.

It took about fifteen minutes for them to reach a low, square building made of blocks of the same concrete as the pavers. It had no verandah, no windows, and no front door, just a black rectangular hole that sucked in all the light that tried to enter it. Inside, the air was stiflingly hot, and Zara's eyes burned with trying to see anything beyond the bright light of the street outside.

Gradually, shapes swam into view: two backless stone benches beneath a row of five iron rings embedded in the bare wall; another of those odd table and chair combinations, these of battered pale wood; a file cabinet so familiar in shape Zara experienced a moment's dizziness, as if a piece of Tremontane had burst into appearance before her; and a door, banded and studded with iron. The lock was rusted and big enough for Zara to fit her index finger through. A tiny square window, heavily barred, showed nothing but darkness beyond.

A woman dressed like the *godozi* stood up from the desk and straightened her robe. The ha-ha man said something in Karitian, holding out a sheet of paper. The woman took it and read it, slowly, glancing at Zara on occasion. Zara did her best to look humble but assertive, which was probably impossible, but the alternative was hurling herself at the woman, shrieking, and tearing her apart until she found the key.

Finally, the woman folded the paper, took an iron-banded stick from beside the prison door, and banged on the bars of the window. After a few seconds, a grouchy voice said something, and the woman responded briefly and handed the paper through the bars. Light flared, as of someone striking a match, then bloomed into a brighter glow. Zara had to remind herself to breathe normally, but it was all taking *so long* and the urge to scream was growing harder to ignore.

The paper poked back through the bars, and the light receded until there was nothing but darkness again. The woman smoothed out the paper and put it away in the file cabinet. "Thank you for your generosity," Zara said. The woman sneered at her, but in a way that told Zara she didn't speak Tremontanese. She tried again in Eskandelic and got a better reaction. *"The prisoner's family is very grateful to Dineh-Karit for its understanding."*

"Foreigners are nothing but trouble," the woman said.

"We understand and are happy to pay for your trouble. One hundred fifty meshet *is a generous price."*

The woman's brow furrowed. *"One hundred fifty?"*

"Yes. Twenty meshet *for the fine, one hundred thirty for administrative costs. But the offense was grave."*

"Indeed." The woman went back to the cabinet and removed the sheet of paper, looking closely at the bottom, where the signature was. *"That is a steep price."*

"The godozi *thought it fair."* Zara smiled. *"He was very clear on the amount."*

The woman put the paper away again. *"I imagine he was."*

Zara made an astonished face. *"I am so sorry, I forgot,"* she said, and withdrew one very small gem. *"The* godozi *did not mention it, but I am sure there is a processing fee here as well. Thank you for your patience."*

Now it was the woman who looked astonished. *"Of course,"* she said, rallying. *"You are well-mannered for a northern savage."*

Zara wasn't sure how to respond to that, but it didn't matter. The *godozi* was going to be in a lot of trouble for the size of the bribe he'd extorted from her, and if there was any justice in the world, he'd end up taking Ransom's place in prison. Anyone who tried to crush Zara North was due for a world of suffering.

At that moment she realized the darkness beyond the square window was lessening, and her heart began hammering again, hard enough she could feel it in her ears. Then the key turned in the lock, and a man pushed the door open. He was short, with hair longer than any she'd seen on a Karitian man before, and that was all she had time for, because he stepped aside to let Ransom shuffle through the door.

Zara found her fists were clenched so tight the nails were cutting into her palms. He was shackled, hand and foot, his head drooping as if a great weight were pulling it down, and even with the pace imposed on him by the leg irons, she could tell he was limping. It had only been a day, a single damn day, who could possibly have done this to him in so short a time?

"Is this the kind of treatment you give prisoners?" she said coldly, then instantly regretted it as the woman turned around fast to give her a disdainful look. Ransom twitched at the sound of her voice, but didn't look up.

"We do not give kindness to prisoners. It is uncivilized," the woman said in Eskandelic.

She spoke rapidly to the short man in Karitian, and he produced a key from somewhere inside his filthy shirt—he wore shirt and trousers, not a robe, Zara noticed, though all her thoughts seemed to be coming from very far away, somewhere beyond the red haze filling her vision. He removed the shackles, draping them over his arm, and Ransom just stood there, his hands dangling at his side. *"Thank you,"* Zara said, hesitated, then went to Ransom and said, quietly, "Can you walk?"

"Put your shoulder under my arm, and pretend you're helping me," he said in a remarkably strong whisper. She did as he asked, and one slow step at a time, they left the prison.

Outside, two *nakati* waited, somewhat impatiently. "You will to come," the man said, and the two began walking rapidly in the direction of the harbor. Time for part two of the day's adventure.

"Pretend you're hurt worse than you are," Zara whispered, then called out, "Wait. He can't move that fast."

Both *nakati* came back. "You must to go now," said the woman.

Ransom let out a groan. "We have to go more slowly. He's hurt," Zara said.

"To be go," said the man, and began striding away again. The woman hesitated.

"Please, just…give us time? We won't talk to anyone. See, there's not even anyone to talk to." Zara gestured with the arm that wasn't pretending to hold Ransom up.

The woman *nakat* called out to her companion, who replied at length and with some impatience. "We have duties," the woman said to Zara.

"We don't want to keep you from them, but he's hurt, he needs to rest." Zara gave the woman her best expression of pleading worry. "Couldn't you…leave us somewhere for a while? We know how to return to our boat. I swear we won't cause any trouble. Just an hour, two hours, and we'll be gone. And you can go tend to your duties now and not be late. That's all right, isn't it?"

The woman looked even more reluctant. Her companion came back and said something, but she cut him off and replied, gesturing at Zara and Ransom. Zara reached into the pouch, awkwardly thanks to her burden, and took out a couple of small stones. Too big a bribe, and they'd be suspicious. "Here," she said. "To show you we're honorable. You shouldn't have to wait on foreigners like this. We'll find a quiet place, out of the way, and rest for an hour or so. We'll be gone before sunset, promise."

The gems shut them both up. The man said something, not taking his eyes off the sapphire he held. The woman looked at Zara again, then at Ransom, and her chin firmed. She spoke to her partner, in a tone of voice that clearly told Zara she knew what was right and she intended to do it. Then she said, "Come this way."

They followed her between the shops until they came to a street no wider than Zara's outstretched arms, along which were houses about the size of the narrow buildings on the docks. Each had a single door and a curtained window—more of the famous Karitian individuality—and the street was still and empty. The *nakat* went to one of the houses, rapped on the door, then opened it. Her partner spoke, and she responded dismissively, waving at Zara and Ransom to enter. Zara "helped" Ransom limp through the door and sit down on a lumpy, narrow bed covered with a blue blanket of equally lumpy weave. There was a table and a chair and a chest, and that was all the room contained.

"It is empty. No one lives in," the woman said. "Stay. Rest. Then leave."

"We will," Zara said. "Thank you."

The woman nodded. "That is wrong," she said, indicating Ransom with a jerk of her chin, then shut the door behind her. Zara listened to their receding footsteps until the street was silent again—the walls were so thin they'd be able to hear anyone approaching, and probably anyone inside the nearby houses, too.

"They're gone," she said.

Ransom stretched and stood smoothly, arching his back, bending at the waist to touch his toes, and then extending his arms until his fingertips brushed the ceiling. Then he sat on the bed with his chin in his hand the way he had the night they'd met. Zara gasped. One of his eyes was swollen nearly shut, and there was a long cut along his left cheekbone that had bled heavily and been imperfectly cleaned. "You look awful!"

"Thank you," he replied drily. "It looks worse than it is. I couldn't exactly heal myself without them realizing my inherent magic. If they had…I would have been a prisoner in Manachen for years."

Zara didn't feel a need to respond to that. "I'm sorry it took so long."

Ransom gingerly prodded his eye. "I thought I told you to send a negotiator."

"The Karitians won't listen to an official Tremontanan negotiator. So they sent me instead."

"That was incredibly dangerous. If you'd made even one mistake, you might have been imprisoned as well."

"Well, it wasn't as if we could let you rot here. Especially once the ambassador found out you're a De Witt."

Ransom groaned and lay back on the bed. "Why did you tell them that?"

"It was the only way we could get her to take us seriously. I'm sorry if that interfered with your nobly getting yourself beaten in a Karitian prison."

"It's not important. What matters is—actually, I can think of any number of questions, starting with 'why are we still here?'"

"Well, that's a long story. How long will it take to heal yourself?"

"I've already healed the internal damage—"

"Internal damage? Ransom, what did they do to you?"

He closed his eyes. The puffy one was already looking better. "You don't want to know the details," he said, "and I'd rather not talk about it. The important thing is I'm free, and I can finish healing, and *you* can tell me a nice story while I'm doing it."

Zara dragged the chair next to the bed. "Don't interrupt, because this is complicated," she said, and told him everything that had happened from the time they arrived at the embassy. She'd already worked out what to say about Jeffrey, and told Ransom only that the King had decided, as long as Zara was going into Manachen, she could complete the task Alfred had been meant to do.

When she wound down, Ransom was silent. He was silent for so long she began to wonder if he'd fallen asleep, and she was about to prod him when he said, "I don't care if he *is* the King, that's not a task to put on a civilian. No matter how capable she is."

"It's not that dangerous. And I've already said I'd do it."

"Rowena, you are out of your mind. We need to return to Tammerek right away."

"I'm supposed to meet with these people somewhere in the city. They don't know I'm coming, so I have to hope they'll be there. Can you help me?"

"No. I don't know more than the docks of Manachen. Are you going to make me drag you to the boat?"

"And make the kind of scene that gets us both thrown into prison?"

Ransom sat up and swore. "If we get caught, prison will be the least of our worries."

"We won't get caught. Turn around. Or close your eyes. I have to change clothes."

"Into what? You're not carrying anything." But he turned his back on her.

Zara stripped off her shirt and trousers and swiftly turned them inside out. Reversed, they were a dull brown that had a few stains on the tunic and were well-worn at the cuffs. She removed the pouch from her neck and handed it to Ransom. "I didn't read the letters," she said. "I showed your signet to the ambassador. It was very convincing."

"The letters aren't important. Just a couple from my Uncle Ransom and one from my sister."

"Even so, they're private. You didn't say everyone thought you were lost."

"It wasn't relevant. It certainly doesn't change how my family feels about me."

Zara ran her hands through her thick hair, tangling it further. "You can probably ask the ambassador not to tell them where you are. Turn around now if you want."

Ransom turned around. "That's quite the transformation. But no one's going to believe you're a servant. Not with the way you move."

"Karitians don't look at northern savages if they can help it."

"I'm not going to help you."

"Then don't. Wait here, and I'll be back soon."

"You know I can't let you go alone."

"That's up to you."

Ransom cursed again. "Give me ten more minutes, and I'll be fully healed. Though I'll still look scruffy."

"That might be a benefit."

She sat down again and waited in silence, watching him as he sat with his eyes closed and his hands clasped loosely in his lap. He'd asked all the questions, but there was one she was burning to ask him, one she wasn't sure she wanted an answer to. It was the wrong time to ask, just before they both risked their lives on behalf of their country. And it probably didn't mean anything, anyway.

"You kissed me," she said.

Ransom smiled, his eyes still closed. "I was wondering when we'd come around to that," he said.

"Why did you do it?"

"I was going off to my almost certain death and thought I wasn't likely to get another chance."

"You said it wasn't goodbye."

"It was only almost certain death. I wasn't sure."

"But...why kiss me at all?"

Ransom said nothing for a long moment. Then he opened his eyes and looked directly at her. "Because you're the most extraordinary woman I've ever known," he said, "and I am deeply attracted to you, and that kiss gave me something to hang onto in the darkness. I don't care that it's only been seven days—"

"Eight days," Zara said, then covered her mouth in embarrassment at how eager that had sounded.

"It's been eight days and already all I can imagine is spending tomorrow with you, and the next day, and the next, just to see what happens. I don't even care if all we do is argue. I'd rather argue with you than trade smiles with any one of the debutantes my parents threw at me."

"I'm old enough to be your grandmother!"

"My grandmother doesn't look nearly as good as you. Besides, you said you never think of my age."

"Yes, but I sure as hell think of mine! I'm too old for this, Ransom. I—" She let out a deep breath. "It's easier for me to leave my life behind if I'm not too attached to the people in it. Leaving behind my grandniece's family...it's going to hurt for a long time. And I've probably got another century or more in me. There's no way you're going to live that long."

Ransom rose and came to stand in front of her, his eyes fixed on hers in a way that made her for the first time in her life wish she could hide, anything to get away from the depth of emotion in his eyes. "I'm not asking for a lifetime's promise, Rowena. I'm asking for the chance to find out whether what I feel for you can grow into something more."

"And if it does? I've come to terms with the way things are. Making friends is worth the pain. Making a deeper connection..." She shook her head. "I don't want to go through that again, burying someone I love."

"You might do that even if you weren't deathless. That's how life works." He took her hand in his. "Don't you even want to take a chance on happiness?"

His hand was dry and warm and gripped hers firmly. "We barely know each other. That's not much to build happiness on."

"Every happy couple started out as strangers. We're just taking that path more quickly, what with the shipwreck and all. It's been a very full eight days."

"'We'? You're so certain I want what you do?"

"I am."

"You're impertinent."

"And if you didn't care about me at least a little, you'd have shut me down hard five minutes ago. You see how well I already know you?"

That quirky, amused smile, his hazel eyes gone dark and serious, left her breathless. She stood and removed her hand from his. "We have to go. We can talk about this later."

"Rowena," Ransom said, putting his hand on her shoulder.

"I'm not saying you're wrong, I'm saying I have to focus on what J—what the King wants me to do."

"I know. I just—"

She'd begun to turn away, but let the gentle pressure of his hand bring her back to face him. The smile was gone; his eyes searched her face for something, she had no idea what. "I just," he repeated, took a step closer, and then his lips were on hers, gentle this time. Instinctively she put her arms around him and drew him closer, and kissed him back.

It was sweet, and tender, and it had been so, so long since anyone had kissed her she'd forgotten how wonderful it was to be kissed by someone who wanted her, body and soul. He smelled awful, like the prison, but she didn't care, because his arms were around her and his kisses grew fiercer, more passionate, until she could hardly breathe. He buried his hand in her hair, his fingers tugging at the tangles in short, sharp twinges, and carefully she withdrew from him, with one last kiss, and saw him smile.

"Don't tell me you're indifferent to me after that," he said.

She was having trouble catching her breath. "I guess I'm not."

He lightly kissed her forehead. "Let's get this over with," he said, "because if all our conversations are going to end that way, I want to have another conversation, very soon."

"Ransom—"

"I know. We'll talk about it later." He opened the door and bowed. "Where do we go?"

Zara removed the sketch map from her pocket and turned it around. "We go...south. And hope we find them soon." She put the map away and touched the Device in her other pocket. *Yes, let's get this over with,* she thought. *Later can't come soon enough.*

CHAPTER EIGHTEEN

The afternoon sun was, if anything, hotter than it had been at noon, and Zara wiped sweat from her forehead and prayed they'd find Jeffrey's agents soon. The alley outside their bolt hole was still empty, the cobbles hot beneath the thin leather soles of her sandals, and a scant breeze ruffled the curtains and then was gone, carrying with it the faint smell of the ocean but providing no relief. Manachen lacked all the smells of a northern city, both the pleasant and unpleasant ones, and between that and the emptiness, Zara felt they were walking through, not a real city, but a life-sized model, built to house the dead. She dismissed the feeling irritably. She didn't need her imagination distracting her from the job at hand.

The great plaza-street was as sparsely populated as before. Heat waves rose up from the concrete pavers, shimmering like a vast, dry sea, and they were so bright Zara's eyes watered. She and Ransom walked side by side, Ransom slightly behind to show he would follow her lead. The eerie silence was like a thousand whispering insects humming at the limits of hearing.

She let her shoulders slump and scuffed her feet along the pavers, trying to exude that same aura of defeat the other Tremontanans she'd seen possessed. Most of those about at this hour were northerners, and now that she knew they were likely working off heavy and unjust fines, her body fizzed with anger. She'd lived too long and in too many places to be chauvinistic about Tremontanan culture, but there were limits to her tolerance, and Manachen had exceeded all of them. Those "servants" might as well be slaves.

Following Blackwood's map in memory, she counted streets, then turned right into a neighborhood of four-story buildings that looked to be only one room wide, their glass-paned windows casting bright glints over the street and blinding Zara further. This street was busier than the other, filled with Karitians in their bright robes passing in and out of doors.

Zara kept her head down, glancing up only often enough to keep from running into anyone. She saw mostly feet and hems, and noted the feet were often dirty and the hems were usually frayed and faded. So Manachen did have a lower class, though she'd wager all of them still felt themselves superior to any northern savage, no matter how wealthy.

She bumped into someone, glanced up in time to see the Karitian recoil, then begin speaking rapidly in his language. Zara cringed, and hoped it would be enough. Ransom said something in uncharacteristically halting Karitian, then added, "We are sorry."

The Karitian glared at Zara again, spat at her feet, and walked away. Ransom put a firm hand on her wrist and murmured, "Be glad it wasn't your face."

"I'll be so glad when we're out of here."

"Well, we'd better walk more quickly, because we're drawing attention. I don't think that map distinguishes the neighborhoods where it's safe for northerners to go."

Zara shuffled faster, counting off streets again. Stupid bigoted Karitians and their stupidly hot city. She was never going to complain about Tremontanan summers again, not that she'd ever really complained. She hoped she wasn't misremembering the map; she couldn't exactly pull it out to look at it. More Karitians took to the streets as the sun sank in the western sky until the murmur grew loud enough to make Manachen finally sound like a city.

She took a left turn and kept going. Their path was taking them through some seedy neighborhoods, limp weeds growing up through cracks in the sidewalk, chips in the stone walls of the dwellings. She smelled food, though she couldn't identify anything beyond yams and squash cooked in animal fat with cinnamon, and it reminded her she hadn't eaten dinner. Maybe they'd be back at the embassy in time for supper. Her stomach rumbled, and she sent it a silent promise of food soon.

"I hope we're almost there, because I don't like the way these people are looking at us," Ransom said.

Zara took a quick look around. "Three houses down," she said, "but we should go past and double back, just in case."

She'd been told to look for a house with two chairs on the verandah, purple curtains, and some long scratches on the door, as if *najabedhi* had come calling and left disappointed. The house looked empty, but she could smell yams being cooked inside. She strode past without staring at the house and moved off down the street. The few people who passed ignored them. She walked past three more houses and hesitated. If she turned around and walked back, that might draw attention.

"This way," Ransom said, pointing at another narrow alley too small for them to walk side by side. "I think it circles back around to the main street."

He led the way down the alley, which was not only deserted but also cluttered with trash. It was the first sign Zara had seen that Manachen wasn't the model city she'd imagined. It stank of human and animal refuse, and she tried to breathe shallowly through her mouth. It didn't help. The agents had certainly chosen well when they picked this part of the city. No one would come here who didn't have to.

They exited the alley and came past the house a second time. No one was looking at them. Zara guessed they were all going off to their suppers, based on the delicious smells that barely overrode the stink of waste. They climbed the few steps to the verandah, which unlike the rest of the house was solid and didn't creak underfoot. Keeping her head bent in what she hoped looked like defeat, she knocked on the door, and they waited. No one answered. She knocked on the door again with the same result. She had the feeling someone was watching her, and glanced around, but saw only Ransom, his face still dirty and with traces of blood on his cheek. He shrugged. "Someone's home," he said.

"Let's go around to the side and see if there's a window we can look through," Zara said, and followed Ransom around the corner of the verandah, out of sight of the street. There were no windows on this side of the house and none on the neighboring wall for a nosy neighbor to peek through. The verandah appeared to completely encircle the house. "Back wall?" Zara said.

Ransom nodded and walked quickly around the back of the house. Zara heard him grunt in surprise and hurried after him. "Did you find—"

The world went dark and scratchy as a bag went over her head. A hand covered her mouth through the bag, rubbing its rough weave painfully against her mouth. She struggled, but a strong arm pinioned her arms to her side and lifted her off the ground as easily as if she were a sack of flour.

She kicked out, felt her foot in its inadequate sandal connect with something, and pain shot up her foot and leg. Her captor shook her roughly, dizzying her, then carried her into someplace dark and cool, cooler than outdoors at any rate, and threw her to the ground. She landed hard on her right wrist and cried out, heard a door slam, and then male voices speaking in Karitian, very rapidly. She tried to stand and rough hands grabbed her, yanked her hands behind her back and tied them with rope as scratchy as the bag.

From nearby, Ransom responded, his voice muffled, and Zara's panic subsided. She was tied up, he probably was too, but at least they hadn't been separated. Ransom sounded calm, but there was an edge to his voice that worried Zara. Then he said, "We aren't servants. We're from Goudge's Folly."

That silenced the men. Zara waited, debating whether to speak. What should she say? Then one of their captors said, in broken Tremontanese, "You liar. No Tremontanans come from the island."

"Are you—" Zara swallowed against the dryness of having the bag jammed into her mouth. "Are you Bull and Lion?" Blackwood had refused to give Zara the agents' real names, saying they wouldn't respond to them anyway.

"You say nonsense. We animals are not," a second voice said. "Why are you here? We know no one with Tremontanan servants."

"We're not servants," Zara said. "King Jeffrey sent us. He needs to communicate with you."

"Who?" The man sounded genuinely puzzled, and Zara closed her eyes and silently cursed. They'd come to the wrong place.

"King Jeffrey of Tremontane," Ransom said. "You're agents of the Crown, we know you are."

Both men laughed. "We Karitian," the first said. "You are wrong. We will call the *nakati* to take you where you not a threat."

Zara went back over everything she'd been told. Two deep cover agents, code named Bull and Lion. The house with the purple curtains and long scratches on the door. Now, if she were an agent of the Crown in an enemy city, her life in danger if her identity was revealed, and two strangers came knocking on the door, what would she do?

"I can prove we are who we say we are," she said. "There's a Device in my pocket. Take a look. It's for the King to communicate with you." She rocked until she was lying on her side with her hip in the air, revealing the hidden pocket. Someone knelt beside her and reached inside her pocket with one hand. With his other hand, he squeezed her bottom briefly and chuckled. Zara didn't react. That was no doubt what he wanted.

The man stood and crossed the room, his sandals making the wooden floor creak. "This Tremontanan is Device," he said. There was silence. Zara heard Ransom breathing heavily nearby and hoped it didn't mean he was hurt. Not that that mattered to him.

Sandals came back toward her, and then the man knelt beside her again, grabbed her shoulder and wrenched her upright. "Name the Tremontanan ambassador," he said. His Tremontanese was suddenly fluent, his accent that of the northwest.

"Calliope Blackwood," she replied.

"And her secretary?"

"James. I never heard his surname."

"What color are his eyes?"

"Blue."

"Who is agent 10254?"

"I don't know. I'm not an agent, just the woman on the spot. But Blackwood gave me a pass phrase for you she said would prove we're who we say we are. She said to tell you, 'Loosen your belts.'"

The man was silent again. Then he released her, making her lose her balance and fall to the floor. "Of course you're not an agent. No agent would have done anything so ham-fisted as you just did. Didn't it occur to you we might be watched?"

"I thought we were being careful. Would you untie us now?"

"I'm still not sure," the other man said. "This could be a trick. She could have been primed with those answers and the pass phrase. Not that I'm saying it means anything."

"You don't believe that, or you wouldn't be speaking so freely," Zara said. "And you've already proved you're Tremontanan."

"You think you're smart enough to work that out on your own?"

"I think no Karitian man would have touched me the way you did a minute ago."

"Rowena," Ransom said, his voice low.

"Now, untie us and we can talk like civilized people. Another thing the Karitians aren't."

The room was silent again. "We'll untie you," the first man said, "but you'll leave the bags on unless you want us to dispose of you permanently. We can't afford to compromise our identities and I'm still not completely convinced you are who you say you are."

The ropes around her wrists loosened, and she freed herself, then sat cross-legged as calmly as if her heart weren't beating far too fast. "Use the Device, and that will prove it," she said, rubbing her wrists. Beside her, she heard Ransom moving around, and then his hand briefly touched her thigh and withdrew. She had no idea what he meant to convey, but it eased her mind to have him nearby.

"We don't know how," the second man said. "And we're not about to trust your word."

Surely this level of paranoia was unwarranted. It was starting to annoy her. "The Device will let you communicate by voice with anyone who has the same Device, anywhere in the world," she said. "It's better than a telecoder because it can't be intercepted. I'll tell you how to work it, and you'll speak to the King himself. I hope you'll trust his word more than mine."

"Talk," the second man said. "We'll see."

Zara ran through the instructions Blackwood had given her and heard the tiny distant tick-thud of the Device's innards engaging. One of the men drew in a sharp breath; the Device had probably started glowing. "You might want to go into another room, if there is one," Zara said. "I don't think we should hear whatever instructions the King gives you. Is that sufficiently paranoid for you?"

"Shut up," the first man said, but without malice. Footsteps crossed the room, and a door opened and swung shut. Zara let out a deep breath. Maybe this would work after all.

They waited for a while. The door opened. "Come here," the first man said, and more footsteps receded across the room. The door shut again.

"Did he hurt you?" Ransom said.

"Of course not. He squeezed my bottom. It's not worth worrying about."

"Forgive me if I worry about what those two men might do to you if I weren't here."

"I don't think they see either of us as a threat. A physical threat, I mean. Obviously they see us as a threat to their safety from the Karitian government."

"I hope they believe the King is who he claims to be. I have no doubt those men would kill us to protect their secret."

"I agree. But I think they're coming to accept what we have to say."

Ransom let out a deep sigh. "Have I said lately that this is insane and you are a lunatic?"

"Not in so many words."

"Well, this is insane. And you're a lunatic."

"A lunatic who got you out of prison."

"Thank you for that. I'm not sure I said it earlier."

"I had to make sure it wasn't goodbye."

Ransom chuckled, a dry sound thanks to the bag. "You're remarkable."

The warmth of his voice made her blush. She was too old to be so easily moved, and yet... "I've just lived a long life."

"And that's not remarkable? I want to know everything about you. Who you've been. What you've seen."

"I want to know why the name Daniel is so offensive to you. It seems perfectly nice to me. Not as nice as Ransom."

"So you know that too, eh? Daniel. Rhymes with 'spaniel'. Which is what the other children called me until the day I went to medical school and left it behind. It's an unpleasant reminder of my childhood."

"I'm sorry I asked. I promise I'll never call you that."

"Now I wish I knew *your* real name. Turnabout and all that."

He'd moved close enough his thigh was pressed against hers. "What makes you think it's not Rowena?"

"I think you've probably used a dozen names in your lifetime. I'd like to know the original."

"I...ask me later. When this is over," she said, and immediately regretted her words. She absolutely could not tell him who she was. That was a secret that could bring down a kingdom. *You trust him*, she thought, and brushed it away. Trust had nothing to do with it.

"I'm starting to become impatient with these fellows. Surely the King can't have that much to say — "

The door opened. "Take the Device and go back to Goudge's Folly," the first man said. "And forget about this place. We have to move now you've found us."

"We're sorry," Zara began.

"It's standard procedure. Go. You can remove the bags once you're out our back door. We don't need you seeing us, just in case."

Zara stood. The man took hold of her shoulders. "Straight ahead," he said, then slapped the Device into her palm. She pocketed it and fumbled her way to the door. Beside her, Ransom stumbled and cursed quietly. Then the door opened, and she felt warm air, and then she was on the shady verandah and the door closed behind her. She quickly removed the bag and combed through her disordered hair. Ransom was doing the same. He dropped his bag and grinned at her.

"I guess we convinced them," he said. "Now, back to the docks. Do we have a ride?"

"I hope so. She said she'd come back every hour. We might need to hire transportation if they won't let us linger on the docks, especially if we still look like servants."

"You could change back into your finery."

"That would take too long. Let's just go." She closed her eyes and remembered what it had felt like to be one of those downtrodden Tremontanan servants, but that made her angry, so she slumped her shoulders and bowed her head and went around the corner of the verandah. She was certain the agents were watching them go, making sure they *did* go, and it annoyed her even as she reminded herself they probably were justified in taking so many precautions.

There were a few Karitians in the street as they reached the stairs. Zara ignored them. She was a servant, nothing worth noticing, and it would take less than an hour to reach the docks—

Someone shouted something in Karitian that sounded like a command. Ransom grabbed Zara's arm. "He wants to know what we're doing here," he said in a low voice.

"Tell him we're…running an errand?"

Behind them, the door to the agents' house opened. Zara turned to see a Karitian man, or someone who looked Karitian, standing in the doorway. He shot a fierce, furious glare at her, then began yelling something in Karitian. Ransom's grip grew tighter. "He's accusing us of theft," he said. "Run. Now."

Zara took off down the street, Ransom just behind her. Her thin sandals struck the pavers with harsh thuds that sent sharp streaks of pain up her shins with every running step. She wasn't sure where she was going, wasn't sure she was retracing their route exactly, but she could tell she was going north, toward the docks, and that way lay safety. "Why did he do that?" Ransom panted.

"We drew attention," Zara said. "Paranoid—if someone drew—the wrong conclusion about us—could mean someone might—ask the wrong questions."

"So they threw us to the wolves."

"Yes." It was too hard to talk and run at the same time. Zara concentrated on running. She heard the crowd before turning a corner and running into it, people laughing and talking as if the silence of the morning had been a mistake. None of them made room for Zara the way they had earlier, though none of them looked at her either. She ran into someone, apologized, and turned around. Ransom was gone.

She stood, craning her neck, looking for some glimpse of him and trying not to panic. He was there somewhere, he was blond, for heaven's sake, he ought to be obvious among all these dark-haired Karitians, but the crowd might as well have been a caiman for how thoroughly it had swallowed him up. She took a calming breath. He was probably looking for her and she should stay where she was...unless he'd decided *she* was looking for *him* and was staying put.

People were starting to look at her, and one or two of them looked like they wanted to know why she was there. *He knows to go to the docks*, she thought, *we'll meet there*, and she pushed her way through the crowd and took off running again. North, to the docks, then back to Goudge's Folly. Simple. Nothing to it.

She got lost.

It was the identical houses that did it. At first, she thought it was just that all the neighborhoods looked alike. Then she realized she'd passed the same dark stain on the wall twice. She stopped running, bent over and pressed her hand to her side. She needed to go slowly and pay closer attention to where she was. Go north.

After about half an hour of fruitless wandering, the sun was beginning to set and she was becoming nervous. If only she could find the river! It was enormous, and she couldn't imagine how she hadn't stumbled on it before now. The streets were deserted, with everyone no doubt safely inside their identical houses. It left her once again feeling she was in a city populated by the dead, though why the dead would need the light that shone from most of the windows, she had no idea.

She was starving and light-headed and tired of the pain in her feet her healing magic couldn't relieve quickly enough. The *nakati* almost certainly patrolled the streets at night—it seemed like a Karitian thing to do, keep the undesirables off the street—and eventually one of them would find her, and then...prison, probably, where she'd be for a very long time. What would the Karitians do when they found out she wasn't aging, wasn't staying injured? She couldn't conceal it the way Ransom had.

And Ransom. What would he do when she simply disappeared? What could any of them do? They'd probably guess where she was, but with the prisoners never identified by name, the chances of them finding her were small. Her best hope was to be allowed to work off her debt, then she would slip away, go to the harbor and coerce someone into taking her to Goudge's Folly, maybe steal a boat—

She stopped in the middle of the narrow alley she'd been following and closed her eyes, then cursed. She was thinking like she was already captured. Well, Zara North didn't give up. She followed through until hope truly was lost, and that had never yet happened to her. She would find the main street, and then the docks, and she would return to Goudge's Folly, and then she would leave this stinking country and never return.

She turned right onto a wider street and saw a Karitian woman coming toward her, filmy gauze over-robe covering her head. "Please," Zara said, "can you help me? I'm lost."

The woman sneered at her and said something in Karitian. Zara repeated herself in Eskandelic and then in Veriboldan, but the woman just shook her head and continued on, giving Zara a wide berth as if she were contagious. Zara stopped, closed her eyes, and swallowed a scream of frustration. What she needed was a Tremontanan servant. She started walking. She was never coming back to Manachen again.

The street widened, turning into a row of short buildings that looked more like shops than houses, with their iron-banded doors and barred windows. Zara walked more quickly. Those shop owners expected thieves, which made this the kind of neighborhood she didn't want to loiter in. All the windows were dark; no help from that quarter.

She heard footsteps approaching. A group, maybe four or five. *Nakati*, probably, traveling in a pack. She slipped between two of the shops and crouched low in the shadows. The steps drew closer. Whoever they were, they weren't talking, and it sounded like they were wearing boots. Zara flattened herself against the wall and ducked her head to conceal her eyes. She hadn't seen any Karitians wearing boots all day; they wore sandals, usually nicer than her thin-soled ones, or went barefoot. Even the *nakati* didn't wear anything sturdier than sandals that laced up their shins.

The footsteps slowed as they drew closer. *"Around the corner,"* someone said in Eskandelic, then the footsteps were running, they were almost on top of her, and she burst from her hiding place and ran in the opposite direction. Whoever they were, they were looking for her.

She took turns at random, doubled back once or twice, listening for the sound of boots hammering the pavers behind her. Manachen was a maze, and she was lost in it, and someone was hunting her. Part of her brain was screaming at her to stop panicking, but dread of being caught had taken her over. Finally, when she couldn't hear the boots anymore, she dropped to her knees and crawled under a verandah, and lay there, breathing heavily. Why would anyone be searching for her? Let alone an Eskandelic—

She heard boots again, rapidly coming in her direction, just as it came to her. There was only one Eskandelic who would be looking for her. She curled into a tiny ball, praying they'd move on past. She was invisible in here, there was no way they could see her. The booted footsteps grew louder and closer.

Zara held her breath until she saw spots, then let it out slowly, silently. She could see them now, from the knees down, four or five Karitian robes that were dull in the light of the setting sun, four or five pairs of booted feet showing below the hems of the robes. They were coming toward her as surely as if she wasn't hiding. *How can they possibly know?* she thought. *They can't track the Device so accurately!* She held as still as she could.

The boots stopped next to the steps of the verandah, and everything was still, so silent Zara wanted to scream just to hear something other than the blood pounding in her ears.

One of the figures knelt and looked under the verandah. She held a pistol pointed directly at Zara's head. "Come out, or I shoot," Ghazarian said.

CHAPTER NINETEEN

Zara considered letting the woman shoot her. It would hurt, and depending on where Ghazarian shot her, it might take a while for her to recover, but it would spare her whatever torture the pirate captain had in mind. On the other hand, Ghazarian might not shoot to kill, and if she did kill her, she'd probably search her body and find the Device. Zara crawled out from under the verandah. Hands grabbed her, pulled her to her feet and immobilized her. She didn't bother struggling.

Ghazarian thrust the pistol into her waistband and took two steps, which put her inches from Zara's face. She was a little taller than Zara and about the same age, at least as old as Zara appeared. She smiled. "You see I have found you," she said. "Take her."

"How did—ah!" One of the pirates wrenched her arm painfully behind her back and gave her a shove. "How did you find me?"

"Walk," Ghazarian said. "Not talk."

The pirate steered Zara through the streets, apparently counting off intersections the way she had earlier. Zara still didn't fight back. There was no point, when they had her outnumbered, and she needed time to make a plan. They had some way of tracking her, so running away was pointless even if she could get free. She needed more information.

They turned down one of the narrow, stinking alleys no wider than her outstretched arms and walked past a row of houses with one door and one window each until they came to a house whose window was dark. One of the pirates kicked the door in, and Zara's captor shoved her inside. It looked the same as her and Ransom's bolt hole, though without a blanket on the lumpy bed. *This is taking mass production to an unhealthy level.*

The pirate shoved her down to sit in the chair. Another pirate produced a rope from beneath his narrow robe—it made a lumpy outline, but she guessed none of them cared about fashion—and tied her hands behind her, then looped rope around her to tie her to the chair.

Ghazarian shut the door behind them. "The Device," she said. "Take it."

Two of the pirates pawed her, patting her all over, including in places the Device couldn't possibly be hidden. Zara ignored them. Showing fear would only make them torment her worse. "How did you find me?" she said.

One of the pirates pulled the Device out of her pocket and handed it to Ghazarian. She held it up and turned it around in the dim light. "Light," she said, and one of the pirates took out a matchlighter and lit the lantern on the table. It threw strange shadows over Ghazarian's face, exaggerating her eyebrows and the curve of her lips. Ghazarian took the Device to the lantern and held it close to the flame. "How does it work?" she asked.

"I want to know how you found me first," Zara said. *Stall. Find a way out of this.*

"You do not demands to make," Ghazarian said. "Tell how it works."

Zara didn't speak. Ghazarian whipped out her knife and held the blade against Zara's throat. "Tell."

"If you kill me, you'll never know," Zara said. "Look, I'm curious. Tell me, and I'll talk."

Ghazarian snarled at her. The knife blade pressed closer. Zara held as still as she could. Getting out of this was going to be difficult, particularly if she wanted to get the Device back. *Don't taunt, be reasonable,* she thought, but to what end? She really needed a plan.

Then Ghazarian grinned. Her canines had been filed to sharp points. She set the knife on the table and took a familiar wooden box with a glass top from within her robe. She showed it to Zara. "You must thank the Karitians. They show me how best to use this."

"How does it work?" Zara said, discarding a number of defiant responses.

Ghazarian grinned again, those canines catching the light of the lantern and the bluer light of the moon that now filtered through the small window. She flipped open the glass top and displayed a square of fine-grained leather stretched taut. It was deep red and pulsed like a beating heart. "We have this from its maker," she said. "It gives you how close you are to the Device but not where it is. It uses little source."

She closed the lid and turned the box upside down, pressed her thumbnail into a nearly invisible slot, and another lid popped open. "This we do not know before the Karitians find it. They thorough are." Zara saw a quivering arrow like the needle of a compass, pointing directly at the Device on the table. "This uses much source, but shows where the Device is." Ghazarian closed the box and picked up the Device, then held it up so the brass case caught the light the way her teeth had. "So. What does it do?"

"I don't know," Zara said.

"You know what it does. You will tell."

"You chased it down, followed me all this way, and you don't know what it does? Why did you want it so badly, then?"

Ghazarian kicked Zara in the stomach, making her cry out. "You tell," she said. "Its builder did not know."

"I don't know either," Zara lied. "How could the builder not know?"

Ghazarian kicked her again. "It complex is. Many parts," she said. "The builder makes only one, then the Tremontane government takes it to put all together. The builder knows only what his part does. So he makes this." She waved the box in Zara's face. "It follows the part. It went to your city, the Aurilien city, then it left to the south. It—he follows the Device to Umberan. He cannot follow more without a ship. So he hires me." She set the tracking Device on the table next to the lantern.

"What happened to him?"

That canine smile again. "He tell me the story. He say the Device valuable is. He tells all and then—I do not need him more."

That chilled Zara despite the muggy night. "Well, I picked it up from a dead man, so I don't know how it works. I thought it was a watch."

"I do not believe."

"I'm sorry about that. I'm telling the truth." *Please don't have Telaine's gift.*

Ghazarian picked up her knife. "I think you do not." She stroked Zara's tangled hair, then wound a lock of it around her fist. With a stroke of the knife, she cut it off. It didn't hurt, but Zara gasped in surprise. *Oh, yes. It's going to be torture.*

Now what? Zara went furiously fast over her situation. She was outnumbered. She was tied up and unarmed. The Device was out of her hands. Ghazarian was the sort of person who enjoyed hurting others. She'd go on hurting Zara even if Zara told her how to work the Device, which meant no matter what Zara did, this could only end one way—in her death. The question was, how could she make that death count?

She let her eyes go wide and panicked. "No, don't! I swear I don't know anything!" she exclaimed.

Ghazarian set the tip of the blade at Zara's temple. Zara whimpered as the knife cut a long, thin line down the side of her face and along the line of her jaw. "Do you not? Maybe I take your ear next. Or a finger."

"No. Please."

Ghazarian took the arch of Zara's left ear in her fingers and pulled it away from her head, setting the edge of the knife beside it. "Tell."

Zara cried out, "All right! I'll tell you! Just stop!"

The tiniest pain ran down Zara's neck as Ghazarian made a cut in the fleshy part of her ear, then withdrew the knife. "You weak are," she said. "Tell."

"It's too complicated," Zara said. "But I can show you."

"You think me to trick?"

"No. I swear. It really is too complicated to explain."

Ghazarian sheathed the knife and stepped back, gesturing at the pirates. One of them cut through Zara's bonds, and she breathed out in relief. She was still going to die—Ghazarian had given in too easily for that not to be the outcome she had in mind—but at least she wouldn't have to untie herself when she finally recovered. She rubbed her wrists, stalling for time.

"What is?" Ghazarian said.

"I'm not completely sure," Zara said. "Like I said, I took it off a dead man and it was hard to work out that it did anything." She held out her hand, and Ghazarian hesitated, then handed her the Device.

"It makes noises when you turn the stem." Zara demonstrated. "That changes these bumps on the surface, so it probably does several things, but I only found one." She went through the sequence Blackwood had shown her, and the Device began to glow green. The pirates crowded around her, stifling her. Ghazarian shouted at them, and they stepped away. Zara turned the stem a few more notches, then pulled up on it. Nothing happened. Exactly as planned.

She made a face and pulled harder. "It's stuck," she said.

"Try harder, or I take a finger," Ghazarian said.

"I'm trying." Zara shoved the stem in, then pulled it out, wiggling it. The thing couldn't be that tough, could it? *Come on, damn you*, she thought at it, then whacked it hard on the table. Ghazarian grabbed it and tried to take it away from her.

"You will break it," she said. "Let me."

"No, I almost have it," Zara said.

"Give it to me."

"It's almost free—please, give me time—"

With a snap, the stem came free from the Device. Ghazarian, holding the case, stumbled back a few steps. The green light vanished. Zara clutched the broken stem. "You broke it," she said.

"I? I do not to break. You do this thing, you fool."

"I was doing fine until you had to interfere," Zara shouted. "Now it's broken and neither of us will get any benefit from it. You're the stupidest person I've ever met!"

Ghazarian drew her knife. "You do not speak so to me," she said in a low, menacing voice.

Zara struck, not at her, but at the tracking Device on the table, sweeping it to the ground. The case cracked, the glass lid shattered, and metal coils and gears spilled out of it like it had been gutted. "I'll speak to you however I want! Stupid, impatient, arrogant! I don't know why anyone obeys you, if this is what you do when you capture ships. Do you sink them with the cargo on board? That's the sort of thing I'd expect from an idiot—"

Ghazarian roared and ran at Zara, grabbing her by the shoulder and thrusting her knife up and under her ribcage. It burned cold agony all the way in, and Zara screamed, not caring who heard or what they thought. "Who is the idiot?" Ghazarian whispered to her, then shoved her away to fall hard on the floor.

Zara lay looking up at the ceiling. Hadn't it been lower just moments before? She brought her hand up to touch the wound and felt hot blood pouring out of her. If Ghazarian hadn't reached the heart, this could go on for a while. The pain was gone now. Instead she felt cold all over, which was nice after the heat and humidity of the day.

Far away, she heard someone speaking, but she couldn't understand the words. It might have been Eskandelic—but surely she would have understood that, because she was almost certain she spoke Eskandelic. Then her heart gave an erratic leap, fluttered a few times, and stopped. Gratefully, Zara slipped into death. *Twice in a week*, she thought, *I really need to be more careful.*

Hot sunlight burned Zara's face. She blinked, then closed her eyes again and turned away from the bright sun. Her bed was hard and gritty, which seemed odd. Surely by now she should smell coffee, if the light was already that bright. But this didn't seem to be her bedroom—

Memory returned. Ghazarian's knife. The Device. She pushed herself up and looked around. The tiny house seemed smaller in daylight, its lumpy bed farther away. She rolled to her knees, stood, and had to grab the chair to keep from falling over. The cut ropes still lay on the floor around it like headless snakes. She kicked them to make sure they weren't actually snakes, then had to sit down and put her head between her knees, she was so lightheaded. That had been a ridiculous thought. She must have lost a lot of blood before her heart stopped beating.

When she wasn't quite so dizzy, she sat up and looked around. The lantern was still on the table, the tracking Device lay shattered on the ground, but Alfred's Device was gone. A sick feeling passed over her. Of course, there was no way she could have stopped them taking the Device, but it still felt like failure.

Then she remembered. She opened her right hand and let the stem of the Device fall onto the table. They had the Device, but no way to use it. Not the ideal solution, but better than letting them have a working communication Device. Though she had no idea how they'd use it if it *were* working, if Jeffrey had the only other one. It didn't matter. She picked up the stem again and put it in her hidden pocket. Might as well not leave any trace of it behind.

She contemplated the broken tracking Device. It was no good to anyone anymore, but she crouched and gathered up all the tiny pieces and tucked them away in her pocket too. It made a funny bulge, but maybe Theo could do something with it. Assuming she could get it to him.

Now, what day was it? Zara stuck her head out the window. Morning, probably not later than ten o'clock. The pirates had found her at sunset, but which day? She prodded her gory tunic. It was completely dry, stiff with her blood, which could mean it had been more than one day she'd lain there, or it could mean things dried quickly even in this climate.

She knew about how long it took her to heal many injuries — fifteen minutes for a deep scratch, two days for a broken bone, seven days for being shot through the head — but she thought she'd been healing faster in Dineh-Karit. And she'd always healed more slowly in Eskandel and Veribold than in Tremontane. Her guess was her healing was directly related to the amount of source available, which meant it might be true Dineh-Karit had more source even than Tremontane. Not that she had time for philosophical analysis. She had to get back to

Goudge's Folly, and she had to do it soon, no matter how long she'd been gone. Blackwood needed to know what had happened to the Device.

She looked down at her tunic again. There no way she wouldn't draw attention in it. And as far as drawing attention went, why hadn't anyone come to investigate the shouting and screams coming from this house the night before, or two nights before, or whenever it was? She opened the chest and found it empty. If the house was unoccupied, that might explain the lack of interest, for which she was grateful. Heaven only knew where a Karitian might have hauled her "corpse." She shook her head and had to sit down again. She was still not thinking clearly. It didn't matter why no one had come. What mattered was getting to the docks and finding a boat.

She stuck her head out the window again. The alley was empty. She heard no noises from any of the houses. Carefully, she opened the door, looked to either side, then moved on to the next house and knocked. No one answered. She tried the knob; the door was unlocked. She went inside and leaned against the door briefly. This house had the same furnishings as the others, but the blanket was red. Individuality? Or had the store simply run out of blue blankets?

She threw open the chest and began rummaging through it. Cup and bowl, a comb and — thank heaven — a change of clothes for the owner of this house. She pulled out tunic and trousers, both a dull gray that didn't suit her coloring, not that it mattered. What mattered was they were both made for someone two sizes larger than she. Well, she'd have to make do. She could probably wear her own trousers, especially since she didn't want to give up the advantage of the hidden pocket, but the new tunic...

She stripped out of her own clothes, reversed the trousers after a moment's consideration, shrugged into the oversized tunic, and folded the ruined one with the bloody side inward so it looked like an ordinary bundle. Then she went back to the house of her captivity and found the longest rope to use for a belt.

She stood in the center of the room and took a deep, relaxing breath. It was probably a good thing she couldn't see herself, because she no doubt looked ridiculous, but as long as she looked like a Tremontanan servant, she didn't care. There was a pitcher of warm water on the table, and she used the too-large trousers to wash her face free of dirt and blood. She'd forgotten Ghazarian had cut her. She settled her bundle comfortably in her arms, tugged the tunic down to conceal the bulge in her pocket, and sent up a prayer to ungoverned heaven this would work.

She'd forgotten how lost she was until she exited the alley and realized she had no idea where to go next. *No. No despair.* She checked the position of the sun, which was already hot and sending up prickles of sweat under her hair and beneath her breasts, and started walking eastward. She knew she was west of the river and the great plaza-road, and if she could find those, the route to the docks would be obvious.

Heat radiated from the concrete pavers, burning through the thin soles of her ridiculous sandals. She kept her head down and her shoulders slumped. It was the heat that made the pose feel so natural and not her emotional exhaustion. Physically, she felt fine, but the city weighed her down with its monotonous construction and the constant silence and the knowledge that her face made her a potential victim of this system.

She thought about Ransom, about whether he'd made it back, and prayed she'd find him again. The way he'd looked at her...he was nothing like Hank, and yet he had that same intent, searching look she remembered so well. The look that said he saw past the face she showed the world to the woman she was inside.

She remembered a long-ago conversation about not being afraid to care about people just because those relationships inevitably ended, and her friends in Longbourne, and how even though it hurt to leave them, it would have hurt worse never to make those connections. But love, romantic love, wasn't that different? Or was she just afraid? Because Zara North was never afraid of anything, and if that was what stood in the way —

She bumped into someone and cursed herself for daydreaming in

226

an enemy city. The person she'd run into didn't recoil, just took a step back and made a funny bow. She carried a parcel much like Zara's and her red hair hung loose around her face. "You're Tremontanan," Zara said.

"So are you," the woman said in a dull voice. "Excuse me."

"Wait," said Zara. "I'm lost. Where is the river?"

The woman's dull expression turned suspicious. "What?"

"The river? I am new here, and I don't know where anything is."

The woman pointed back over her shoulder. "Just there." She still looked suspicious.

"Oh, how foolish of me," Zara said. "Excuse me." She made a clumsy imitation of the woman's bow, then hurried away. She could feel the woman watching her, and the prickles of sweat turned into droplets. She'd been afraid of attracting the attention of the Karitians; it hadn't occurred to her to worry about northerners as well. She walked faster. There was nothing to worry about. That woman wouldn't betray her. Probably.

She came out on the riverside so abruptly she stumbled and went to one knee, throwing out a hand to stop herself falling. The heat of the concrete burned her palm, and she snatched her hand back, blowing on it to cool the skin. A few Karitians passed, paying her only enough attention to step around her. Sticking out her other leg to trip their smug faces would be satisfying, but that would draw far too much attention, so Zara kept that impulse to herself. She waited for the Karitians to pass, then got to her feet and headed north.

She passed one of the docking platforms, empty now, and took the first bridge she came to. If she hadn't heard the distant cries of the sea birds, if not for the scraping of her soles on the square white stones of the bridge and the sound of the river, she might have believed she'd gone deaf. She once again felt like screaming or singing, anything to break the unnerving silence. What kind of country *was* this? Why the silence? Why the identical houses? She was tired of being fair-minded. Anyone who lived like this had to be crazy.

The east side of the city was laid out in regular, straight streets at precise intervals, and finding the plaza-street was so easy she wanted to weep in gratitude to ungoverned heaven for making one thing go right in all of this. Of course, if heaven cared at all about her, it had a funny way of showing it. Heaven probably wanted her to show self-reliance.

She had no idea how far she was from the harbor, couldn't do anything but keep her head down and put one foot in front of the other, over and over again. *One more step. One more step.* No one spoke to her or called out accusations in Karitian. She refused to feel encouraged. Time enough for that when she was on the island. Premature celebration could get her killed. Again.

Gradually, the hot, wet air took on a briny smell, and she imagined she could feel salt brushing her cheeks, and then it was incredibly hard to keep from feeling eager. Zara glanced up. Ahead, the great street narrowed to go through the arch leading to the harbor. No doors stood open to welcome visitors; there were no doors at all. Maybe Dineh-Karit was so confident in its military might it didn't fear any attack that might come by sea. Or maybe it was arrogance rather than confidence. Either way, seeing a pirate fleet sail into the harbor to sack Manachen...no, she wasn't callous enough to wish that on any city. But it would have cheered her to see red and blue *nakati* run screaming.

She slowed her pace as she neared the arch, then veered to one side and ducked behind one of the shops lining the road. She tossed her bundle into the space behind the shop and quickly combed through her hair with her fingers, straightened her stolen tunic, and emerged, stiffening her spine and holding her head erect. She strode toward the arch confidently, focusing her gaze on a ship far out in the harbor. She heard nothing but the sea birds, her shoes, and, finally, the creak of wood and the snap of sails and ropes. No one shouted after her.

The heavy arch cast a welcome shadow over her briefly, then she'd left the concrete behind for hard-packed earth that kicked up in tiny puffs around her feet as she walked. Ahead were the warehouses, beyond that, the *nakati* houses, and then there were the piers and, thank holy heaven, dozens of brightly colored boats tied up to them. Cerise and her hat couldn't possibly still be there, so she'd need to hire—

Her reflexes, and her fear of discovery, kept her walking without a stumble or hesitation, but her body felt turned to stone. Ransom had the pouch full of gems. She had no way to pay someone to take her to Goudge's Folly.

She passed the warehouses with little more than disinterested glances from the men laboring there. Thank heaven there were some people in Manachen who didn't feel it was their duty to harass foreign women. The *nakat* who'd sent them to Goudge's Folly after Ransom had been imprisoned had just spoken to a pilot, hadn't offered her any money that Zara had seen. Maybe Zara could convince someone to give her a ride on the promise of a lot of money when she got to her destination. *And maybe I'll strip down to one of those brassiere and loincloth getups and dance for the* nakati *in the middle of the street.* But it was the only option she had.

A *nakat* emerged from one of the little houses almost in her face. He glared at her and said in Veriboldan, *"You should more carefully walk, foreigner."*

"I apologize," Zara replied, and backed away a few steps.

"Stop." The *nakat* took hold of her shoulder. *"Where are your papers?"*

"I am a private negotiator. I have no papers."

"All negotiators have papers."

"Not the Tremontanans," Zara said, switching to her own language. The man's eyes narrowed. Zara guessed he didn't speak Tremontanese. *"I am returning to Tammerek. I will leave immediately and I will not speak to anyone while I am here,"* she added in Veriboldan.

"We will see of your credentials. You will wait for authorization," the *nakat* said, and went back into the little blue house without shutting the door. Zara heard him speaking in Karitian to someone inside. The other person didn't sound happy. Zara gauged the distance between herself and the piers. Casually, she began walking away, a fast walk

that wasn't quite a run, scanning the piers for what she needed. Any minute now, that *nakat* was going to come out of the house—

Someone shouted in Karitian, then said in Veriboldan, "*Stop now!*" Without looking back, Zara broke into a run.

CHAPTER TWENTY

Her feet struck the wooden pier, sending up echoes that harmonized with the slap of her sandals, *THUD-slap, THUD-slap.* Behind her came more shouting, far too close, and the thrum of running feet on the pier behind her. The rush of the waves, the cries of the birds, all seemed too loud, even as the roars and purrs of the boat Devices seemed too far away. She had no time to negotiate for passage, no time to argue, and no Karitian would help someone pursued by the *nakati* anyway. But there was one option she hadn't considered, and it was the only one left to her.

She jagged right, turned left, and threw herself into the bottom of one of the empty boats. It rocked, sending splashes of water over the side to dampen her knees. She grabbed the loop of rope tethering it to the pier and yanked it free, making the boat rock more and drift away with the waves.

Five *nakati* pounded up the pier toward her, shouting. The boat Device was tilted at an acute angle, its tail waving idly in the air. She pushed on it, leaned her whole weight on it, and it slowly tipped toward the water, the tail submerging. Something went *click* and the Device became warm under her hands.

"Stop or we shoot you!" one of the *nakati* yelled in Veriboldan.

Zara fumbled around for the button to start the Device and mashed it hard several times. The *nakati* pulled out gun Devices and leveled them at Zara. She spun the wheel as hard as she could, and the Device roared and the boat shot forward, knocking Zara over.

Projectiles sang through the air past her head and shoulders, then a sharp pain like the bite of the world's largest insect erupted in her left arm. Her vision went blurry for a few seconds, then came into surreal clarity. She reached around and pulled out a dart the length of the first joint of her finger and as big around as a candle flame. It had the tiniest blue feathers that sparkled like diamonds, and the needle point gleamed silver. It was so beautiful Zara forgot to steer and heard cursing from another boat that had to swerve to avoid her.

It's poison. She gripped the tiller hard to focus. It would pass quickly; she just needed not to crash into anyone until it did. *Or after,* she thought, and giggled for nearly a minute at the thought of crashing into another boat.

She thought to look behind her and saw two boats full of red and blue *nakati* coming up fast behind her. *They want to be friends,* her addled brain thought, but her fingers wouldn't turn the boat around. They were not friends. They would try to take her back to Manachen, and there was no way she was going back to that dead, hot, silent city.

She spun the wheel to full and steered wide around a ship coming into the harbor. She had a good head start, their boats didn't seem to be gaining on her anymore, and there was no reason she couldn't reach Goudge's Folly before them, then run at top speed to the embassy and claim asylum. Unless the Karitians didn't believe in the sovereignty of foreign nations. Would Jeffrey be willing to go to war over her? Would she let him?

The spot where the dart had hit her was swollen and hard, and rainbow glitters outlined everything she saw. Her heart was beating rapidly, her stomach was sick, and her head ached as her body slowly converted the poison into something harmless. It wouldn't kill her, it was probably just a powerful sedative, but if it incapacitated her… Her hand closed on the tiller so hard she was afraid she might break it. *I am not going back there.*

The minutes stretched out into hours — no, that was wrong, it only took half an hour to get to Goudge's Folly from the mainland. It was the poison, playing with her perceptions again. The rainbows really were beautiful, how they made the dull gray ships look bright and cheerful. Maybe everyone in Manachen needed a dose of that poison, just enough to make them see things differently.

Zara glanced back at her pursuers. They were still following her. Her fuddled brain tried to remember the laws about national jurisdiction over the waters a certain distance from a country's territory. Was it two miles, or three? Though Goudge's Folly didn't belong to Tremontane, so maybe that didn't matter. And Karitians might not have those laws at all. She was so lightheaded, tired and hungry and desperate, and she worked the wheel, but the boat didn't go any faster. It was only her imagination that the *nakati* were getting closer.

More minutes. Goudge's Folly emerged from the misty distance, and she thought she could see the Tremontanan embassy from where she was. The rainbows were dimmer; the poison was working its way through her system. She glanced back for the hundredth time. The *nakati* were definitely closer.

She should have made Ransom show her how to do that trick with the motive force. With her luck, she'd only blow herself up. Maybe if she were in a million pieces, she could finally die. The thought cleared the last of the fog from her brain. She didn't want to die, not that way, not any other way. She was eighty-seven years old and she wasn't ready for death. She steered the boat more directly at the island. If they were going to take her, she would make them work for it.

More projectiles whistled past her head. She ducked, letting the Device shield her. *Thank heaven they don't have bullets. I wonder if it's occurred to them that destroying this Device would let them capture me easily?* She made the boat swerve from side to side, and the projectiles stopped. She was so close she could make out the little Device-powered boats tied up at the piers, zipping around the mouth of the harbor. So close.

"Stop now and we will let you live!" The voice echoed strangely, sounding much like Jeffrey's had through the communication Device. Zara looked back to see one of the *nakati* holding what looked like an oversized coffee cup with no bottom and speaking into it. *"We will punish your country if you stop not."*

Zara ignored him. Dineh-Karit was already angry at Tremontane; if they hadn't attacked its property on Goudge's Folly yet, they weren't going to go to war over one escaped Tremontanan. The boat was slowing, not much, but she could feel it, as if she'd pushed the Device beyond its capacity. She steered a straight line again, straining to see a place where she could dock. She wouldn't have time to make it to the embassy. She'd have to try for the harbormaster's house instead, and hope the woman would be willing to defend her.

The piers were approaching at an alarming rate. Zara grabbed the wheel and prepared to slow. She didn't dare look behind her at the oncoming boats. *Almost there…*

She spun the wheel all the way in the other direction, shutting down the Device and letting momentum carry her to the pier, where it slammed into the posts with a sharp, grinding crash. Zara pushed off from the crippled boat and dragged herself up and over the edge of the pier, and then she was running, pushing herself past the limits of her endurance, willing her body to replenish itself enough to keep her going.

Behind her, the *nakati* boats thumped against the piers, and she could hear them following her. She dodged sailors and pilots, tripped over a crate and rolled to her feet and kept going. Where the hell was the harbormaster's house? They'd come in on the other side of the docks the last time, none of this looked familiar, she was going to be caught because she was too stupid to pay attention to where she was going.

Her legs burned with exhaustion. Her chest felt as if someone had rubbed her lungs with sandpaper. Her eyes watered with the pain. Everything was blurry, even the brown and green signs… There it was. The brown and green triple peaks of Tremontane. She put on a final burst of speed and flung open the harbormaster's door, bowling over the person who was about to exit and tumbling with that woman to the ground.

"You again," the harbormaster said. "Why are you always in such a rush?"

"Help me," Zara said. "The *nakati* are after me. I'm a Tremontanan citizen and they want to imprison me."

"Get off me, or I'll help them," said the woman she'd knocked over. Zara rolled over and lay panting on the floor. "*Nakati,* here?

You're delirious. Looks like they shot you with one of those fletchers of theirs."

The door flew open again. Five *nakati* shoved past the woman who had just risen from the floor, almost knocking her over again. "Do not to interfere," said the one in the lead. "She is prisoner."

"What's she done?" the harbormaster said, as casually as if armed *nakati* burst into her offices every day.

"Nothing," Zara said, getting to her feet and backing all the way to the far wall. "I'm a negotiator and they think I was there illegally. Send word to the embassy, they'll tell you I'm telling the truth."

"Why run you, then?" the *nakat* said. "You guilty. You will come. Do not to interfere."

"*Please* don't let them do this," Zara said.

The *nakati* all raised their weapons at once, pointing them at Zara. The harbormaster had backed away behind the counter. Zara kept her eyes on the *nakati*. What would being hit with all those darts do to her? Nothing good.

"Walk away to us," the *nakat* said. Zara pressed herself flat against the wall. She was *not* going back.

There was a click, and the sound of metal sliding against metal. Zara saw the harbormaster lift a rifle Device to her shoulder and sight along its barrel. "I'm not letting you take a Tremontanan citizen off what's Tremontanan soil for the next thirty-eight years," she said. "If she's done wrong, our government will make amends. Until then, get out."

"You do not to shoot us all," said the *nakat*, whose weapon didn't shake.

"I've only got two shots, it's true," the harbormaster said. "But that means two of you might be going back to Manachen in shrouds. So you maybe want to think hard about whether you want to take a chance on being one of those two."

Zara continued to watch the *nakati*. Their leader's face was growing red, and his hand had started to shake. Finally, he lowered his weapon and gestured to the others to do the same. "You will be punished," he said, and Zara couldn't tell whether he meant her or the harbormaster. Then he turned and left, followed by the others, the door slamming behind them. No one moved. Then the harbormaster lowered her rifle Device, and Zara slumped against the wall, sliding down it until she was sitting on the floor.

"Thank you," she said.

The harbormaster put the rifle away behind the counter. "It's not the first time I've had to scare off those red and blue bastards. Hence the rifle. It's good and dramatic and tends to make my point for me."

"Did you really break their law?" the other woman said.

"Only by being there without proper permission. But even that can land you in prison." Zara leaned her head back and closed her eyes. "I'll get out of your way as soon as I've rested for a bit."

"Stay there and I'll send a messenger to the embassy," the harbormaster said. She tilted Zara's chin. "Looks like you've had a rough time. There's blood on your face."

"It's nothing." She must not have been as thorough cleaning herself as she'd thought. It was a miracle she'd made it out of Manachen. "Really, I can walk." She pushed herself up, then wobbled and sat down hard on the floor. "Or not."

"Sit. They'll send a carriage for you."

Zara nodded and closed her eyes. The harbormaster's house was warm and muggy, but it smelled pleasantly of salt brine, and the floor was soft, and so was the wall. She slid down to lie curled up with her formerly injured cheek pillowed on her hand and fell into a not-quite-asleep state. Birds were chirping all around her, not sea birds but sparrows and blue jays, some of them with deep voices and some of them lilting sopranos. Someone huge lifted her and began bouncing her on his knee as if she were an infant, then she was floating along through a chilly field, skating on ice, and she fell into a pillow of a snowbank and finally fell asleep.

When she woke, it was full dark, and moonlight struck the foot of her bed, turning it silver and charcoal. She lay there, eyes open and staring at the squares of the paned window, thinking of nothing as she listened to her heart beating. It made a nice slow rhythmic counterpoint to her breathing. She wasn't disoriented, as she'd been when she woke up from being dead; she guessed this was the embassy because the room was as cold as an ice cave. The light blanket covering her did nothing to warm her. She rubbed her bare feet together to warm them, then stretched. It was so nice not to hurt anymore.

Something hard moved against her leg when she shifted. The tracking Device. She reached into her pocket and fingered the irregular edges of the gears and coils. She should get this to Theo—no, she needed to tell Blackwood what had happened to the communication Device first. She sat up, then closed her eyes against dizziness. She wasn't as well as she'd thought.

She waited a few seconds, then stood and felt around for the lamp switch. She could make out dim shapes, something that might be a wardrobe and a lower rectangular box that was probably a dresser— had they put her in the room she'd slept in the night before? If it *was* the night before. She still had no idea how long she'd been dead.

The light clicked on, blinding her because she'd inadvertently been staring directly at the bulb. She sat back down and rubbed her eyes. They felt gritty and her hair was filthy, and there was still dried blood on her chest. Talk to Blackwood, talk to Theo, and then a bath was in order.

The hall outside the room was empty and still, and she shivered, not from the cold but from the reminder of Manachen's silence. Surely there were people here, and they were talking and laughing and not walking around with their heads bowed as if weights were bearing down on their shoulders. This was the room she'd been given, so the stairs were to the right.

Her bare feet were silent on the carpeting, the thick gray pile swallowing up all sound, and she walked faster and faster until she was running and she could hear the faint thudding of her feet on the stairs. Around the curves she went, her hand trailing along the well-waxed banister, until she was on the first floor with its hardwood tiles and her feet made reassuring slaps across them.

Distantly, she heard voices, and made herself walk toward them. Running was foolish, she was being foolish, those were no doubt her friends…but was Ransom there? She'd assumed he'd made it out of the city, but what if he was still there, trapped? Her head began to ache with worry, and she walked faster, terrified now of what she might find.

The sounds led her to the formal dining room, made to seat thirty people. Doors glazed with tiny panes separated the hall from the dining room, so all Zara could see were swirls of color like smudged paint and the minute movements of people eating. She set her hand to the door latch, which had a brass thumb plate shaped like an oak leaf, told her heart to stop battering at her, and pushed the door open.

Six people looked up at her entrance. Calliope Blackwood, presiding at the far end of the table. Theo, Arjan, Cantara, Belinda — and Ransom, setting down his fork and looking at her with a calm, indifferent expression that struck her to the heart. "You didn't wait supper on me?" she managed to choke out. Her voice sounded scratchy, as if she hadn't used it for a week.

Then everyone except Ransom and Blackwood was shoving back chairs and standing, exclaiming and pelting her with questions. Belinda and Cantara threw themselves on her, Cantara in tears. "She tell us you dead are," she murmured into Zara's shoulder.

"Who?"

"Ghazarian," Belinda said. "She has the Device—how did you survive?"

"I…she knocked me unconscious, and she must have believed she killed me." Zara extricated herself from her friends. "I take it she contacted you?" she said to Blackwood.

"Yesterday morning. Sit, you must be hungry, after sleeping all day." She rang a bell positioned at her left hand, and a servant emerged from a door behind her.

"All day?" Zara felt dizzy again. She had missed far too much. "How long was I gone? I…feel so muddled."

"It's been two days since you rescued me," Ransom said. "May I?" He rose to lay two fingers along the pulse in her wrist, then closed his eyes. He looked perfectly well, but then he'd had two days to heal himself fully. After a silent, awkward minute in which no one spoke, he released her and went back to his seat. "You seem entirely recovered. Fortunate, because head injuries can be serious. I imagine you were only exhausted."

"But what were you doing all that time?" Theo said.

Zara sat down and picked up a fork, twiddling it. The cold silver made her fingers tingle. Did Ransom guess what had really happened? "I'm going to eat first," she said, and Theo made a noise of protest, "and then I'll tell you everything. But you can tell your story first. What did Ghazarian demand?"

"More than we can pay," Blackwood said. "Probably more than the treasury at Aurilien could manage, even. She told us she'd killed you and had the Device, and she demanded five hundred thousand guilders for it."

"She could have been lying about the Device."

"She sent a lock of your hair along with the demand. It was very convincing."

It wasn't something Zara would have taken as evidence, but she was older and more cynical than the ambassador. "So you turned her down."

"We had no choice. Even if we'd had the money, it's our policy not to deal with pirates."

"I think this Device is more important than that policy."

"And give everyone from Eskandel to Manachen the idea we're weak? No, Miss Farrell, we don't negotiate with criminals."

"It doesn't matter. What did she do when you sent back your reply?" Not that it was hard to figure out.

Blackwood harrumphed and scooted back an inch in her chair. "Taunted us about how she was going to take it to the Karitians."

Of course. "That must have taken most of yesterday. What are you going to do now?"

"Find Ghazarian's ship," Blackwood said, "board it, and take the Device by force."

"It's lunacy," Belinda said. "You're going to get a lot of people killed."

"Yes, and most of them will be pirates," Blackwood said.

"I beg your pardon, but where will you get a fighting force? Recruit sailors?" Zara realized she'd paused with a forkful of peas to her mouth and quickly set it down. "You're not in a position to raid a pirate ship."

"Two-thirds of the embassy staff are soldiers out of uniform," Blackwood said with a grim smile. "Our security, should the Karitians decide their agreements with regard to Goudge's Folly are null."

"Even so—"

"Miss Farrell, I appreciate that the King respects your abilities, but you're a civilian and unattached to the Tremontanan government in any official capacity. Please keep your opinions to yourself."

The sound of metal clinking against china ceased. Out of the corner of one eye, Zara could see Arjan looking at her as if waiting for direction. Blackwood looked placid, but the expression on her face was stony. *She's afraid I'll force the issue, though what she thinks I can accomplish, I have no idea.* Zara gave her a cool, indifferent look. "Of course," she said. "I'm sure the King has already given you his instructions. No need for me to do his job for him. Though you'll want to pass on some crucial information."

"What's that?" Blackwood continued to look impassive, but her expression was cracking around the edges.

Zara began pulling out fragments of the tracking Device. Theo leaned forward. "What's that?"

"It's how Ghazarian was tracking us—more accurately, tracking the communicator." She found the tiny stem and held it up. "Which no longer works."

Belinda gasped. Blackwood snatched the piece out of Zara's hand. "Is this part of the Device?"

"It is. Ghazarian's prize isn't worth anything without it."

"But that's wonderful!" Belinda said. "Isn't it?"

Zara glanced at Blackwood, who didn't look happy. They were once again on the same side, though who knew how long that would last. "The Device is still mostly whole," Blackwood said. "If Ghazarian can convince the Karitians it's valuable, they can take it apart and work out how to repair it. This only delays the inevitable."

"Ghazarian's had a day to contact the Karitians and work out an arrangement," Zara said. "Depending on whom she talked to, she could have a deal in place right now."

"We believe Dineh-Karit knows of the communication Device from its interception of our telecodes, though not how to use it," Blackwood said. "We've detected a larger than usual number of telecodes being sent between Manachen and the capital Esfanyar. They're still negotiating. Presumably their reluctance to deal with foreigners is at war with their desire for the Device. When that traffic dies down, we'll know they've agreed to her terms. Or rejected her entirely."

Blackwood wiped her mouth with her napkin and pushed her chair back. "Excuse me. It's good to have you back, Miss Farrell." Her expression didn't match her polite words. Zara realized she was holding her knife too tightly and set it down on her plate. Reacting to Blackwood's insults was beneath her, and anyway, Blackwood was right: it wasn't Zara's business. Not anymore.

CHAPTER TWENTY-ONE

When the door had swung quietly shut behind Blackwood, Theo said, "I need tools."

"You're going to sit up all night with that thing, aren't you?" Belinda said, teasing.

"Wouldn't you?" Theo tried to fit the two pieces of glass together, then dropped them on the tablecloth. "We need to get that Device back."

"What 'we' is that?" Ransom asked. He sounded as sardonic as he had the night Zara had met him.

"Uh…I didn't mean us, just…Tremontane. That 'we.'"

"I don't feel all that much attachment to my country," Ransom said. "Not that I wouldn't want to give Ghazarian a poke in the eye, but there's not much any of us can do."

"There must be something," Cantara insisted. "I Tremontanan am not, but if Ghazarian sells the Device to Dineh-Karit, it will be Eskandel that suffers as well."

"Her men caught me unawares," Arjan said. "Let us catch them first and we will see who suffers."

"You want to go after Ghazarian's pirates?" Ransom laughed, a short, bitter sound. "A fighter—"

"Two fighters," Cantara said. "*Arakeli* is more than dance."

"Whatever. Two fighters, an apprentice Deviser, a sharpshooter, and whatever Rowena is, against dozens of pirates who are all well-armed and ready to kill if it suits them? You're out of your minds."

"Nobody's proposing we go after them alone," Belinda said, "just that we want to help. And I notice you didn't include yourself in that list."

"Because I'm not a madman. I'm going back to Dineh-Karit in the morning, now that Rowena's restored to you all, and I'm going to put this insanity behind me."

242

"I thought—" Belinda said.

"I don't care what you thought. I got you to Goudge's Folly, as promised. And now I'm going to bed. I want to get an early start so I can avoid those *nakati*." He shoved his chair back roughly and strode from the room.

"I don't get it," Theo said. "Why is he so angry?"

"I don't know," Zara said, "but he—" She threw down her napkin and ran out of the dining room. Ransom was halfway up the winding stairs. "Ransom!" she called out. He ignored her. She ran up the stairs, the carpet prickling her bare feet, and saw him go into a room across from hers. "*Ransom!*" she shouted, and pelted down the hall, stumbling to a halt at his door. She knocked. "I want to talk to you!"

Silence. She was so sick of silence. She pounded on the door. "Open this door and talk to me!"

More silence. "Ransom, I am going to stand here all night if I have to. And I'll be here in the morning when you leave. So you can either try crawling out your window, or you can talk to me like a civilized person."

The door flew open. "I might have known you wouldn't have the decency to take a hint," Ransom said, his voice tight and angry.

"And *you* don't have the decency to say what's really wrong. We are your *friends*. How dare you turn on us like that?"

Ransom closed his eyes and lowered his head. His jaw was clenched tight. "Fine," he said. "Say it. Whatever it is, say it and then leave me alone."

"What I have to say shouldn't be spoken in public."

"More secrets?" Ransom let out a heavy, sharp sigh of frustration. "Am I going to get rid of you any other way?"

"Of course not."

He stepped back and waved his hand toward the empty room. "Then let's get this over with."

Zara walked past him into darkness lit only by the wedge of light coming through the door, which vanished a moment later. "Don't you want the light on?"

"I prefer the dark. It means—never mind. Say your piece."

"I want to know what's wrong with you. You're not acting at all like yourself."

"We've known each other for ten days. You don't have any idea what myself is like."

"What happened to…what you said? About—"

"About what?"

That afternoon, the day he'd told her how he felt about her, seemed so far away. "Apparently nothing," she said, feeling her heart freeze over to match the chill in the air. "You let yourself be imprisoned to keep the rest of us safe. That's not the action of a man who's indifferent."

"I told you I occasionally break out in a rash of chivalry. I usually regret it."

"That's not it. Something happened to you, and I want to know what it is."

Ransom moved toward the window and stood looking out, making himself a black silhouette against the moonlight. "It's none of your business."

"Your favorite phrase. I'm making it my business."

"Nobody likes a snoop. Let it go."

"No."

"I said *let it go!*" he roared, turning on her and making her take an involuntary step backward. "Did it never occur to you maybe the world isn't yours to rule? That people might deserve a little privacy? Or is it just that you've decided you're old enough to know better than anyone else how things should run? Maybe you ought to take a good look at yourself and figure out why you have this need to pick, and pick, until you've laid a problem bare that you should have left alone in the first place!"

Breathless, Zara closed her fist against an angry reply. "Sweet heaven," she said. "It's eating you up inside."

"What are you talking about?"

"Guilt," she said. "You had to leave me behind."

244

Ransom's shoulders sagged. He turned away from her. "Just go. Please. I can't bear to look at you."

"This room's too dark for you to see me. We were separated, and you left me, and now—"

"Is there *any* way I can get you to shut up and leave?"

"Talk to me, Ransom. Please." Zara fumbled around until she found a chair, and sat. She heard him breathing in time with her, filling the silence with a rhythm that soothed her frozen heart, melting it. At least in one way, they were in harmony.

"I lost you," Ransom said, so quietly that if her ears weren't accustomed to silence, she couldn't have understood him. "It was so sudden—you were there, and then you were gone. I got out of the crowd and hoped you'd do the same, and I waited, and I didn't see you. Then the Karitians began to notice me, stopped pretending I was invisible, and I couldn't stay any longer.

"So I went to the docks and I waited there, but the *nakati* could tell—I looked awful, like an escaped prisoner, which technically I was—and I had to take the first boat I could. I *had* to leave, Rowena, don't you understand? They would have captured me again, and I could have endured it if I'd known you were safe, but..."

He leaned on the window sill and pressed his forehead to the glass, which in the moonlight looked as cold as the room. "And Ghazarian captured you. In all my nightmares, that was the one I never thought to consider. She killed you, didn't she?"

"Ransom, it's not important—"

"*Answer me!*"

Zara clutched the upholstered arm of the chair, crushing the velvet. "Yes. But I made her do it."

Ransom let out a groan that seemed to come from his innermost soul. "Rowena!"

"It was either that or let her torture me to death."

He groaned again and flung himself away from the window. She heard the bed creak as he sat down on it. "Please, no more."

"It's all right. You shouldn't feel guilty. You did exactly what I hoped you'd do when we were separated."

"It is *not* all right!" Ransom shouted. "I should never have left. I should have searched until I found you."

"Absolutely not. Ransom, that woman was able to track me down no matter where I went. If you'd stayed with me, and we'd both been captured, you'd be dead now. I would have woken up next to your corpse. This was the best outcome."

"The best outcome would be for those damned Karitians never to have imprisoned me in the first place. Don't try to make this better."

"Then stop trying to make this all your fault. You think you failed? Then I forgive you. You need to forgive yourself."

Ransom laughed that bitter laugh again. "For a canny old woman, you don't understand anything."

"No? Then explain it to me. Explain why you're beating yourself up so badly you lashed out at people who care about you."

Again she could hear nothing but his breathing, faint like a breeze barely touching new leaves. "Rowena," he said finally, "I want to be someone you can depend on. Someone who can defend you from the things you can't fight. And I failed you so completely I can't believe you can bear to speak to me, let alone forgive me. The whole time you were gone—"

"Stop," Zara said, moving to sit next to him on the bed. "Just—stop. I was sick with worry over you the whole time, not knowing if you were safe, blaming myself for not making the right decisions. So I think we might have failed each other."

"It's not the same—"

"I'm not finished." She felt around until she could take his hand. His lay unresisting in hers, so she squeezed it and said, "The first man I loved…well, I don't know that I really loved him, but I thought I did…anyway. He told me I wasn't someone who needed to be cared for, to be protected, and he was right. I never gave anyone a chance to do that for me. Then my husband, Hank…we were partners, he and I, supporting each other, but he never tried to fight my battles for me. And I liked that. But now…"

246

She squeezed his hand again. "I'm an old woman, and I've changed a lot over the years, and I've learned having weaknesses means giving others the chance to use their strengths on your behalf. That you want to do that for me means more than you can know. You gave up your freedom so I didn't have to. You think I don't know I can depend on you without question?"

His hand closed gently on hers. "I take it back. You're possibly the wisest person I've ever met."

"I don't usually feel wise. Other people are easy to understand, but myself...half the time when I do things I surprise myself. And half of those times I do the wrong thing."

"That's hard to believe." Her eyes were accustomed to the dark finally, so she could see the outline of his face, the dark smudges of his eyes and lips, which curved in a smile.

"You've seen me make all sorts of wrong decisions," she said.

"Really? Name one."

"Well...I might have told someone I didn't want to fall in love again. That it wasn't worth the heartache."

"And that was wrong?"

"Isn't love worth taking a chance on?"

"I certainly think so," Ransom said, putting his arms around her. "Maybe you should tell that person you've changed your mind."

"I think I already have," she whispered, and he pulled her close and kissed her. There was nothing gentle about it; they kissed desperately, as if they'd never have the chance again. Everything she'd endured, every moment of fear for herself and for him, turned into longing for his touch. His hands were tangled in her hair again, and that reminded her of how filthy she was, how awful she must smell. She drew back, and he went from kissing her lips to kissing the place where her neck and shoulder met. "I need a bath," she said.

"Don't care," he said, his hand moving from her hair to settle on the curve of her hip. "Sweet heaven, I've never wanted anything more than I want to kiss you, right now."

"Well, I care," Zara said, laughing. She gently pushed him away.

"And we're not ready for more than kissing."

"I know. But kissing is pretty damn wonderful all on its own." He brushed his lips against her forehead, then hugged her tightly. "Never mind. You're right, you smell terrible."

"You realize in all the time we've known each other, we've never both been clean at the same time?"

"I wonder what that would be like. Is your hair ever not tangled?"

"Sometimes. You seem obsessed with it."

"It's beautiful even when it's dirty and tangled and…there's blood on your face. How did that happen?"

"Don't you dare fall back into self-loathing. It's unattractive. I'm fine, you're unhurt, and we're both moving forward."

Ransom sighed and released her. "And what does 'moving forward' look like?"

"I…don't know. I was planning to go to Veribold after this, but…I want to get to know you better."

"I've never been to Veribold. I hear it's nice, even if it is full of Veriboldans."

"After the Karitians, Veriboldans are friendly and outgoing. Would you really come with me?"

He clasped her hand. "I don't think we should make each other any promises, but I'm not ready to let you go. So…yes. But on one condition."

"Conditions? I'm not sure I know you that well yet."

"I just want to know your original name. You did say to ask later, and it's later."

Cold dread crept into her heart. *I trust him*, she thought. *I can't tell him*, she thought. And how would he look at her when he found out the truth? Memories of Hank emerged, memories of her reasons for never telling him who she'd been. They'd been good reasons, but they'd been cowardly as well, and Zara North was no coward. Or wasn't anymore, at least. "Ransom," she said.

Someone knocked on the door. "Ransom?" Belinda sounded uncertain even through the thick wood. "Miss Blackwood wants to talk to all of us. If that still includes you."

Ransom gave Zara's hand one final squeeze, then went to the door. "It does," he said to a nervous-looking Belinda, "and I'm sorry I behaved like that. Did Miss Blackwood say why?"

Belinda shook her head. "She just wants us to come now." She looked past Ransom at Zara, and Zara could almost feel the questions she wasn't asking.

"Rowena?" Ransom said, and offered her his hand. Zara rose and took it without hesitation, and Belinda's eyes went wide. "I suppose, as she's our host, it's polite to obey her wishes."

"Yes," Belinda said. She looked as if she were suppressing a dozen exclamations. She'd have a dozen questions for Zara later, and what a conversation that would be.

They went downstairs and crossed the house to Blackwood's office, where the other three already waited. Blackwood noticed their clasped hands, but only raised an eyebrow at Zara, who returned the look coolly. "Sit," she said, and Zara had to let go of Ransom to take her seat. Her hand felt so cold after the warmth of his. Of course, the entire room was as cold as winter, which it still was back in the north. Little Zara would spend half the day sledding on the short hill behind the forge, shrieking laughter and crying out to her father to watch her do it one more time. She closed her hand on the memory.

"I've spoken to the King," Blackwood said, "and told him you weren't dead after all. He expressed his relief at the news." She fixed Zara with a calculating expression. Zara remained impassive. Poor Jeffrey. He couldn't exactly have told anyone she was still alive. "I don't suppose you want to be more forthcoming about your...special status?"

"If his Majesty didn't tell you, it's not my place to say," Zara said.

Blackwood shrugged. "I've called you all here as a courtesy, given that you risked much to bring the communicator here. The King has ordered us to retrieve the Device as quickly as possible. We'll be sending out boats in the morning to find Ghazarian's ship, then our soldiers will board it and take the Device."

"Won't the Karitians have a problem with you attacking someone in their own harbor?" Zara said.

"We're not convinced Ghazarian is in the Bay of Avizi," Blackwood said, "though we won't know until the Deviser arrives to repair the tracking Device." She held out her hand to Theo. "Mister Jenkins, I'll have that now."

"But—" Theo began. Blackwood fixed him with a cool, firm gaze. Scowling, he dug up the pieces of the tracking Device and handed them over to Blackwood. She put them away in a drawer.

"In any case," she went on, "the Karitians won't intervene in a conflict between two northerners, so it won't matter what they think."

"This seems like a dangerous proposal. They might see it as an opportunity to take the Device themselves. Wouldn't it be better—"

"As I said, Miss Farrell, you're not an expert, whatever the King thinks of you." Blackwood stood, pushing her chair back. "We're grateful for your help, and we'll be happy to reimburse you—all of you—for your time and trouble, but it's best if you continue on to your destinations. Feel free to spend the night here."

"Thank you," Zara said, staring Blackwood down. The woman didn't flinch. She might be a fool, but she wasn't easily cowed. Zara wished that made her feel better. She stood and nodded to the ambassador. "Good night."

"'Good night'? Rowena, are you going to let her get away with that?" Theo barely waited for the door to shut behind them to speak. "It's a bad plan, and it's going to fail!"

"It will cause greatest loss of life," Cantara said. "They will fight and they will die."

"Not much we can do about it," Ransom said, "given that we have no authority."

"But we have to do *something*," Theo insisted. "Rowena?"

"Why are you looking at me?"

"Because you're smarter than Blackwood is, and you don't want the Device to end up with the Karitians," Theo said.

"I also don't have Blackwood's resources. It's best if we let her handle it." Zara headed off toward the stairs. "It's not our responsibility. Ransom said it—"

"I was being cranky, Rowena. Don't hold it against me."

"I'm not. But you were right. Two fighters, an apprentice Deviser, a sharpshooter, a healer, and…I don't even know what I am. But the six of us are not enough to fight pirates who won't blink at killing us."

"Then we don't fight them. We trick them. Rowena, we can do this. I know we can."

"Theo…" Zara put her hand over his. "It's over. You need to go to your aunt. I have a job. We all have lives that have nothing to do with the communicator. Go to sleep. That's what I'm going to do." She turned away so she didn't have to see his face. This wasn't her fight and it wasn't his either.

Chapter Twenty-Two

She bathed, sloughing the last of Manachen from her skin, then went to her room and lay wakeful in her bed. Sleeping all day probably hadn't been a good idea, not that she'd had much choice. Was she wrong? Did she have a responsibility to retrieve the communicator? What would Jeffrey tell her? Not that it mattered, since she had a history of disrespecting her nephew's commands, but he was sensible and clever and, she had to grudgingly admit, had a good grasp of the political realities. She needed to let him be King and not try to usurp his role by challenging Blackwood's authority.

She rolled on her side and squeezed her eyes shut, wishing her hair was dry and not chilling her further. This nagging feeling of guilt was irrational. She'd done as Alfred asked and more. She felt the cold blade sliding beneath her ribs again and shuddered. Done far more than anyone had a right to expect of her. She burrowed deeper under the blankets and eventually fell asleep.

She dreamed of storms, not the wild ocean tempests where the winds blew in every direction at once and the ship dove down cliff-steep waves, but the thunderstorms of her mountain home, noisy and boisterous. A crash of thunder woke her, and she sat up, disoriented at how the winds didn't rattle the panes. Pale light turned the glass pearly gray. Sunrise was near. Another crash echoed in the distance, and she realized it was the sound of the front door opening and slamming shut.

She slid out of bed and padded barefoot to her bedroom door. Loud voices, unintelligible with distance, filtered up the staircase. She moved silently down the stairs until she couldn't go any farther without being seen from the entry hall below.

" —didn't expect that," a man said. "I take full responsibility."

"You should," Blackwood said. "They're just pirates, for heaven's sake, you should be embarrassed at being so easily defeated."

"It was no defeat," another man said. "We captured the ship at the

252

cost of too many Tremontanan lives."

"And lost the communicator," Blackwood said. "Retrieving it was the point of this raid, Captain Thurman, or have you forgotten that?"

"No, ma'am," Thurman said. He sounded as if he were talking through clenched teeth. "But we couldn't—"

"Don't make excuses," Blackwood said. "That pirate captain has escaped with the communicator, and you've lost the tracking Device. What do you propose we do now?"

"We'll post a reward for Ghazarian's apprehension," the first man said. "And we'll interrogate the prisoners. This isn't the end, Miss Blackwood."

"I'm sure his Majesty will be completely reassured by that. See to your men, captain. I'll have new orders for you later." Footsteps sounded across the entry hall, more doors opened and shut, and then there was silence.

Zara crept back up the stairs and to her room, where she went to stand next to the window. The glass was cold against her hand, though that probably wouldn't last long into the heat of the day. Far below, she saw the lights of the harbor like specks of gold on the early morning mist, and brighter, paler specks moving beyond that where even at this hour boats traveled into the bay. So. Blackwood's attack had failed, Ghazarian had escaped with the communicator, and…how had they lost the tracking Device? That seemed uncharacteristically careless.

Zara shrugged and went back to bed, snuggling under the blankets to warm her chilly feet and nose. It wasn't her problem. Blackwood had made that clear. Zara had done what Jeffrey asked and now she would…she had to find Falken and Daughter, resign her job, send a telecode to Jeffrey asking for money—that might be a problem, but she'd been killed in the line of duty and that deserved some reward.

That communicator is important. True, but still not her problem. *Jeffrey would want you to help.* He had plenty of helpers here in the embassy, all of whom were better armed and better informed than she. *You don't want the Karitians to gain the upper hand.* And if she were still

Queen, what she wanted might matter.

She lay restlessly in bed, watching the square of the window grow lighter, until she couldn't bear it any longer. She got dressed and went looking for something to eat. An early start wasn't a bad idea.

The smell of hot coffee and bacon drew her onward to the mausoleum room, where the low round table at the center of the room was covered with silver dishes bearing eggs, sausage, bacon, porridge, and flat cakes. Blackwood was treading the fine line between hospitality and wanting to be rid of them quickly, or she'd have laid on breakfast in the dining room. It was such a familiar, reassuring presence of home Zara loaded her plate fuller than she really wanted and poured herself a generous cup of coffee. An early start with a hearty breakfast, *that* was a good way to begin the day.

"Good morning," Ransom said, shutting the door quietly behind him. "Are you an early riser, or is today special?"

"I couldn't sleep," Zara said. "Though I admit I'm eager to make a fresh start."

"I agree." He sat next to her and leaned over for a kiss that made Zara tingle all over with pleasure. An early start with a hearty breakfast *and* kissing, definitely her new favorite way to wake up. "I was thinking we should make a plan," he added.

"Do you need to return to the village for Nettles?"

"More to the point, I need to return their boat. It was delivered to the Tremontanan docks early yesterday, in perfect condition except for not having a motive force. Something else I need to get. And I've got to send messages to a few other places so they'll know not to expect me."

"I could come with you. If I —"

The door banged open. "Rowena," Theo said. He was carrying a strangely-shaped oak box about two feet long and was breathing heavily. "I need to speak to you alone."

Zara exchanged glances with Ransom. "Why is that?"

Theo shook his head. "I just...I planned this all...couldn't we please speak privately?"

"Is it a secret?" Ransom asked.

Theo shook his head. "Look—never mind. He might as well hear." He shoved the door closed behind him and deposited his burden on the velvet sofa next to Zara. It was a clock—no, the oblong case of a clock, filled not with the delicate gears of a clock Device, but crude, heavy pieces of metal, two of them glowing with purple light. A metal bowl was wedged into the place where the clock's face had been, buckled in places where the sides had been cut and overlapped to fit the small space.

"Theo, what is this?" Zara said.

"A Device," Theo said. "A tracking Device."

"And it tracks...?" Ransom said. He lifted the glass door of the casing and withdrew his hand when Theo slapped it, lightly.

"The communicator." Theo pointed at the center of the metal bowl. The tiny brass stem of the communicator clung to one of its sides, quivering slightly from the opening of the door. "I figured out how to make the stem resonate with the communicator. We can find it now."

"Theo, that's Miss Blackwood's job. And how did you know they would need this?"

"I didn't. I built it for practice. And because I was mad about what she said to you. The Deviser let me use her shop—she doesn't think I'm good for anything, as an apprentice—and I was still there when the raiding party came back from attacking Ghazarian's ship. One of the soldiers told me they left the tracking Device in one of the boats, and it was overturned in the fight, so they lost the Device. That means this is the only way we have of finding the communicator."

"Theo," Zara said, "you need to take this to Miss Blackwood immediately."

"No." Theo's face was set in a scowl. "No, Rowena. We have to use it to go after Ghazarian."

"Theo—"

"Just *listen*. Miss Blackwood doesn't think Ghazarian is anything but an ordinary pirate, but we know she's clever and ruthless and is going to keep tricking anyone Miss Blackwood sends after her. You're the only one who can outwit Ghazarian, you know that."

Zara looked at Ransom, who shrugged. "He's right," he said.

"See? And Miss Blackwood's already failed once, so what's the chance she'll get it right the second time? *And* there are only a few pirates with Ghazarian, our troops captured all the rest, *and* she doesn't have a ship. If we hurry, we can catch up to her before she makes a bargain with the Karitians!"

"That's incredibly dangerous even if Ghazarian doesn't have many pirates with her. It will take soldiers. You're not even a combatant!"

"If Miss Blackwood sends soldiers, they'll be under the command of someone else who doesn't know how to defeat Ghazarian. She'll never put you in charge. And it has to be you, Rowena."

"I'm not..." Theo gave her a look of appeal that wouldn't have been out of place on a puppy, despite his age. "It's too dangerous. I'm not going to ask everyone to risk their lives like this."

"Then I will."

Theo was out the door before Zara could stop him. She closed her mouth on more objections and covered her face with both hands.

"You're not considering this, are you?" Ransom said.

Zara raised her head. "I...he made some good points. Letting that Device fall into Karitian hands could be devastating to Tremontane. And Blackwood clearly is at a loss here."

"He's right that you know better than Blackwood how to fight Ghazarian, but it's not your responsibility. If you go after her, people are going to get hurt, probably killed. That's unacceptable to me."

"I could go alone."

Ransom swore and stood abruptly, making his chair rock on its back legs. "That is *not* going to happen. I don't care how indestructible you are, that's insanity."

"So it's acceptable to let Blackwood send more troops after Ghazarian and let *them* be killed?"

"It's just a Device, Rowena, and a broken one at that. How much damage can Dineh-Karit do with it?"

Zara set her plate to one side. "Communication is key in warfare," she said, "and Dineh-Karit is our enemy, which means war is always a possibility. It's not just about keeping an advantage, it's about preventing our enemy from gaining that advantage. Tremontane will be able to reproduce that Devisery, but we'll be playing catch-up with Dineh-Karit, and if their Devisery is as advanced as I've seen, heaven only knows what else they'll be able to invent based on it. Recovering the Device is urgent, and Blackwood knows that. She just doesn't realize what kind of enemy she's facing."

"That still doesn't make it your job. You could advise Blackwood."

Zara laughed. "She'd never listen to me." Even revealing why Zara was so close in Jeffrey's confidence wouldn't make a difference, not that she could do that. "I might be able to persuade her I know something of Ghazarian's plans, but that's it."

"So do that. You can't seriously intend to drag the others into this? It's far too dangerous."

Zara hesitated. "I don't—"

The door banged open again. "We're all agreed," Theo said. "We're going after Ghazarian."

"Rowena, what's he talking about?" Belinda said.

"We're not going after Ghazarian," Ransom said.

"That Miss Blackwood's job is," Cantara said.

"*Stop,*" Zara said, "and sit down. Theo, what did you tell them?"

"That we have a tracking Device and you're going to lead us to get the communicator back."

"That's not a given," Ransom said.

"It's the only thing that makes sense."

"Slow down, Theo," Zara said. She sat back in her chair and closed her eyes briefly. "I don't know how many of you have heard, but Blackwood's attack on Ghazarian's ship failed to recover the communicator. It sounds like Ghazarian took it and escaped with some of her men. Worse, the soldiers lost the tracking Device, so they'll have to resort to other ways of finding a missing person. Theo, who was either foresighted or obstinate, built a second tracking Device, which means it's still possible to track the communicator. But Theo doesn't want to give it to Blackwood, he wants us to find Ghazarian and retrieve the communicator from her."

"But...we're not soldiers. Isn't that dangerous?" Belinda said.

"Rowena is the only one who can beat Ghazarian," Theo said. "I'm sure she can find a way to make it less dangerous. It's certainly better than letting more soldiers tromp around and fail."

"I afraid am not," Arjan said, "and Cantara and I willing to fight are."

"But Theo's no fighter, and neither am I," Ransom said.

"You can shoot a gun," Belinda pointed out.

"Not very well. And I thought you were more sensible than that."

"I am," Belinda said, "and that's why I think we should do it. Yes, it will be dangerous, but if we give Theo's Device to Miss Blackwood, she'll do the same thing she did before that's already failed, and more people will die. She'll never put Rowena in charge of those soldiers. Ghazarian can't have many men, and I'm confident we can trick them."

"People will die," Ransom said. "Are you capable of shooting to kill?"

"If it's what I have to do to protect the people I care about, yes."

"We're all in agreement," Theo said. "What about you, Rowena?"

Zara looked at each of them in turn. Arjan looked belligerent. Cantara looked confident. Belinda was pale, but her jaw was set in a way that said she wasn't going to let fear conquer her. Theo was as certain as ever. "You understand this could mean our deaths," she said. "Are you sure you want to risk your lives for a Device?"

"For a Device we don't want the Karitians to have," Belinda said. "You've already risked your life for it. That tells me it's important. So...yes."

Zara turned her attention to Ransom, who was standing a little apart from their circle of chairs, his head bowed. "It's going to take all of us," she said. "If Ghazarian has gone to ground in the jungle, we'll need someone who knows how to find their way and won't get lost. And I'm not superstitious about saying we may need your inherent magic."

Ransom sighed. "I think it's lunacy," he said, "but you've convinced me it's a chance worth taking. I'm in. But if I have to use my magic on any one of you, I won't be gentle."

"Understood," Zara said. "Now, eat up, and I'll tell you my plan."

Zara sat beside Ransom at the stern of the boat, which bounced along the waves made by the morning tide as if it were as eager to find their prey as she was. The morning mist had all but burned off, and it was going to be another scorcher of a day. She wished she had dressed Karitian-style in loincloth and twisted brassiere, the way Cantara had, but she and Belinda were too pale to do anything but burn under the hot Karitian sun. So they had opted for sleeveless tunics and thin, wide-legged trousers, with sandals and broad-brimmed Veriboldan hats she hoped might throw observers off.

Arjan and Theo had stripped down to short pants, while Ransom wore a sleeveless Karitian shirt and trousers rolled to the knee. He was too blond to pass as anything but Tremontanan, but Zara hoped the six of them in their varied attire and appearance would look like northern sailors, on business in the Bay of Avizi. The harbormaster had given them all a look of extreme disbelief, but had rented them a boat without comment. For once, Zara hadn't knocked anyone over upon entering. She hoped it was a good omen.

"Steer left," she told Ransom. Theo made a noise of protest.

"We're moving away from Ghazarian!" he exclaimed. "We need to stay on course."

"Ghazarian will be watching carefully for any signs she's been discovered, Theo," Zara reminded him, "and a boat making a straight line for her will be extremely suspicious. Just keep telling us where the Device puts her."

"She's still to the west. We're almost out of the bay. We're going to look suspicious anyway if we're the only two boats in the area."

"Don't worry about it. Let's move closer to Manachen now."

"I see three large ships in the direction the Device indicates," Belinda said. She had a rifle lying across the tops of her feet, well below where any observer could see it. "You're sure that's where she'll be?"

"It's the only thing that makes sense." Zara squinted off in the direction Theo had indicated. "Blackwood's soldiers captured her ship and most of her men, so she needs a new vessel. Ghazarian can't stay in Dineh-Karit without risking the Karitians apprehending her after their deal, not to mention she can't live in the kind of luxury that bounty will buy her. So she needs a ship that will take her across the ocean."

"But those are all Karitian ships. How would she get one of those?"

"Stole it, probably," Ransom said. "One more reason for her to conclude this transaction rapidly." He turned the tiller and the boat zipped away in a new direction. "I think I'll bring us around the far side of those ships, see if we can't identify which one is Ghazarian's."

Zara nodded, keeping her eyes on the distant vessels. One of the ships had what she thought of as traditional lines, several masts with sails furled as it sat at rest. It was bigger than Ghazarian's captured ship, and Zara concluded it was not their quarry. Ghazarian had been left with barely a handful of pirates after Blackwood's raid, not enough men to crew a ship that size.

The other two didn't look like sailing ships at all. They had no masts, and their prows curved high out of the water, sheltering the rest of the ship and making them look unbalanced. Giant Devices, scaled-up versions of the one propelling their boat, were attached to the sterns. One was tipped up out of the water and figures were tending to it, while the other was turned to low and idly propelled the ship forward barely faster than the waves could move it. They didn't look like anything that could survive the open ocean, but Zara had a healthy respect for Karitian Devices and figured they knew better than she did what their capacities were.

"It's one of the two funny-looking ones," Theo said, confirming Zara's guess. Ransom made another course correction.

"Let's not get close enough to see their faces," Belinda said.

"If we can see them, they can see us," Arjan said. "Best to stay away."

260

Cantara, sitting in the bow, half-turned to look back at Zara. "It is the ship with the broken Device."

"How do you know?"

"They tentative are, like ones who do not know what they doing are. They Karitian sailors are not."

"Theo?" Zara asked.

"She could be right. Turn left again." Theo rotated the tracking Device in his lap. The heavy oblong case turned awkwardly, as if it weighed much more than it did. "It's them."

Zara stared at the ship, committing it to memory. Its dull wooden sides had giant eyes with orange irises painted on them, monstrous things Zara was glad weren't pointed her way. She felt, with a twinge of superstition, that Ghazarian might through some sympathetic magic be able to see through those eyes. She straightened her spine and said, "Make one more loop around, then back toward the Karitian docks. Now we can make a plan."

No one pressed her for details, which relieved her mind. Her plan up until now had been to gather more information so she could generate a real plan, one which would end with her in possession of the communication Device. Now that she had information, though, the plan which presented itself to her looked like a terrible idea: board Ghazarian's ship and take back the Device, killing as many pirates as necessary while not getting killed themselves. Blackwood had succeeded in taking Ghazarian's first ship, but it had been a deadly exchange, with far too many soldiers losing their lives. They would be at a serious disadvantage. But they had to retrieve the Device before Ghazarian sold it to the Karitians, which could happen at any time.

"Theo, keep track of Ghazarian, please," she said.

"Of course," Theo said scornfully. Zara realized her preoccupation had pushed her toward condescension and shut up. How could they eliminate some of the pirates and nudge the odds in their favor? Belinda could get off two shots before the pirates realized anything was wrong, and if she was as good a shot as she claimed... Zara wished she knew how many pirates they were talking about. Surely no more than fifteen, but probably no fewer than five. That was a lot of enemies to eliminate, particularly if they were all armed.

"They have repaired the Device," Cantara said. "It in the water is."

"They're moving," Theo said. "Moving away."

"Away?" said Zara.

"I think we should follow them," Ransom said.

"Is that safe?" asked Belinda.

"Better than losing sight of them entirely. And suppose they're heading off to the rendezvous?"

"Do it," Zara said, moving to join Cantara in the bow. "Without looking like we're following them."

"You don't ask much, do you?" Ransom said, sounding amused, but the Device roared higher and louder, and they accelerated toward the distant ship.

The wind of their passage, brine-scented and cool, tangled Zara's hair even though she'd tied it back. They passed a couple of the flyspeck islands dotting the bay and the coast, most of them barely big enough to hold one of the *nakati* huts, but a few lushly overgrown and tempting Zara to explore. She adjusted the brim of her hat and kept her eye on Ghazarian's ship. A few other boats zipped past, some of them putting in at what must be private docks west of Manachen proper. She hoped they were effective camouflage.

Ahead, another island loomed, this one larger than the others but still apparently uninhabited. The ship approached it slowly, without displaying any urgency that might indicate they'd noticed their shadow. Zara watched it, conviction growing in her heart. "Faster," she told Ransom. "Get us to the far side of that island, *without* looking like that's what we're doing."

"We can't beat them there, Rowena," Ransom said even as he steered the boat in a new course.

"We don't have to. We just have to beat her sentry." It was all falling into place. "She's going to make the sale here. It's far enough from Manachen not to attract attention, it lets her choose her ground, and if she gets a sentry in place, she'll have warning if the Karitians try to double-cross her. Which I'd bet they will. I know I would."

"But they will see us," Arjan said.

"Take a look at the island's profile," Zara said, not pointing. "It curves up to a high point left of center, perfect to have someone watching for treachery. But it's also far from where she'll land, if she keeps on course. So if we can land on the far side—"

"I understand," Arjan said. "We conceal the boat and there nothing for the sentry to see is."

"Then what?" Belinda asked.

Zara's blood was fizzing with excitement. It had been far too long since she'd gone up against an opponent wily enough to give her a challenge. "Then," she said, "we take back what's ours."

CHAPTER TWENTY-THREE

Ransom steered them to a sheltered cove no bigger than twenty feet across, and they all waded to shore, Arjan and Theo dragging the boat up the beach. "All the way," Zara said when they reached the high tide mark. "Into the undergrowth. We can't have anyone noticing this boat."

When it was concealed under the greenery, she said, "Back into the trees."

"Were we fast enough?" Theo asked.

"If we weren't, we'll find out soon." Zara wiped her palms on her trousers. "Now. We can't go rushing in there without knowing how many pirates we're facing. And we don't want anyone raising the alarm. So, Arjan and Cantara, I want you to climb to the top of the island and take care of whoever Ghazarian puts there. There might be more than one sentry, though I doubt it. It's essential he or she not be able to alert Ghazarian we're coming."

Arjan nodded. Cantara said, "Where do we go when that is done?"

"You'll come back here. Ransom, you'll scout ahead and see how many enemies we're dealing with. Ghazarian will have to leave a few of her people on the ship, but she'll want as many as possible with her to keep the Karitians from getting any ideas about overpowering her. If she's smart, she'll have limited the size of their party in her demands. It doesn't matter, because we'll have retrieved the Device before the Karitians get here, but we should expect to be outnumbered."

"Yes, ma'am," Ransom said, his hazel eyes twinkling with amusement. Zara smiled back. By heaven, it felt good to be in command again!

"Come back as soon as you've scouted the place—I don't have to tell you to be careful, do I?"

"I'm always careful," Ransom said. He kissed her swiftly and disappeared between the trees.

The rest of them gaped at her in astonishment, even Belinda. Embarrassment crept over Zara, and she willed her blush away. "Arjan, Cantara," she said, and the two Eskandelics started out of their reverie and vanished in the direction Ransom had gone. Zara found a fallen tree and sat on it. The memory of Ransom's kiss lingered on her lips. She had no reason to feel embarrassed, but...it was just that they'd all been so close on their journey, and now that two of them were even closer, it felt awkward, as if their relationships all had to alter to make room for a romance.

Belinda cleared her throat. "So...what should Theo and I do?"

Grateful for the distraction, Zara said, "It depends on what Ransom finds. The best outcome would be for us to find you high ground to shoot from, but the moment you fire that first shot, that's the end of secrecy. So we'll want to eliminate as many pirates as we can before that happens."

"And what about me?" Theo asked.

"You're not a fighter, Theo," Belinda said.

"So I'm supposed to just sit there and watch the rest of you?" His belligerent voice echoed off the trees, and Belinda shushed him. "I hit that pirate back by the river, remember? I'm not weak."

"No one's saying you're weak," said Belinda.

"Then let me fight. What about a gun? I can fire a gun. They don't take much skill. No offense, Belinda, but you know what I mean."

"I'm not a fighter, either." Zara pushed off from the log and faced Theo. "Are you saying *I'm* weak?"

Theo blinked. "Well...no."

"Theo, my father taught me a long time ago—" *a* very *long time ago*—"when you're facing an opponent, you should match your strengths against their weaknesses and not the other way around." She'd learned so much from her father, King Sylvester, that had shaped the woman she'd become. All those years ago... "You want to fight because right now it looks like that's the kind of battle this is. But you've already beaten Ghazarian because you built the Device that let us find her. That's your strength. If you want to go in with your fists

265

flying like Arjan, I won't stop you. But you'll be matching your weakness to their strength. Think about it."

Theo nodded once, slowly, like he was digesting her words. "I just don't want to be useless. There's a strong source on this island, I can smell it from here—I can imbue your gun Devices—"

"That would be pointlessly dangerous. And you're not useless. I want you to stay with the boat and have it ready to launch. If we retrieve the Device without killing or incapacitating all the pirates, we'll be leaving here at a run. If you've got the boat in the water and its Device ready to go, we might actually make it out alive."

Theo had looked like he wanted to protest, but by the time she wound down, he was nodding again. "I understand. I can do that."

Belinda had taken a seat on Zara's log and was examining the rifle Device. "Are you sure you're ready to fire that thing?" she said, indicating Ghazarian's pistol, jammed into Zara's waistband.

"I probably won't do anything more than frighten people, but yes, I'm ready." Zara sat beside her. "I hate this part."

"The waiting? How often do you fight pirates that you can call it 'this part'?" Belinda teased.

Zara shrugged. "It's always the same, no matter what the challenge. The hardest part is waiting for others to do their jobs so you can do yours." Memory surfaced, of facing down the Magistrix of the Scholia in her throne room, her nerves keyed to the breaking point waiting for all the pieces to fall into place. It was essential not to let the waiting break you. She let out a long breath and surreptitiously rolled out her shoulders. She was much older now, and better at waiting. It didn't make her like it more.

They sat in silence, listening to the birds and the insects, for what felt like hours. Zara had no watch, and it wouldn't have mattered anyway, because she could not make Arjan, Cantara, and Ransom move faster. Moving faster might be deadly for them, too. She let herself fall into a waking fugue, her eyes sweeping the jungle, her ears tuned to listen for the sound of returning footsteps, her lungs taking in wet, hot air and expelling it slowly. A couple of times, she began daydreaming of traveling to Veribold with Ransom and had to stop herself. She needed to be alert, not distracted.

Distantly, she heard someone moving through the undergrowth. She gestured to Belinda and Theo to hide themselves, though she had no illusions about how well any of them might do that. If this was a pirate and not one of their friends, their only hope was to try to overcome him before he could return to Ghazarian with news of their presence.

"We have returned," Arjan said, his deep voice almost a whisper. Zara emerged from behind the tree where she'd sheltered. Arjan and Cantara looked as if they'd been in a fight, but neither looked wounded or moved like they were in pain. Cantara was smiling.

"Two of them," she said. "They did not see us coming, and now they will tell no one we here are."

"Did you...kill them?" Theo's whisper was even quieter than Arjan's.

The smile fell away from Cantara's face. "We could not subdue them and risk them getting free to make a warning. They will tell no one anything ever again."

"That was the right choice," Zara said, shooting a warning look at Theo. "Thank you."

"They would have killed us," Arjan said with a shrug. "Though I cannot say I will forget how it felt. I have never killed a man before."

"Nor I," said Cantara. She rubbed her fist, running her fingertips over her knuckles reminiscently. "It was...too easy."

"That's two pirates who can't help Ghazarian fight," Zara said, hoping to distract Cantara. "Ransom will return soon, and we'll know better how many are left."

"Ransom is back now," Ransom said, emerging from the thick growth. "You probably shouldn't all stand out in the open like that."

"What did you learn?" Zara asked.

Ransom crouched in the dirt next to the log Zara and Belinda had sat on and drew with his forefinger in the thin topsoil. "There's a place where the trees thin out—it's not really a clearing, but it's big enough to hold a good twenty people if they all like each other very much. Ghazarian had a couple of pirates clearing the undergrowth, which tells me this is where she plans to make her stand."

"You saw her?"

Ransom nodded. "Somebody got off a lucky shot during Blackwood's raid, because there was a bloody bandage wrapped around her left leg. It didn't do more than give her a limp, so we shouldn't count on it incapacitating her in a fight. Anyway. The clearing. I saw Ghazarian and five other pirates, one of whom left to go to the shore as I watched. I don't know what orders Ghazarian gave her, because she spoke in Eskandelic, but the path she took only leads to the beach."

"Do they have a longboat, then?"

"Pulled up on shore. I circled around to make sure the ship hadn't slipped around this side of the island."

"Ghazarian still has the Device," Theo said. He pointed at the bowl of the tracking Device, where the stem clung as if magnetized to the side about halfway between the lip and the center.

"Good," Zara said. "Then it's time for the next part of the plan."

She wasn't as certain as she sounded. The ideal plan would have been to get everyone into position before Ghazarian arrived, but they couldn't know where she planned to make her stand until she reached the island. So that possibility was eliminated. "We're going to draw away some of Ghazarian's support, distract her, then attack when she isn't expecting it," she said. "But we need to move quickly. If they're preparing the clearing, they're already not as alert as they could be, and we can use that."

"I'll lead the way," Ransom said. "Follow as closely as you can, and for heaven's sake try not to make noise."

That was probably wishful thinking, Zara thought. The ground was thick with undergrowth, wide-lobed plants and grasses with blades as broad as her palm, all of which rustled as they passed. The lush greenery grew most riotously where they walked between the trees, which were fewer than on the mainland but every bit as tall. Zara had considered putting Belinda in one of them, to give her a better vantage point, but their trunks were straight and branchless for the first thirty feet. She glanced at Belinda, who wasn't breathing heavily but whose face was red. Getting her into a tree, even one with plenty of spreading low branches, might have been difficult.

Ransom moved easily, but with awareness of those following him. He held bushes aside for them to pass rather than hacking them with his notched knife, and silently pointed out ground vines they might trip over. The rich green smell of vegetation wafted up with every step as they crushed plants underfoot despite their care. Zara was grateful for the high canopy, shielding them from the morning sun. One way or another, this would all be over before the scorching heat of afternoon was upon them, but the air was already warm and wet and clinging like a second skin. She once again dismissed thoughts of the dry heat of Veribold and focused on ducking past a shrub bearing purple berries, probably poisonous if Dineh-Karit's wildlife was representative of the country.

After about fifteen minutes of walking, Ransom held up a hand to signal a halt. "They're another fifty yards ahead," he whispered when they'd all gathered around. "What next?"

Zara listened, but heard no sounds of human movement, only the raucous birds in the trees and the rustle of the undergrowth when a stray breeze passed through it. "Ransom," she said, "I want you and...Arjan...to approach as close as you can. When you're within speaking distance, get their attention and then say something in Karitian."

"The idea being to make them believe they've been double-crossed?" Ransom grinned.

"And I will overcome the ones who come after us," Arjan said. "It is a good plan."

"It's part of a plan," Zara said. "The rest of us are going to move around to the other side of the clearing. When the pirates leave to investigate Ransom and Arjan—it won't be all of them, but even one would be enough, and I'm betting Ghazarian will send two—we'll jump the others. Belinda, you'll need to take aim on Ghazarian and shoot her if she tries to run. Cantara, you'll fight the ones who are left until Arjan and Ransom join us."

"You have great faith in me," Cantara said with a smile. "Suppose there are many?"

"I've seen *arakeli* dancers before. I'm certain you can keep them busy."

"What about you?" Ransom asked.

"I'm the final distraction." Zara smiled, fierce excitement filling her. "Ghazarian thinks I'm dead. When she sees me…I don't know what she'll do, but it will rattle her enough I can retrieve the Device." She remembered how bloody she'd been, lying on the floor of that tiny house, and the furious joy on Ghazarian's face when she'd driven the knife home. Saying she'd be rattled was an understatement.

"Then let's go," Ransom said, taking Zara's hand briefly and squeezing it before turning away. She watched him and Arjan for a few steps, then gestured to the others to follow her. How had they ended up divided by sex, men and women? It didn't matter. What mattered was retrieving the Device. She sent up a short prayer that her plan wouldn't get them all killed.

She led them forward, not as silently as Ransom had, but without sounding like a party of women tramping through the undergrowth. She hoped. At the very least, they needed to be quiet enough that they could hear Ghazarian's men if they strayed from the clearing. Too late, she realized she should have arranged a signal to let Ransom know when they were in position. She quickened her steps. If Ransom and Arjan acted too quickly —

The trees grew more thickly together where they were, and Zara slipped from trunk to broad trunk, hoping her guess was correct and she was keeping the thick boles between herself and the still unseen clearing. Her ears practically quivered with the strain of listening for anything out of the ordinary. If she'd been an animal, they'd be swiveled forward, tilted to catch the smallest sound. The idea amused her.

She tripped and caught herself on a tree, scraping her hand. She examined it briefly and was startled to see the abrasion fading already, her skin turning pink as it healed. What had Theo said — that there was a strong source on the island? And she felt energetic, not at all winded or tired. Maybe she was right, and her healing magic worked more rapidly and effectively the closer she was to a source. She must be practically on top of it. She wiped her now-uninjured palm on her trousers and kept walking. Not being shot by a pirate suddenly mattered more, if she wanted to keep her secret. The image of a bullet shooting back out of her rapidly healing flesh made her shudder — or would she heal around it? Even worse.

She heard someone stumble and turned to see Belinda leaning heavily on the rifle as if she'd caught herself before falling. She gave Zara a reassuring nod and used the rifle to push herself upright. Then her eyes widened. She swiftly brought the rifle to her shoulder and fired past Zara. The shot echoed, sending the birds into a screaming frenzy.

Zara whipped around. A woman dressed in the castoff clothing of three nations swayed there, her eyes as astonished as Belinda's, her chest a gory mess. A pistol slipped from her limp fingers to disappear into the undergrowth. Reflexively Zara leaped to catch the woman as she sagged, then dropped her and stepped away. No point in trying to keep this quiet. More gunshots sounded in the distance, then shouting. Zara swore and said, "Run for the clearing!"

CHAPTER TWENTY-FOUR

They ran as best they could through the thick undergrowth, tripping on ground vines and dodging around trees. Cantara was faster than Zara and soon outdistanced them. The cries of fighting were louder now, filling Zara with dread. So much for the plan. Now she had to make it up as she went along.

She and Belinda saw the clearing before they stumbled into it. Zara grabbed Belinda to keep her from continuing into the open. The clearing was a confused mass of motion, Cantara darting past to slam into a pirate twice her size and taking them both down, more pirates shooting wildly into the bushes. There were far too many people, more than Zara had anticipated. Where were Ransom and Arjan?

Belinda brought the rifle up again and tracked the movement of one of the pirates who had his back to her. "Wait!" Zara said, but Belinda had already fired and was reloading. The pirate collapsed, blood spreading across his narrow back, and his companion turned to see where the shot had come from. Belinda's hands moved feverishly fast, and she was swearing under her breath, a long stream of invective. The pirate, his pistol held high, headed across the clearing, his pace gradually increasing until he was running.

Belinda swore again. Zara knew nothing about guns, but she had a feeling something was wrong with this one. The pirate barreled down on them, close enough now Zara could see his face contorted into a snarl. Desperate, Zara stepped forward into the clearing and braced herself. She could slow him down long enough for Belinda to finish loading. With luck, he'd be a bad shot and only wound her.

Her sudden appearance startled him, and he skidded to a stop, confusion replacing anger for the moment. "Back away, and you might survive this," Zara said, fixing him with the blue-eyed North gaze.

To her surprise, he took a few steps back. "*You,*" he said in Eskandelic. "*You were dead!*"

"*Not for long,*" Zara said.

The sound of the rifle bolt ratcheting into place almost made her flinch, but showing weakness would be fatal. Belinda stepped wide around her, the rifle pointed at the pirate's chest. The pirate swore, turned, and ran. Before he reached the far side of the clearing, and the path to the beach, another shot rang out. Half the pirate's head exploded, scattering flesh and bone and blood in every direction. Belinda cried out and lowered the rifle. "That wasn't me," she exclaimed.

A tall figure stepped out of the sheltering trees into the clearing. "I do not tolerate traitors," Ghazarian said. Smoke wafted from the black powder pistol she held.

Zara grabbed Belinda's arm and put her friend behind her. "I'm not surprised."

Ghazarian focused on her, and her face went slack with astonishment and fear. "You," she said as the pirate had. "I killed you." The pistol fell out of her hand, but she didn't seem to notice.

"You thought you killed me. You should have made sure."

Ghazarian took a few steps forward, slow, hesitant ones. "I have killed many. I was sure. What are you, that you do not die?"

Zara held still, keeping Ghazarian's attention on her. Where was everyone, and why hadn't Belinda shot Ghazarian already? Well, she'd wanted a distraction, and she'd gotten one. It was her own fault she hadn't told anyone what to do with it. "Give me the Device, and maybe I'll tell you."

"It my Device is, until I sell it. The Tremontanans had a chance and wasted it. The Karitians more intelligent are." Ghazarian's hand drifted to the hilt of the archaic long blade she wore at her hip. "I will have to kill you more this time."

Belinda brought the rifle up again. "Hand over the Device," she said. "I won't hesitate to shoot."

Ghazarian's lips curled in a mocking sneer. "Then shoot." Her eyes were fixed on Zara, as if despite her words the two of them were the only ones in the clearing. Zara gazed back, certain if she looked away, Ghazarian would attack. *Shoot her, Belinda!*

Belinda cursed, then in a low voice said, "It's still jammed. I was bluffing."

She spoke so quietly Zara could barely hear her over the shouts and screams, but Ghazarian's sneer became a vicious smile, the smile of someone who knew she'd won. "I kill you all," she said, drew her sword, and advanced on Zara.

Zara backed away, reaching for the pistol jammed into her waistband. "Run, Belinda!" she shouted, and then Ghazarian was upon her, sword thrusting for her midsection. Zara flung herself to one side, but Ghazarian followed, slashing at her legs. A sharp sting turned into a dull ache as Ghazarian scored a hit on Zara's thigh. The ache burned and then vanished. They had to be right on top of the source. Zara pulled Ghazarian's pistol free of her waistband and nearly lost it as the pirate captain brought the sword around in a heavy two-handed blow that almost took Zara's head off. Zara rolled awkwardly out of the way. She needed to stop fighting a defensive battle.

She turned and ran, dodging pirates and Arjan, who was locked in hand-to-hand combat with a pirate whose shirtless chest gleamed with sweat. There was no place she could make a stand that Ghazarian couldn't reach her. She stopped near the path leading to the beach, or at least she assumed it led to the beach from what Ransom had said, and wheeled to face Ghazarian, squeezing off a shot. It went wild, but Ghazarian ducked anyway, then lunged at Zara. Before Zara could move, Ghazarian's sword plunged into her chest.

It was as icy as the knife had been, sharp enough that at first the pain was minimal, no worse than the bite of a paper cut. Ghazarian grinned and thrust the sword deeper. *Now* it hurt. Zara screamed, heard Belinda echo her, then fell as Ghazarian pulled the blade out and gave her a shove. "I watch to see you dead," Ghazarian said, gloating.

You're going to watch a long time. Her body burned like molten honey, a strangely pleasant sensation. For the first time, she could feel her body healing, felt her heart sealing around the wound inflicted by the sword and the flesh of her chest knitting. The flow of blood slowed, then became a trickle. Every breath filled her with life, searing hot. It was amazing.

She became aware she was kneeling slumped on the undergrowth the pirates had crushed to make their clearing. Ghazarian stood over her, legs akimbo, leaning on the bloody blade so it flexed outward. The noise of the fight was greater than it had been, with Belinda's screams filling the air like the cries of the birds who had surely all fled the melee. Zara drew in another deep, molten, wonderful breath and raised her head. Ghazarian's smile was vulpine, the look of a predator who'd bested a rival. Zara smiled back, and saw Ghazarian's expression falter. Without a word, Zara raised the pistol, Ghazarian's own gun, and shot the woman in the chest.

The shot was unnaturally loud even against the backdrop of screams and shouts. Ghazarian staggered backward, dropping her sword and raising her other hand to clutch her shattered chest. Zara rose, keeping the pistol trained on her enemy. It had been a good, clean shot, but she wasn't so stupid as to assume that meant Ghazarian was no longer dangerous. Ghazarian continued to back away from her, her eyes glassy and fixed on Zara as if they were the only two people in the clearing. "What are you?" she said, her voice barely more than a whisper, almost inaudible against the noise.

"Someone you should never have trifled with," Zara said, matching her tone for tone.

She kept pace with Ghazarian's halting retreat until the woman stumbled and fell. Her bloody chest heaved with exertion. She reached inside her coat, a heavy leather mantle far too warm for this climate, and pulled out the communicator Device. She thrust it at Zara. "Take it," she gasped. "Just…do not let me die. Use your magic on…"

Zara took the Device. "I wouldn't spare you even if I could," she said coldly. "Heaven knows how many lives you've taken. You killed me once. I'm just balancing the scales."

Ghazarian's eyes flashed, and she snarled in defiance. "I…" she began, then sagged, her eyes closing.

Zara heard footsteps disturbing the undergrowth. "Is she dead?"

Belinda said. She began to kneel beside Ghazarian's body. Zara grabbed her shoulder and hauled her up. She prodded Ghazarian's side with her sandaled toe, flipping the coat open to reveal Ghazarian's hand clutched on the hilt of a wickedly long knife. It trembled, rose a few inches, then fell still.

"She had one more surprise in her," Zara said. "Not that it would have mattered. Is everyone all right?" She looked around the clearing. It was empty of pirates, living ones, anyway. Ransom knelt before Arjan with his hand on the big man's bloody shoulder, his head bowed in healing. Cantara paced the circumference of the space, alert and unwounded.

Belinda was silent. Zara glanced at her, then took a longer look. Belinda's eyes were wide and stunned, her jaw slack. "Are *you* all right?" Zara said.

Belinda swallowed. "I saw her stab you through the heart," she said. "The heart, Rowena. I *saw* it. But you're...sweet heaven, you're covered in blood and you're standing there like nothing is wrong—"

Zara's unwounded heart lurched. "I don't suppose I can persuade you to forget you saw that?" she said, trying for a light tone.

Belinda shook her head. "Rowena, what kind of magic is it? It has to be magic—"

The sound of a pistol being cocked rang out in the stillness of the clearing. A voice spoke in Karitian, then in Tremontanese added, "We will be taking the Device now."

Zara turned slowly, her hands wide to show she was unarmed, then remembered she still held the communicator Device and cursed herself. She might have been able to bluff if she'd kept it hidden. No choice now but to brazen it out. Beside her, Belinda made a move as if to aim her rifle at the speaker, then subsided. Even Belinda's reflexes weren't that quick.

Four blue and red *nakati* armed with pistol Devices flanked a Karitian man dressed in the narrow robe and enveloping gauzy over-robe Zara thought of as civilian wear. It was probably not a good idea to make assumptions at this point. The Karitian party stood at the head of the path leading to the beach, fanned out to block their exit, if Zara had had any intention of leaving by that route. The Karitian's face was broad and fleshy, fatter than any Karitians she'd seen so far, but his brown eyes were sharp and Zara felt it would be a mistake to believe him indolent just because he was large and sweating in the mid-morning heat.

The Karitian stepped forward, not far enough to separate himself from his guards, and said, "You will to me give the Device."

"It's not yours. It's Tremontanan property," Zara replied.

"We have the weapons. It is our property now."

"It's theft. Our government will consider it an act of war."

"Who is to see, out here where there is nothing and…no one?" The Karitian glanced past Zara at whichever of her friends stood there, out of her sight. As a threat, it was effective, but Zara was too old and too canny to be drawn by it.

"If you intend to kill us all anyway, why should I make it easy on you?" she said. The Karitian twitched, but that was the only sign her shot had gone home.

"Let's discuss this like civilized people, shall we?" she went on. "You Karitians pride yourselves on being civilized — that should appeal to you."

The Karitian inclined his head slightly, indicating she should continue. Zara prayed her friends wouldn't do anything stupid. "There are only three ways this can play out. One. We give you the Device without a fight. You let us go free. We return to the embassy and report the theft of a valuable Tremontanan Device, giving our country the pretext for going to war. I don't have to describe what happens next, do I?

"Two. You attempt to take the Device by force. It's true, you're well-armed, but I'm standing beside the Tremontanan sharpshooting champion, and I'll bet she can drop at least a few of you before you take her down. Maybe you succeed, maybe we do, but it's guaranteed none of us are walking out of here unscathed."

Zara took another wonderfully life-saturated breath. She could get used to this. Probably she shouldn't get used to it. "And then we come to three. We both walk away. The Device is broken, so it's not useful to you. Nobody dies. Everything returns to the way it was three days ago, except the world is rid of a vicious criminal. You're welcome, by the way."

The Karitian's brows rose. "Why am I welcome?"

Zara pointed in Ghazarian's direction without breaking their gaze. "Heaven only knows what kind of depredations she's wreaked on your shipping, starting with stealing a ship and murdering its crew. You were willing to trade with her to get the Device, but she'd have been a problem for you for many years if you'd let her get away with it."

"We had plans for Ghazarian," the Karitian said. He pronounced the name with a strange emphasis, as if it tasted bad.

"It was a mistake to assume you could control her. Be grateful she's dead. And walk away from this."

The Karitian pursed his lips. "You assume my government will this find an acceptable outcome. Perhaps it is better for me to return dead."

"I don't think you believe that. You don't strike me as someone who lets political tides overwhelm him. I'm certain you know how to spin this your way."

One of the *nakati* shifted. The Karitian held up a quelling hand. "You speak well," he said, "but I think you understand not the demands of my government. We need this Device."

Zara smiled. She couldn't help herself. *Never give away more than you have to.* "Well, we don't," she said, and enjoyed the look of startled puzzlement that flitted across his face before he controlled himself. "We'll build another. It's not the Device that matters, it's the Devisery. Do you really think we're willing to give up our advantage?"

The Karitian opened his mouth to reply, and Zara overrode him. "You're not stupid. You know as well as I do the winner in a negotiation is the one who's willing to walk away. Now I'm going to tell you what will happen. My friends and I are going back to our embassy. *With* the Device. You're going to turn around and return to your government and tell them the Device was…destroyed." Her lips curled in a mirthless smile. "The pirates had a falling out. I'm sure you can make it believable."

She took a step toward the man, then another, conscious of the guns trained on her but with her whole attention focused on the Karitian. "You're going to do this because, sir, the alternative is death. Not only for you, but for thousands, perhaps hundreds of thousands. And I'm betting my own life that matters to you." She came to a halt some two feet from the Karitian. "This is the only deal I'm offering. Take it."

The Karitian swallowed. "Who are you to make such an offer?"

So many possible responses flooded her mind Zara felt choked by them. "Jeffrey North's voice, in this place, at this time," she finally said. It was as true as anything.

The same *nakat* brought his gun to bear on her. Quicker than a man his size ought to be able to move, the Karitian spun and snatched the weapon from the man's hand and threw it on the ground. He spat out a few words in Karitian that made the *nakati* back up and lower their pistols. Zara didn't move. The Karitian turned to face her and said, "Go now, and remember — this is not over."

It *was* over, but she could leave the man his dignity. Zara nodded and turned her back on him, her spine itching at the proximity to all those unfriendly guns, even if they weren't currently trained on her. She didn't wait to see if the others followed, didn't care whether she was going the right way; all that mattered was to get out of that clearing before the spell she'd cast over the Karitians broke.

They crashed through the undergrowth, no longer caring about not making noise. Zara slowed to let Ransom take the lead. He passed her silently, with no more than a glance that said nothing of what he was feeling or thinking. Good. Time enough to talk about all this when they were safe.

"Rowena," Belinda said, then fell silent before Zara could shush her. That was a relief. It wasn't as if they needed to be quiet, it was just that Zara didn't feel equal to having the conversation Belinda no doubt wanted while they were fleeing through the jungle. How many of the others had witnessed Ghazarian's blow? Had anyone but Belinda seen Zara heal herself? Maybe her secret was still safe. Zara trusted Belinda to be close-mouthed, especially if Zara could impress upon her the gravity of the truth. And it wasn't as if she had to admit to being effectively immortal; only a healer would intuit that.

She glanced at Belinda again. Her friend's astonishment was palpable, her expression that of a woman who was holding in a million questions and bursting with the desire to ask them. Zara's heart sank. *And so it begins.* Whether Belinda could keep quiet or not was irrelevant. Every person who knew was one more person who might tell. Keeping her secret had just become a hundred times harder.

CHAPTER TWENTY-FIVE

They came through the trees to the shore and found the boat halfway in the water with Theo at the helm. He stood when they appeared, his slim frame tense with worry, and took in their filthy and gory condition with horror that faded only slightly when he realized they were all mobile. "Did you get the Device?"

"Yes. Back to the embassy, and hurry," Zara said. It had occurred to her on their walk that the Karitians might still come after them, and they were mostly helpless on the open sea. They needed to get away from this island before that Karitian came to his senses. He would eventually realize those four *nakati* were witnesses who might tell his superiors what had happened, and then there would be bloodshed. She couldn't count on the blood shed being his, securing their escape.

They shoved off, and Ransom took his place at the tiller, steering them wide of the island. Ghazarian's stolen ship was gone, either taken by the Karitians or used by the remaining pirates to make their escape. A different ship lay off the coast of the island, similar to Ghazarian's but with random blue lines adorning its prow rather than orange eyes. It was otherwise unmarked, bore no national flag, and Zara shivered when she looked at it.

"It's not moving," Ransom said. "I don't think they're going to follow us."

"Still, let's not take any chances."

"Don't worry, Rowena, I have no desire to see the inside of a Karitian prison again."

"They would likely kill us instead," Arjan said.

Ransom regarded him sardonically. "That's cheering."

"But I think they could not kill Rowena," Arjan added. "Not if Ghazarian could not."

Silence descended, broken only by the hum of the boat's Device and the slap of waves against the boat's sides. "Ah," Zara said, struck suddenly mute. So Belinda had *not* been the only one to see.

"You have inherent magic, don't you," Belinda said. "That's why...Rowena, she stabbed you through the heart, and you survived! How is that even possible?"

So much for her secret. "I...heal myself," Zara said. "Like Ransom, only without thinking about it, and I can't heal others. I wish you hadn't found out."

"Why not?" Belinda exclaimed. "That—even in Tremontane, that's not something to be ashamed of. Healers are accepted everywhere."

"Some people are suspicious even of healers," Ransom said. "I could tell you stories...but we're not talking about me now."

"It unsettling is," Arjan said. "If you my friend were not, I would fear you."

"Don't say that, Arjan," Belinda protested. "It's not true. I wouldn't fear you, Rowena."

"Thank you, Belinda, but Arjan's reaction is more usual," Zara said. "It's a secret because I don't want people looking at me like I'm a monster. I'm just an ordinary woman who happens to have inherent magic."

Cantara laughed. "You have just talked us out of death. You hardly ordinary are."

"Well, you understand what I mean." Zara leaned into the wind of their passage, willing it to cool her cheeks. Cantara's comment made her unexpectedly flustered. "I hope I don't have to ask you all to keep my secret."

"We wouldn't tell," Theo said. "It's nobody's business, anyway."

Zara handed him the Device and his eyes lit with excitement. "They won't let you keep it," she said.

"I know. But I'd like to be the one who returns it, if that's all right. That Deviser was really snooty with me. I want to see her face when she realizes it was my tracking Device that found it."

Belinda let out a deep breath. "I feel so let down," she said, "as if nothing exciting could possibly happen again."

"I do not think I wish for excitement," Cantara said. "I wish for a peaceful life now."

"We're not safe yet," Zara said, which quelled the conversation.

She watched their wake the whole way back to Goudge's Folly, but the unmarked Karitian ship didn't follow them. No one paid them any attention as Ransom zipped between the rest of the crafts plying the bay, but Zara wasn't completely comfortable until they docked and returned custody of their boat to the harbormaster. It was nearly noon, and they trudged up the hill to the embassy in weary silence. The effects of the island's powerful source had worn off, though Zara thought the tiredness she felt was a result of the battle of wits she'd had and not the aftereffects of nearly dying again. She hoped their success would incline Blackwood to letting her have another bath.

Young Dyer was on duty at the gate again, and opened it for them before Zara could ask him to. He eyed her bloody shirt as if he wanted to ask about it, but a glance from her cowed him. Probably she shouldn't feel so smug about intimidating someone as insignificant as Dyer, but she disliked bullies, even small and ineffectual ones. Maybe encountering her would change his attitude.

The frigid air of the embassy once again made Zara break out in a sweat upon entering the foyer. Blackwood's secretary James came trotting toward them and stopped a few feet away, his mouth falling open in dismay. "Miss Farrell—Mister Zakhari—what happened? You're—"

"I want to speak with Miss Blackwood," Zara said. "We have something that belongs to her."

James nodded and gestured to them to follow him. Now they were safely on Tremontanan soil, weariness struck Zara as if she'd run all the way from the docks to the embassy. She straightened her shoulders and ignored it. This wasn't over yet.

James opened Blackwood's door without knocking. They must really have rattled him. "Miss Blackwood," he said, "they...Miss Farrell..."

Blackwood looked up from her desk. Her irritation turned to surprise. "What in the hell—"

Zara gestured to Theo, who came forward and laid the Device on Blackwood's desk. "We got it back," he said.

Blackwood shoved back from her desk and stood in one swift motion. "You did *what?*" She prodded the Device with a finger as if it were an unexploded bomb. "Miss Farrell, I specifically told you to leave this alone!"

"That's not true," Zara said. "You did imply it strongly, though. Would you like us to take it back where we found it?"

Blackwood glared at her. "Don't be flippant with *me*, Miss Farrell. And don't expect my gratitude to change my mind about you. You're still a civilian and you had no business interfering in government affairs."

Zara slapped both hands palm down on the desk and leaned forward, putting her face inches from Blackwood's. "A civilian who got results, Miss Blackwood, results *you* were incapable of. Let me remind you that I have his Majesty's full faith and approval. Just because I'm not free to tell you the details of my role in his Majesty's government does not mean I don't have one. Don't cross me, Miss Blackwood, or we'll find out what *other* results I might be capable of."

Blackwood's gaze didn't falter, but Zara had faced down opponents far more deadly. It was Blackwood who turned away first. "My...thanks, Miss Farrell," she ground out. "I hope you won't imagine this embassy is not grateful for your efforts, particularly since some of you appear to have been wounded in the retrieval of the Device. Do you need medical attention?"

"Ransom De Witt has taken care of that," Zara said. "But thank you."

"Then, if that's all..." Blackwood wasn't bothering to conceal her eagerness to get them out of there.

"I'll take the Device to your Deviser," Theo said. "I have to disassemble the tracking Device to give her the stem so she can fix it."

Blackwood looked confused at the words "tracking Device," but didn't pursue it. "If there's anything the embassy can do for you, just ask," she said, with an air that told Zara she really didn't want them to

284

ask. Zara nodded.

Out in the hall, Belinda said, "She might have been more grateful."

"She embarrassed was," Cantara said. "I do not think she had more gratitude to give."

"So…now what?" Theo asked.

"It's over," Zara said. "And life goes on."

"I'm sorry to have put you to so much trouble," Zara said. "I just don't think life in Dineh-Karit is for me."

Mistress Falken Senior pursed her lips. She was a lean woman in her middle sixties, with a cap of short silver hair and a tendency to tilt her head to one side like an inquisitive bird. With her eyes narrowed and her lips pursed, it was a bird of prey. "We went to some trouble to get you here," she said. "Now we're out the price of your passage *and* we still don't have an employee."

"Well, I had an idea about that." Zara leaned back in her chair, hoping her relaxed pose would put Mistress Falken at ease. "I know a woman who's looking for work. Her name is Belinda Stouffer. She's an experienced businesswoman who's interested in making a change. She used to be a merchant herself and understands the business. I have no doubt she'd be willing to take the job."

"You expect me to hire someone I've never met?"

"You hired me, didn't you?" Zara smiled. "I'll even repay my fare, so you won't be out any money." Technically, she could have made a case for them paying the fare for Belinda, but she was in a good mood and she wanted Mistress Falken to think positively of Belinda.

Mistress Falken pursed her lips again. "I'll consider it. Send Miss Stouffer to meet with me this afternoon. I'll expect the return of your fare at the same time."

"Certainly." Zara rose and offered Mistress Falken her hand. "Thank you for being so accommodating."

Out on the docks, Zara drew in a deep breath of briny air. It had been six days since they'd retrieved the Device, and she'd needed every one of them to put her affairs in order. She missed Ransom, who'd left with Kossrek Tamun's boat only hours after the ordeal. He ought to be back any day now, with *his* affairs in order so they could begin their journey together. In his absence, she'd begun to worry about the decision. Yes, she cared about him, and yes, she wanted to get to know him better, but was a four-week journey aboard ship really the best way to do so? Suppose they got tired of each other? Suppose she'd made the wrong decision?

Her eye was caught by the movement of someone running across the docks toward her. It took her a moment to remember the girl — Cerise, the one who'd taken her to Manachen when she had to rescue Ransom. "Miss Farrell," Cerise said when she came panting up to her. "I've a message from Miss Blackwood. She wants you to report to her at the embassy immediately."

"Immediately?" Zara felt no urgency to obey that summons, but she wasn't going to deliberately ignore it just to irritate Blackwood. "All right. Thank you, Cerise."

The young woman beamed. "I didn't think you'd remember me."

No way to explain Zara had spent a long lifetime remembering people she might have need of later. "You have a distinctive hat," she said, making Cerise laugh.

Zara took a carriage to the embassy, not wanting to be wilting and sweaty when she arrived. She hadn't seen Blackwood in the six days since last leaving her office, and she didn't want to be at a disadvantage when she already didn't know why the woman wanted to see her. It certainly wasn't to thank her.

The foyer was empty when Zara arrived at the embassy, so she strode down the hall toward Blackwood's office, not feeling inclined to wait on James's schedule. She knocked, and entered at Blackwood's muffled, "Come in."

Blackwood concealed the briefest look of irritation when she saw who her visitor was. "Miss Farrell," she said. "The King would like a word with you."

"The communicator is repaired?"

"My Deviser is a crafty woman." Blackwood removed the

286

communicator from a drawer and turned and pressed the stem in a complicated series of movements. The communicator glowed green, then purple, then green again, and Blackwood set it on the desk. "Miss Farrell for his Majesty," she said, her voice a little too loud as if she were speaking to someone hard of hearing.

"*One moment,*" a voice said. Blackwood stood and nodded to Zara, then left the room. Zara waited. It was longer than a moment before Jeffrey said, "*Rowena?*"

"It's me, Jeffrey."

"*I'm not sure where to begin. Thank you for retrieving the Device. It's more than I asked of you.*"

"Someone convinced me it was my duty. You're welcome."

"*I hope I didn't make you feel obligated. I know you've left that behind you.*"

"Well, I hope you don't feel I usurped your authority. You're the King, Jeffrey, and I...well, you wouldn't believe me if I said I'd obey your orders." Jeffrey laughed, an odd, hollow barking sound. "But I don't second-guess your decisions. That's not my job."

"*I'm grateful for it. Sometimes I wonder what might have happened if you...hadn't left. I hope you've had a good life, and you don't regret anything.*"

"No more than anyone does." She thought of Ransom, and for the first time in nearly a week did so without any reservations.

"*Is there anything I can do for you? By proxy, that is. Anything you need?*"

"I could use some money. I've decided to travel and I need to repay my fare for getting here."

"*I'll tell Calliope to make some of the embassy funds available to you. Anything else?*"

"I...don't think so. But thank you."

"*Let me know if that changes. I regret that you had to leave Longbourne. It's small comfort that Mother was able to see you before she died. I know she missed you, all those years.*"

"I missed her, too. Missed all of you."

"If there were a way — "

"I know, Jeffrey. Don't you think I've given it thought?"

"I want you to know you're not forgotten. Imogen and I know where you are, and Telaine and Ben. You don't have to be alone."

She thought of Ransom again. "I'm not. I'm starting a new life. And for the first time…I don't feel resentful of losing the old one."

She left Blackwood's office in possession of a purse full of guilders and went in search of Belinda at the lodging house they'd both taken rooms in. "Mistress Falken is agreeable to meeting you," she said when Belinda opened her door. "The rest is up to you."

"No worries," Belinda said. "I'm good at making people like me. And the job sounds interesting."

"I wouldn't be surprised if you worked your way up to partner someday. Working in Dineh-Karit has its challenges, but you're more than a match for them."

"So long as they don't involve sleeping on the jungle floor and eating snake, I'm sure that's true." Belinda gestured to the room's lone chair and took a seat on the edge of the bed. "Ransom's not back yet?"

"He had a lot to do. He should be back any day now."

"I can't believe you're traveling to Veribold together. It's so romantic."

"I hope so. That is, I hope it's romantic and not stupid."

"You're well suited, for all you were at each other's throats at the beginning."

Zara smiled in memory. "Only room for one queen in a hive, was it? Fortunately, we realized we weren't in competition."

"Oh, you're still the queen," Belinda said. Zara coughed and waved away Belinda's concern and the offer of a glass of water. "I mean," she continued, "Ransom's used to doing things his way, but you're used to other people doing things *your* way. I almost wish I could go with you to see who you end up being."

"Maybe we'll come back here someday," Zara said, and let Belinda hug her. She was getting better at displaying affection, but friendly hugs still made her uncomfortable. Past time she got over that.

She introduced Belinda to Mistress Falken a few hours later, when she brought the money for her fare, then strolled back to the lodging house along the docks. That was Belinda settled; Zara had no doubt Mistress Falken would see the benefit of hiring her. She was probably a better choice than Zara, who had no experience with the business. It was tempting to think this was all how heaven had intended it to be, but Zara didn't think heaven was quite so bloodthirsty as to have wanted it all to play out with so much loss of life.

Theo was happily ensconced in his aunt's home, taking up his interrupted apprenticeship. Mistress Jenkins had been thrilled with his tales of adventure and hadn't begrudged them the loan of her gems, once she knew to what use they'd been put. Zara had seen him several times when the affable lady had invited all of them to supper. It was a relief to know he'd found his footing, and she hoped it would be a good long time before he had to set foot on a ship again.

The Zakharis, on the other hand, had disappeared into the Tremontanan enclave. "We dare not be Eskandelic," Cantara had said, "for fear someone will recognize us."

"But you'll stand out among the Tremontanans," Belinda had countered. "Isn't that just as bad?"

"There nowhere safe is," Arjan said, "but Tremontane is better than Veribold, who does not accept foreigners easily. We will make our way as best we can."

"Good luck," Zara had said. She hadn't seen them since. She prayed Dineh-Karit was, in fact, far enough to hide them from the wrath of the Takjashi.

Someone fell into step beside her. "You look as if you're thinking of something unpleasant," Ransom said. "What can I do to change that?"

Smiling, Zara took his hand. "You've already done it."

Ransom kissed her lightly on the lips. "I have returned the boat, sold my supplies, found a home for Nettles, and sent off a dozen messages. I am entirely free of responsibilities and am ready to take on an ocean voyage with you."

"Funny, I was just thinking my responsibilities here are at an end. Shall we inquire after fares to Veribold?"

"I did that when I arrived. There's a ship to Veribold leaving on the evening tide. I hope that's not too soon. It's a cargo ship, but they have a few berths free."

"You *are* eager."

"I just don't believe in wasting time. What about it, Rowena? Are you ready for another voyage?"

Rowena. The name hung in the air between them. There was one more thing she had to do, that she wasn't going to do standing on the docks of Goudge's Folly surrounded by hundreds of people. "Let me pack my bag," she said, "and we can leave."

Zara packed her spare shirt into her new bag and fastened the toggles. She couldn't remember how long it had been since she'd done this the first time, back in Kingsport. All her possessions in a single bag, a purse full of enough coin to take her through Veribold—she probably could have gotten more out of Jeffrey, but that would have felt like being beholden to him. So soon, to start a new life, this one with a companion who might turn out to be something more. But if it didn't, what then? Her old doubts resurfaced. Would he resent her for dragging him away from the jungles where he was so needed? He hadn't seemed at all put out by the idea of going off to Veribold, where he didn't speak the language, but anything could happen in four weeks—

A knock on the door brought her out of her reverie. "The ship's leaving in two hours," Ransom said through the door. "Are you ready?"

Zara took a deep breath. No more cowardice. "I am," she said, opening the door, "but—"

He stopped her words with a kiss. "That's in case you were about to tell me you'd changed your mind. Just a reminder of why we're doing this."

"That's not it. Will you come in and shut the door? I need to tell you something."

"That sounds ominous." He was still smiling, but there was uncertainty in his eyes. What would he think, when she told him? He was clearly expecting something awful.

"You wanted to know my original name," she said, and relief replaced uncertainty.

"I didn't think it was such a serious thing," he said. "Well?"

Zara took another deep breath. "My name is Zara."

To her astonishment, Ransom laughed. "That was my maternal grandmother's name. I think there must be half a million Zaras in that generation, named after the infant princess. Zara North left her mark..." His voice trailed off. "You were part of that generation, weren't you?"

"I was." Her throat was too dry for more. She didn't know how to go on. "They—I wasn't named after the Queen, though. They were all...named after me."

Ransom blinked. His mouth went slack with astonishment. "Queen Zara died," he said.

"Queen Zara was shot through the head. No one could survive that."

"No one," Ransom said. He took a lock of her black hair in his fingers. "Sweet holy heaven. No wonder the King trusted you. You're Zara North."

"You can see why I couldn't just tell you my name."

"I do. Rowena—Zara—"

"Rowena. I can't use the other name, even now."

Ransom sat down heavily on the bed. "You weren't aging," he said.

"Imagine if I were still Queen."

"I am. What a nightmare. Everyone would know—sweet heaven, are you the only one in the North family with inherent magic?"

"That's irrelevant. All it takes is one, and the people start to question our fitness to rule. And then there's chaos as the provincial lords go to war over who should rule instead."

"I know. Did you—you must have faked your death. How?"

"I can't answer all your questions until you've answered one of mine." She swallowed again. Was her throat going to be dry forever? "Does this…change anything?"

"What—you mean, about you and me?" He looked up at her. "Aside from how I am now incredibly intimidated by you?"

It felt like a blow to the chest. "I see," she said, feeling her eyes begin to ache.

Ransom stood and wrapped his arms around her, holding her close. "That was a stupid joke. I'm sorry. Of course it doesn't change anything. I think you've never stopped being Zara North just because you've changed your name. It explains absolutely everything about who you are."

She returned his embrace, resting her head on his shoulder. "You're the first person I've ever told this to. Everyone else who knew found out by accident."

"Like your grandniece. The King's daughter?"

"No. Princess Elspeth's only child."

"That's Telaine North Hunter. I had a crush on her when I was young. Sweet heaven. You haven't seen history, you *are* history."

"That makes me feel very old, Ransom."

"Sorry. Is it all right if it takes me a while to get used to this?"

"Just so long as you don't start looking at me in a funny way."

Ransom drew back enough that she could see his face. "Just this way," he said, and kissed her, his lips lingering on hers.

EPILOGUE

Four months later

The narrow stairwell was dark enough Zara had to tread carefully as she climbed, lifting her enveloping robe out of the way of her feet. She ascended the last flight of stairs and, slightly out of breath, pushed the door open. It creaked as it always did — she kept meaning to oil the hinges, but there were always other things to do, and she didn't come up here very often, anyway.

The fragrance of desert flowers, heated by the early summer sun now dipping below the horizon, wafted over her as she crossed the rooftop garden to look out over Haizea. It reminded her of Aurilien, at least what she remembered of it — all those tiny light Devices outlining streets and making the larger buildings, like the opera house and the Jaixante, the residence of the Veriboldan King, look as if they were burning with color. Unlike Aurilien, Haizea's lights were dozens of colors so the city sparkled like a dowager Countess's jewelry cabinet, and while Zara retained a loyalty to her home city, her eye was seduced by the Veriboldan capital's beauty.

She leaned against the wall and looked down the five stories at the street below. It was busy with pedestrians, none of whom looked up or noticed her at all. It was fun to watch them pass by and try to guess where they were going, though most of them were no doubt going home to supper. She ought to make supper before Ransom returned, but she was an indifferent cook and had never wanted to improve, so they were likely going to the restaurant down the street again. It wasn't fair to make him cook when he'd had such a long day.

Faint music drifted to her ears from a couple of streets over. One of the large families that lived there was celebrating someone's birthday. They should stop by, say hello; ordinary Veriboldans weren't as standoffish as the ruling class, but it was good to maintain those friendships nevertheless, remind them that foreign didn't have to mean

293

alien. And Ransom had tended to the grandmother, who had an illness healing couldn't fix but medicine could. Watching him work...it filled her with such love for him.

It should have been a surprise, falling in love with him on the ship going north after only two weeks of travel. Two weeks in which they'd spent nearly every minute together. She'd never been bored. She'd never been sick of his presence, never found excuses to get away from him.

It wasn't just the kissing—there hadn't been much of that, really, what with limited privacy and her feeling that they shouldn't be alone together in her berth. It was the joy of talking to him, of telling him things she'd never told another soul and letting him do the same for her. It was finding out all the things they had in common and arguing over the things they didn't. And now she couldn't imagine being without him. That he'd fallen in love with her just as quickly...Zara didn't believe in destiny, not after the life she'd led, but it was hard not to think of their love as meant to be, whoever or whatever it was that did the meaning.

She saw Ransom approaching then, moving against the tide of the crowds. She always recognized him no matter how far away he was, though his blond hair wasn't uncommon in Haizea and he wasn't taller than the average man. She just knew him, knew the way he held his shoulders, the way he greeted people, even strangers. The confidence that set him apart from other men, self-assured without being cocky.

She leaned out farther and watched him approach. He wasn't moving as if he were tired, though he'd seemed distracted earlier that day, when she was translating for him at a new mother's bedside. Supper, then the party, then an early bed if not a shared one.

Zara bowed her head and closed her eyes. What did she want? If she loved him, and wanted nothing more than to spend the rest of her life with him, why didn't she propose marriage? It wasn't Hank's specter; he wouldn't have wanted her to pass on happiness out of remembered loyalty to him. It wasn't fear of being rejected, because she could feel Ransom's love for her in his kiss and in the look in his eyes, every day they were together.

She clenched her fists and her eyes tight shut. He was going to die someday, and she wouldn't. That was it. She liked to tell herself she was no coward, but the plain truth was she couldn't bear the thought of losing him the way she'd lost Hank. *He's not leaving, even if you never marry*, she told herself, *you'll outlive him no matter what vows you do or don't make*, but her heart quailed at the thought, as if marriage would make the loss greater.

The door squealed, startling her. "I thought you might be here, when your room was empty," Ransom said. He crossed the garden to stand beside her and kiss her, a light, welcoming kiss. "Anything wrong?"

"I just wanted to see the city." Zara turned back to watching the streets. Facing him felt uncomfortable, as if she'd already betrayed him by not wanting to make their relationship permanent. "Are you hungry? I was thinking we could eat at the restaurant."

"I think we may do that too often. We should be saving money."

"I'm sorry I'm not a better cook."

"That wasn't a criticism, Rowena. I was being practical."

"I know. Sorry. I'm a little tired."

"It was a long, hot, busy day." Ransom put his arm around her. She tensed involuntarily, and he let his arm fall. "Something *is* wrong."

"Just…really, it's nothing."

"Nothing you can tell me, you mean."

"What's that supposed to mean?"

Ransom leaned on the wall beside her. "You think I don't notice your silences? The times you brush me off with 'it's nothing'? I thought we were at least close enough to share our troubles."

"We are."

"I think you've just said we're not." Ransom pushed off the wall and went toward the door. "I'd rather not eat just yet. I'm not hungry." The door squealed shut behind him, leaving Zara with nothing to say and no one to say it to. How had their conversation gone so wrong, so quickly? And then he'd left. It was her fault, she hadn't known how to speak to him, and now he thought heaven knew what about her. She realized her hands were shaking and squeezed her eyes shut against tears, feeling as if she'd lost something precious. This was just a fight, wasn't it? Their love was stronger than this, it had to be.

She wrenched the old door open, descended two flights of stairs, and went down the short hall to knock on Ransom's door. His rooms were opposite hers, a bed-sitting room and a tiny kitchen the mirror image of hers. It was easier that way, easier than sharing an apartment with bedrooms close together. They'd agreed not to sleep together until…come to think on it, neither of them had said the word 'marriage' during that discussion, so what did that mean?

The door opened. Ransom's expression went from irritated to concerned. "You're crying," he said. "I'm sorry, Rowena, I shouldn't have been so accusatory—"

"Can I come in?" She'd thought her few tears were all gone, and wiped her eyes again. She wasn't going to manipulate him with tears.

Ransom stood aside and gestured for her to enter. His tiny rooms were as neat as he was, with no clutter of belongings or clothes to make the small place feel smaller. "It's just that you were right," she said as he closed the door. "There are some things I don't want to burden you with."

Ransom guided her to sit on the bed, then took a chair and sat opposite her. "Do you think I'm resentful when you ask for my help? I love doing things to ease your burdens. I love you. Don't deprive me of the gift of showing that love."

Tears threatened to fall again. She firmly reminded herself Zara North never cried. "You're right," she said. "I'm sorry. I do love you, you know."

He smiled at her, the warm, wonderful smile he saved for her. "Then tell me what's troubling you."

"It's…complicated."

"It can't possibly be more complicated than reattaching a finger, which is what I did this afternoon while you were gone. The man was so excited I was concerned he might be offering me his firstborn daughter in marriage or something in repayment."

"All right, it's not that complicated." His mention of marriage had her stomach twisting itself around her other organs, trying to find a way out. "Just…sensitive."

"Now I'm frightened. You're not leaving me for the vegetable seller on the corner, are you? I've seen how he looks at you."

"Ransom, be serious."

"I am serious. You really have me worried."

Zara took a deep breath. "I love you, I want to marry you, and I don't want to watch you die."

Ransom blinked. "I'm not sure what part of that statement to respond to first."

"I told you it was sensitive."

"I'm not going to die, Rowena."

"Someday you will. I know, I said I was willing to take a chance on love, but I can't bear the thought of losing you."

"And you think not marrying me will make that easier?"

"Yes. No, that's not—I'm sorry, I'm doing this all wrong."

"I'm not sure there's a right way to do this. You really want to marry me?"

"Don't sound so surprised."

Ransom sighed and rubbed the bridge of his nose. "I mean, is that a serious offer?"

Zara looked at him, at his handsome face and blond hair, at how his strong chest was visible past the deep V-neck of his sleeveless shirt, and thought of all the things that made her love him that didn't show on the outside. "I love you," she said, "and I want to spend my life with you. I just wish I couldn't see the end so clearly."

Ransom rose to kneel in front of her and took hold of her hands. "Sweetheart," he said, "nobody really sees the end from the beginning. I want to be with you every day, for all the days I have left, and I don't care how many of them there are. I just don't want to know that every day you're wondering if this is the last one."

His words sent a chill through her. "I didn't think I was doing that."

"Of course you are. Not that I can blame you. But if you start thinking in terms of the end, you'll miss out on everything that happens after the beginning. I want to marry you, but only if you'll let those fears go."

"Is marriage really something that should begin with a bargain?"

"Why not? We promise to be the strength to each other's weakness, and what's that but a different kind of bargain?"

"I—"

He knelt up so they were almost face to face. "I'm going to kiss you now," he whispered, "and I want to know if I'll be kissing my future wife."

It felt as if the hot desert wind blew through her, scouring all her fears away. "Yes," she said. He smiled, and kissed her so tenderly she thought she might burst into tears. When had she become so emotionally fragile? She returned his kiss, threading her fingers through his hair, and he pulled her off the bed so they were both sitting on the floor, her practically in his lap. "I want to marry you soon," she said between kisses. "I've been waiting so long for more than kisses."

"As soon as we find someone to officiate," he said in her ear, nipping it with his teeth and making her moan. "Do you think we could manage it tonight?"

"Veriboldan ceremonies aren't complicated. I imagine Arkaixa could do it, if he's willing to leave the party for a few minutes…oh, do that again."

"If I do that again, we might not make it past the door of this apartment." He kissed her cheek, then helped her stand. "But we'll also need to be married the Tremontanan way."

"I know. And I want you to adopt into my family."

Ransom took a step backward. "You do?"

"I didn't think you'd mind."

"I don't, but…it's not every day you get asked to adopt into the royal house of North."

"And I'm going to ask Jeffrey to do it."

"You don't do things by halves, do you?"

Zara laid her palm along the curve of his cheek. "I want to be married in my own name this time. We'll still go by Farrell in public, but—"

"Ransom North. It sounds good." He gave her his familiar sardonic smile. "My parents are going to have identical heart attacks when they find out, but they can't exactly argue about whether or not I love someone. Well, no, they probably will. I'm sorry."

"I'm still Zara North. I feel no fear at facing down your parents."

"You wouldn't, would you?" Ransom took her hand. "Let's go. Or do you want to change into something fancy?"

"Ransom, the first time you saw me I smelled like jungle. And you fell in love with me anyway. I don't care what I'm wearing so long as I'm marrying you."

He laughed and kissed her hand. "Then let's find Arkaixa, and make this another night to remember."

Zara stretched, reveling in the feel of Ransom's skin against hers. She fumbled for his hand in the darkness and squeezed it. "Are you glad we waited?"

"If I'd known how good it would be," he said, his voice unexpectedly deep, "I'd have married you months ago."

"It was beautiful. I love you." She curled up against him and ran her fingers along the line of his collarbone.

"You're not...comparing at all?"

"Of course not. It didn't even occur to me. We're the only two people in this bed, Ransom, and that's always going to be true."

"I hope so. There's no room for anyone else, even if I were inclined that way." He chuckled. "We should move to a new apartment."

"I have a place in mind. We'll go in the morning." Zara stretched again and yawned. "I feel so relaxed. I hope you don't mind that I'm falling asleep."

"No...actually, there's something I wanted to tell you."

His voice sounded strange, distant and faint as if he were yards away instead of breathing softly across her forehead. "Can't it wait for morning?"

"I thought it could. But now…I had reasons for not bringing it up earlier, but now it comes to it, I'm wondering if they were bad reasons. So if you're going to hate me, I'd like to know immediately."

Zara realized she was breathing more rapidly, in time with her quickened pulse. "It's bad enough you think I might hate you? Shouldn't you have told me *before* we had sex?"

Ransom's laugh sounded forced. "It's not about the thing itself. It's about not having told you sooner."

Zara pushed herself up onto one elbow and felt around until she could turn on the light Device. Ransom covered his eyes against the brightness. "Talk," she said, not caring that she sounded harsh.

Ransom lowered his hand. "Zara," he said, and her heart beat faster, because he only called her by her real name when things were serious. "Haven't you ever wondered why I'm always clean-shaven even though I don't own a razor?"

That was not a question she'd expected. "Ah…actually, no, I've never thought about it, though now you mention it, you did stay clean-shaven the whole time we were in the jungle. I didn't realize you don't have a razor. I guess I assumed you don't grow a heavy beard."

"I don't, but that's not why. The reason is I keep those follicles suppressed. Not really, but the details are complicated and wouldn't interest you. Healing is all about manipulating living tissue, and there are all sorts of things healers can do that don't have anything to do with repairing injuries. It's why almost all healers become doctors, to understand the consequences of those manipulations."

"That's interesting, but I'm sure it's not what you are so worried about."

Ransom sat up, dislodging the blanket. "What I haven't told you is that I'm capable of healing much more than gross injury. I can heal very small injuries. Such as…such as the ones caused by aging."

For a moment, she didn't understand.

Then she did.

She found herself pacing the floor without knowing how she got there. "You didn't tell me," she breathed. Then she shouted, *"Why didn't you tell me?"*

"Because it would have made a difference!" Ransom shouted back. "I didn't want you to know because I would always, *always* have wondered if you wanted me for myself or because I was the only man in the world you could grow old with! I love you, Zara, and I was afraid—don't tell me you don't understand being afraid of losing what you love!"

"You didn't trust me."

"I'm sorry. I told you I thought they might be bad reasons. I hoped you'd understand anyway."

Zara paced more rapidly, trying to outrun the thoughts that swept madly through her brain. "You were—sweet heaven, I can't—" she said, and then she was crying, huge, painful sobs that wracked her whole body. She could tell Ransom had come to stand next to her, though he didn't touch her, and she wasn't ready to go to him for comfort. She covered her face and sobbed without knowing what she was crying for. It hurt, yet she couldn't stop. Finally she sank to the floor and sat hugging her knees as her tears wound down. "I'm sorry," she said.

"You're sorry?" Ransom knelt beside her and tentatively put one hand on her shoulder. "I'm the one who did everything wrong."

She looked up at him and blinked away the last of her tears. He looked utterly anguished, as if he desperately wanted to comfort her but was afraid of being rejected. It broke her heart. "I love you," she said, and put her arms around him. "I love you. I'm sorry, I was just overwhelmed."

He took her in his arms and cradled her, kissing the top of her head. "Forgive my stupidity and cowardice?"

"There's nothing to forgive. I wish I could say it wouldn't have mattered, but you're right, it would have changed how I saw you. It's just...my greatest fear, and all along you knew it was groundless. It's dizzying."

"Come back to bed, and let's hold each other," Ransom said, helping her up, "while you get used to the idea that you're not the only deathless person around here."

She laughed, sniffled, and wiped her eyes. "Not exactly."

"No," Ransom said. Zara snuggled into his arms and sighed happily. "It's not as efficient as your magic seems to be. I have to consciously direct it, for one, so I'm not as indestructible as you are. I'll still age more rapidly than you will. Fortunately, you have a bit of a head start on me, old woman. And I don't intend to start doing it for another five years. I'd like to look a little less like you're robbing the cradle."

"Ah, vanity. It will be your downfall."

"Probably. Suppressing my beard growth could be seen as showing off, if anyone knew about it. It's just easier than shaving."

"Is this something all healers know about? Is there some secret underground cabal of ageless men and women?"

Ransom shifted. "I don't know. We rarely discuss it, even privately—you understand how unsettling ordinary people would find it. And when we do, it's conversations about the ethics of it, and the practicalities. That's also something you understand, outliving everyone you love. I imagine most of us have tried it at one time or another. How many of us have reason to keep it up, I don't know."

"It sounds much more appealing from the outside, I can tell you that." She thought of Dr. Trevellian, who had died more than twenty years ago…or had he? Suppose he was wandering the world, never staying long in one place, making a living as a traveling healer? If he was ageless, he hadn't confided in her, even when he knew they had something in common. She hoped he had let himself age naturally.

"So…are we all right?" Ransom asked.

"Do you mean, am I going to run naked into the street looking for a divorce? No, my love, I am not. One of the things I know about marriage is that keeping score is the fast way to end one. We've each done our share of hurting one another, so I'm not going to hold this against you. But…now would be a good time to tell me any other secrets you've kept hidden."

"That was the only one. What about you? Anything more than the little matter of being an unkillable former Queen of Tremontane?"

Zara fell silent. "We've never talked about it, because I assumed you knew, but…I'm barren."

"I know. I'm sorry. There's nothing I can do about that."

"And the truth is, I feel too old to be a mother even if you could fix it. But I don't like—"

"Don't worry about me. I love the woman you are, just as you are." He trailed his fingers down her bare side, then lower. "And I'd like to show you how much I love you, if you don't mind."

Zara rolled over to lie atop him. "Mind?" she said. "I positively encourage it."

ABOUT THE AUTHOR

Melissa McShane is the author of many fantasy novels, including the novels of Tremontane, the first of which is *Servant of the Crown;* The Extraordinaries series, beginning with *Burning Bright;* *The Book of Secrets,* first book in The Last Oracle series; and the Convergence trilogy. She lives in the shelter of the mountains out West with her husband, four children and a niece, and two very needy cats. She wrote reviews and critical essays for many years before turning to fiction, which is much more fun than anyone ought to be allowed to have. You can visit her at her website **www.melissamcshanewrites.com** for more information on other books and upcoming releases.

www.ingramcontent.com/pod-product-compliance
Lightning Source LLC
Chambersburg PA
CBHW071110250626
47159CB00002B/674